Paper Conspiracies

Paper Conspiracies

SUSAN DAITCH

City Lights Books • San Francisco

All rights reserved.
Cover and book design by Linda Ronan.
Front cover photo: "Paris Exposition: night view, Paris, France, 1900." Night view includes the Ponte Alexandre III. Brooklyn Museum Archives, Goodyear Archival Collection.

Library of Congress Cataloging-in-Publication Data
Daitch, Susan.
  Paper conspiracies / Susan Daitch.
    p. cm.
  ISBN 978-0-87286-514-3
  1. Dreyfus, Alfred, 1859–1935—Fiction. 2. Trials (Treason)—France—Fiction. 3. Jews—France—Fiction. I. Title.
  PS3554.A33P36 2011
  813'.54—dc22
                    2011014523

City Lights Books are published at the City Lights Bookstore,
261 Columbus Avenue, San Francisco, CA 94133.
Visit our website: www.citylights.com

For Nissim

AFFAIRE ESTERHAZY

Identité absolue des Ecritures

Le BORDEREAU est l'œuvre du Commandant Esterhazy

Les Fac-simile ci-dessus qui forment un tout complet, sont composés l'un d'un fragment du Bordereau, suivi d'un fragment de lettre du commandant Esterhazy; l'autre par moitié de l'écriture du Bordereau et par moitié de l'écriture du commandant Esterhazy, alternant deux lignes par deux lignes. Les deux écritures se confondent absolument à tous les points de vue.

Train-Eating Sun Blinded by Eclipse

How many stories could begin, "What are you doing here, you're supposed to be dead?"

The door opens, light shines into the dark hall, and the curve of a cheekbone appears vaguely familiar. Other guests, innocent family members in the back of the room don't notice the new arrival. You think it can't be possible that he or she might only be visible to you. No, it can't be. You shut the door, looking up at the transom, then down at the gap between the bottom of the door and the threshold to be sure no shadow has slid into the room.

The encounter might take place on the street, in a train station, a busy intersection, a back alley, *you're supposed to be dead! What are you doing here? What do you want from me? Leave me alone, please.* You're in trouble. Calling the police is useless because a history of guilt and complicity on your part isn't entirely buried and forgotten. Could the likeness be only a coincidental double, not the real person, not the actual birth-certificate-waving human, not the citizen who might have made your life a living hell? That's how I felt at work when restoring old movies. Shadowy figures assembled into frames began to look familiar, to hum and vibrate with amorous longings, embarrassment, coyness, the desire for evening old scores, or simmering with rage, they fade into an indistinct background.

A silhouette skating like a banshee over pebbled glass, a profile reflected in the rearview mirror of a parked car, I twisted around quickly, not believing it possible. *Is that you? Wait a minute, let me be certain.* I grew up the only daughter of two people who didn't know where they wanted to or even could go, so they ended up in a small city halfway between New York and Montreal. Both of them, but my mother in particular, were not destined to feel at home anywhere. The idea of home stood on shaky ground: a house, an address on a steeply inclined plot of land on which sprouted a one-story house called a ranch but there were no palominos or branding machines on this idea of ranch. It was just a one-story house so you didn't have to go up or down stairs. There were no grandparents, no uncles, aunts, or cousins. One distant cousin landed in Argentina in 1940, but his children were disappeared in that country's dirty war of the 1970s, and he ended his life jumping from a balcony shortly thereafter. His letters, written in a hybrid of Spanish, Russian, and Yiddish were kept in a drawer along with tax forms, photographs, fliers for discounts at car washes. I was unable to read them completely, and no one was willing to translate his macaronics for me. In one letter I could make out *Nokh a kish funa gonif, dezehl iber dayne tzende* (If you kiss a thief, count your teeth) and figured someone was carrying on with someone they shouldn't have, but the specifics of who was tangoing on the wrong street, I couldn't make out. I'm not sure each page really revealed much anyway. The letters were murmured over when they arrived; a few years later my mother wept over them. Alone, sneaking the pages out of a drawer at night, I figured out some of the Spanish parts that referred to quotidian details of an increasingly frightened life, as if by burying the anticipation of death squads under details about a trip to the doctor's, the fear might be buried, too. Houses broken into in the middle of the night, children going into hiding in country houses, in the jungle, in museum basements. My mother, a woman who fought chaos with chaos, snatched them from my hands, saying she'd heard all this before, and I didn't need to hear it at all. When I turned fifteen, around the time the letters from Argentina stopped, she spent a lot of time wandering around a newly built windowless shopping mall looking for light switches (prices slashed), wrapping paper (after holidays), out-of-stock paint colors, and other semiuseless objects because you never knew when there would be shortages or how these things could become useful if flight or hiding became necessary. Both my parents were talented at putting mechanical detritus to good use: radio innards were used to fix the telephone, a turntable mutated into a gizmo used to stir prints in my father's darkroom, a speaker made of plywood the size of a refrigerator box blasted music all over the house. As a child I was convinced they could turn a desert junkyard into a phalanx of robots. The one-story house became a vault for packages of jeweler's screwdrivers (what if you have to fix a watch?), picture hooks (could pick a lock), rolls of tape of all kinds, and tins of sardines and vacuum-sealed bags of raisins with expiration dates from before the camera was invented. While my mother was preoccupied with this kind of shopping my father spent more and more time tinkering with electrical machinery and a homemade computer as big as a bathtub, with disks the size of dinner plates. Chaos reigned. No one would answer my questions. I only knew I was named for someone whose name began with the letter *F*, someone who was born in a town whose name was made up of consonants and couldn't be found on any map.

My mother couldn't use an oven and cooked quickly over a stove, burning pots and pans, throwing them out whenever possible. Food that was canned or frozen presented a language that, for all its simplicity, held hidden dangers, the breaching of food taboos. What was she seeing in the turquoise packaging of a frozen macaroni-and-cheese dinner? The bits of bacon rendered it inedible, and the whole thing had to be taken outside and put in the garbage. The staring into space got worse after my accident, which wasn't really an accident at all, but a letter bomb directed at all of us. I was the one who opened it.

"Where will we go? Rio?" My father grew angry at my mother's hysteria, useless and irrational, as far as he was concerned. "Shall we join your cousin whose children were dropped out of a helicopter over the Atlantic Ocean?"

"You're always the last one to get it. You stay behind until the wolf is at the door, until his tail wallops the glass, and then it's too late." My mother dumped the contents of her bag on the floor, looking for her keys so she could make an exit. "Frances, were you going through my things again?" I'd just gotten out of the hospital and I wasn't going anywhere. Half my face was bandaged over, my hair hung limply out from under white strips of gauze.

We weren't going to go anywhere. My father had a stable job teaching biology in a high school. In the spring when he got to the unit on evolution a few of the English teachers who were creationists would somehow have sniffed this out and, during lunch, they would try to convert him, but in this task there lay madness. Perhaps they saw the classroom charts that mapped relationships between family, species, and genus laid out in green and blue lines like the veins of a leaf. In Darwin's theory of natural selection they saw the cosmos reduced to chaos. The collector of beetles and carnivorous plants who rode a tortoise in the Galapagos opened the universe to random terror. This cracked my father up. He didn't take the creationists seriously. He might notice them peering at him as he rode into the parking lot on his motorcycle, but he never described them in condescending terms. As far as he was concerned, the argument could be parsed into two obviously warring camps: evolutionists whose soldiers could refer to the Salk vaccine, the H-bomb (even though it had to be tested many times and even though it could be said to be a dubious achievement), walking on the moon. The soldiers on the other side drove their stake into ground with the solidity of the Everglades, and though they unfurled their banner with conviction, it was true, what did they have to brag about really? Galileo under house arrest because he wrote that the sun was the center of the universe? My father lit a Marlboro and tapped ash into a glass ashtray in the shape of the Apollo 11 rocket.

To my mother the creationists were nauseating, a grave affront. Pour water on them and they would melt into the floor in a plume of smoke. To her they were all complicitous bombers, and she longed for cities with narrow streets set at odd, unpredictable angles where the shadow of Nosferatu or a golem gliding across a wall would be as prosaic as meeting a friend in a café where you could talk about movies, plays, show off new clothes, and gossip in a language all your friends understood. Your feet made noise on the pavement instead of the silence of asphalt parking lots. After the letter bomb she embarked on fits of driving, traveling to the far-flung provinces of provincial life. On her journeys she discovered apple stands and strip malls, cut-rate carpet dealers and fish fries, public libraries set up in defunct churches, and covered bridges on unmapped roads.

My initial fifteen-year-old response was to try to blend into the town my parents had picked out of nowhere. I daydreamed in school, drawing relentlessly in notebooks, the margins of textbooks, on desks. I still have a few of those sketches of futuristic cities based on my mother's stories of buildings honeycombed with crowded apartments which I imagined were Gaudí-like, glittering with tesserae, built like huge stalagmites. It was a means of imagining my way out. In the meantime I made an attempt to be anonymous, but the project was useless. After the letter bomb I realized it was impossible to hide behind ordinary clothes and straightened hair that only lasted for a few hours before it boinged back to its curly state. I went to Ravi Shankar and Nina Simone concerts, but if I cheered when she exhorted the crowd by saying *if a few white men can run this country you can take over this university,* nobody cared or noticed my enthusiastic response.

I encountered my own equivalent of the creationists. My classes were full of small-town boys, mediocre athletes with buzz cuts and monosyllabic names whose lives seemed fixed if not gated. My parents blinked and saw the lot of them crammed into Mr. Wizard's Way Back Machine. All of them were the descendants of the Gaston who had joined the Children's Crusade and all were ready to march on infidel-filled Jerusalem if their draft number came up. The letter bomb proved it. I wasn't so sure.

What happened when they, these boys who knew little of life beyond the next town, ended up in Vietnam, Beirut, the Persian Gulf? One bearlike boy who read *Soldier of Fortune* magazine bragged he would go to Afghanistan or Zaire, names he proudly mispronounced. The ingredients for explosives lurked in their cellar workshops, with how-to manuals hidden in drawers full of jock clothing; they were my suspects. I never knew exactly which one or ones created me, turned me into a target, one-eyed and angry, with no effective means of striking back at them. My parents who looked like Persians with Boris and Natasha accents made me an easy mark. My mother, in particular, was a sitting duck for mimics, and I knew it. Since I'd lost an eye to the anonymous letter bomb I was a sitting duck myself.

In school I had wanted to study Latin and Greek — as if dead languages might explain how images were first connected to words. I imagined hectoring mobs of things (lions, columns, arenas, aqueducts, toga pins, constellations) marshaled into categories: nouns, verbs, syntax — but my family insisted that I do something practical, so I studied the most insubstantial thing I could think of: light.

The job posting was the stamp on my ticket: *Library of Congress Film Restoration Project, Paid Internship.*

I was charmed by the idea of working in film, but intensely camera shy and happy to work as a kind of handmaiden to "the industry." All right, I thought, at least I have a hand or an eye in something. Here, I wouldn't be a target, wouldn't be stared at, few questions asked, go on with your business, please. The process of learning how to put a brush to aged celluloid gave me a sense of professional identity, saved me from the night shift at a movie-rental shop with a large independent section, answering urgent questions about matrixchopsockeystarwarsdirectorscut. Now I had a hood I could pull over my head, a burrow, a bunker, a fallout shelter with a periscope.

I left for Washington at the end of the summer so my departure could be confused with going off to school, and it was still hot, but in a last gasp kind of way. Department store windows displayed artificial leaves while children on our street still ran through hoses and hydrants in brilliant fuchsia and purple bathing suits. My mother said good-bye at the house; seeing me wave from the window of a train was not possible for her. I kept looking out the car window all the way to the station, armoring myself against her resentment and despair, her sense of betrayal that chased me no matter how much my father, imitating Peter Lorre, said *full steam ahead, Frances.* Since we were early my father and I stopped at a Dunkin' Donuts near the station.

"What do you think about Cuba?" he asked, stirring and staring into the parking lot.

"What do you mean, what do I think about Cuba?" My father, who was a very calm man, was making me nervous.

"They're looking for science teachers."

"You can't go to Cuba. You're a United States citizen. If you moved to Havana you'd never be able to come back."

"I've left a lot of places that I can't and don't want to return to."

"You've lived in Israel. You won't be let in."

"That was a long time ago. Maybe they won't notice."

"What about Mom?" The point I feared was that she occupied one of the places he didn't want to return to.

"I need to get away from here. Between the creationists who guarantee me a life in everlasting hell, who think petri dishes are something you hang from a Christmas tree, and your mother, who mistakes family photographs for expired discount coupons and tosses them out, I think for me, personally, it's time for a change."

There was no arguing with him. I didn't know if he would apply for Cuban citizenship or not, but I knew now that I was leaving, he would as well.

"I want to give you something before your mother makes a clean sweep of everything in the house." He handed me a faded sepia photograph of a small girl, about four years old. I turned it over. On the back was written *F. Baum, 1940.* This was my father's sister.

"So keep this in a safe place."

Our conversation dwindled in the minutes remaining. Finally he dropped me at the station then went back to his machines. I didn't want to get on the train, didn't want to see him return to his mammoth computers, coverless radios, old turntables spinning wildly on the cluttered floor. By giving me this photograph I'd never seen, he was tearing some part of me away, as if to say, you'll never be able to come back here, and you'll never be able to leave. The train pulled out of the station, and the red brick apartment buildings, the flyblown variety stores already giving way to Kmarts and then Walmarts moved out to the horizon as if they were on conveyor belts, parts of changing sets.

In Washington in a cheap, hastily rented studio apartment I put my tiny aunt's picture in a frame made in China and set out to learn the art of conserving film.

This kind of resuscitation required a steady hand and a life in dark rooms. When beads from a sweater bought in a thrift shop, for example, fell onto an editing table, jamming a reel, it was, for the actors, akin to an avalanche of glass. Every thread, hair, drop of coffee had to be kept out of the danger zone. In my position as assistant to a film archivist at the Library of Congress I wasn't paid much, but I soon became a skilled surgeon of lost performances, an ambulance driver for long-dead actors.

What about my own ghosts? They lived and died in a town I never saw; they drank coffee in bare provincial cafés, had lives circumscribed by rituals and holidays whose meanings organized each year like shifting but predictable constellations. Yet when I watched movies and cartoons made before 1939 I couldn't help but pretend to inhabit those faces known only through photographs, wondering if they had watched these too, and in that projection back, the ghostly clusters took on a mixture of strange and familiar features. Also, and this makes their summoning even more troublesome, they appeared horrifyingly modern, not part of someone's acute but aged set of memories. The murdered live next door, or almost. You can't say: look at their clothes, they belong in another time, because with their fairly well-cut suits and dresses in geometric prints they look as if they could live in the same cities I have lived in, travel in what are essentially the same kinds of cars, respond to the same news of elections and atrocities, although this is impossible. What I mean is they have become personalities I'm capable of trying on although I never met a single one of them. They died before I was born. If this sounds arrogant it's only because they've been at my door persistently, despite my family's need to look the other way.

The new city engulfed me, and I plunged into my job with intensity. Taking on the role of the animating but anonymous power that revitalized Buster Keaton as his eyes grew sadder and (I thought) more disillusioned, or pumping up a flimsy, short-haired Myrna Loy revealed an odd kind of romance I sometimes had with these images. Or maybe it was a case of antiromance, the romance of solitary, imaginary pleasures. I used to notice old men and sullen boys in movie houses and wonder how far removed I really was from them. What kinds of illusions did I labor under? It's a job, I kept telling myself, one I felt fortunate to have.

"Hello, this is Alphabet Films, please hold."

I pushed hair out of my eye. I had worked overtime and so was sleeping late. The call not only disrupted my sleep but the edgy equilibrium of a life lived in dark rooms.

"Hello, is this Frances L. Baum?" A man's voice, respectful but authoritative boomed in my ear.

"Yes."

"This is Julius Shute, director of Alphabet Film Conservation. You were recommended to me by . . ." Groping for my eye patch in the dark while he searched for the name of my current boss, a displaced Iowan who, though he had no complaints about my work, saw me as a rootless cosmopolitan who would soon move on, the phone slipped from my shoulder and fell into the space between the bed and the wall. I was alone, I didn't need the eye patch, but felt as if a public event were taking place, as if this Shute were watching me sit up in the middle of a twist of bedsheets. "I'd like to ask you to consider working for me at Alphabet." His muffled voice came from somewhere under the bed. In the silence while I felt for the phone, Shute continued to speak, filling the void. "Occasionally people are reluctant to leave the Library of Congress for West 22nd Street. Arbergast, that was who recommended you."

"Yes, that's my boss."

Apparently, unbeknownst to me, Arbergast, a faultless technician with a phenomenal memory for film trivia which he regaled us with constantly, was greasing the rails of my move which, he believed, was inevitable. I managed to tell Shute I was interested in West 22nd Street, wherever that was.

"I'm traveling to Washington in a week to testify at congressional hearings on film colorization, and thought I could set up an interview with you while I'm in town."

We agreed on a time and place, then I hung up as if nothing unusual had happened, but in my excitement I was completely unable to find matching socks. Mentally I began to prepare my answers to his questions, believing when we met he would back out of his offer as instantly as he'd extended it.

How did you lose an eye? Does it impair your ability to do painstaking work?

Am I wearing glasses?

No.

I see perfectly well with my left eye.

Responding to the usual second question and avoiding the first, I had learned how to be a master at evasive answers when they were needed. It's difficult to say: *a letter bomb* and let it go at that. People want to know more. These kinds of bombs have been delivered in Rome, Istanbul, Argentina to scientists and governors but rarely to isolated high school students. I didn't want to explain the arrests, the trial, senders not convicted. I knew Shute's name had originally been Shulevitz, but his mother had changed it. In the name Shulevitz there might have been sympathy, but I was no longer looking for it.

Despite Julius's eagerness to meet and his effusiveness about my work, I felt unprepared, a one-eyed amateur, a fraud who should back out of the interview, but lulled by the man's voice, I was prepared to go ahead and make a fool of myself. Alphabet had an international reputation, and I wanted to move to New York.

One week later we met at a Greek diner. Julius disliked expensive restaurants. They made him uncomfortable. Any place with a maître d' was like a hair salon with a perfumed atmosphere, as far as he was concerned. He needed to walk in and find his own place to sit. From a distance he looked like a young Frank Sinatra in thick glasses: angular face; calm blue eyes that drew you in, meaning no harm, interested in only you absolutely, but when one walked closer, sat across from him at a small table, one could see the fraying around the edges, and he was much older than a young anybody. You could still smoke in restaurants back then, and he did, with the kind of assurance that came from years of practice. But Julius was not overly confident either. Despite his accomplishments, his expense account must have been limited, or so his choice of the diner signaled to me. A man who meant business, who didn't bother with the language of extravagant lunches, meals that stretched into the afternoon were of little interest to him. I was too nervous to eat anyway. My spanakopita remained a square brick on my plate, and although I tried to concentrate on Julius's questions, as well as his descriptions of his business, my eye wandered to the revolving display of heavily frosted cakes ringed with glazed cherries, mountainous meringue pies, and other desserts positioned just behind Julius's head

He was a man without a niche so he used expressions that would appear to give him one, to make him seem to be *in the swim* and *a heavy hitter, sounding me out from the get go*. He knew all about the films I'd worked on. I wondered if English was his first language. I asked him how his testimony went.

"Colorization is like tossing a ball into a cocked hat."

The hearings had been somewhat controversial. Many celebrities and film stars had appeared. Julius enjoyed rubbing shoulders with them and denounced the colorization of old black-and-white films, a process he viewed with disgust and refused to undertake, no matter how lucrative coloring might be.

"Painting Barbara Stanwyck's dress red in *The Lady Eve,* for example, sends a signal to the audience that she's duplicitous. Let them figure it out for themselves."

It was an argument I would remember when Julius and I would discuss how far to go in conserving a particular film.

"Even the word *restoration* represents a threat. To restore often means to impose someone's idea of what a picture should look like, means a heavy dose of tampering, means this: going too far. Colorization, like putting arms back on Venus, is out of the question." He turned around and asked the waitress for more coffee, then just as abruptly changed the subject.

"I grew up in Los Angeles. My mother worked in the costume department of Universal Studios," Julius said, and I imagined the man I barely knew sitting across from me as a child careening around this or that set. "I stole a costume once from a stuntman who was doubling for Clint Eastwood in *Hang 'Em High*. It was a great cowboy suit with these Technicolor yellow suede chaps with green fringe. I wore the suit to school thinking other kids would pay attention to me. They did, but not in the way I imagined."

He didn't reveal what kind of attention he received, but because of this story I felt some affection for him, and this was a mistake. Julius knew how to elicit sympathy and attention, and my response, my laughter, made him comfortable, so he plunged on. Actually, I'd worked on *Hang 'Em High*, admittedly restoring only one section of the film, but couldn't remember Clint Eastwood in yellow chaps. Perhaps the scene with that particular stunt had been cut when the film was edited. In any case I said nothing about it.

"She used to get calls from gossip columnists because actors, even extras, often made startling confessions during fittings, revealing liaisons and uncomfortable memories as if she knew magic words of absolution, as if she had the answers which, believe me, she did not. She was as good as they were at theatrical expressions of shock and sympathy that she recycled from the movies, and sometimes when I'm working on a film I see her raised eyebrows or hand over her mouth. The talent also spoke to one another as if she was invisible, and in this way more gossip was overheard. An uncle got me into the preservation business because they thought I was brainy and useless, but I learned from my mother. My telephone number is unlisted."

Julius, a displaced Californian who took his profession east, was never entirely at home in New York where hundreds of miles of trains rumbled underground, where the odds of an actual earthquake were small, and business was conducted in dark rooms high above street level. He was constantly a bit bewildered, as if looking for a switch in order to turn on the light. Yet Julius could read damaged and deteriorating film history as if it were a large-print book. The old films became a pedestal he lectured from. *Without me, you're nothing,* he'd say, and this always got a laugh from whoever was in the room.

Julius was meticulous, this I knew from his reputation, but ill at ease with responsibility, the kind of man who belonged nowhere and who had landed in a profession that only once in a while demanded he communicate with a live human being. He didn't like the idea of exercise, was gym phobic, but every once in a while would take the stairs. Julius lit another cigarette but held it so his hand dangled over the edge of the booth.

"I don't want to blow smoke in your eyes. Eye," he corrected himself and turned red. I wasn't annoyed, in an odd way his embarrassment and the dangling hand were persuasive.

Over the cash register a television was suspended. The Garwood case was being discussed briefly on the news. *Garwood, a Vietnam POW — some believe he was falsely accused of treason.* We stood up to leave, and I had my eye on that particular story when suddenly Julius kissed me good-bye awkwardly but deliberately. As he bent over I noticed he colored his hair orangey brown (against colorization but dyed his hair) and his eyes were shut. Somehow he made me feel I'd asked for that kiss since I'd laughed at his self-deprecating jokes. His implication was that there was more where it came from; still, I accepted the job. I guess at the time I didn't mind all that much.

When I left the Library of Congress to work for a private company in New York I cut my hair so that no strand would accidentally fall across the frame, and I tried unsuccessfully to quit drinking coffee, which was making my hands shake a bit if I was tired. I made more money but still affected an appearance that combined seriousness with attention to certain kinds of ironic details, like narrow-waisted jackets that looked as if they'd been pinched from old movies and frayed trousers because I wore clothing until it fell apart. This created an image of studied slovenliness, as if my mind were completely on my work and not on the body I actually inhabited. A ten-dollar good-luck ring set with a square, magenta piece of glass was my prize possession until I lost it in a public swimming pool my first week in the city. No longer working with a large number of people as I had in Washington, and knowing no one in New York, I could go for days barely speaking to anyone. I felt like a prisoner in my own skin and began to wonder what the relationship might be between my sense of physicality, my vanity, all unacted upon, and my vocation that was so concerned with preserving the display of others.

The editing rooms of Alphabet Film Conservation are in the Mayflower Building downtown. You walk in through the main entrance, a double door centered like a mouth, windows for eyes. A sculpture, a large statue of Hermes built into its own recessed aedicule above the door; that's the nose. Hermes is sinewy, his arms and legs an abstract collection of metal rods, yet in his winged cap he is identifiable as the god of rogues, gymnasts, and travelers. Other mouths: curving balconies, Gaudí-like but functionless flourishes since no one uses them. More windows resemble other pairs of eyes. How is an office building like a human body? Banks of elevators function like arteries, the furnace is a giant sweat gland, air-conditioning ducts are drawn-out branches of lung. The building directory located in the lobby might be the brain, flat and simple, tin and industrial felt, a banal yet practical mind.

Alphabet is on the fifth floor. The labs where the films are treated branch out from the reception area and offices of the director, Julius Shute, his assistant, and the accountant. The walls are covered with framed posters from a few of the films we have preserved: *Go West, The Cameraman, Wages of Fear, Out of the Past, The Runaway Bride,* and photographs of Julius as a boy shaking hands with Charlie Chaplin in one picture and Montgomery Clift in another. Julius believes that in the eyes of our clients these photographs are the equivalent of medical school diplomas.

Chaplin bent over to meet Julius's gaze and smiled broadly, cane stuck out behind, yet this was an older Chaplin, perhaps tired of little boys, although perhaps not. Montgomery Clift playing Freud didn't look happy. He may have been pressed for time, the shutter snapped, and Julius, a confused but polite boy, thanked him and disappeared back into the ranks of the crew. *Peanut lights, 200-watt midget solarspot, stingers* (a 25-foot extension cord), *horsecock* (feeder cable), *Mighty-Moles, Mickey-Moles, inkies, tweenies, leekos, optima 32s, brutes,* and *HMI 6Ks.* He could hear gaffers' and electricians' banter, and he ducked behind a trailer grabbing a doughnut as he ran. *Behind the camera, behind it, not in front, stay out of harm's way, kid. Do us a favor. Get that boy out of here. Keep him out of the light.* And so they did. The photographs of Julius represent his history, and at the same time the images have the aura of standard publicity shots.

The waiting room also contains a Mr. Coffee, newspapers, magazines, and a few plants, but only a few, since the work done in Alphabet is performed in the dark. On a table near the receptionist are stacks of letters addressed to members of Congress and institutions representing the motion-picture industry, letters of protest against the colorization of old black-and-white films.

When she isn't reading or answering the telephone, Antonya, the accountant and occasional receptionist, suggests that anyone visiting Alphabet should sign one or more of the letters and mail them to Washington and Hollywood. Washington and Hollywood, Washington and Hollywood, she repeats every few hours.

———•———

Julius increasingly shaved days or weeks off the amount of time needed to complete a job. There had always been quarters of any given year when Alphabet wouldn't have made any money without quickly turning around a number of jobs, but it was happening all the time now. The urgency was caffeinated and articulated in tones bordering on hysteria. Only Antonya was relaxed. "Deadlines have nothing to do with me," she said when Julius wasn't around, and plunged back into her martial arts books with enviable composure.

———•———

"He's a compulsive gambler."
"What do you mean?"

"Look at this, girlfriend."

Antonya showed me a log of accusatory letters from people who claimed Julius owed them money.

"Why did you take them out of the office?"

"I don't know."

"He doesn't talk to me about this kind of thing. Do you listen to his phone calls?"

"Sometimes. Then he talks to himself. He's pissed at Shylock this and Shylock that. One more thing about these letters, I figure these are the people who write letters, you know what I'm saying? There are others who made him loans who may not put their terms in writing, if you know what I mean."

Antonya and I were having lunch at Burrito Fresca. Her cousin was a manager, and we got free meals when he was on a day shift.

"Shute's got a son who's always calling asking for hand-outs and whatnot, and an ex-wife who hates his guts." Antonya splashed more hot sauce on her rice. "Sometimes I wake up and I wonder how I ended up in this job. All I've got here is my cousin and my two kids." She jerked her head in Luis's direction. Apart from her daughters, aged five and seven, Antonya didn't talk about her family very much. The one time she mentioned them was when we decided to get tattoos pricked into our ankles. She wanted to have a quetzal, half-bird, half-snake, painted permanently on her body. Alphabet was in a neighborhood that was no stranger to tattoo parlors, tai chi studios, boxing gyms, X-rated video stores. We simply went across the street during lunch. She persuaded me to have one done too, and although at first I had no intention of joining her, I agreed to get small wings on my ankles. We started out small because both our absent mothers would have exploded if they saw our bodies decorated with patterns that had no meaning for them. That was the only time Antonya talked about her mother, and I stupidly realized only after it was done just what tattoos meant to mine. For this reason I wore black tights the few times I visited her in Florida.

A stretch limo with smoked-glass windows pulled up in front of the Burrito Fresca, and a chauffeur opened the door for a man in a leather suit who ran into a yellow brick apartment building across the street. His suit looked like an ordinary business suit fashionable about a decade or two ago, but it was obviously new and the reference to another decade meant expensive irony — and it was leather. He looked vaguely familiar, maybe a man from talk television, some kind of actor, I wasn't sure. Antonya swiveled around and stared as if to imply the oversized car and passengers were a mystery that had no business in our neighborhood.

"How can he live like he does?" She pointed with the stick of a purple-brown lipstick before running it over her lips, but I wasn't sure she meant the man in leather or Julius, who teetered on the edge of bankruptcy. "Someday I want to make a film called *What Do You Do?* I'll go into restaurants, knock on doors, ask people what they do for a living, what are their jobs, how do they afford to live where they live, eat what they eat, drive what they drive, and so on. I, personally, would pay money to see a movie like that."

Antonya had little interest in old movies. The accounting job allowed her an H-1 working visa while she finished school.

———•———

"Méliès," Julius said.

I opened the can. "Mealies," I said.

Inside were long shreds of film, glutinous and flaked. Single reels looked like hockey pucks, gummy sweat exuding along the edges. These were rare films whose footage was almost obliterated, yet they continued to cling to life. Old silent films are the most difficult to preserve or restore. They are brittle, shrunken; images are distorted as if burned, or figures appear drowned under a bubbled, warped surface. The films' perforations, round or straight edged with chamfered corners, won't fit on the

Steenbeck editing table whose teeth are designed to accommodate only film with the standard square sprocket holes. Unless the teeth are filed down, the machine will only shred the film. Prints have to be matched to the original, if possible, but in the case of some very old prints, no original has survived.

"Be careful with these. Remove the film slowly, as if you're moving through Jello." Julius spoke to me as if I was a child, and I winced.

"I've done this kind of work before, you know."

Julius's eyes were weak and strained so he himself could no longer spend long hours at the Steenbeck, although in his examination of films he still compared himself to a mortician who wouldn't give up, there was always one more line to draw or bruise to cover. Ordinarily we worked in separate rooms and he left me alone once a job was assigned.

"Once I beheaded a horse and obliterated an actor known for upstaging everyone on the set."

"Don't joke with me, Frances. This is one of the most serious projects I've assigned to you. Blow this and you can start packing. This is a big job and the future of Alphabet depends on it being done right and both of us getting paid." Julius took the can out of my hands and replaced the lid.

"What's going on, what's so special about these?"

"In 1907 fifty negatives were stolen from the New York office of Star Films. They were never heard of again." Julius paused, bent his knees, then straightened them quickly in what seemed like a gesture copied from an introduction to a martial arts class, as if he were saying: beginners, stand like this. He often looked as if he were saluting another officer the way Erich von Stroheim did in *Grand Illusion*.

"What would thieves want with films of unassigned value?" He posed a question to which I had no answer.

"It's easier to strip copper wires than to extract silver from film emulsion." I didn't really know what I was saying, but I wanted to give the impression of participating in the conversation. Not unique paintings, Greek icons, or antiquities from the Aegean which could be held for ransom, these bits were considered the medium of cheap thrills, worthless multiples, and in 1907 no international black market existed for pirated silent films. Why would anyone bother?

"When the lock was picked and the door to Star Films gave, the thief must have been surprised to find little more than chintzy office furniture."

"How do you know what was in there?"

"I'm guessing, Frances."

So perhaps like the thief who put a lot of effort into breaking into a bus locker only to find a chewed pencil, he must have wanted some kind of compensation for his work, and just as the pencil was pocketed, so too the films were probably stolen for the sake of taking something. Even negatives whose whereabouts are documented often disintegrate into chips of celluloid, shreds of landscapes and chopped-up figures, pratfalls and botched rescues.

"For the lost negatives of Star Films there was no hope," Julius appeared to conclude. "There were rumors that the films contained coded military secrets. If people were looking for the figure in the carpet what did they expect to find in Méliès's fantastic acrobatics? The design of a canon secretly outlined in an underwater fantasy filmed behind a large fish tank, a superfast trigger mechanism clandestinely outlined in the trajectory of a tumbler's flips, troop maneuvers signaled in *Every Man His Own Cigar Lighter*?"

I glanced at the newspaper on his desk, comparing the language used to describe crude images fleeing across screens of security cameras to film molecules, particles of nothing eddying into the corners of drawers. Julius cleared his throat. "I'm listening," I said. When a job arrived Julius often felt he needed to give the staff some history, some background tracing the provenance of the films, but now he was talking about some kind of espionage. When I asked him whether he believed there was something in these old films or thought it was just a rumor, he ignored my question.

"Leon Schlesinger, producer of *Looney Tunes* and *Merrie Melodies*, managed to acquire many of Méliès's prints, believing they would someday be worth a fortune."

"When did he acquire them?"

"Probably in the late 1930s, after Méliès himself died."

I imagined a man standing in a room with a view of the Pacific Ocean on a day so bright he pretends he can see Easter Island, the Bikini Atoll, Honolulu, but not Pearl Harbor, not quite yet. He has his back to Europe, but a flood of refugees are working for him, so many that he occasionally feels he's working not in Los Angeles, but strolling though the Babelsberg studios just outside Berlin. Even the newly acquired *Looney Tunes* venture, even their comic castles are built on the pratfalls of the Méliès's canon so there's no getting away from it, no one can have his feet as firmly planted in the New World as he thinks.

"My mother worked with some Schlesinger people, of course." Julius cleared his throat again. "When Schlesinger died, his widow kept these films locked up. For years she sat on the Dead Sea Scrolls of cinema, allowing only limited access to Maronites in sunglasses, but finally the archive of prints was released." Julius waved at stacks of cans and boxes labeled in French and English. I'd seen *A Trip to the Moon*, but the others were new to me. He pointed to one box as if it contained a bomb.

"These Méliès films have come from all over the world, Frances," he turned to me. "Do we have enough Wet Gate in stock for this job?"

"We can't use Wet Gate on these films." According to the label on the can, *The Dreyfus Affair* was made in 1899.

Sometimes I'm convinced Julius had a penchant for slickness in all its forms, that his apartment was coated with Formica and shellac, mirrors partially framed by cutouts from soft-core pornography printed on coated paper. As director of Alphabet he always preferred an image with as little visual static as possible, and so Julius loved Wet Gate, a substance that fills in abrasions and scratches. But Wet Gate, slippery and odorless, was no blessing. Every treatment has its risks, and it had been recognized for some time that old films treated with Wet Gate began to take on a Wet Gate look: images processed this way became too perfect and too sharp, as if photographed yesterday. Some felt it was a kind of fluid amber, but the image preserved underneath wasn't necessarily true to the original.

"Drawn flames may be more believable when applied with dyes and chemicals than when photographed. We've seen it happen." Julius preferred the synthetic choice more and more often. Like overheard conversation you repeat to one friend after another, the dialogue you invent may actually sound more realistic. "A little artificiality can enhance the image and restore accuracy," he argued.

"1903, 1907." I pointed to can after can, reading the dates out loud. "We agreed to interfere as little as possible in films made before 1940." I shook my head in an attempt to make Julius appreciate the gravity of his decision. Some of the cans had notes on them, a short catalog of the other labs the films had passed through. The notes also described how they had been treated and what had been done to them. He held up a film labeled *The Dreyfus Affair.*

"Captain Dreyfus was tried *in-camera.*"

I told Julius I didn't know what that meant.

"In a private, closed room, judged by a committee, not an open court."

"A secret session."

"Yes. Listen, no one remembers the Dreyfus trial, but I've got a lot of money riding on this project. And pay special attention to the last few feet of film." Something had slipped. Julius Shute, known for his meticulousness, a conservator committed to each and every film, no matter how obscure the subject, now had glazed eyes. What was he hinting? Alphabet was in trouble and could afford to cut a few corners with multiple payments due, the exigencies and urgencies of the present were shoving Dreyfus and Méliès, Chaplin and Keaton onto a short moving sidewalk and out the door to make way for the next late blockbuster in need of a quick fix.

"Am I looking for codes about nineteenth-century military maneuvers, secret weapons munitions, buried treasure?" As a believer in signs, portents, conspiracy theories, the existence of the thing under the bed, I wasn't being entirely sarcastic.

"Tell me first if you find anything unusual at the ends of the reels." Julius was dead serious, his voice dry as bones.

He picked up his papers scattered on the table. Julius seemed oddly calm, like a man so sure of himself as he emerges from his personal helicopter that he forgets he shouldn't get in the way of the blades when he stands up. Maybe it was a sedated kind of tranquility. Before leaving the room, he repeated the deadline for the restorations, and then I was left alone. It was night by the time I cleared my desk of previous projects and was able to turn to these very earliest of short, silent films. Instead of *The Dreyfus Affair*, one of the films Méliès made based on an actual event, I unspooled one of his "preconstructions," those fantastical films that first introduced the idea of special effects.

Every Man His Own Cigar Lighter. A man, a pedestrian with good intentions, is unable to find someone who will light his cigar. He gestures to people on the street as if asking: puts his cigar in his mouth, pushes his face slightly in their direction, but he is ignored. Flaneurs, boulevardiers, and streetwalkers either don't understand his gestures or think he's deliberately offending them in some way — since there was no sound track, I was just guessing. Desperate, he creates a double of himself who will light the cigar for him. This one I liked. There are times when it's impossible to ask anyone for anything, all you can do is rely on yourself, split yourself in two. On the street, you're too paralyzed to get a word out, everyone passes you with extreme hostility: Who are you? Who do you think you are? Don't interrupt me with petty needs such as an inquiry after the time or directions. I don't like your face. Get lost!

In the dark, huddled over a light box holding a magnifying loupe, looking over a strip of film, I talk to myself. What happened to these actors? *You're supposed to be dead,* I tell them, *you came within an inch of being taken out with the trash years after being lost, stolen and forgotten, lying around in a warehouse or a* Looney Tunes *archive.* They were filmed in a glass house, Méliès's Star Film Studios on the outskirts of Paris, a building whose interior I imagine as frozen yet full of potential for movement, a structure like the Visible Man who could be assembled and studied, organs glued together or snapped apart. Open jars of paint are blood cells, and Georges Méliès himself is iris, retina, and cataract. Under his critical surveillance set designers who fabricate volcanos, lunar surfaces, underwater wrecks react to his criticism like nerve endings about to explode. *I've had it, Georges! Piss off!* The Oedipus of early cinema, Méliès destroyed many of his films himself, behaving like those long, flexible pencils you see in joke shops that can be bent around to leave a trail of erasure rather than a line of words. What am I looking at? A girl travels to the North Pole in a vehicle labeled *Aérobus de l'ingénieur Maboul.*

———————

"Hello, is this Frances L. Baum?"

"Yes."

"My name is Jack Kews of Omnibus Film Archives, London. I'm calling about a film entitled *The Dreyfus Affair,* which I believe your company is working on."

"What did you say your name was?" He had said it quickly, as if sneezing one word run together, and he repeated his name just as fast.

"What do you want to know about the film?" I had just gotten to work and was surprised to get a call this early in the morning. I hadn't yet shut the blinds in my studio or even visited the Mr. Coffee machine. A half-eaten orange lay beside the unused Steenbeck; I hadn't looked at a newspaper or spoken to anyone in the office.

"I'm in New York, and I'd like to take a look at the footage in your possession."

"I've never heard of Omnibus Film Archives, London." If this place really existed, I would have known about it.

He rattled off an address that meant nothing to me. His voice sounded youngish, but the Cary Grant mid-Atlantic accent and the politesse of a stranger asking for a favor frayed, and the voice betrayed its American roots. "While Méliès was shooting *The Affair,* the man who played Dreyfus disappeared, maybe was killed, and I think there are some answers as to how and why in that footage."

"Whatever you're going to discover, it's old information, and you're talking about a thirteen-minute silent film in terrible condition. It's not going to tell you much." Taking off my shoe I rubbed loops into the carpet pile with my left toe. "Anyone alive in 1899 would be dead now anyway, and whoever murdered him would be long gone as well."

He paused for a long time as if deciding what to answer, then I heard a long, drawn-out *yes.*

"Look, I know about you and I know about your work, Frances. A film sputters into life; it's silent, black and white. The figures move in the choppy, disjointed fashion customary to films made in 1899. They wobble and jerk from the rue du Bac, past shop windows crowded with mannequins: half men in high-collared shirts and headless women in long dresses like fluted columns. The crowd turns down a street filled with cheap theaters, garish posters cover the walls with images of acrobats, huge, gaping, laughing mouths, freaks, and so on. Entrance tickets are only a few centimes, and there are a fair number of choices. Which one does the crowd pick?"

"You're giving me a lot of detail for early cinema."

"Stay with me, Frances. The crowd descends on one theater in particular. Guess what? Méliès's *The Dreyfus Affair* is playing. Because we're not in real time, but in collapsed film time, the mob is swept in and out of the theater in seconds, but they've seen the film, you can assume that. Now they realize Méliès thinks Dreyfus is innocent, and so the mob is enraged. *No, he's guilty!* Even the subtitles appear in the jagged lightning-line typeface that indicates urgency and wrath, but maybe even terror, too. Faces are angry, screaming, distorted from grimacing. The jerky figures are yelling, throwing rocks. Angry at the film and the man who made it, they're rioting: smashing windows, breaking into fisticuffs. When the crowd disperses a man lies murdered on the street, apparently trampled to death, but as the camera closes in you notice a neat wound that would indicate he's been stabbed."

"What are you trying to tell me?" Half-afraid he would hang up, I held the receiver close to my ear so I could be sure to hear his answer.

"I made up the film I just described, but after the 1899 screening of *The Dreyfus Affair* there were riots in the streets; people were trampled to death. The film was banned in France until 1950, and no film could be made about the trial until 1974. The death I just described to you, however, was deliberate, not a random thing, not simply a man who found himself in the wrong place at the wrong time. And I believe that after the riots Méliès filmed a second ending that revealed what actually happened to that man and disclosed the identity of his assailant."

"And you believe these scenes were tacked on to the reel in my possession?"

"Yes."

I knew something of the story behind *The Dreyfus Affair* but didn't really understand how this subject could turn what had previously been a form of cheap popular entertainment into something so incendiary. It was as if an invention associated with gum balls, pinballs, barkers, and shills had traveled to the province of cluster bombs and Molotov cocktails, and did so in little more than a wink. I was skeptical.

"The owners of *Looney Tunes* were curators of the remains of Bugs Bunny and Daffy Duck, not of Alfred Dreyfus, falsely accused, or the real spy, Esterhazy. They made films in which ducks and cats fall off cliffs, are smashed against doors, and bounce back completely. *Looney Tunes* was as far removed from the intrigues of a nineteenth-century espionage trial as possible. They wouldn't have been interested." I imagined cans of film stored in a safe, next to diamonds wrapped in flannel sleeves, securities and bonds, the deed to the house, and a will tucked into a manila envelope, accumulating dust and controversy.

"Just because they owned it doesn't mean they watched it. It's in bad shape and can't be threaded up on any old projector. Even if it were to be screened you have to know what you're looking for." He had a point. It was unlikely Schlesinger or anyone else had looked at the film after 1899.

"I can't just spool to the end. The film is so fragile I have to examine the whole thing first, and I have others I'm supposed to work on before I get to it." I had opened the can and seen the condition of *The Affair*. It was possible the end had deteriorated beyond repair. "Give me your number and I'll call you when I get to it."

He then hung up on me.

How can you know what's at the end of a film if you've never seen it? I said into the dead phone like some Dagwood Bumstead jabbering into a busted old rotary. I felt oddly numb, as when a relative or friend puts the receiver down, terminating the call with no warning or polite good-bye and you're left wondering what kind of toes you inadvertently stepped on. Who was this Jack with a husky voice who knew my name and what I did? I imagined a man in a T-shirt with holes around the neck, tanned arms, leaning in a doorway and pinging rubber bands into a wastebasket across the room as he spoke.

I pushed the Dreyfus can aside as if it contained a long dormant explosive that could be sparked again at any unpredictable moment, tried to forget about the call, and went back to work on *Train-Eating Sun Blinded by Eclipse*.

A lewdly winking sun is about to swallow a locomotive when gradually an eclipse with a female face overshadows eyes, nose, and mouth. I began to think about what men did or had done to them in these films, and who or what was assigned a female identity. Comets, selenites, keys, houris, and musical notes were female. An advertisement for *Parisian, Love on Credit* came to life and the figure of a sinuous woman chased a few men around the set. Devils, astronauts, deep-sea divers, scientists, and planets were usually male, as well as travelers and most of the main characters. Men had things done to them, women were the agency of vexation. Women were more mutable than men, more susceptible to transformations that appeared painless, unlike the men whose bodies split or whose heads exploded. Men were tricked over and over with nothing left to do but raise their hats in order to scratch their heads. There were exceptions to this theory, but on the whole I would say roles were divided along those lines. Whether the stories were driven by the travels of a central character or by plot, the victims and travelers alike were generally men.

By evening I needed to rest my eye and took a walk down the hall. When work is slow Alphabet rents out some of the extra editing rooms. There are ten of them lined up on either side of a short corridor, each one behind a numbered door. They are rented out like any other kind of office space, and none of the doors are completely soundproof. Finding one's way down the hall, listening as each sound track runs into the next, is like walking past a series of apartments whose doors have all been left open so that arguments, conversations, polemics, and shouting matches can be heard, one after the next. I used to walk to school past one house and then the next, and even if they were dark and locked up, as I walked past I knew what went on in a few of them. In this house a bully slept, a girl who picked her victims at random but with the finality of a court sentence. With the sound of gravel underfoot, breath misting on a cold early morning, I ran past hoping she wouldn't be sitting on her screen porch or playing with her dog, an oversize highly strung dalmatian named Teency. She didn't use her fists like scrappy or tough girls, but was a master of the taunt delivered in private when no one else was listening; each one was something you could take home with you and worry about like a time bomb that would go off in bursts over and over.

You and your family are always right there where the money is.

I'm going to do an experiment. If I drop a quarter will you pick it up?

Next door was a man who shot deer and brought them home, strapped to the top of his car. We watched from across the lawn while he smiled and called out to us to take a look at this or that beauty. I imagined they bled all over his garage.

There is a basic confusion concerning the newsreel film. They said that Lumière invented the newsreel — it was actually Méliès.

I stopped and listened. The sound track was in French, but someone was translating the dialogue aloud into English.

Lumière photographed train stations, horse races, families in the garden — the stuff of impressionist painting. Méliès filmed a trip to the moon, President Fallières visiting Yugoslavia, the eruption of Mount Pelée, Dreyfus.

I knocked and opened the door. Someone froze the frame. On the screen a woman's face peered out from behind stacks of Mao's little red books. Two annoyed faces turned in my direction.

"We were told we'd have complete privacy and quiet here. This is the third time we've been disturbed," a woman in black-framed glasses snapped at me. "I paid good money to rent this space. Every Tom, Dick, and Harry seems to have a question to ask or something to announce as soon as they get to this door."

"I was walking by and I wondered who was talking about newsreels and Lumière."

"Jean-Pierre Léaud in Godard's *La Chinoise.*" She pushed her glasses up on her head in exasperation at my stupidity and pointed to the screen.

Before I could thank her for the information and apologize for the interruption, I was pushed aside by a delivery boy from the Chinese restaurant down the street. He expressed frustration and in his agitation had nothing but blind disinterest in the image on the screen that held us transfixed. He had gotten lost and was sure the food in the bags he carried had gone cold.

"We ordered Mexican!" The Godard people rolled their eyes in disgust at our collective ignorance and slammed the door in our faces.

We stood side by side in the hall. He was silent, holding the cold food by the edges of the bag as if it contained a dinner he would spend the rest of the night trying to deliver. I walked back down the hall with him, noticing he'd left his bicycle leaning against Antonya's desk. Had he chained it outside the Mayflower it might have been stolen, but she would be angry that he'd left it parked against her desk; its handlebars had been shoved into her papers, causing a miniature landslide. I didn't know where she'd gone. The waiting area was empty, and books and files had been put away as if she were preparing to leave for the night. I moved his bicycle away from her desk while he dialed the restaurant. It turned out the delivery was for Alphabet City Typeface. We looked it up, and I directed him a few blocks away. I wasn't in a hurry to get back to work and watched him until the elevator came. Antonya emerged from it just as he pushed his way in. Turning off her computer, putting the last of her papers away, and jangling her set of keys, she collected her things and asked me if I would lock the door after her.

A moonlit deck is a woman's business office. I recognized Barbara Stanwyck's voice. Walking back down the hall the sound track of *La Chinoise* was followed by sounds of gunshots in dry air — a Western, I thought, and then from the next door came English accents and rainfall implying a jungle or a London street, it was hard to tell what the situation was. A faucet dripped somewhere, a real drip, not a recorded one, and out a corner window as I turned down the hall I could see lights beginning to come on as night fell. Again I was reminded of walking down the middle of a silent, empty road when it began to grow dark early, and just when there seemed to be no one in any of the houses for miles in any direction, I would hear a dog bark and a girl's voice ring out.

I began to unspool *The Dreyfus Affair*. I knew the beginning of the story. In 1894 French intelligence discovered that someone was selling military secrets to Germany. Only a high-ranking officer with access to this kind of information could have been the agent of the espionage, and Alfred Dreyfus was accused. I unwound carefully, setting up the film: on the Steenbeck Dreyfus has just been arrested. He is taken into a room that resembles an office. He writes while a man with a faintly obscene-sounding name, Major General du Paty de Clam, dictates. I know that the paper du Paty holds in his hand is a letter that Esterhazy, the real spy, actually wrote. It was delivered to him via the "Ordinary Track," a night cleaner who retrieved it from the trash at the German embassy. When the two letters are compared he will indicate that the handwriting is identical, although the lines weren't the same at all. Dreyfus is handed a pistol. *Go ahead, do it, kill yourself.* He refuses and is taken away at gunpoint.

Sitting in the dark watching Dreyfus stand in a prison yard, I felt as if I were at the beginning of a tunnel, and somewhere at its end were black and white figures, mute, moving stiffly, who didn't know that mustard gas, dynamite, and the airplane were about to be invented. Touching the negative by the edges I held the brittle film up to a light. Dreyfus's face was faded to an almost featureless disk. The film, once considered too explosive to be shown in France, was about as sturdy as cigarette ash. I had nightmares about film breaking down at a crucial scene, the rest of it disintegrating in the can. At that moment my hands weren't the most steady they had ever been.

The telephone rang. I jumped.

"Hello?"

The line went dead.

I tried to picture Jack Kews. He called from an identical dark room, sat leaning back in a swivel chair, feet on his desk displacing papers, books, reels of film. He chomped on a Cuban cigar, laughing too hard at his own jokes, wrapping the telephone cord around his index finger. He called from a park bench, binoculars around his neck, subway map in a back pocket because he's new to the city. He called, like Groucho Marx, while eating crackers in bed, and wanted me to come join him. He called from a tattoo parlor, the same one Antonya and I had recently visited. He pays cash for tattoos of ironically kabbalistic significance winding around his arm and across his back, so I'll have a way of identifying him when we finally meet. So I can be sure, even with his shirt off, that Jack Kews is really Jack Kews.

Look, I know about you, and I know about your work, Frances.

What did this Jack know, and how did he know it? In what crowded auditorium had I unknowingly brushed against a stalker? Perhaps he knew about my father and the creationists, he knew Julius was three months behind paying for the electricity that kept us in business, perilously close to not meeting even Alphabet's small payroll, needing a small fortune in cash by the fifteenth of the month or down the hole we all would go: Charlie Chaplin, the Godard girls, Dreyfus, free lunches at Burrito Fresca. Did he also know Julius was an aficionado of dark rooms in the worst way? Julius, slow to figure out how bad things really were until the creditors carried out the furniture, would say everyone is entitled to their own private worst *ways.*

Jack was simply a disgruntled employee of *Looney Tunes.*

Jack knew who delivered the bomb that took one of my eyes, or he had been the errand boy himself.

I'd had too much coffee and turned the call into one of those dreams in which something is chasing you, some creature, some threat you will never outrun, and the corridor down which you flee stretches out, getting longer and longer. It could have just been a crank call, right? I tried to shift my focus to the job at hand.

The Affair tugged at my shirtsleeves. I was afraid to spool too much of the film, yet while it was eating me up with curiosity, I ate up the idea of the actual trial. What I remembered was the saying that some people, had they not been born what they were, might not be on their own side. The trial said, among other things, that you can try to hide a Shulevitz inside a Shute, but it might not work out. My parents didn't really talk about other cities they'd lived in, and I didn't talk much about them either, but all those unspoken histories were packed away, little signifiers of identity ready to burst out uncontrollably, more embarrassing or painful for the fact that they had been hidden than for what they were. And what are the boundaries of embarrassment anyway? Where is it for the person ahead of me in line who turns around for a second then turns around again, for a teacher I tried to impress, for all those who stare, who can't help themselves? When they're aware I'm conscious of their gaze, they look away. Instinct precedes compassion, and you may hope compassion will overtake and educate instinct, but this isn't always the case. What I look like betrays my identity as soon as I'm asked: How did you lose an eye?

I turned off the light table and opened the blinds a crack. It was night; the street was almost empty apart from a woman looking under the hood of her car. She slammed it shut, wiped her hands on her pants then walked to a phone booth to make a call. In profile she looked like a Roman senator with short gray hair. It was late, but even from the fifth floor I could read her expression. She was annoyed. She wiped her hands on her trousers, thrust them into pockets looking for change, then got back into her car, rummaged around in the glove compartment, and slammed back out of it again. Under a streetlight, she pounded the telephone. She couldn't have been more irked. I stretched my arms over my head, went back to the film. When I turned from the window I noticed a note had been slipped under my door. At first I thought it might have been another take-out menu, or an angry note from the Godard people, but the envelope had my name on it. I unfolded the paper, creased into thirds, and read:

Dear Frances,

There is some information you might need to know as you work. In 1937 Méliès was asked to write his memoirs for an Italian magazine, *Cinema,* but what he wrote was in the third person, as if actualities, the brass tacks of daily life, coffee cups and ashtrays, belonged to someone else.

(When riots threatened his film production company and assassins plotted to kill him, he continued to work on his preconstructions. Resolute and resilient even in the face of imminent shipwreck, he searched for the trick card somewhere up one of his sleeves or the rabbit that could somehow be pulled out of a hat. He believed he would bounce back even if bouncing back meant working in a toy shop in a train station. He watched people loitering aimlessly, drunkenly, or as they rushed past; he looked at each with curiosity as if awaiting some cheerful metamorphosis.) I'm making this up, but you get the idea. If no object in Star Films was stuck to its identity, if everything was continually metamorphosed into something else, then perhaps the author and producer of these transformations, Méliès himself, didn't want to be pinned to one identity either. The distant third person was a stand-in. For a man fond of cryptography (especially cases where one set of words becomes a substitute for another) and jokes with names, this makes sense. Are there more traces of biography in the actualities than in the preconstructions?

Both Méliès and Dreyfus had granddaughters named Madeleine, but there are no other similarities between them that I'm aware of. Georges, drawn in by his cousin Adolphe, was sympathetic to the Dreyfus cause, supportive to the point where he had to break off with his brothers. Although the trial did divide families, Méliès was a public figure, and therefore easily victimized for his position as a Dreyfusard. Many were ridiculed: Émile Zola;

Femande Labori, Dreyfus's lawyer; Prime Minister Clemenceau, and others found their caricatures on postcards, posters, painted on chamber pots, printed in newspapers and on the boards of children's games. They were the butt of all kinds of cartoons. Like Zola and the rest, Méliès was a physical target, easily recognized, the first film celebrity to have to go into hiding from the press. He acted in most of his own films, as you know, but what you may not know is that he also had a double, a man who played Méliès as a kind of stuntman. This man who looked like Georges was the one who had to take the fall time and time again. A head explodes, a deep-sea diver is swept away, a figure explores the polar ice cap in a hot space suit, all of these were filmed using a stunt double for Méliès. Méliès made films after 1899. We know he wasn't murdered, but the double, his substitute, never appears again.

Yours truly,
Jack Kews

I opened the door, looked down the empty hall. *New reasons to be afraid,* came the voice of an actor from behind one of the doors. The note could have been lying on the floor for hours, but I'd only just seen it. No one answered when I called out. Sounds came from behind the Godardistes' door, but they didn't respond to my voice. Everyone else had left. I shut the door and leaned my back against it.

I put the note on top of the light table. It was typed on plain white typing paper. The *J* of Jack's signature vaguely resembled Julius's *J*s — he began his capital *J*s and *T*s with the same broad hook at the top, a kind of roof supported by the stem of the letter — but the *Jack Kews,* the sneeze that remained, had a different slant and bore no resemblance to Julius's handwriting. Jack's *K* was angular, and Julius's capital *K* always had a loop in the center as if lassoing a pole. I turned the note upside down and put a magnifying loupe over *Jack Kews*. The *J* looked like a fish-hook or a nose seen in profile. (Du Paty de Clam had said that if the *bordereau,* a detailed note or list, matched Esterhazy's writing then it would only prove that Dreyfus himself had produced a good forgery. Esterhazy had lied so many times that when he admitted to having written the *bordereau*, no one believed him.) I didn't suspect Julius. He wouldn't, I don't think, have tried to scare me in this way, changing his voice, leaving an oddball note, a few harebrained conclusions deduced from Méliès's memoirs. The office tricks Julius played were blatant and obvious slapstick, like coming to work in a gorilla suit when we were preserving an old print of *King Kong*.

So maybe there really was a Jack Kews, inquisitive but skittish, a man who supposed, as did Julius, that these films might not be as harmless as they appeared. In spite of Jack's belief that this bit of silent film had caused riots, looting, vandalism, murder, there was nothing incendiary left in *The Dreyfus Affair* that I could see. Whoever Jack Kews was, those two down the hall might have seen him. While looking for me, he probably knocked on their door, turning into one of the Tom, Dick, and Harrys the women referred to with such annoyance. I wanted to ask them if they remembered what the other interlopers had looked like, but was afraid to knock on their door again that night. I walked past it instead and tried the entrance to Alphabet just past the corridor of editing rooms. The front door was unlocked, just as I'd instructed Antonya to leave it, but I decided to secure it now. The dark hall, the sound of a running toilet coming from down the corridor, unlocked stairwells where anyone could do anything were all ominous in the range of possibility they offered. I sat at Antonya's desk, pulled out a telephone book, and looked up Kews just in case that London business wasn't true.

> Kew Gardens Florist
> Kews, F
> Kews, Lilly
> Kewshansky, Tatiana (probably Tchevshanska, originally)

Expensive black leather coats tight around their bodies, the Godardistes approached. I put the telephone book back in a drawer and spun around in Antonya's chair. They were leaving for the night, carrying bags of tapes and speaking to each other in loud, emphatic voices. They were in agreement in their disgust and disappointment about something or other. The illusion the two women presented as they walked toward me was that the carpet had been transformed into a conveyor belt. As if on a people-mover found in airports, they appeared to glide effortlessly in my direction. I was a motionless sitting target until their hip bones abutted Antonya's desk, and, assuming I was the receptionist, they handed me the key to their room along with a bag of detritus from their Mexican dinner. I threw it in the trash on top of Antonya's junk mail and day-old newspaper.

"There was no garbage can in the viewing room," one said with a slight French accent.

I apologized as if it were my job to provide furniture and services, then asked if they could describe anyone who'd interrupted their work besides myself and the delivery boy.

"Short, sort of a goatee, moustache, and wire rimmed glasses. He was wearing a jacket and underneath his jacket he wore a sweatshirt turned inside out."

"What did he say? Anything?"

"Wrong room."

"That's all?"

"Yes. He knew he had the wrong room and he left us in peace, which is more than some people have done. Can we leave these tapes with you? We don't want to carry them around all night."

"No. I'm not the concierge. You should have locked them in the editing room." They headed for the elevator, smoking, fuming, chattering like monkeys, brittle, hard as nails. Dreyfus waited for me in the editing room, shackled to a prison bed, and I didn't know exactly what to do with him. Why was this worth saving? I could smell the coil of old nitrate film lying dormant in a can as it had for years and feel its crumbly slickness under my fingernails, but could make little connection between the life of a man delivering take-out food who had been smuggled into the city in the trunk of a car with holes punched in the top for air and the value of saving old film. Some part of me remained unconvinced.

I step into the shoes of the man who shot deer, tied them to the back of his car, and waved with glee at the people who stared at him in disgust as he drove down the interstate. As if by knowing this neighbor well and by playing with his children, I have more than a glimpse into a life organized around utilitarian motivation; more than a passing acquaintance with a house dominated by the maypoling twins of hunger and satisfaction, one continually chasing the other. There is no room for history, no reason to preserve the feeble or antique. Why not melt the films down for boot heels? This is a dangerous and actually false confession for someone with my job, but sometimes the cobwebs stick to my hands, the reasons elude me, and for a moment I'm watching deer cut from the back of the car or truck, fascinated by torn fur, looking over the surface of the carcass for the evidence of the wound. This confession might mark me as a slacker who sees only futility in the project at hand, but I'm not, I'm very good at conservation and very careful. I would never rub out an actor or a scene, despite jokes to the contrary and perverse temptation.

Why bother with Dreyfus taken away at gunpoint? Are new Dreyfuses born every day? Julius traveled to Paris during the two-hundredth anniversary of the French Revolution and returned with Charlotte Corday and Marat cigarette lighters for everyone in the office, as well as condoms printed with pictures of Robespierre that he only claimed to have and showed to no one. For the anniversary of the trial will there be Dreyfus (innocent) lighters and Esterhazy (guilty) condoms, already torn and punctured with sneaky pinprick holes?

Julius was yelling into the phone. I needed to talk to Antonya, but we both listened to him instead. It was unavoidable. The door to his office was open. Antonya was circling want ads with a yellow highlighter.

"Listen, Ratner, you have my deposit just in case, but what I'm saying to you is we've got a big contract here and as soon as that payment clears I can catch up on rent."

Pause.

"La Société de la Preservation du Cinema. That's who's got the contract."

Pause.

"Yes, I'm pronouncing it correctly."

Pause.

"I know. I know I can't pay you with celluloid."

Pause.

"Look, Ratner, you can't impound my equipment. I'll never be able to pay you if I can't work."

Pause.

"Well, suit yourself."

Pause.

"You have a point, but if I don't pay my electric bills and the power is turned off I can't work either. My company vanishes into paperwork. I declare personal bankruptcy, and you get zilch."

Pause.

"I know someone else will pay three times what I'm paying in rent, but if Alphabet goes Chapter 11 you better collect top dollar from whoever moves into this dump next. We're the last in the industry, Ratner. For your information what I do is a dying art."

Pause.

Julius looked up, saw us listening, put his hand over the receiver, "He just told me to take my extinct horseshoes to

Williamsburg — not the Brooklyn one, but the one he heard is in Virginia."

"You're no Trump, Ratner, you're a small-time dinosaur yourself."

Pause.

"Listen, Frances, prepare yourself," Antonya whispered. "He's already spent that contract money he's talking about. Don't count on being paid anytime soon. I do the books, so I know. There isn't any Société paying for this job. It must be some other outfit."

"Frances, how much longer on the Méliès job?" Julius called out to me, hand over the receiver once again.

I held up seven fingers although I really wasn't sure how much longer it would take. Julius frowned and kicked the door shut.

———

The sound of breaking glass interrupted my concentration on a scene from *French Cops Learning English*. Thinking the noise came from a nearby sound track I tried to ignore it. In the Méliès film four French policemen were learning bilingual puns. The teacher wrote on the blackboard *What a fair fish!* One of the police responded by writing *Va ta faire fiche* as if that were the French translation. Then she wrote *Very well, thank you.* He replied by writing *Manivelle Saint Cloud*, holding a chalkboard up for the audience to see. The end of the film was chaotic. Four English girls, clearly actors in drag, invaded the classroom and sat on the policemen's laps, danced with them, and then the whole scene degenerated into wild cartwheels and gymnastics. The sound of things being thrown around persisted.

I looked out my door toward the reception area. The door to Julius's office was open, and a man I'd never seen before was screaming at him. The room was in disarray. Tables overturned, papers scattered. One of Antonya's martial arts books had been thrown down the hall and lay a few feet away from me. She was out of the office, perhaps at lunch or doing errands, the whole place seemed deserted, as if the man knew when Julius would be alone or nearly alone. The telephone lay on the floor, disconnected. It would not have been possible to plug it back in and call the police without drawing the intruder's attention. The only way out of Alphabet was past him, so I was trapped. The man was small and well built, bug eyed. I could make out a pierced eyebrow and elaborate multicolored tattoos of intertwined snakes and ferrets crawling up his forearms. He was scary in the way a rodent is scary: it could run up your pant legs, your dress, it could gnaw into you, you wouldn't be able to stop it, so you inch your way down the wall, trying very hard not to provoke the creature or man, whoever he was. Then I noticed that he had a knife in his hand, which somehow seemed more dangerous than a gun, which would at least have made some noise. I reached for the Mr. Coffee, not knowing whether I could hit him over the head with it, but then he turned, took it from my hand, and smashed it against the wall, holding a large, curved shard up against my only functioning eye.

"You have three days left. That's it," the man said to Julius. Then he left without saying a word to me.

I reached for the phone, but Julius caught my hand.

"Don't call the police." He picked his glasses up off the floor with dignity as if the intruder had been nothing more than a phantom, a film projection, something that never happened and should be easily forgotten.

"You're okay." This was not a question. "We can get on with our work here and not mention our visitor to anyone." Julius shut the door to his office, and I wouldn't see him again for a few days.

I was shaking too badly to return to work that required a steady hand, and so I sat at Antonya's desk for a few minutes. My impulse was to start cleaning up, but this was a crime scene, and it needed to remain untouched, even if the police were not to be called. When Antonya returned she called the building's janitor. Asking no questions about the cause of the mess he proceeded to clean up as if minor indoor tornadoes happened every day. As I watched them from my doorway I considered how it might be a good idea to start looking for another job.

———·—·———

Everything in Dreyfus's world was fixed, stable, he was set on a particular course until his own personal letter bomb was found in the trash, conclusions were drawn and never entirely withdrawn in some quarters. But the accusations leveled at him weren't completely the result of confusion over handwriting. The army targeted him because they believed he belonged to a rootless tribe and that nomadic nature, according to his accusers, was inherited, not learned. His allegiance to the army must therefore be unreliable. Of course he was the spy. Who else?

It was only a matter of time before apartment walls, furniture, books of family records and photographs all went up in flames. In the scheme of things Field Marshall Pétain and Pierre Laval were only a few decades away, so his stolid, solid life was doomed anyway. It's easy, looking back, to speed up time so it all passes in a blink. Méliès was busy constructing what it meant to see, record, to bear witness, but he too was threatened by erasure by that same blinking mechanism that reduces years of quotidian misery to the half life of a twinkle.

Stuck in traffic, I daydream. I could be anywhere, bouncing from city to city, my path traced by an animated dot on a turning globe. Driving down Sunset Boulevard, boulevard du Montparnasse, or the Cross Island Parkway approaching the Throgs Neck Bridge, I'm traveling in an unassigned city, a city that becomes a character with arms, legs, hands, and feet of clay. This borough is the head, the people on this block will spill out and clog an artery, this corner was torn up and never rebuilt: the city, an amputee, erases itself. From a distance, it's a candy city, apartment towers look as if made of waffles with Life Savers water tanks perched on rooftops. I drive closer to them and the metaphor of sweets falls on its face. Barrackslike buildings near a train depot have been gutted, fire escapes and catwalks dangle from crumbling walls; ailanthus, sumac, orange hawkweed, and yarrow grow out of the wrecked foundations. An area of warehouses is transformed into expensive apartments: the city rewrites itself.

The radio is on, tuned to a talk station. *General Schwarzkopf,* the host says, and a caller picks up the topic, responding with the general's nickname, *Stormin' Norman,* he agrees, *the Bear,* but his voice has nothing to do with the view from my car window and I listen indifferently. Image, meaning, plastic: I look at my work as three choices, three pools to dive into, and usually I pick the third. Assessment and repair of the material is my job, but meaning often throws me for a loop. For the Dreyfus job, repairing 780 feet of incendiary film (thirteen minutes, the longest of the lot), I have found out one or two things about the trial of Alfred D. The windows are open as I drive, the radio is on, and I think of another soldier involved in the Dreyfus affair, the German attaché, Schwarzkoppen, who carried on a long affair with Madame de Weede, the wife of a Dutch diplomat. Schwarzkoppen was flirtatious, handsome, a lover of men as well as women: in a careless gesture he tore her letters into twenty pieces later collected by a cleaning lady who became known as the Ordinary Track. He and the Italian attaché, Pannizzardi, had a mysterious informer whom they called "Jacques Dubois" after the swindler who proposed to sell them "smokeless gunpowder." The swindler, Dubois, was actually Esterhazy, the real spy, also known as D or Z.

Dubois = D, who was really Esterhazy also known as Z, not Dreyfus, at all, therefore D = Z.

The incriminating letter signed D signaled Esterhazy. Panizzardi wrote to Schwarzkoppen under the name Alexandrine, calling him Maximilienne: *My darling all yours and on the mouth . . . Yes, little red dog, I shall come for your pleasure. I would be capable of stuffing a meter of swaddling in you and all the fourteen-year-old com-*

mandants if needed. Their letters are now stored in the archive of the French Ministry of War in a file dated February 1896. Were they a pair of comic bunglers, a Laurel and Hardy of the foreign service?

I pass a car with children fighting in the backseat and a rusting Dodge Dart, windows open and the driver tapping her steering wheel to a turned-up recording of "Bitch with an Attitude." On my radio the host makes a smooth transition from the war in the Persian Gulf to the need to punish countries who support international terrorism. He speaks of them in terms of badly disciplined children who must be kept in line because they don't know what's good for them. Metaphors of weakness, femininity, lunacy roll off his tongue without, it would seem, second thoughts, rehearsal, or plan. All of his speech has the impression of being delivered off the cuff. *Hello, you're on . . . Welcome to . . .* A caller points out that America had been pouring military assistance into Iraq for many years. Desert Storm, the caller says, seems to her to have been a very bad idea: misguided, all about oil, really. He cuts her off. *You've always had people like Patty Hearst around. People who are easily duped into believing revolutionary rhetoric. So-called revolutionary.* Implying the caller is one of these, a woman easily fooled, he savors his own cynicism. *Whatever happened to Stephen Weed?* he asks with a fat laugh. His voice has a cunning, know–it–all, yet slightly self-deprecating tone. It smells of old socks and tickets to the game. I imagine he weighs five hundred pounds, a moon face behind the microphone. No one ever sees him. The traffic moves more quickly, and I turn the radio off. Pigeons or gulls fly overhead in patterns of boomerangs and lotuses.

So far Méliès himself has appeared in many of the reels, especially notable as the leader of the Institute for Incoherent Geography. In this role I imagine him sitting in the passenger seat as I drive. He whistles along with the radio, comments on passing scenery, directs me to turn left or right. Let's get lost, I say.

"Hello, Frances? It's Jack. Have you gotten to the end of *The Dreyfus Affair* yet?"

"No, no yet, but I have a theory about the murdered man." I suggested the German and Italian attachés. "Both Panizzardi and Schwarzkoppen knew that Dreyfus was being framed by the Army General Staff, so it's true some would have wanted them dead. Perhaps the dead man was one of them."

I took another swallow of coffee, suddenly aware of Jack's breathing on the other end. It was slightly wheezy as if Jack had asthma from time to time.

"Do me a favor, Frances, I don't have much time; try to unspool the rest of the Dreyfus film."

"Would you like to come in and see the first minute? That's all I've worked on so far."

There was a pause filled by a little more wheezing.

"I thought that's what you wanted, to see the film." I really wanted him to show up but was trying not to say so. It would have been very simple, just ask, but I was afraid he would outright refuse if I did.

"I do, yes, that's the idea, but I need to be alone with it. I know how to work a Steenbeck."

"I can't allow that. Why can't we meet? Have we already met? Do I know you?" I leaned back in my chair, put my feet on the editing table.

"I'll call you soon to arrange a time for me to view the film," he repeated.

"Impossible without me present." I enjoyed having what I thought was the upper hand and, now intrigued, wanted to goad him into a meeting, but he was also beginning to make me feel nervous.

"Then this is the last time I'll be able to telephone you."

The second, much thicker note arrived a few days later. It was leaning against my door.

Dear Frances,

Some notes:

At the beginning of the affair Dreyfus was nearly released for lack of evidence. History hangs by a drying thread. Meeting at the Section of Statistics the generals covered up for the real spy by inventing documents, and they blocked evidence that would have been damaging to them by claiming that national security was at stake. National Security is a phrase one hears echoed over and over. Let me give you some examples. (Note: what was eventually to be located down the street from the Section of Statistics on the rue de Lille? The famous waiting rooms of Jacques Lacan.)

1972 Break-in at the Democratic headquarters at the Watergate Hotel. At first that case, too, looked insignificant: a matter of small potatoes, lack of evidence to prove otherwise. The trail that led to the president began with initials written in the burglars' address books: HH and WH. It was difficult to get anyone to talk. "There was a pattern in the way people said no." The bungled felony appeared to be just a case of five flat-footed burglars, and there was no need to investigate further. But as history now knows, secret cash funds whose purpose was to sabotage the candidates and activities of the other party were eventually traced. The expression "dirty tricks" enters the language in a new way. Also the words "double-cross" and "ratfuck." The trial goes beyond middle-class lawyers and irked FBI agents. Connections revealed through an examination of checking accounts, telephone and hotel bills led to the Committee to Re-Elect the President and from there to Mitchell and Haldeman. Nixon supervised extensive cover-ups, had documents fabricated, lists shredded, and so the unmasking of bigwigs required a great deal of perseverance. Again secrecy was maintained on the basis of the claim that national security would otherwise be at risk. The notion of shredding became linked to the word *cover-up*. *HH* stood for Howard Hunt, who besides working for the CIA, wrote spy novels.

1981 El Mozote, El Salvador. American-trained soldiers massacred over seven hundred civilians, mainly women and very young children. The Reagan administration denied the story and tried to discredit the *New York Times* and *Washington Post* reporters who visited El Mozote and wrote about the murders. No one in the State Department ever asked to see their photographs, and so with a clear conscience they were able to release a statement that declared that "no evidence of a systematic massacre" had been found. Because it was necessary for American military assistance to continue, every attempt was made to smear the reporters. They were accused of invention, of hallucination, of being dupes of guerrillas who didn't speak English. Years later forensic anthropologists found the bodies of 131 children under twelve years of age who had been bayoneted, shot, and hung. The anthropologists determined that the children had been lying on the floor while someone stood over them. Few, if any, had been buried.

One can, as in the Dreyfus case, manufacture anything, and create the context, the circumstances necessary for a story to be believed, and in a lake of whitewash submarines will float. So while *The Dreyfus Affair* languished in its can turning into jagged crumbs, residue, and grit, forgers were at work producing letters, doctoring photographs, smearing Zola, who publicly accused the generals of being "diabolical artisans" who "committed outrages against humanity." His language may sound overblown and heavy handed (in fact it was said in criticism of his writing: "A naked crime is a hundred times more horrible than a crime clothed in adjectives") but he got the result he was after: attention. When a judge who had been in the army's pocket convicted him on charges of libel he fled to England during the night under the name Mr. Pascal.

Perhaps the murdered man at the end of *The Dreyfus Affair* was the man who knew too much. It's a fact that Zola had many enemies who desired his death, but the murdered man isn't EZ — that isn't how he died. Was the man a friend of Zola, someone who might have aided and abetted him in his escape and therefore became a target?

1987 Iran-Contra Affair or Contragate. The National Security Committee operated as a kind of parallel government, setting up illegal deals to continue funding the Nicaraguan contras or "freedom fighters" who burn fields, starve out families, murder children. The hearings revealed an "underworld of arms dealers and financial brokers into which Lieut. Col. Oliver L. North and his fellow National Security Council staff members descended" ("Reagan's Band of True Believers," Frances Fitzgerald, the *New York Times*, May 10, 1987).

1897 Felix Gribelin covered his googly eyes with dark blue glasses. He was about to enter a public urinal in the Parc Montsouris. A man whose long, drooping moustache would not have set him apart from any number of other middle-aged men in the Paris streets that spring, he didn't need much of a disguise but felt the dark glasses were important, if not essential. Gribelin was the archivist of the Section of Statistics, an agency something like the FBI, but he didn't approach the arranged meeting with Count Esterhazy as if it were all in the course of an ordinary day, because it wasn't. He had been summoned by the General Staff for this appointment, and he had to carry out their wishes.

Gribelin was startled to see a large woman exiting the small stone building just as he was about to enter. Her face was veiled, and she opened an umbrella to shield herself from the rain. He turned to look at her back and the folds of her skirt as she disappeared, making her way through the park. Despite the somber tailoring of the woman's clothing there was something gaudy about the way she put herself together. Her green brocade jacket was very bright as well as close fitting, and he had seen many rings on her gloved hands before she opened the umbrella in his face. He assumed she was a prostitute, but what he didn't know was the woman was actually Major General du Paty de Clam. Once she was out of sight, Felix entered the urinal to find the Count leaning against a tiled wall, coat unbuttoned, humming a tune, waiting for him.

As long as they were determined to condemn Dreyfus, the real spy, Esterhazy, had only a slight chance of being convicted, and he was arrogant with the knowledge that although guilty he was almost untouchable. They needed him, and the deeper the General Staff dug in asserting Dreyfus's guilt, the more they needed him. The Count was fortunate that the letter signed D found in the garbage at the German embassy had been misattributed to Dreyfus. Had the D been assigned to a Drumont or Deroulede or d'Ormescheville, Christians all of them, the outcome would not have been so clearly in the Count's favor. Du Paty de Clam was powerful, a man who arranged convictions, promotions, a man who moved without restraint, a man so confident of his position that he could wear a dress, and no one could say *I have the goods on you,* a man beyond blackmail.

In the dim urinal, made considerably murkier by his dark glasses, Felix made out the shadowy form of the Count. Water dripped, gaslights sputtered, the tile smelled of chlorine and salt. The two men shook hands. Du Paty had told Felix that national security issues were at stake in the Dreyfus trial and therefore the conviction must stand. Esterhazy made Felix a little uneasy, which was unusual because after all his years with the Section of Statistics, few people did.

Just as du Paty's General Staff was an agency of parallel government arranging deals in public urinals, creating evidence of crimes where none existed, so too was Oliver North able to manufacture the fraud he was the architect of, or perhaps he genuinely believed in it. His project, however, operated on a global scale, getting one group of thugs to bankroll another. Again, North's testimony was bracketed by deletions and assertions that "national security issues were at stake."

1992 John Lennon's file is still sealed. The FBI claims national security is at stake.

Do you see what I'm getting at? Méliès wrote: "The scenario is simply a thread intended to link the 'effects' in themselves without much relation to each other." In other words the individual stories are less important than the parallels they represent. The who's, where's, when's and why's might be interchangeable. The scenario is a means to the end. Evidence of mistrials and cover-ups, the forgeries and lengths of shredded documents are only a series of similar patterns. Yet all these machinations make a mockery of even the notion of gullibility. I want to believe what you're telling me is true, I yell childishly at the radio, television, and microfilm. I want to believe the lives of John Lennon and Salvadoran children were corrosives eating away at a filigreed and imperiled democracy, but face it, Frances, don't you find all this a little difficult to swallow?

Some "national securities," so important at the moment, turn into exercises in clownish paranoia, the butt of curatorial or custodial jokes in a museum of ancient history, and while some conspiracies deflate when subjected to the pinpricks of the late twentieth century, others are born and gain momentum fed on underground springs. It was believed Napoléon died from stomach cancer. We know now that Napoléon died of arsenic poisoning.

Méliès's slogan was *Star Films: The World Within Reach.* He really believed any event, from kidnapping to a flash of lightning, could be caught and preserved, made accessible through the camera. It was an optimistic slogan. I think he was saying that because of the camera, the truth couldn't be perverted. Little did he know.

One thing I should add, someone stole the two books on Méliès from the New York Public Library. Settling down at the Donnell branch I called for the books only to find they were long gone, so most of what I'm telling you about him was learned while I worked at Omnibus. When I arrived back in the States I thought I would have access to more information and may yet, but so far I'm coming up empty handed. Not only are the books missing, but I've found microfilm tampered with by someone armed with pins and needles keen on riddling the strips with strategically placed pinprick holes and minute slashes so that any information I sought was rendered inscrutable. Most references to him have been poked or sliced out. When one of the books I searched for was found, the sections about Méliès had been torn out, replaced by chewing gum, tissues, or nothing at all.

Last week I was followed from the library into the subway at Broadway and 66th Street. It was early evening, just past rush hour, but the underpass that connects the downtown and uptown sides was surprisingly deserted. How do I know I was followed? I don't, but I think I was, although I heard no footsteps. A figure came up suddenly from behind me, and an abrupt blow to the jaw almost knocked me out. I didn't get a good look at her, but I'm certain it was a woman. She was a pro and moved quickly and gracefully like a figure from a Jackie Chan movie. Punjabi dance music floated down from the news kiosk on the subway platform just up the stairs above my head and the sounds of tabla and sitar threaded in and out of my consciousness until I was able to stand up and make my way to the stairs. I groped toward the sound, comforting and familiar from my years in London. Finally I reached the steps, damp with spilt liquids, and sat down again, my head in my hands. I swallowed my screams because this is a crime I'm unable to report. I'm here in this country illegally although I was an American citizen at one time and suppose I still am. I held my arms against my stomach rocking back and forth, unable to go to the hospital for exactly the same reason. No one paid any attention to me. When I was able I made my way onto a train although it was going the wrong way. My wallet was gone, which means someone has my address and Alphabet's. My assailant knows I'm living in New York, and I worry about you as well. They surely know you have this film and that you are working against the clock to preserve it.

Yours truly,
Jack Kews

I remember watching the Watergate trial on television. The screen flickered. Our reception wasn't very good. Howard Hunt with his pencil moustache. Liddy with his burned hand and love of Nazi propaganda films. Round-eyed Maureen Dean, a name with rhyming parts. We sat around the kitchen table watching. I remember the scene as if it were evening although it may have been during the day, and because I was very young I probably didn't know exactly what was going on. Houseplants and lumpy pottery made in grade school framed the talking heads. When a television commentator expressed shock, I had a sense of imminent catastrophe and shame, but it wasn't personal shame, and I didn't know who to attribute this shame to. Everyone sitting around the table talked back to the television.

"A thief. I always knew it."

"Magruder," my mother said, "like the sound a flat tire makes slapping the road."

"If they don't want you to know something, if it's really big and ugly and makes them look bad, don't think for a minute the thing will surface on national television. Don't be naive," said Mr. Levine, a neighbor who was considered an alarmist but one with interesting theories about conspiracies that he even exposed to children. As he paid you for mowing his lawn he might explain the connection between former president Johnson, an unlabeled complex of cinder-block buildings down Route 2, and a Coca-Cola commercial which co-opted sports imagery. "It's a racket," he would always say. There were no guns in his house, no freezer full of deer parts and bloody footprints on the concrete garage floor, and he refused to vote.

Paty de Clam. Patsy de Cline. I put the letter into a desk drawer beside the first one and reached for the telephone, then replaced the receiver without dialing. The notes didn't threaten or harass, they only proposed schemes like those hatched by the long-dead man down the road, links between assassinations of popes and presidents, between the deaths of Marilyn Monroe, John Lennon, and Aldo Moro, as if suicide, shooting, and kidnapping were all hatched from the same committee, a cartel shrouded in secrecy that exerted power over every unconscious citizen.

As I fit the film over the viewing machinery and examined each crumbling frame, I was afraid of what I might learn, but if I learned anything from my mother staring into space and my father plotting against those who believed Adam and Eve were parentless, it is that there is no safety to be found in pretending the facts aren't staring you in the face.

Even up on the fifth floor a fly had somehow gotten into Alphabet, and I watched it collide with the strips of venetian blind. I shut the door behind me and walked down the hall, letters in hand. *Felix the Cat* was being restored next door. The jingle, played at the beginning and at the end of the cartoon, was repetitive on its own but run over and over as the film was spooled back and forth, the lyrics could easily become the kind of episodic torture used to drive someone mad. I knew it was the actual cartoon that was being played not something spliced together or borrowed and used as a weapon in an imaginary setting, but the knowledge didn't keep the song from being any less penetrating. As I walked past Julius's office I could hear him talking loudly. Antonya sat with her feet on the reception desk, writing notes in the margins of a book on martial arts. Her glasses were pushed up on her head; replacing them in order to look at me she peered through black-rimmed eyes and lenses smeared with hair gel.

"Did a man come in this morning, wearing wire-rimmed glasses, jacket, sweatshirt turned inside out?" I asked her.

"No, but I've only been here an hour. The temp who comes in while I'm at class might have seen someone yesterday." I showed her the letters.

"A crackpot." She only glanced at them, then shrugged in dismissal, but she did call the agency, got the temp's number, called her home and left a message anyway.

"Why don't you leave Kews a note asking him to knock next time so you can actually shake hands."

"I don't want to shake hands with a stalker who doesn't want to meet me anyway. He writes about old magazines and Napoléon."

"What if he thinks he's Napoléon?"

"Look in the book. Did Julius have an appointment with Napoléon yesterday?"

With a twist Antonya turned the appointment ledger around so I could read it. He had meetings with a woman from the British Film Institute, a man from Kodak, a pair of researchers compiling a catalog of silent Westerns, a man who had a collection of films made on early cameras, the Mutigraph and the Mirograph, and the list went on. Jack Kews could have been any of them.

"Why don't you go to the police?"

I shook my head. *Could you spell Méliès for us?* they'd ask, the note having been sent to another department in order to determine what kind of old typewriter had been used to produce it. The female officer might open her drawer for a second and I'd be able to see a glint of handcuffs, keys, unused chopsticks, Rolaids and Juicy Fruit. Perhaps Kews had a record, a police file that could be called up on a computer that would reveal a past I'd no knowledge of: tax fraud, armed robbery, credit-card and identity theft. I would lean over the screen and try to read what he'd been apprehended for: *resisting arrest and assaulting an officer, loitering with intent, blocking the entrance to a church.*

"Whaddaya think? They're going to issue a restraining order for a phantom or place a guard at the door?"

For a moment she reminded me a little of Mr. Levine, the man who had watched the Watergate trial with premonition and enthusiasm, the man who saw the figure in the carpet, who thought everything was a swindle of some kind. With very little information she could construct cathedrals of imagined crimes, and yet Antonya was only humoring me.

"You got nothing better to do than worry about some couple of notes that don't even make sense?"

My explanations, stories about surrendered sunglasses, aimless trips to shops, emptied drawers that had long been cleaned out of anything meaningful, all these statements were left half-finished, stuttering. For Antonya the way to keep ghosts at bay was to figure out how many free meals you could tolerate at Burrito Fresca, because if you could put away a certain amount of money each week, you might hope to return to the city where your family had disappeared. She calculated and didn't reflect, taking a pragmatic approach, losing patience with my stuttering and obsession with the Dreyfus trial.

"Could he be charged with trespassing? He wasn't even seen for certain. Any messenger could have delivered the letters."

As far as I knew the police had never been to the offices. I imagined them arriving on the fifth floor to dust for fingerprints. They'd pick up copies of anticolorization letters stacked in the reception area, not with the intention of mailing them, but only to file away somewhere. They'd tell me that as long as my life wasn't threatened, there was nothing they could do. *It was just a prank, sweetie.* I went back to work.

At six o'clock Antonya knocked on my door. The temp had called back.

"She remembered only two visitors who didn't have appointments: a woman who inquired about renting an editing room, and a man who claimed to have rented space, but he left a few minutes later, saying he had forgotten something. He didn't return while she was here."

———•—

Three days later the following note arrived by mail:

Dear Frances,

I changed my mind. Meet me at La Chinita Linda's at 7:00 this Tuesday. I have short brown hair, wear glasses, beard, and moustache. Will wear a black T-shirt and a plaid jacket.

Yours,
Jack Kews

I tacked the note to the bulletin board above my light table, my eye wandering up to it when tired of examining and preserving the fleeting images of tiny men and women. Dreyfus read a letter from his wife, Lucie, and looked as if he would disintegrate with anguish. The prison as Méliès had designed it in 1899, gray and minimal, looked very modern. The emptiness of the prison cell wasn't the result of film-stock degeneration; the film at this point was in good shape. Lucie's letter, a surprisingly stark white square, fluttered to the ground. I worked on this scene all afternoon until my eye began to hurt. Toward the end of the day I showed the third note to Antonya.

"He didn't ask what you look like."

"So he knows. It's not like the notes are responses to an ad placed in a personals column."

"He knows your name, too. You better watch yourself. You want me to come with you?"

"Sure. Why not?" I tried to sound offhand, but Antonya was right. What did I really know about this guy?

Jack Kews was a fin-de-siècle Terminator, programmed, relentless, fixated on the twists and turns of a forgotten trial, obsessively cracking bilingual puns, pretending he's Georges Méliès disappearing around corners and reappearing already sitting in your chair when you open your door. On the other hand, why me? I was such a bit player in this. Why target the restorer of an obscure silent film? It was as if by setting his sights small, as if looking for a toehold, a footnote might be produced that would alter the course of the story or change how its meaning might unravel.

I locked Alphabet for the night. Offices had long ago emptied out, and the deserted Mayflower Building would make anyone jumpy, but after the notes from Kews I felt prone to hearing footsteps, seeing shadows down the halls, and catching silhouettes against doors when clearly even maintenance workers and guards had gone home. We stepped into the night. The air smelled like overturned earth, but dirt that was full of metal filings, asphalt, and loose parts of archaic machinery. A road crew worked on part of the dug-up avenue, steam from pipes or Con Edison ducts partially obscured their legs so that the workers' heads appeared disembodied, floating above the street.

We stopped in front of an appliance store whose display window was full of televisions, an entire wall of televisions turned to different channels. The one in the center was not tuned to any particular station. It was broadcasting pictures of us. A video camera had been set up to look at the street and transmit the picture to a monitor so you could see yourself and the scene behind you as if you were on television. Antonya and I stared into the screen while she combed her hair, our breath misting in the cold night air. I stepped to one side, my image reflected over a baseball game. There was no sound piped outside, the window display wasn't a segment of a Tower of Babel; there were only pictures.

My father used to take me to these kinds of stores, concrete shells with deep-discounted appliances arranged in long rows or grouped into a square as if a kind of model room. We didn't buy much in them, they were more a source of ideas. He used to love to take cars and machines apart and put them back together again. Spinning parts of the clothes dryer became a turntable. His workshop was a hospital for darkroom timers and short-circuited ceiling fans. Scores of radios were taken apart, their tubes and wiring, like miniature futuristic cities, transformed into other, more powerful radios. At night he would drink black coffee, listen to Jean Shepherd broadcasts from New York City, and laugh to himself.

In another window all kinds of telephones were on display. Some were ordinary dial phones, the kind not seen in years; some were gag phones. One instrument was in the shape of a pair of lips, another contained push buttons embedded in a silver high heel, a third was a clear plastic telephone with a green neon light running around inside it. Maybe Jack Kews slept with a green neon telephone beside his bed. He might proudly show it to guests as a symbol of an ironic sense of humor. Those who possessed a telephone designed to operate from a pair of red plastic lips or a fake shoe might at least feel sure of the direction their day would take when they got up in the morning; they would feel no chagrin at refusing to answer questions they didn't understand, and if their day turned into a nightmare they might have the strength of their convictions to tell everyone who crossed them to piss off. Antonya took one last look at herself on the screen, traffic halting in the background, and we crossed the street to the restaurant. A neon palm whose trunk blinked and buzzed sheltered about half the letters of *La Chinita Linda,* but its three fronds, once the shape of the Great Lakes, were out.

It was a few minutes past seven so we took a booth, ordered tea, and waited. I sat facing the door, watching everyone who entered. At twenty minutes past seven a man in a Mets cap appeared. He swiveled his body to the glass counter from the door as if his shoulder was attached to its hinges. Leaning against the register he told the cashier that he was a homeless veteran looking for work; if they needed a dishwasher, he would be happy to wash for them. He spoke in a loud voice, but the woman didn't answer him. She only shook her head. He took a handful of toothpicks and left. At 7:45 a group of thin young men entered wearing black suits with narrow ties or black leather jackets and sunglasses although night had fallen hours ago. They rolled up their sleeves to reveal tattoos of barbed wire, birds with talons exposed, and other designs I couldn't make out. Crowding into a booth, they seemed to know everyone who worked in the restaurant and spoke to them by name. One waiter looked nervous, another shrugged.

"Maybe they're related to the owner," Antonya said, watching them push sunglasses up on their heads and light each others' cigarettes. They were brought plates of rice and soft-shell crabs without any one of them looking at a menu or ordering.

It grew dark outside. La Chinita Linda's window reflected

nervous colored light from the inconstant palm. At a nearby table a child held a hand over one of the lanterns placed on her table, causing her fingers to turn red and translucent. Eavesdropping on a man sitting at a table to our left we observed the fact that he shared noodles with a blond girl easily less than half his age. In a tutelary voice he described the endings of French irregular verbs, leaning close to her, chopsticks pointing to lines of print on a piece of paper, probably leaving trails of sauce.

"You can see by the ending that it's almost regular, but then there is a corruption here." He had a thin, lined face, long curly hair, a stagy accent.

"Who gives language lessons in a Cuban-Chinese restaurant?" Antonya whispered. The man was doing most of the talking while the girl, about sixteen, giggled. He turned red but kept talking: *je, tu, il, elle.* Although we were obviously staring he paid no attention to us. We weren't sixteen.

"I have a nightmare," Antonya said loudly. "I'm stuck in a bridal shop during an earthquake, and I'm suffocating in red lace from bridesmaids' dresses. That's how I'll die."

The man looked startled and stopped talking for a few seconds. I laughed but at the same time, strained to see if Kews might have come on the heels of this group or that couple, but no one resembling Jack Kews entered La Chinita Linda as far as I could tell. It was possible he had seen Antonya and left, but since we were sitting in a booth, it was also true that he might not have been able to glimpse the back of Antonya's head at all. I tried to determine if the top could be seen from behind and decided it just about could. Or he might have seen only me but guessed from my gestures that I was talking to someone. I played with the small lanterns on our table. A boy behind us was drumming on the table with chopsticks, impatient for his dinner. Antonya asked for a beer, then as we got hungry we ordered salt-and-pepper shrimp, red beans, and brown rice.

"If he hadn't given himself a beard and moustache, I might have guessed he was one of the women who came in last night.

Jack Kews might be Jackie Kews," Antonya said, "might be a woman."

Antonya was annoyed with those renters of editing space who complained about the noise from the air conditioner as if she could stop the moaning sound issuing from the vent and could do so with nothing more than a pocket screwdriver. She was annoyed with people who asked for the key to the bathroom every twenty minutes when she was trying to do the accounts, she was impatient with Julius's debts, with me, with people who reserved space but who canceled at the last minute, costing the company money, with letter writers who didn't show up. Money flowed out, not much trickled back in. Preparing to take offense as soon as anyone called or walked in to Alphabet made her efficient. Antonya wanted to hang up on those who wasted her time. People yelled at her through the telephone receiver: "What do you mean you don't have any editing rooms?" or "I need to speak to Shute right away. It's urgent. I can't hold." Killjoys and crackpots fueled by what seemed to her a false urgency over saving old movies made her life miserable.

"Julius will never learn the old dead have to make way for the new dead." Actually, I thought he had come round to doing exactly that. Antonya, however, wasn't convinced Alphabet's backwards mission was such a lifesaver tossed to a drowning man. What did any of this crumbling film and archival narrative matter? At the same time she was saying: New Dreyfuses are born every day. Or are they?

Washington and Hollywood. Washington and Hollywood. She recapped lipstick and pens, clipped shut mirrors and notebooks, dismissed the bicycle messenger service with professional finality. Pulling the beard off Jack Kews or pasting it back on, either way wasn't going to make or break her days. Julius's lawyer had handled Immigration and Naturalization for her, but that in turn meant she couldn't legally work anywhere else.

"You better hope Alphabet stays afloat."

She shrugged.

I played with empty cups and bowls, stacking and arranging them as if they were futuristic architectural models. The backs of our legs stuck to red vinyl seats. The plastic was printed with an ice-cube pattern, but La Chinita Linda's, with only a plate-glass window, grew hot from the kitchen. Despite the cold outside, ceiling fans spun uselessly above us. Antonya looked at her watch. We both had other things to do. Jack Kews wasn't going to show up that night. The palm tree that looked like a map of the Great Lakes sputtered overhead as we left.

———·——

My hands had the sweet raisiny smell of old film. I'd been work-ing a long time at the Steenbeck. I stood up to stretch, closed my eye and walked into the hall that lead to the waiting area and Antonya's desk. I knew where I was going, or thought I did. I looked like a sleepwalker. My hands hit a fur wall. I opened my eye.

"Who the hell are you?"

It was Judy Holliday back from the dead. I mean, it was the former Mrs. Julius Shute in a short fur coat. Mrs. Julius had had some work done, but when looking around the office she wore a my-husband-is-a-bum expression. Her face was tight, eyes sunk-en, mouth like a stretched-out red rubber band. Yet Mrs. J. was no dummy. She spoke five languages and read several newspapers every morning. On her right hand, which flailed in my direc-tion, a topaz the size of a cough drop glittered.

"This is Frances Baum. She works for me," Julius said while showing her to the door.

"Does she always play hide-and-seek in the office?"

Before Julius could answer she went on. "Look at this place. I don't know why I ever bought into your half-baked ideas."

"There's nothing half-baked about Alphabet. It's an indus-try, an art." Julius grabbed her by the elbow and steered her toward the elevator.

"Fine, now I want my money back . . ." Her voice trailed off as the door shut.

———·———

"Frances, a word." He tipped his head toward my room as if to say, the jig is up. Inside the editing room he looked at what I was working on. I threaded up *Divers at Work on the Wreck of the "Maine,"* one of Méliès's *actualités.* This one had been tricky because Méliès had shot through layers of gauze to give the effect of swimming under Havana Harbor.

Julius squinted, then frowned.

"These prints should reflect the original with all its granularity and visual static," I defended the careful hand I'd taken in the restoration.

"Then the image on the screen will be nothing but grain. There won't be any clear picture, only fountains spilling piles of black and white M&M's. No clear picture. Maybe a hand or a face will appear once in while if you're lucky."

"The Wet Gate look has become less desirable, Julius. You know that. These films aren't supposed to look as if they were made yesterday."

I loved the archaeology of these crappy prints, and when making a copy of a film I photographed the whole surface, preserving whatever was there, including the dust and fingerprints. This was information Jack Kews would want, but that Julius, for reason of profit, wanted to get rid of. I wanted to race to the end of the film, but because it was so terribly fragile I had to proceed one frame at a time.

"Relying on what the film looks like to the naked eye is important because the emotional punch may matter more than the quality of the image. Don't paint the dress red." He stood very close. I inched away but kept talking.

"Noir films, for example, should retain scratches and grayness. Sometimes you want a rich gray scale; it depends on the subject. Comedies, we've agreed, should have sharp black and white contrast."

"Apart from *Dreyfus,* most of these *are* comedies," Julius argued. "Frances, you don't understand. These films have to look clear and crisp, yes, as if they were made yesterday. Otherwise, the client will be unhappy with our work, and according to our contract we won't receive the last half of the payment due us. This isn't the subsidized Library of Congress. I told you, I'm sacrificing *Dreyfus* in order to keep Alphabet afloat. I don't care if you have to use so much Wet Gate that Dreyfus has a halo at the end and flies up to fluffy clouds above his prison on Devil's Island. Frances, my life depends on this."

The heathered gray soundproofing that covered the studio walls loomed as if the walls were slightly tilted and pushing in on me from all sides.

"What are you saying?"

"I want *The Dreyfus Affair* to have a happy ending. The guilty verdict is impossible to believe because he was so clearly innocent. Over time, for those who care to dig and sift through forged documents and trial records, it will look only more ab surd. Eventually if the trial is remembered at all, many readers will stop at the evidence which points to innocence and close the book."

Julius wouldn't tell me who bought the *Looney Tunes* archive, but he did tell me that what we had in the office was the last known copy of the Dreyfus film. Few living people had ever seen it, he believed. Certainly all the original rioters were long dead.

Of course, I doubted his claim. He couldn't be certain this was the only copy of a rarely seen and, as far as he was concerned, barely documented film. Besides, written descriptions of the film must have existed in a book or two. If the film were to convey the astounding assumption that Dreyfus went free without the trials he did have, ammunition was taken from those who would charge the prosecution with fabricating evidence, of in fact protecting the real spy. Julius didn't see it that way.

The innocent verdict, Julius explained, is a victory; history as it was meant to be, not a whitewash of the guilty, not in the least. He wanted to pull one bit of victory/success out of the morass of prison cells, firing squads, nooses, gas chambers, even if it was a fantasy. Delirious, sleep deprived, "Why not?" he said. "Who can it hurt?" Fluorescent lights flickered overhead.

"It doesn't just make me look better," he whispered. "It doesn't just save the business from bankruptcy. I have a bigger picture in mind. There are, as you know, revisionists who say now we know, now we can say it: Alfred Dreyfus really was guilty all along."

I'd been up so long assessing the damage done to Méliès's rockets landing in the moon's left eye that I'd almost agree with Julius if he told me my parents had finally seen the light, joined the creationists, and were now burning classroom charts connecting amoebas, eventually, to man.

"You can't reshoot a scene from over one hundred years ago. You can't rewrite history."

"Cut the end. Cut the guilty verdict. Dreyfus's case was so convincing the audience will assume he was found innocent without seeing the verdict read. Cut the degradation scene where his sword is broken, cut the scene where Dreyfus is returned to prison after the trial. Just cut all that footage. We're on a deadline. Say it was too screwed up to save. No one will ever know. What does it matter if a few French generals and their henchmen are given a whitewash? Dreyfus was innocent. Everyone knows it. Let it go at that. We're just taking a shortcut to get to the same end result."

"What if someone asks what happened to the end of the film?"

"There wasn't any viable film stock left to unspool. I've been offered a lot of money to change the ending, and that's what's happening."

I had visions of Julius deliberately damaging the film in the middle of the night, squeezing chemicals from an eyedropper onto the film so as to look like natural erosion, mimicking the corrosive nature of the passage of time and humidity, blaming an archive that used improper storage.

Julius was sweating slightly, like he'd had way too much coffee and just wanted to get on to the next task at hand, regardless of how outrageous the suggestion he had just made was. I asked him if he was trying to lose his business or change history or both. He just kept talking.

"Before Disney took over Times Square there were these booths where you could talk to women for a dollar. I not only liked to go into them, but I wondered about the other men, like myself, who paid a dollar for what didn't amount to much, really. Was there some kind of fusion between my interest in degenerating film stock and what many would have considered degenerate practice?"

"Julius, why are you telling me this?"

"I don't know. Maybe what I'm saying is that sometimes what the client of the moment wants trumps what a long-dead director actually shot. It happens. Also, we need to get paid as quickly as possible."

There was a boy who stood so close to me in a film preservation class that there was barely a molecule of air between our sleeves. We shared editing tables, joked about rewriting movies and adding Godzillas where they didn't belong. I thought he was just a work buddy, but then I wasn't so sure an arm was just something for reaching for the next canister. I wondered what he saw in me, and what projection of his fantasies I might have been. Images of a one-eyed woman were too obvious and unbearable to think about.

Hey Cyclops, what makes you think you can be so choosy?

I pretended to examine the Méliès film in which a man was turning himself into a cigarette lighter, and in the silence Julius walked out

I could make two copies: a doctored version for Julius, an accurate copy for myself. One of the two I would clean up, using gallons of Wet Gate, drawing into the emulsion if streaks of rain or lightning bolts had faded, but in the second copy I'd leave every mark, scuff, and crack. The negative can't be read with the naked eye, but with copies I can experiment. There is no master, no original. After five copies, degradation of the image makes it unreadable. The Air Force once tried making numerous copies of surveillance films. What they were left with proved Julius's M&M's theory. After a certain point you get diverticulation, the emulsion falls off. Russian satellites or Iraqi tanks disintegrate into bottle shapes and tin cans, a Méliès-like transformation from signifiers of harm to pedestrian bits and pieces: an unwitting but complete conversion of swords into plough shares.

"Hello, Frances?"

"I was waiting for your call. What happened? You stood me up. Don't ask me for any more favors. You can take your exploding heads and buy yourself a watch."

"You weren't alone."

"So what?"

"I didn't want an audience."

"Are you two years old, or what? I don't know anything about you so I brought a friend."

"While in prison one of the General Staff's star forgers in the conspiracy to frame Dreyfus, a man named Colonel Henry, slits his own throat." Jack resorted to Dreyfusspeak.

"How do you know that's the scene I'm working on now? The print is very worn here. His razor emerges with a grand sweep, an arc of light. Henry's body is so blurred and grainy, the image gives the impression that a disembodied arm has appeared from foggy atmosphere and severed a head which has already been guillotined." I backed up the film, thinking I might have missed a figure entering his cell. "Now he's only sitting at his desk writing a letter to his wife."

"Doll-like and unseen, Madame Henry will be capable of hysterical courtroom outbursts when the judge, Bertulus, refers to the late forger, Henry. The mystery of Henry's suicide, never solved, was that a shut razor was found in his hand. Had he slit his throat himself he would have had no time to calmly shut the razor, lie down, and prepare to expire."

Then the phone went dead.

"The Count and Countess Pecci-Blunt gave an elaborate costume ball in their house and garden in Paris. The theme was white; any costume was admitted but it had to be all in white. A large white dance floor was installed in the garden with the orchestra hidden in the bushes. I was asked to think up some added attraction. I hired a movie projector which was set up in a room on an upper floor, with the window giving out on the garden. I found an old hand-colored film by the pioneer French film-maker, Méliès. While the white couples were revolving on the white floor, the film was projected on this moving screen — those who were not dancing looked down from the windows of the house. The effect was eerie."

Man Ray, *Self Portrait*, 1963. Courtesy of Jack Kews

The snippet had arrived in the mail along with the usual kinds of advertisements for film equipment and personal inquiries about specific jobs that I occasionally receive at Alphabet. Colonel Henry's suicide splashes over a skirt. One of Méliès's heads explodes at an elbow. A rocket lands in someone's eye. Apart from the Dreyfus film, which is somewhat stark, these films are crowded, packed with images. Méliès nearly always filled black space as if he had a fear of emptiness. No cave, room, door, fireplace remained black for long, sooner or later something would emerge from it. In *The Conquest of the Pole,* a huge figure eats the explorers, but the barren tundra is soon inhabited when the monster throws them up again. I stood in the dark, relatively empty room. I waited for Jack Kews or anyone to burst in. Nothing happened.

———·—

I worked through the night to try to reach the end of the film, but there was too much damage, and it was slow going.

After Henry's suicide Dreyfus leaves Devil's Island, returning to France for a second trial at Rennes. Although a great deal of evidence to prove his innocence has been established, he will again be found guilty, but for the moment there's still hope. He lands at the port of Quiberon in Bretagne. I held the film up to the light. A storm has been brewing. The forks of lightning that were hand drawn on the film have all but disappeared, only traces of them remain. Figures of Dreyfus and his guard ascend steps leading to the quay. Sailors, probably sitting on the floor, sway back and forth as if they're rocked by actual waves in an actual boat; otherwise the scene is gray and static like a nineteenth-century sculpture garden.

Prints from the 1890s are very dark. I turned out the light and laid the carefully unspooled strips across a light table. I wanted to jump ahead, but the storm needed repair. Too many frames had degenerated to dotty atmosphere, pointillist and vague. As creditors threatened and Alphabet's accounts had the dry heaves, Julius wanted all these scenes dissolved. Kews, on the other hand, sent notes and left messages: preserve what you can then cut to the epilogue.

Louis Kahn wrote that a boy walks around the city and the city tells him what to do with himself. Architects may not be the only ones who look at the exterior of buildings and the layout of streets, parks, and bridges as a kind of visual or tactile guide indicating appropriate behavior and suggesting what to do next. I think his theory about walking around the city works well for girls, too. During lunch I went to the public library. The main branch was just a few blocks from Alphabet, its steps already littered with fallen leaves, and its hours reduced. Others on their lunch breaks brushed the detritus aside in order to sit on the steps and eat hot dogs, slices of pizza, drink sodas, and stare at the street. As I climbed the steps, I felt I ought to have been watching the street too, balling up paper wrapping and reading headlines over someone's shoulder, yet I continued up the steps with a sense of purpose, aiming toward computer terminals and the smell of binding glue. The process would take about an hour. I looked up *Artificially Arranged Scenes: the Films of Georges Méliès, The Affair: The Case of Alfred Dreyfus, All the President's Men,* the testimony of Oliver North and other transcripts from the Iran-Contra hearings published in book form, and a biography of John Lennon. I handed my list to the librarian, but he came back empty handed. None of the books were on the shelves. He checked the computer and told me the same person had taken each out, and all were overdue.

"We'll send him a postcard to see that they're returned. Try us again at the end of the week."

"I think I know the man who took them out." There were hundreds of thousands of people with library cards who might have taken out these books. "Jack Kews."

"Look under Zola." The librarian spoke with a Russian accent. *"J'accuse.* You want I should look it up for you?"

"No, it's a man's name."

"This I can not tell you."

Light bounced off the librarian's glasses so his eyes were difficult to see, and he winked at me. I couldn't wink in return. Dust motes floated in the air above his black and gray hair.

"Jack Kews." I repeated his name. No one was watching us. Awkwardly, I pulled a twenty-dollar bill out of my wallet and slid it across the worn wooden counter.

"A fine," he turned to a woman behind the counter who suddenly turned to look at a computer screen. After consulting an index card, the librarian wrote Jack Kews's address and telephone number on a piece of paper. So I entered a silent deal or bargain with a man who hated his job, who wanted to sabotage the head librarian, who mis-shelved books.

A frieze ran around the hall, a leftover from when the shelves were organized differently and the images on the wall directed the reader to the area he or she searched. Egyptian figures, Greek gods, elm trees, elephants, whales, knights, birds in flight were markers of a now obsolete and long-abandoned visual lexicon. There was no place in the frieze for a symbol for books on microchips or superconductors.

The librarian, used to the complicated tenses and acrobatics of Russian, might find the expansiveness of English — the way it absorbs words and sentence constructions from all over, New York English with all its accents, dialects, and to say nothing of all the pidgins — chaotic, impossible to take seriously beyond what's required for the job. Why not subvert the hard-to-pin-down order should the opportunity present itself. When asked about the disorder he created he looks at the frieze circling the hall and states the obvious. At night all the illustrated creatures come down from their respective perches and mix things up.

"Whatever you want, *babechik*. Books disappear every day."

I tried to fix a noncommittal or businesslike expression on my face while in fact I was nervous, as if I'd been caught defacing a book and stood captive at the librarian's mercy.

"Remember he can't just hand them to you. He has to return them to us first." He looked into the distance at a woman who was putting books in her bag until it was quite weighted down. "Mr. Kews always looked like he was stealing books from the reading room. We noticed he put books in his jacket as if he was thinking about stealing, but he did check them out."

"Is there any particular day he comes in regularly?"

"No."

The librarian walked over to a cart, pulled a book out, and handed it to me.

"He returned this one a few days ago. It hasn't been reshelved yet. You know, at first I thought Kews was one of these, because others come and ask questions about him, then I don't see him anymore. Now if you will excuse me."

Trying to look as if I didn't understand what he meant I took *Captain Dreyfus the Story of a Mass Hysteria* from him and found a seat at a table. The room was nearly empty. The stacks and carrels were without any sign of industry; no sounds of writing or pages being turned were audible. A man sitting a few chairs to my left snored over a paper, arm stretched out across the table, glasses abandoned a few inches from his hand. Before beginning the book read so recently by Jack Kews I turned it over and over, finally opening it to the acknowledgments then thumbing through the first fifty pages. About a third through *Captain Dreyfus the Story of Mass Hysteria,* one line was marked.

While the rigidly restricted investigation by General Pellieux went droning on, the legal blinders making it [the trial] like the study of a book whose pages could not be opened. . . .

There the marking ended, but in the margins someone had written: *I would like to open this book*

———·——

Méliès was taunting me, saying look at me, choose me, you'll be seduced, entertained as you never have been before, and you won't regret it either, not for a minute.

I picked up other cans and read the titles written on their labels, one after another: *Pharmaceutical Hallucinations, Dreams of an Opium Fiend, Delirium in a Studio* (Julius had said it was based on a Delacroix painting), *Scheming Gambler's Paradise, Melomaniac, Dislocation Extraordinary, A Terrible Night, Every Man His Own Cigar Lighter, Four Troublesome Heads.* Not all the hockey pucks would unspool. You can easily give up or try to soften them, then make copies as quickly as possible. It's like Russian roulette. Once unsealed they disintegrate rapidly because the base is breaking down. Unrolling film is like following a map that might break diagonally any minute. The strips are so brittle they snap if you so much as look at them. You put the pieces back together again with mylar. Dreyfus, the American invasion of Cuba, and dismembered body parts are all mixed together. Where is the real Méliès? Does Méliès ever turn to the audience or to his workers as they hammer and paint, does he ever turn to them and say, *Sorry, I don't feel like myself. Threatened by bankruptcy and violent family members, I can no longer make sound decisions, but keep the camera rolling anyway. The* mixture of despondency with bursts of gallows humor reminded me of the moments when my mother used to quote Max Lieberman's remark on the subject of the Nazis marching through the Brandenburg gate: "You can't eat as much as you would like to throw up."

The next note to come in the mail was a series of cartoons, unfolding like an accordion as I slit the tape that bound them.

They were drawn on the backs of postcards, one attached to the next. The postcards were tourist attractions from Paris: the Eiffel Tower, Montmartre, Les Deux Magots, the Champs d'Elysees, the Musée d'Orsay, the pyramid in front of the Louvre. The cartoons on the back were drawings of Emile Zola in New York done in ballpoint pen. He went to the top of the Empire State Building, visited the Lower East Side and the Fulton Fish Market. I wouldn't have recognized the figure and buildings; they were drawn with very simple lines, but each tableau was labeled.

———•—•———

Jack lived in Brooklyn. Not in my neighborhood but in a building much closer to the river. There was a parking garage on one side of it and a laundromat on the other. Above the laundromat were the offices and classrooms of a technical school, and Antonya pointed out Styrofoam heads looking down at us, wigs pinned to their scalps. To the left of the laundromat was a Mail Boxes Etc. A man strolled out of it, walked to the front of Jack

Kews's building and positioned a milkcrate with his foot so he could sit on it as he looked through his mail. I wondered if the man was Kews, but he had white hair, was clean shaven and wore a pork-pie hat. He looked our way but didn't speak to us as we stepped into the entrance. The hall was painted half-red, half-yellow, and its mailboxes were battered, the little doors swung off their hinges. Tenants probably rented the boxes next door in order to receive mail. We pressed a buzzer labeled Kews. No one answered, but Antonya pushed the front door. It was open. We walked up five flights of stairs and knocked on number 5B.

"There isn't going to be anyone home if he didn't answer the front door bell."

"It might be broken."

I knocked softly. Antonya knocked loudly. We heard nothing, standing in silence for a few minutes until a voice from behind a door across the hall called out to us.

"Hey girlies, girlies, come over here. You looking for Jack?" Antonya jumped.

From a crack in the door we could see a face pressed against the door chain. He smiled like the Coney Island laughing boy, aggressive and intimidating, an attempt to entice and threaten at the same time.

"Jack's not in," he told us.

"We know."

"Do you know where he is? He owes me money. I lent him fifty dollars. Jack's here from London illegally, you know," the nearly disembodied voice croaked.

"Jack went to England years ago to avoid the draft. He had a low number like two or something." He laughed to himself. "So he left, then he came back, and now he's here, or he was here. I shouldn't be telling you this, but he owes me money." The man rested his chin on the chain. "Another woman was looking for him yesterday. I told her the same thing. She could have been a *nofky*, or a ghost sent from immigration, from the police, or she could have been his girlfriend for all I know. It's nothing to me what happens to him now that he's skipped out. She could have been sent by a ghost of the draft board. Hey, *be all that you can be in the army."* He snickered and sang off key. He appeared to salivate, white foam collected at the corners of his mouth, and although we only saw a sliver of him, it seemed that he was completely naked.

"What did she look like?"

"Like you, the one with short hair." Antonya, who had been standing behind me, stepped out of his line of vision, almost slamming her back against the wall beside his door so he couldn't see her, but I was the one with short hair.

"I can't go out regularly, see, or I'd try to find him myself. I'm in a wheelchair. Jack used to help me out when the mood suited him." He must have been supporting himself somehow, braced on shelves or ledges on either side of the inner jambs so he could stand.

Antonya rolled up a five-dollar bill and put it up to the man's face. He opened his mouth so the could clamp the bill in his teeth, then he turned his head to spit it out somewhere behind him.

"Why won't you open the door?" I asked out of a perverse streak to see if he could be completely unleashed.

"Nothing doing, girlies," he said with obvious contempt, then the door slammed in our faces, and that was that. It was getting late, and we had to get back to Alphabet.

Downstairs by the mailboxes we looked at the labels beside the buzzers. The name on 5C was Lewisohn.

"What's a *nofky*?"

"A prostitute." It was a word I hadn't ever heard during my childhood, not that I could remember. As an adult I was driving somewhere downtown with my mother when we saw a woman in a red dress with Christmas gnomes and reindeer printed along the bottom. It might have been made from an old tablecloth.

"There's Dell, the *alte nofky*. Do you remember her?"

"No."

"She was the school secretary, but she had another life."

"How did you know?"

"I heard."

Then I guessed what the word meant. She said it with some sadness as if beyond meaning *prostitute* the word implied that anyone could end up wearing dresses made from tablecloths and think no one noticed.

The way my mother said the words *alte nofky* meant, as I remembered, that we all conceal something — a past, pretensions, something, and we deceive ourselves into believing that we do so with success. An *alte nofky* lurked inside Lewisohn, Antonya, Julius, me, the librarian in impenetrable reflective glasses. Jack Kews was a stew of hidden identities. Maybe it was time to give up on him.

When I got back to the office I checked the postmark on the last letter he'd sent me. The print was barely legible, but the zip code looked like the same code as Alphabet's. It must have been mailed within a few blocks of the Mayflower Building. If he had gone to Spartacus, a few hours' drive north, I couldn't imagine when he would have mailed the last letter, but there were enough gaps in the correspondence so that I wouldn't have been able to account for his weekly movements even if I'd saved all the envelopes. He might have had someone else do the mailing for him. He led me to believe he had been following me around for a long time whether we came from the same city or not. I shook the stack and a small postcard I hadn't seen before fluttered to the floor.

A twelve-year-old girl goes missing in Paris after this riot. Méliès is suspected. Star Films is searched by the police who overturn volcanoes, the North Pole, and the moon looking for her.

This was written on the back of a postcard from the 1939 World's Fair. The date was circled, and he didn't have to tell me of its significance. Never entirely dormant, the furies stirred up by the trial were in 1939 given an opportunity to boil over again. I propped it up in front of the can containing the newly preserved *A Terrible Night*, in which a man was attacked by giant bedbugs. There is no peace in his bed, no possibility of sleep, only aggravation. He hits them with a broom. Tough luck. When is a bug not really a bug? My bed was haunted by an insect who sent notes, who held up a corrupting mirror, who wouldn't let me treat the Dreyfus film as a job like any other, who wouldn't let meaning be. To everything I did he seemed to say, *you think this is precious stuff? It's all been recycled.* These shadowy, grainy figures left the refuge of the literal and abandoned the realm of the simple pictorial situation; he nudged them out. *You think it's just a strip of plastic,* he seemed to be saying in his notes, *think again.* He loomed over the sheets, laughing and pinching. I would like to have blown up a frame of the traveler haunted by bugs and tacked it to my office door, but Alphabet wasn't going to have a door much longer.

Dial 1-800-HISTORY.

On the television screen children in shorts and T-shirts stuck their heads into pillories while a voice overdescribed colonial forms of criminal punishment. Men wearing wigs pounded anvils, and women, also in wigs, smiled back at them. A family in tennis whites was transformed: mother and daughter swished from stable to parlor in long dresses, father and son suddenly carrying lanterns instead of camcorders, braids grown down their backs. My eye ached. I had nothing to do, so I reached for the telephone.

Thank you for calling Colonial Williamsburg. All our reservation agents are busy at the moment. We take your call very seriously. Please stay on the line. This message will not repeat.

The man next door hammered into our adjoining wall while singing along with the radio. Telephone wedged between ear and shoulder I reached for a pencil, but as I listened to him sing and as I considered the deadlines I faced at work, the idea of a colonial village where tobacco was harvested but no one smoked, a place where slaves smiled, baked bread, and walked unhindered by chains made me anxious. *I've got you under my skin*, my neighbor sang. Pocahattans played by students on summer vacation handed the villagers what looked like pemmican and peace pipes, then held out their hands and were given, in turn, strands of glass beads. The colonial family was buying the Chesapeake Bay. Terrified, I hung up the phone, then fell asleep.

Waking a few hours later I could now hear my neighbor's television through the wall. He was watching *Entertainment Live from Andrews Air Force Base*, singing along with Bob Hope as if his heart would break. I didn't want to interrupt his pleasure, but during a commercial for L'Oreal Eye Defense I banged on the wall. He turned the sound down, but it was still impossible to sleep.

I had become conscious of men in crowds, found myself turning around to see who was behind me, and felt a little haunted by the fact that Jack knew what I looked like while my image of him was blurry and vague; he refused to hold still for the camera. He knows what you look like, Antonya had said, his letters, his quotes from Man Ray's memoirs were little fluttering baits at the end of a line. He was taunting me, terrorizing me into finding him. Jack could have been anyone, the kind of person who faded into the woodwork, going unnoticed unless you knew where to look, or he could be daring and flamboyant, right there in front of you, an irritant in the public eye all along.

Perhaps he was someone I grew up with, but I never knew him. This new possible Jack tapped me on the shoulder and jerked his thumb north, to indicate that other, much smaller city I hadn't thought about in a long time. Had we ridden school buses together, stood in line at the Great Adventure or Storytown? Had he snickered when others called me Hawkeye, and by snickering so included himself in their group? There had been no surprise smart alecks at my school. No one who would grow up to drop notes about Méliès under my hard-to-find door. If there was someone who had pretended to be Orwell writing about the Spanish Civil War between shifts at Mr. Subb's I think I would have known. Still, I could imagine Jack in a diner, sitting cross legged in one of the booths, shunned by everyone, even the few who protested the war. Had he been one of those who dealt drugs bought in the projects, exploded illegal fireworks, shoplifted from time to time? The boy, Jack, turns around. He's been kicked, beaten, glasses on the ground, Orwell tossed in the gutter. He's teased, gets angry in turn, sets fire to some derelict building in which an illegal squatter is accidentally killed. Never convicted, Orwell smiles and offers him an escape. He wears a beret to school, which is a big mistake. Life gets worse for him. The beret is grabbed, fit over a Frisbee. It flies through the air, little felt tag stiff in the breeze.

This time the note contained a Xerox of a letter that had been printed in a newspaper, but the margin had been torn off so that where it had appeared was impossible to determine.

January 13, 1969

President Richard M. Nixon
The White House
Washington, D.C.

Dear Mr. President,

As I watched my draft card burn last night I imagined what it would be like to be an herbicide, say, Agent Orange. Okay, here we are in Vietnam, and I am a molecule of exfoliant, floating toward a banana leaf, dissolving through it, landing on a woman's arm, eating through bone, finally resting on the ground, burning a monkey's paw, or searing a snake as one or the other passes over me. With a wind I drift into a rice paddy, and anyone who eats me becomes a mutant and has mutant offspring for many generations. As a molecule, or if I really were a molecule, I would want to thank you for putting me to work in such an exotic setting, and I would ask you what more could I do that would be as mindlessly destructive of innocent civilians and verdant jungle? Advancing up the food chain of weaponry I might prefer to be a mine, a piece of shrapnel, a bullet or a bomb. Unleashed in the middle of a firestorm I aim my pointed head at bamboo huts because you never know, there might be tunnels to Moscow underneath. I pass through walls and limbs as if they were no more substantial than crackerjacks. I've never had so much fun, but I'm none of these things. My card is burnt. I flush the ashes down the toilet.

I write to accuse, to point a finger at you, Henry Kissinger, and the other architects of this degrading and inhuman war. We should let the people of Vietnam decide their own future. I am writing to you to express alarm and outrage over the war. We have no right to be there. Like the bully on the playground who gets his own way by force, not by compassion or by engendering reason among others, nothing can be won or achieved because there is nothing to win by bombing Vietnam into the Stone Age. American actions in Southeast Asia are nothing short of genocide.

Yours very truly,
Jack Kews

———·•·———

A man (Jack Kews?) stared at me as I looked in the window of the appliance store next door to Burrito Fresca. Children were making faces at themselves in the self-broadcast television. I stood to one side so I could watch them and myself while they rolled their eyes back into their heads, stuck out their tongues, and called each other names. There were two of them, and the one who clearly had the upper hand was quick to goad the smaller one, taunting while her friend lagged a little, mesmerized by the process of seeing herself reflected on a regular television. *See, this is you. This is what you look like.* Someone who resembled my idea of Jack walked behind me. I turned around quickly, but as the man crossed the street he darted around a truck. I couldn't see where he went, and traffic prevented me from following him. By the time the truck moved, and I was able to cross the street, he was gone, leaving nothing but an afterimage. *It hits you between the eye and the eyeball,* Louis Kahn also wrote, but I couldn't remember what *it* was. The thing that hit me between the eye and the eyeball might have been an afterimage of a running Jack Kews, might have been Méliès's lost negatives, might have been a bottle of Wet Gate smoothing the abrasions and scratches so that everything looked as if it were shot yesterday. 1-800-HISTORY turned out to be a useless number after all.

I went back to Jack's apartment building. I didn't think he'd be there, and I was right, he wasn't, but the man who had read his mail in front of the building stepped out of Mail Boxes Etc just as distractedly as he had done the last time, stumbling and looking around. The hour was the same. He looked in my direction as if he recognized me as well. It turned out he was the building's super; he lived on the ground floor and had keys to every apartment.

"I'm looking for Kews in 5B."

"Haven't seen him in weeks. Did you lend him money? One of the other tenants wanted me to break the door down because he was owed." He stuck a thumb in a belt loop of his plumber's pants, creating structural stress on the pants. There was a distinct possibility they would fall even further, perhaps down to his ankles.

"No, but I'd like to talk to him."

"A lot of people would like to talk to him."

Anticipating this, I reached into a jacket pocket and handed him a twenty. Jack's building had a way of reaching into wallets.

"You know, this is highly irregular," the super said as he gestured for me to follow him upstairs. "But I haven't seen him in some time. It's worth checking out. Once we had a tenant who ate rat poison. Didn't find the body for *days,* and let me tell you, it wasn't a suicide or an accident."

"Somebody was forced to eat poison?"

"You don't believe me?"

"Well, no, sorry. I don't think I do."

"Suit yourself."

Holes had been punched in the walls and dry plaster crumbled from them, yet the surrounding surfaces seemed damp and shiny as a result of a glossy red paint job. I heard a child's voice screaming as we approached one apartment, and I banged on the door shouting to whoever it was to stop. The super grabbed my hand and told me the screaming wasn't what I thought it was. We reached the entrance to Kews's apartment. Even from the outside each door in the building bore the marks of a history of bolts and screws, presumably associated with locks, installed and then removed by successive tenants.

"It was the only time anyone died while I worked in this building. There were a lot of aliens here at the time. Some of the women were forced to do things, you know what I'm saying? One woman discovered the art of rat poison and thought that was her ticket to freedom. So what I learned is, it doesn't hurt to be nosy once in a while, but don't bang on that door," he jerked his head in the direction of the apartment where the screaming had come from. It was quiet now. The pants shifted about an inch lower. "If a stiff's in here, we would've smelled it, but's still worth having a look, you know." He took a last gulp from a bottle of orange soda and deposited the empty on the floor beside Jack's door. Taking a key from a back pocket he unlocked the door and flipped a light switch.

Jack lived in a one-room apartment with a small kitchen stuck into a kind of alcove. A bathtub with ball-and-claw feet jutted out from beside the sink, but the first thing I saw was that his bed, pushed against a wall, was wrinkled. I walked over to it, put my hand on the dented pillow while the super made a beeline for the dripping tap. The sheets still felt warm. There was only one window, and although it faced the street, light was blocked by the adjacent building whose bay windows projected further out, encroaching on the sidewalk. It was mid-afternoon and very cold. The room darkened quickly.

While the super looked under the sink I walked over to Jack's desk, which had been positioned in front of the window. Photographs of Jack with various people and photocopies of articles had been taped to the walls. I glanced at one about POW Garwood, falsely accused of something I couldn't make out. *Bug Suspect Got Campaign Funds. Radio Hanoi.* . . . An article about mining strikes in England, written by Jack Kews, was tucked into a beat-up copy of Zola's *Germinal*. I had to be careful the super didn't catch me snooping. The articles were eclectic, and the walls' contents made the room resemble that of a student writing papers for an array of classes that might not, at first glance, have much to do with one another. A jar of Wonderbond Plus glue and a staple gun lay on top of some papers, and enclosed in a paperweight was a scene of a hillside with a shovel stuck into it. When I shook the plastic bubble, snow fell. The desk served as a kitchen table as well. A plate of fried eggs and toast lay to one side, on top of a pile of books. I touched it, and to my surprise the food, too, was still warm.

"You sure you haven't seen him?"

"I'm not always sitting out front. He could have left while I was next door picking up mail."

While the super continued to inspect the dripping tap I began to open desk drawers as quietly as possible. I found a box of thumbtacks, envelopes, letterhead stationery taken from a London newspaper, and a yellowed clipping from a paper about, as far as I could read very quickly, a business which stored and collected personal information of all kinds, released to anyone for a fee. At the bottom of the drawer I found a list of names and addresses. The page, a sheet of lined legal paper, looked as if it had been compiled many years ago, but it was impossible to know for certain. *DRL, Draft Resisters League* had been written across the top, and I quickly folded the list and put it in my pocket. In the next drawer were two sealed letters addressed to me at Alphabet Conservation.

"No stiffs in here. As long as he pays his rent I can't allow you to go through his drawers." Having quickly confirmed that the tap did indeed leak and there was nothing he was going to do about it for the moment, the super had turned around and caught me riffling through Jack's things.

I straightened up, embarrassed, but he hadn't seen me pocket the DRL list.

After we shut the door and the key clicked in the lock, the door to 5C opened. A man in a wheelchair rolled into the hall.

"Let me into that apartment, Ed. He owes me fifty dollars."

The super shook his head. Lewisohn rushed toward us, naked in his wheelchair, screaming that he had no money and he was sick of it; there were drugs he needed and medicines, and nobody cared if he lived or died. I ran to the edge of the stairs, but he blocked my getaway. Bald and rheumy eyed, he was simultaneously plaintive and terrifying. He had heavy bags under his eyes, and with a gold earring pulling down one earlobe, he was already the ghost of a pirate.

"Ever try to find a vein when you're half paralyzed?"

His viciousness, directed at me, had to come from somewhere, but I'd done nothing to him that I could think of. His raw fury was spectacular. He was like a small animal, a rat or a snake whose frenzy seems personal although it really can't be, and even though you're much bigger, you feel cornered. It was impossible not to look at his veined, emaciated limbs and shriveled genitals, but in looking I felt even more vulnerable, as if he had baited me. Yes, I was caught looking at the forbidden, yet how can you not look? Lewisohn snarled, pulling back as if baring teeth or fangs, as if he was saying, I know you, I know all about you, don't think for a minute I don't. Once a woman pushed me aside in the subway saying, *move, fuckhead,* and I felt that although she was a stranger she knew some kind of hidden truth about me; a useless person who wastes time listening to a neighbor sing along with the radio, lacking the nerve to tell him to stop. Lewisohn unleashed a farrago of barely comprehensible accusations. I had betrayed him. I had made promises. I had no right to enter the building, to walk around, to breathe.

"Don't shrink away from me. I can accuse you if I choose." His voice echoed down the stairwell.

Pinned to the wall, a stand-in for I didn't know who or what, I never wanted to help him, didn't want to listen to his insinuating incriminations. The super stood by in silence staring at the naked man in the wheelchair. I had no obligations to this Lewisohn snarling, nipping at my heels. Would I have pushed him before a moving train, given the chance? I don't know.

"You didn't go after him," I accused Lewisohn, jerking my head in the direction of the super. The ability to run away was meaningless. I was sure he would flatten me even as I shrank down the stairs. Lewisohn's anger had the force of a cartoon electric fan, high powered and out of control, blowing all the furniture to one side of the room. I threw twenty dollars at him.

"You sure you want to do that?" the super asked me, and I nodded. Between me and Antonya we'd paid off half Jack's debt. As I walked down the stairs the building was completely silent. I couldn't remember which door the screaming had come from, and still don't know why I believed the super when he said the shrieking wasn't what I thought it was.

———•—·—·———

"People think in packs," Clarice said.

Her name had been written on the back of the DRL list, like a kind of recent afterthought, and her entry was in a darker, more liquid ink, like a fountain pen, where the others on the list had been written in ballpoint.

"There was no way Jack was going to get a fair trial, even representing himself, which might have been a stupid thing to do, looking back. He was convicted of violating the Selective Service Act. There were guys we knew who got five-year jail terms as conscientious objectors. Between conviction and sentencing, he jumped bail, getting to the UK through Canada." She said "the UK" like an American who had lived there. "For a while he became interested in other people's trials. I haven't seen him in weeks. I'm going back to London. He wants to stay here."

"When you lived with him, did he ever talk about silent movies?"

"Yes, often enough when he worked at an old film house. Omni something. I didn't always listen, but I remember it got broken into a lot, not that there was much to steal. Some of the films disappeared, and Jack's boss, who was a bit off, used to say, 'If you knew what I knew, you'd be dead, my girl.' He was murdered shortly before we were finally able to leave London and return here."

"Did you find that strange, that he'd been murdered, after he said he was the man who knew too much? Do you think it's true, that someone killed him because of his business?"

"How should I know? I only met him a couple of times. The last time I saw him, it had been raining, I remember that, so I went into the bathroom to comb my hair. There were never any paper towels, so I wiped my hands on the flocked paper, and the fuzz would come off, so then you had to wipe your hands on your pants. There was a big window, odd for a bathroom, and it didn't have bars on it the way it would have in New York. That's probably how they got in. Out in the lobby, there was a painting of a parade of actors, all of them together, cheek by jowl as if they had all known each other as the most intimate friends: the Marx brothers, Marilyn Monroe, Jimmy Stewart, Cary Grant. The door to the projectionist's booth, little more than seams in the wall behind the popcorn machine, was covered by Barbara Stanwyck with Peter Sellers at her elbow."

"Jack was a projectionist?"

"Yes, what did he tell you?"

"Nothing."

"The manager always had a telephone wedged between ear and shoulder. A large man wearing a tie that depicted flags of all nations, chain smoking, bits of ash falling on the tie, he was annoyed with me, with everyone. 'Knock on that door and ask for Jack.' Like I wouldn't know that. 'Nothing's out of focus, my dear.' As if I cared.

"So I knocked on someone's left eye. A voice that sounded as if it came from far in the back of the booth told me to come in, but there was no doorknob, no way to push the panels in. After a few minutes the door swung open. At first I didn't see anyone and banged my head against a shelf of empty reels. Several large projectors looked like army tanks capable of firing something, not necessarily waves of light. If I'd stumbled across them in a junkyard, I wouldn't have been certain what they were, but they whined into life, reels spun, and a cone of light shot into the theater. The booth was a mess. Jack was distracted, looking for a film that he was never able to locate. He had this nervous habit of twirling empty reels, the smaller ones, around his index finger. Then the night shift guy came, and we left. The next day the manager was found with his throat cut.

"Jack was distraught when he heard. You might say, who wouldn't be? One minute the man was there, the next day, gone. Jack was especially close to him and believed whatever nonsense the man spun about stolen films, conspiracies, bits changed and added on, scenes found at the very ends of reels. I only half listened, if that. I don't believe there was some association of revisionistas tinkering with select bits of history. Who would bother? I can still see the big fat man in that little theater. He could barely move anywhere in it. When they came for him with a knife, whoever they were, where could he run to? Who would want to kill a harmless old bugger? Junkies, I'm guessing. The police wanted to question Jack because he worked there and all, so it was time for us to return home, but as I said, it's nothing to do with me, and I'm not staying here."

"When is your flight?" I balanced the receiver on my shoulder, prepared to write.

"Next week."

"Don't you think Jack will want to see you before you leave?" I was prepared to meet him at the airport if I knew he would be there.

"Maybe. Maybe not. It wouldn't be the first time he left me in the lurch. How did you get my number, anyway?"

Jack the two-timer, the good-for-nothing, Jack who's always late, who owes money to everyone, Jack who loses his grip from time to time, anything. Jack, who tapped me on the shoulder then disappeared, only to repeat the performance again and again, always winking, always just out of reach. Jack, the man who falls asleep next to you on a plane then picks up your suitcase at baggage claim in order to see you again, but the exchange never actually takes place. Both the man and your stuff vanish into a foreign city.

"I don't know why I'm talking to you," Clarice said as if it had just dawned on her, and she hung up on me.

<hr />

I was looking at the third-to-last scene of the Dreyfus film, the scene entitled "Battle of the Journalists." In an ordinary-looking room men and women argue about the verdict, and within seconds a fight breaks out. Besides casting himself as Labori, Dreyfus's lawyer, Méliès has also cast himself as one of the journalists. He's hopping all over the tiny screen. Perhaps he and Jack Kews are alike in that their good intentions are easily undercut. They look quizzically at those who flee from attention, who write anonymously or broadcast without call letters, those who think they have a message but poke the image of a messiah in the ribs. The fight among the journalists appears so realistic and violent that if I had just spooled to this scene at random without knowing what was on the film, I would have believed I was looking at a documentary, unstaged and shot completely as it happened.

"Enough people didn't believe he could be found guilty a second time, as I told you, so you can cut the court martial scene."

I jumped. I hadn't heard him, but Julius had opened the door to my office without knocking. He glanced over my shoulder at the film.

"Let me see the courtroom scene."

I ran the film forwards, a tiny square of light in a dark room.

"The image is fairly degraded. Dreyfus salutes the judges. Okay. It's hard to know exactly what's going on here except when the verdict is read. If we could change the expression on Dreyfus' face, if he looked happy or if the face were to be blurred by Wet Gate and you could do a little harmless airbrushing, then Dreyfus is a free man and less of the film faces the guillotine."

"I can't do it."

"No one remembers this trial, Frances. I want to stay in business, to retire handsomely to an offshore destination. I don't want to lose my shirt. Everything evaporates eventually. Dreyfus is innocent."

In front of the troops in the yard of *Les Invalides* Dreyfus is stripped of his medals. This is the scene of his degradation. A man I assume to be a general breaks Dreyfus's sword over his knee.

"Yes, but by changing the end of the film you're giving the judges credit for something they didn't do."

"So you've said. Listen, Scholom Aleichem wrote a story, "Dreyfus in Krasilov," in which the citizens of a remote Russian town read about the Dreyfus trial in installments that arrive in a newspaper mailed from France. They know all the evidence proves he's innocent, that he was framed by corrupt generals and poorly executed forgeries. They don't see how Dreyfus could be found guilty a second time. The guilty verdict isn't possible, not in Paris, so they tear up the town's only newspaper. It could only be a hoax. "

"Méliès resisted the temptation to change the fantastic verdict into the correct verdict: innocent. He let the unbelievable conclusion stand. He shot the actuality, as improbable as it was. Who's paying for this restoration?" This was a question I had never asked before.

"I can't say."

"You told the landlord it was someone in France."

"The landlord needs whatever false assurances I can give him that the back rent here isn't a lost cause."

"Do we even have an air brush?"

Julius nodded.

"I'm just asking. I haven't said I'll use it."

"A happy ending is money in the bank. Remember that."

A line of frayed thread connected me to the Russian librarian, to someone who might long for an expensive coat when winter comes, especially if he now owns little more than a second- or third-hand gray suit. I no longer have any idea of the sort of image I presented. Was my shirt tucked in, hair flat, hands in pockets? Or were buttons askew, stains on blouse, dark circles under my eyes, did I have a manic twitch, were phrases tumbling from my mouth one after the next? In speech did I confuse characters from the Dreyfus trial (Picquart, Esterhazy, Zola, du Paty) with attempts to remember to buy soap, toothpaste, eye drops before the drugstore closed?

"The last scene is supposed to be one of terrible humiliation," I said.

"Degradation can take many forms." As he leaned closer I thought he might explain what he meant. How did this icon of degradation, the sword snapped over a knee, translate into the electronic present?

"The general's face is barely visible. As the sword snaps, don't you think some kind of expression would have registered?" Julius asked.

I carefully removed the Dreyfus film from the Steenbeck and showed him another one I had finished, *The Man with the Rubber*

Head. Méliès's head grew larger and larger, finally exploding, the force of the explosion blowing his assistant out of the frame.

"The man who mistook his head for a Coney Island white-fish," Julius said.

He turned off the light table and we sat in the dark. He made me uncomfortable, and I moved my chair closer to the wall, hoping he wouldn't notice I was, as usual, edging away from him.

"Frances, we offer a service for which there is less and less need."

I didn't want to hear his confession, didn't want to be responsible for its weight. I wanted to tell him about the librarian who had left everything he knew on the other side of the world, the hysteric in a wheelchair, the opening scene of *The Man with the Rubber Head,* where Méliès is chain smoking and smiling like the devil. Don't make me responsible if the studio is about to fold, I wanted to say, but didn't. Whatever deal Julius had made or with whom he'd made it, he kept to himself. I suppose all transactions can be read in terms of extortion, there are many who might sell their souls to avoid Devil's Island. Some people, I think, carry their own Devil's Island around like a box covering their heads with two holes punched out for eyes, and if that's the case, the eyeholes are meaningless anyway. I tried to shrug Julius's arm off my back. He kept it there.

Jack's notes seemed to say, if you think there was only one deliberate framing, only one cover-up ever, only one case of forged government documents, only one miscarriage of justice, look how wrong you are, how naive. Julius, embarrassed and defensive, let go, saying his eyes were troubling him, and he left me alone with the silent films.

Listening to Julius's footsteps recede, I rewound, put the Dreyfus film on a shelf with the other unfinished Méliès reels. A few hours later when I got up from my chair to stretch another envelope had been slipped under my door.

It was the middle of the afternoon, and I needed to look into the distance for a few minutes in order to compensate for hours spent with Dreyfus at close range. I went out, intending to at least walk past an address on the list of war resisters. The name was Adam Mercy.

I told Antonya I would be back in a half hour and left swinging doors in my wake, only to stand in the empty elevator feeling foolish; all my urgency was about chasing phantoms. Still, I didn't go back, and instead walked out into the street with no hint I'd entertained second thoughts.

A few yards from the entrance to the Mayflower Building two boys played on overturned plastic buckets held between their knees. The buckets were white and looked new. A third, smaller pail stood directly in front of them for people to drop money into while they drummed. Lately, they had been at their post every day. Inhaling smells of roasted peanuts and skewered meat sold from carts with portable grills I could only think about what I would say when face to face with one of the former war resisters. Hello, Mr. Mercy, we spoke earlier. I'm looking for a man you might remember. It will seem like an impertinent question coming from a stranger, but it would mean a lot to me if you could tell me if you've recently heard from a man I believe you first met many years ago? I'm no longer sure I know his real name.

I finally reached the address marked on Jack's list, but the building had been demolished. The apartment complex next door was partly bricked up. Squatters occupied a few of the floors. Although it was long past Halloween a boy in a steak costume looked out of a second-story window. The steak was cut out of a box, painted red and white. He wore marbled red tights, a red cap, and waved a rubber fork before disappearing into the building. A Blockbuster Video, one story high, made of sand-colored cinder blocks had been erected where Mercy's building must have been. I stood before the display window and watched Robert Redford wait in a parking garage of waffle-paneled concrete for his Deep Throat. Stacks of *Dracula* and *Malcolm X* framed the screen. Inside, two women appeared to be arguing, pointing to another screen that showed the same film. I watched in the cold for a few more minutes then went back to work.

Just as I had tried to imagine Jack Kews I also tried to form a picture of Adam Mercy. They were older than the boys I had known but Jack, his friends, and the ones whose names I've forgotten all looked into the same mirror. I was sure of it. They had long hair and rolled cigarettes whose contents came from wads of tinfoil or plastic bags. What they looked like, how they chose to look, mixed signs of masculinity and femininity in a combination that could be confusing. How you chose them or were chosen by them wasn't thought about under the category of pressure, although the pressure to sleep with them came at every turn, and then I'm not sure. I never heard that word, probably never dreamed about it. It was just what you did. You just did it and then moved on to the next one with no attachments. Clear nights full of stars, warm enough to sleep outside if you wanted to, parents away, friends with cars. Tabs of acid might be brought out from back pockets as if the greatest thing in the world had just been discovered among the linty bits and pieces. Someone always had one of those small plastic bags.

"Jack? Jack? Is that you? I can't believe it!"
　　I turned around quickly, but the man being embraced was little more than twenty years old and looked embarrassed to be recognized by a woman who pulled up beside the curb, got out of her car, and briefly smothered him with kisses. She was quite a bit older than he, and sensing his discomfort, she backed off, embarrassed, got back into her car, and drove away.

WARNING

"In the current rather emotional atmosphere the frequency of procedural errors on the part of the local draft boards has increased noticeably. In reading this *Handbook* please bear this in mind. If your local draft board does not respond as you think it should, contact your nearest draft counselor or Central Committee for Conscientious Objectors at once for advice on remedial action.

"In the best circumstances local boards act very differently — just as registrants do. You cannot prevent their mistakes, but only your own. Several men are in prison right now because of their own mistakes."

This warning, which I took very seriously, is quoted from the *Handbook for Conscientious Objectors* edited by Arlo Tatum, tenth edition, December 1969.

When commenting on the Nuremberg trials Telford Taylor said, "Military justice is to justice as military music is to music." Knowing that, I left for Canada, but in order to survive underground I had to become someone else.

Even in Canada I was always looking over my shoulder, down the block, across the street. I sought out crowds because if anything happened there would be witnesses to the confrontation. You heard stories of deserters and draft exiles being kidnapped in Toronto, Montreal, Vancouver, only to be spirited over the border. A chloroformed handkerchief was put over your nose and mouth, then you were driven straight through customs with no questions asked. I wasn't interested in becoming an experiment in transnational anesthesia, so I went on to England, believing it less likely that the long arm of the FBI would stretch across the Atlantic and back just for one draft resister. I don't like the term *draft dodger*; it implies something cagey and sly, and doesn't reflect the decision to leave as a moral one. We were against the war.

At first in Canada and later in England I felt like a kid trying on Halloween costumes, making the sounds of a gorilla, then speaking like Frankenstein or Dracula in turn, but my false identity soon turned from a kind of curiosity or novelty into a very different condition. It became a vacuum that sucked everything out: memory, history, geography. The identities that were meant to cloak erased the person who lay beneath. Now you see him, now you don't. I won't even tell you the names I traveled under. I became unmoored. My motto was: today is the first day of the end of your life. I was from Chicago, from Los Angeles, from Seattle, from small towns whose names were entirely made up: Red Plains, Whitman Park, Sandy Hook, Los Carneros. I had a lost twin sister or Clarice was my sister. I wrote under a variety of names. My address was a shifting post-office box.

I forgot a great deal and filled the space with whatever came to mind first. I couldn't confide in Clarice because I didn't really trust anyone. Fascinated by skinheads she worked with victims of their attacks, administering counseling, visiting housing estates and caravans. As if answers and then solutions could be found in half-hour interviews. Ask the right, informed questions. Get useful answers. Find a solution. Living with a man who had to keep changing his story might start to feel old. What if, I kept thinking, what if she decides she's had it and goes back to the States with no warning? She insisted she didn't want to go back either, but then I began to worry that distracted, she might slip up under pressure. Clarice often stared out the window when I or anyone was on about something. She wasn't aware of it, and insisted she was listening, and somehow the syntax of other people made it through her daydreams to her spindle neurons, but I could never be sure. That dreamy look, like Wendy waiting for a shadowless boy while Rome burned, was kind of seductive, because there was always the possibility that she really was listening. But it was a risk. I was afraid we'd be at an airport and Customs and Immigration would ask, "You're traveling with your brother?"

"My brother? I don't have a brother. Wait a minute, yes I do," she might say.

So we behaved as if we were strangers who didn't know each other. I tried to lose her on crowded streets, on trains, In large shops. It pissed her off. Living with me, she said, required a lot of guesswork. In the morning I'm at my worst, and she would do anything to try to crack the moodiness that left her out. She would wear my clothes, which looked ridiculous on her, cuffs and legs dragging behind, or describe the pratfalls of her dreams, leaving out the nightmarish parts. She would talk in funny accents, imitating people who had been in line ahead of her at a store or a post office, snippets that sounded like futuristic creatures in their combination of mismatched syllables and abbreviation. Her life was sometimes one continuous narration, I wasn't sure if I was doing more than listening or less. Still, I stayed around while I knew she found herself getting louder, shriller, more ridiculous in the face of my increasing need for invisibility, to lose my shadow.

I learned to be as neutral as possible so people might see in me the reflection of their own attitudes; I provided an arena for narcissism. I had to become an actor. I'm not an actor. The process of slipping into and out of other identities took a great deal of self-control and driving under the speed limit. I didn't, under any circumstances, want to attract attention. A speeding violation could be a one-way ticket to deportation.

For a few months, nearly a year, I worked in London at an old movie house, more of a storefront than a real theater, that showed Méliès's old films. I was drawn to them. He had ended his life in obscurity, and his films had been revived only recently. Like Méliès I tried out a few different heads, then exploded them when they were no longer of any use, and also like Méliès, I found it tempting to write of myself in the third person. (He drove to Canada picking a rarely traveled road where he had to wake up the customs official who just waved him through. He had cut his hair quickly and unevenly. The man didn't notice.)

When the manager and other staff seemed to be getting to know me too well I had to quit the job, but before I left, I learned something about the Méliès films that were about to be sent to you for preservation. I decided to slip back in

In 1973 when President Ford offered "conditional clemency" or "earned reentry" to the forty thousand American exiles, only thirty-four gave it a try. There were five categories under which you could apply for this reentry business, but none of the categories allowed for the position of being *against* the war. We'd committed no felony, unlike Nixon, who was granted a presidential pardon. Why accept a pardon if you haven't committed a crime? A question that was asked of Dreyfus as well. What we had done was refuse to participate in an "adventure" that we considered criminal. We weren't the ones who needed amnesty. That same year I went to the International Conference of Exiles held in Paris in early spring. Sartre, in a letter written to a magazine for American exiles, supported us. His letter has antecedents in Zola. The idea of writers, philosophers sticking an oar into the political sea began, I think, with him. Anyway, Ford's clemency program was a crock.

So if anyone asks, I'm not here.

Love,
Jack

P.S. Let's get to the end of the film already.

It was as if a figure who had been chased for several blocks finally came to a stop and admitted that he did in fact answer to the name repeatedly called out. I read the letter twice. I didn't know whether to believe him or not. The excuse, that his desire was to travel with the films, was just as good a wedge in the door of return as any other. He might have picked a random moment to come back. Why did he trust me? Because I was preserving the films he identified so strongly with? In a way I was coating the underground man with Wet Gate, too.

After he wrote his *j'accuse* letter, Zola's name, in some circles, became synonymous with *le métèque*, foreigner. His motives were seen as nothing more than the antics of a publicity seeker. Both he and Jack became *les métèques*. Clarice knew what was going on, why Jack had to give her the slip from time to time, but it no longer seemed to matter to her. She gave the impression that she looked upon Jack with repulsion, as if he was an illness she used to have. The antibodies to the disease were unknown, and after some searching through medical textbooks and experimenting with a haphazard assortment of pills and syringes, the malady just wore off on its own over time. Perhaps she tried running marathons or sat through hours of silent movies in order to be the sort of person he wanted, then she gave it all up. A woman who looked at her affairs as a series of columns: credits heading one and debits the other. Jack, in her opinion, was Mr. Debit.

So what am I left with? Unfocused pangs for a jackpot of a no-hope romance. Even the invisible Clarice dumped him. Even good-for-nothings are occasionally good for something. There are women who destroy themselves over idiots, dunderheads, liars, cheats, con artists, vacuous slobs, elderly or middle-aged babies who may or may not have the capacity to bankroll lives of leisure. Sometimes they tell their stories on *America's Most Wanted;* they leave you staggering under the weight of the knowledge that desire can be oppressive if it doesn't do you in altogether.

On a map of estrangement there must be a spot marked for the location where one spends the night with a stranger. You may not even know the meaning or exact nature of its geography while you inhabit it, but once that particular landscape recedes you realize exactly what you were about and what you couldn't have known at the time. Once when I worked at the Library of Congress I spent the night with a man who claimed to have stolen manuscripts, rare unguarded manuscripts from libraries all over the world. Like Jack, he knew a lot about me, but when I wouldn't help him, he vanished into thin air.

I didn't really want to meet Jack Kews. I read in the paper of the trial of five men, citizens of a small town in upstate New York, who found a woman they knew passed out in a restaurant bathroom. She had had too many free drinks. The men laid her on a table and raped her. Although they had confessed to the rape they were only fined $750 each, since confession doesn't count as proof a crime has been committed. One needs scars and sperm, the article said. Furthermore, according to the paper, the prosecutor often ate in the restaurant where the rape took place. The establishment's owner was the father of one of her attackers, and the two men were friends. I could see the booths covered in red plastic, coffee slopped into their saucers, men leaning back in their places, not even hunched over on their elbows playing nervously with salt and pepper shakers, but sitting like viceroys with their legs spread apart, as if to say, "Hey, I got a dick, you know?" In the history of stalking, chase, and hunt, the quarry is often a stranger, unknown, the object of a voyeuristic speculation. I was less concerned with the idea of a stranger murdering a stranger. In the history of men and women there is plenty of that. Sartre, of whose moral support Jack felt justifiably proud, reduces rape to a case of the desirer and the desirable. The desirable in the case in upstate New York wrote that she wanted all five men lined up on a platform and hung for what they had done to her.

If I found Jack, he might turn out not to be the man I thought he was. He posed like Zola, ready to expose the false stories, invented conspiracies, and forgeries of aged Generals and Secretaries of Defense; hiding out in England under the name Pasquale, only to return to a Brooklyn apartment with no heat. I know one or two things about him, but just when I'm sure of a situation, something backfires, turns slippery, goes as haywire as a naked man in a wheelchair.

Take, for example, the idea of dinosaur eggs manufactured from a strand of DNA piped out of a prehistoric mosquito caught in amber. The insect had sucked the blood of Tyrannosaurus Rex, but the gaps in the isolated strand that produce a T. Rex had to be filled in by whatever kind of DNA was close and available: a frog's double helix was used for the patchwork. However, the resulting monster turned out to be capable of changing sex midstream. If you ask me every man is a potential Jurassic Park. You never know what you're getting. There is no way of knowing what kind of violence is scheduled at the end.

"Adam Mercy." He said his name as if it were one word. Adamercy. I pictured a man living in a basement, his gray hair tied into a ponytail by a rubber band. "Furtim Vigilans."

"Furtim Vigilans," I repeated, trying not to make my voice go up as if I were asking a question.

"Data-collection services. How may I be of assistance?"

After the usual preliminaries, I asked him if he knew a man named Jack Kews.

"Jack Kews. Jack Kews. Can't say that I did."

"Your name was on a list he kept."

"Perhaps he intended to call me."

"It was a list of men in a group called DLR."

There was a pause, just as I knew there would be. The image of a skinny gray ponytail was replaced by a man in a silk tie swiveling in his chair to survey all the views from his corner office, or maybe his office was all corners, and he already saw everything.

"Yeah, I knew Jack."

"Heard from him lately?"

"Not in years. I thought he was dead."

"Can you tell me anything about him?" I was calling from Antonya's desk because I was on my way out of the office. I almost wasn't going to call Mercy, but on an impulse, decided okay, might as well give him a try. Antonya had gone to a martial arts class.

"Not much. He hid from people. Jack was the kind of person who didn't laugh at jokes and who would make sure, in his silent way, that you felt like a fool for telling them. He ran from the camera, sliding down the flagpole as soon as he saw one." Then he asked, "Who are you, Frances? Why do you need to know?"

"An old friend. He got in touch with me, then disappeared."

"He has a tendency to do that. If you hear from him, please give him my number. I would love to see Jack again."

"What kind of data do you collect?"

"All kinds, Frances. People lie. Evidence tells the truth."

"Except when it doesn't." I felt as if I were an archaeologist brushing dirt away from an object I thought was a figure of an ancient totem or god, only to find when the dust was cleared an obscene plastic troll left by a looter.

"You could say that."

I imagined Adam commanding a league of mercenaries who fanned out into the city wearing jackets with black patches embroided with skulls, claws, and the words *Furtim Vigilans,* Vigilance through Stealth, looking for Jack. Perhaps Jack imagined this, too, or maybe the data-collection mission wasn't imaginary at all.

After I hung up I leaned over to throw out the scrap of paper on which I had scribbled his number. In the garbage I saw a flattened milk carton; a square piece had been cut out of one of its sides where a picture of a missing child had been.

Across the street from the Mayflower was a two-story building that housed William C. C. Chen's Tai Chi Chuan Studio. At night when I looked down a few floors and across I could see the silhouettes of men distorted behind steamed windows moving slowly backward and forward. Red banners with gold writing covered the walls. On the ground floor below Chen's was the Eye for an Eye Video Store on whose narrow glass panels were painted the signs:

ADULT PEEP
ADULT PEEP
and
NO
BODY
BEATS
OUR PRICES

The words *body* and *beats* took on new meaning in their isolation. I watched the men who went in and wondered if Jack Kews might be one of them, killing time before he slipped another note under my door, or did Julius, with the expression on his face of a man who loitered with anxiety, ever go into the Eye for an Eye looking for a film entitled *Wet Gate,* for example? I'd never imagined them unconsciously dogging one another's footsteps, but suddenly the two were mixed up. After all, they both projected their personalities in my direction as if I were a blank screen. I added Jack's most recent letter to the pile in my desk, locked the door behind me, and went home.

I stopped at an intersection. Antonya was playing with the radio. It was beginning to feel like the end of winter, deceptively and momentarily warm, and we'd decided to drive to Coney Island, a relic of its former self, but it was still a beach even if you had to watch out for used needles and broken glass buried just under the surface of the sand. We parked near the subway at Stillwell Avenue. It was a weekday and very quiet. Under the shadow of the blackened Thunderbolt, an abandoned roller coaster, I thought about what is preserved and what is lost. François Mauriac claimed that as a child he had been given a chamber pot with Zola's name painted on it. Had it been manufactured, rather than made by hand, presumably there would be many others, and they are stored somewhere. Who keeps such things now in their attic or auctions them off on some unknown block, bidders collapsing into either knowing or ignorant hysterics? History with a small *h*, not panoramic history as in Dial 1-800.

All that was left of the roller coaster was a kind of a skeleton of a skeleton. Sumac trees and weeds grew upwards through the missing rails, and people lived underneath it. Their houses were constructed from shopping carts, blankets, and fragments of broken beach chairs, webbing flapping in the breeze; bright pink or yellow deflated plastic animals replaced curtains. We continued past a bricked-over bathhouse, medallions of dolphins circling the top, just out of reach of the graffiti. Windows close to the top story were broken, gaping open. Those living under the Thunderbolt somehow managed to scale the walls and get into the vast derelict baths. Businesses, drug deals, and gang meetings were conducted inside its ruinous caverns behind Neptune's head.

I bought a coke at Astroland, the painted tin Astroland boy and girl holding enormous hamburgers overhead.

The Cyclone, the white-heat version of the defunct Thunderbolt, was also inoperative but didn't appear abandoned. It looked like a series of fake de Chirico mountains. "I would throw up on one of those," Antonya said as pink and green cars slid from the outer edge of the wheel.

"The office can only last a week, maybe less."

Despite the cold the boardwalk was full of people, Russians, mostly, in fur coats walking arm in arm, speaking slowly, sounds of observation and complaint, pockets full of cell phones and beepers. A group of beer bottles wrapped in paper bags had been left sticking up in the sand like a series of aggressive noses, bodies still buried underneath. Even in the chilly air the Wonder Wheel beckoned, lazy, inevitably returning riders to the point where they boarded. I watched a woman in a rumpled dress sit on the beach with two young children. They ran around her and dug in the cold sand, but she remained unresponsive, staring at the water. Two men passed her carrying fish they appeared to have just caught. She barely looked at them. Others walked by with radios blaring. *Double trouble*, one blasted, Antonya sang along with it, repeating the lyrics over and over. The children ran out of steam and sat a few feet away. Still, the woman stared at the ocean, gold sunglasses pushed back on her head occasionally turning to yell at the children in a south Russian Odessa accent. I threw my Coke can away and dumped sand from my shoes.

"Soon everyone will be either a spectator or an actor in theme parks where unattended children disappear," I said, trying to be funny. "Without Alphabet hundreds of films will disintegrate." In their place I imagined tableaus or rides based on the life of Charlie Chaplin or Dreyfus: digitalized funhouses attended only fitfully, and finally those would be shut down too.

———•———

The brief thaw ended, and it began to snow again, a last fist of winter, but a heavy one. The Mayflower security guard watched reports of hazardous roads on a tiny TV. Alphabet Conservation was dark when I unlocked the door, and thinking it would be deserted, I was prepared to disconnect the alarm system. The red light on the coffee machine burned in the shadows although there was nothing left in the pot but a ring of sludge. The alarm hadn't been activated, all was quiet. Montgomery Clift had returned and glinted above a calendar. He had turned to face the camera, his arm around young Julius's shoulder as if posing for a father and son shirt ad, except Clift, as Freud, wasn't smiling. Julius had said he himself smiled because he felt he had to, that was what you did as a guest on the set for whom a favor was being done, he felt he had no choice but to smile. There was a light on in Julius's office. I opened the door to find him slumped over his desk. I thought he had fallen asleep and had no impulse to wake him. I didn't want to touch Julius, didn't want to shake his arm or even be alone with him in Alphabet at night. The corridor was dark, light from the street came through two of the windows, and I made my way into my office, silently, without turning on any lights.

During a dark night beside a bridge in Rennes an assassin hides under a bridge. He pulls a gun and Dreyfus's lawyer, played by Méliès, falls to the street yelling for help. The assassin escapes. I was very tired and could no longer tell if it was snowing during this scene or if the film was only very scratched and grainy. I listened for sounds of the office being left for the night. Doors softly shutting in the distance might have been the sound of Julius departing. Ironically, as the story became more tragic, the image grew clearer. The end of the film was in better shape than the beginning. In the last scene Dreyfus leaves the court at Rennes for prison. Soldiers stand in lines with their backs to him as he descends the stone steps. There was no scene of riots or murder. I put the film in a can and went on to the next one. The preservation of *The Affair* was completed. The telephone rang.

"Jack, there's no murder at the end of the film."

"People were killed in the streets following the original showing of the film. People were literally stomped to death, ribs cracking, guts coming out of their mouths."

"But it's not on this film."

"Look again. I'll call you back. It's freezing cold and there's no heat in my building."

"You could come up here to Alphabet. At least the heat's still on." But he had already hung up.

What he described sounded like the riot scene in *Day of the Locust* when Homer Simpson stomps the child actor, Adore, to death, but the murder had happened not in a novel about Hollywood, but in Paris in 1899.

Jack saw himself as an accuser, a finger pointer, but stopped short. Who was the murdered man at the end of the film and where was that ending? Small towers of film taunted me with the possibility of the wrong splice. The answer could have been in any one or none of them.

I read a story once about a woman, Ethel K., who was in love with Harry Houdini. Even aside from the fact that he was already married to Bess Rahner, few personal obsessions could have been more hopeless. She followed him from outdoor exhibitions to staged arenas all over the world. As many times as she watched Houdini escape from any number of contrivances, whether he dangled chained, cuffed, and straitjacketed from a Wall Street ledge, or similarly manacled, plunged off a Berlin bridge, she always held her breath as she watched; his performances left her both aroused and terrified. It would have torn her apart to see someone torture the showman, but she confessed she was mesmerized by his penchant for torturing himself. She waited at stage doors, a round, lovelorn face lost in the crowd, sent letters that were never answered, ran out of money, did odd jobs, even engaged in prostitution when she became really desperate. Once, as he descended from the stage door, she called his name, and she believed he turned and gave her a smile before entering his car. Often she was convinced he looked her in the eye during his escape struggles, making eye contact despite the mob, the sea of other choices, and doing so in the last minute before he finally broke free. It was mostly men, fedoras or homburgs perched on their heads, that made up the crowds, so she wasn't that hard to spot. *Hey, sweetheart, it's me! Your good-luck charm!* The hats ignored her, and the great man never so much as sent her an autographed picture. Houdini was always one step ahead of her, as if it were she herself he was escaping from.

One night, alone in Montreal, Ethel K. considered giving up the chase and going home, though home, at this point, could be wherever she decided to hang her hat. The object of her desire kept running away, disappearing around the corner, just out of reach. If she turned the tables with a *Harrumph to you, Harry*, disappearing herself, would his next show end in disaster? Or, noticing her absence, even if he wasn't exactly clear as to her identity, would he find his way to her door? *Ethel, my darling, please come back!* What she was driving at was a means to shift the story, so escape was no longer the main subject of a given page, but would become a footnote to their romance. Ethel K. was ready for a straitjacket herself.

In one of Houdini's original tricks, he and Bess changed places. He was chained, locked in a box, the box itself wrapped in chains, then she pulled a curtain, obscuring the whole shooting match, and clapped her hands, the magic sound necessary to instigate the mechanics of the switcheroo about to take place. In an instant, he stood before the audience, and she was found in the box. So in the story of Ethel K. and Harry, she hoped he could be persuaded to change places, to make her someone to be desired, and he someone she needed to escape from. In fact, she did need to escape from him, as the seducer she imagined him to be, a role he actually didn't have much of a conscious hand in. Was this story some kind of vaudeville reflection of the hide-and-seek game I was playing with Jack? Yikes. I hope not. To be seduced by a disembodied voice isn't much more substantial than eroticizing that last flick of a wrist in an escape artist's repertoire. If so, I'm not sure who plays which part. Given Jack's affinity for escapeology, I don't know if the thing that he's afraid of, the thing that chases him, even if it's me, is more real or less real than life in rooms above the man in a wheelchair.

Locking up for the night, I passed Julius's office. His light was still on, so I approached soundlessly. The door was ajar, and I looked in again. Packing boxes lay strewn about, he was still sleeping the heavy sleep of the drugged, head on his desk, deaf to everyone, staking his claim to the few square inches where ear and cheek met wood laminate.

The notice in the paper was small. An unidentified man had been found dead in an apartment building near the Brooklyn Bridge. There was nothing remarkable about one more death in a city where many died every day, but his death was noted because it was attributed to negligence on the part of his landlord. There had been a sudden cold snap, the temperature had plummeted, and the man had apparently turned on the gas because his building had no heat. This is illegal, and according to the paper, the landlord was already under indictment for other violations. The address was given. A disabled tenant was quoted as saying the landlord should be forced to live in one of his own buildings. The victim of the accident was unidentified and unknown. My impression of Jack was that he was the kind of person who would turn on the gas, and although sitting in front of the oven, would have been sure to have taken the precaution of opening the window beforehand. I opened the blinds and looked out the window at a vacant lot. Snow fell on an empty overturned shopping cart, the only object in it. Death makes random selections, freak accidents occur, someone is trampled by a crowd, hunted with deliberation, death is foreshadowed by salvos from a man unknown or missiles from a girl who lives down the road. The hunter who shoots at a dash of fur or antlers gets his mark, and that's it. He gives the finger to cars with animal rights bumper stickers as he passes them. Zola had died of asphyxiation in his house on rue de Bruxelles on a cold night when there was no heat. The door had to be broken down, but by the time they found him he was dead. Dreyfus supporters believed he was murdered. Those Zola had charged with invention in his *j'accuse* letter years earlier dismissed his death as suicide. I imagined Jack playing tricks on me. *Look, you think I've disappeared, but I'll be back.* I have a copy of the film in my coat pocket, and I plan to look at the end again.

Le Bordereau

Sans nouvelles m'indiquant que vous
désirez me voir, je vous adresse cependant
Monsieur quelques renseignements intéressants

1° une note sur le frein hydraulique
du 120 et la manière dont s'est conduite
cette pièce.

2° une note sur les troupes de couverture.
(quelques modifications seront apportées par
le nouveau plan).

3° une note sur une modification aux
formations de l'artillerie:

4° une note relative à Madagascar.

5° le projet de manuel de tir de
l'artillerie de campagne (14 mars 1894.)

Ce dernier document est extrêmement
difficile à se procurer et je ne puis
l'avoir à ma disposition que très peu
de jours. Le ministère de la guerre
en a envoyé un nombre fixe dans
les corps et ces corps en sont responsables,
chaque officier détenteur doit
remettre le sien après les manœuvres.
Si donc vous voulez y prendre ce
que vous intéresse et le tenir
à ma disposition après, je le
prendrai. À moins que vous ne
vouliez que je le fasse copier
in extenso et ne vous en adresse
la copie.

Je vais partir en manœuvres.

The Ordinary Track

Paris 1968

The American students play their music too loudly. The
Vietnamese cook who lives below them complains in broken,
hesitant French; the salesman from Marseilles who occupies the
room next door complains loudly to himself and with passion.
I bang on their door, and they turn the volume down sometimes. They live here because it's cheap. Even I have begun to
understand the English words, or at least been able to guess at
the meaning of their records, they play them over and over. Just
before they return to America they'll take my picture in front of
the building. *This old woman is like the super or the building manager,*
they'll write on the back. In May they'll join the riots or retreat,
baffled, this kind of thing doesn't happen at home, or maybe it
does. I've never left my city and have no images of their New
Yorks, Washingtons, Clevelands, *you name eet buddee.*

Last night a friend of one of the Americans fell into a closet that faces the courtyard. Heaving himself up and singing all
the while, I could hear him throwing things out of it. Buckets,
screwdrivers, bottles of cleaning fluid, mops, and brooms were
scattered as if a wind had swept through only this very small
space. I went out into the courtyard and asked him what he
thought he was doing, waking up half the building. He looked
at me with bleary eyes as he clung to a doorjamb and answered
that he was searching for some papers.

"What kind?"

"Dictée. Écriture."

His mouth was open as if he was about to be sick but nothing came out. I called the police while he chanted *mar-toonies*, *mar-toonies* in a singsong voice. He was a harmless, blind-drunk foreigner, but I had to have him and his friend thrown out, reprimanding them sharply, rapidly in a language they barely understood. The Vietnamese in blue trousers looked out of their doorway down into the courtyard, as if watching a kind of theater performance, fastening the black frogs on their jackets while leaning over the railing. The salesman from Marseilles came downstairs in a scarlet bathrobe and yelled at the Americans and at the police. The very drunk one staggered into him and pinched his cheek, a cartoon drunk, before he was hauled off. *"Quel drame!"* he said, making a drinking motion. Above our heads Madame Nguyen laughed. Jean Auric, my retired salesman, tied his robe tighter and scowled up at her.

"The Americans used to be identified by their very short hair and baggy suits. Now they have slightly longer hair," he said, "but they are still the same." It had rained, and the courtyard was so damp that sweeping was useless. We put away brooms, threw buckets of water on pools of soap powder. Bubbles poured out into the street. The Vietnamese children ran down the stairs to chase them into the middle of the night. I called them back; I needed to lock up. I told Auric I was perfectly all right, and I would finish the mopping myself. He insisted that I was too old, I must need help, but I preferred that he go back to his rooms. Cleaning at midnight isn't like drinking alone, the fumes of cleaning fluid provide more nausea than intoxication, but I enjoy the solitude of the courtyard. I don't want to hurt Auric's feelings. Once in a while he takes it upon himself to be helpful, and he has a pushy tenant's way of sometimes taking charge that I occasionally encourage out of laziness and lack of enthusiasm, but there are times when I want to be left alone.

"Who cleans at midnight? No one." He asks and answers his own question.

I walked upstairs with Jean Auric, and we looked into the small room just vacated by the American students. It is the smallest room in the building, and was cluttered with their things. Copies of the *Herald Tribune* lay on the floor, a dying plant by the window. *Boumedienne Suspends Constitution. Establishes Revolutionary Council.* Auric shook his head at the American mess and climbed the rest of the way without me. He was a nuisance with a hound-dog face. I wanted to say, why don't you just find Madame Brigitte and leave me alone, but I knew he couldn't. When he was out of sight I shut the door. In one corner a wooden crate they had used as a chair had been overturned. I sat on it and put on one of their records, very softly so that no one would hear.

I once knew someone who swept through corridors and antechambers with some idea of self-importance, hoarding the crumpled detritus of other people's dark rooms. The more abandoned, the better. The more destitute, the more welcoming.

When my mother found Auguste Bastian, we put her in this room, and she lived here for a few months. Before she came to stay with us, the room had been unoccupied, used for storing pieces of wood, tools, somebody's army uniform. I knew old schoolbooks lay in a battered trunk with a false bottom, and I'd hoped to find other things in it but never did. Since Auguste's departure the room has nearly always been occupied, but she was its first tenant, and she didn't pay.

———·———

I had been sitting in the courtyard singing to myself, poking into rat holes with a stick. My hair had just been cut short, and I could feel a breeze on my neck for the first time. The breeze seemed to tickle the room keys hung on a board near where my mother sat. Otherwise the afternoon was soundless until one of our tenants began to yell. Shutters knocked open against court-yard walls, faces and bare arms appeared in windows smoking cigarettes and drinking coffee, laundry was suddenly pulled in. I thought the tenant might have seen a rat, but her voice came from just outside the building. Those rats weren't our province. My mother ran out, and I followed, but I had no idea what the shouting could mean. I saw nothing unusual on the street, there was only an old woman sitting near our entrance. The woman had called out as if in pain, and my mother told one of our tenants, Madame Gilberte, who had been out walking her ter-rier, to fetch some water. The old woman's face was very red, and her nose was running, but my mother leaned close to her, put her mouth next to the woman's ear, and then put her ear to the woman's mouth. I could see the surprised expression on my mother's face and found it troubling, a premonition of dis-order. My mother, who was tall, helped the woman to her feet and guided the rag pile into our building. When I saw the two of them enter, I felt uneasy. I didn't like the idea of yet another stranger in a building already full of demanding near-strangers. I snapped my rat stick in two and stood in the entrance, a useless midget sentinel.

My mother nudged me with her elbow to move me out of the way.

"This woman is a national heroine. She must have gotten lost. Someone will come to fetch her."

I didn't recognize any national heroine in the old bag. *Joan of Arc. Madame Curie. Sarah Bernhardt.* If my mother thought the woman was a goldmine, or a goldmine waiting to happen, her identity was obscure, deeply buried treasure.

She whispered to me, "This one is rich, miserly perhaps, but she'll reward us for taking her in." I thought my mother was out of her mind.

A girl was quickly hired from the bakery next door to help clean out the storage room while I watched from the courtyard. My mother had pulled the lump of rags in off the street as if it were no more animate than something that had rolled off a delivery truck on its way to the wax museum. I was always suspicious of my mother's largesse and of its recipients; the murkiness of these altruistic transactions often spelled trouble. Soon piles of rusted equipment, wooden boards, empty bottles, the trunk full of books, all of it was carted away in clouds of dust. I arched backwards, the sky was gray, and I wanted it to rain on my naked neck while everyone else was chasing rubbish. Other tenants emerged from their rooms to get a look at whatever was going on before they went to their night jobs. I squatted nearby and watched the small feet and large hands sticking out from the pile of rags. It was about to rain, but I didn't go into our apartment

"Eh, what do they call you?" I pulled on a yellow-striped rag.

The pile groaned or grunted. It was a woman, but she had a mannish face. "What's your name, thing?"

"Auguste Bastian."

That was the name the police had given her. We never knew her real one. Rain began to hit the courtyard. Auguste and I ignored it, only staring at each other with mutual contempt as if she were waiting for me to taunt her *bastards Bastian,* and I was waiting for my mother to become so absorbed in the ragged woman's upkeep that I would be compelled to go around hungry and ignored. While we silently assessed the harm one might do to the other, Madame Gilberte returned from the bakery, throwing crumbs around the courtyard for birds. She often fed them during the rain.

"It's only rats that you're feeding, you know." I kicked a heel of bread, and it scudded into a puddle.

"Little girls should know when to come out of the rain." She waved her black umbrella, inadvertently spattering me with extra drops. The terrier barked at us, and she sniffed at the pile of rags as if she, Madame Gilberte, could move to another place anytime.

"I'm going to tell your mother that the walls of my apartment are infested with bugs. They crawl over everything; they bathe in my coffee. Since you people came this building has gone to the dogs."

I wanted to kick her ugly little terrier, but the animal, I reasoned, was an innocent.

"Then why don't you find another place to live?"

We both knew she wouldn't.

"I saw a rat!" I yelled at Madame Gilberte.

"I smell one." This retort came not from Gilberte, but from the sonambulent Bastian.

"Yeah, and I think it's you." I kicked her, not hard, but still a kick.

My mother leaned over the rail, yelling at me and hurrying downstairs. She apologized to Auguste and guided the large delicate ball up to her new room. I followed, anxious to look into the future goldmine's closet of a space. As far as I could tell peering around the two of them, one tall, the other round, Auguste's room contained only a narrow bed, a chair, and a small table. Auguste pointed at me, said something unintelligible, and my observation period was cut short. The door was shut, and my mother yanked me back downstairs to her station. The building was suddenly quiet. Everyone had gone to work or disappeared behind shutters. I followed closely, leaning against my mother, thinking a display of affection might ward off blows. It began to rain heavily. Keys jangled in the thunder. My mother hit me with the back of her hand. I didn't cry. Another stranger had come between us. It had happened before.

"Who is she?"

"Madame Bastian," she lit the stove, "used to clean the German embassy on the rue de Lille. She was known for going through the garbage collected from wastebaskets and mail slots."

I didn't understand how this would give anyone a bit of notoriety. Had she found a lottery ticket in one of the bins, stuck between a sausage end and slivers of sauerkraut? The leap between what I saw and what my mother promised was too great. "She looks as if she lives in an alley. Why should she want to stay with us? How did she get rich from cleaning?" This seemed impossible to me. Nobody could become rich from cleaning, or my mother would be the first to keep our building tidy.

"She had her job for about ten years, I think, but a long time ago, before the 1900 Exposition." I had only the dimmest memories of the exposition, and knew of it mainly through a few old postcards stored in the basement and souvenir paperweights my mother had placed in a corner near the stove as if the miniature monuments were huddled in a conference there.

Auguste had the mien of a someone used to going unnoticed, but as a presence in this or any other building, she also stood her ground, a man's felt hat jammed on her head and bags clutched in her hands.

"You might try to be nice to her. You might learn something from her." She cut potatoes with impatience as if each one represented my intransigence. I dropped a few pieces in hot oil. A tenant rang, and I tried to think of a way to change the subject because the topic of my behavior toward Madame Bastian was a cul de sac with no hope for me in it, and my mother still hadn't explained exactly how this lunatic would make us rich.

"Tell me about the desert," I asked when she returned. Because her family had been sent to the colonies, my mother had spent her childhood in Algiers, finally leaving for Paris when she was a young woman. She didn't speak about her family. I was under the impression they were long dead. Algeria was an imaginary geography, site of half-buried memories; I had few pictures of it. If she told me about the palms and cafés on the boulevard d'Alger or the vaulted caves of the rue de Impuisance I might understand why a lump of semianimate rags should be treated as if the thing might turn out to be some kind of holy man. In other words, I might discover why my mother believed some things weren't exactly what they appeared to be. As a child I had full confidence in the concept of trusting appearances, and if the appearance of the clod Auguste was clear cut, why not believe she was just as she presented herself? A beggar. A mooch.

What was my mother's problem? The answer might lie in having grown up in a place of constant bargaining, where value was relative and never as stated. Paupers might turn out to be rich men in disguise, and so the offer of shelter could be well rewarded in turn.

"I was ready to leave the heat and shut-in hours behind," she began.

When woken and pestered in the middle of the night by a drunk customer looking for Madame Gilberte, my mother would reminesce about Algiers as a place of great decency where a prostitute's clients wouldn't ever make the mistake of knocking on her door. Even with the tenth or twentieth telling, even if an anecdote I hadn't heard before was added, that bank of images that meant so much to her — the sound of the muezzin calling, cardamom seeds cracking between your teeth, dwellings with no ceilings, and dreams of heat — eluded me. I myself was fairly glad to be where I was, especially when I saw people living under bridges and inside cardboard boxes, but my mother never felt entirely at home in northern cities.

When people complain of not being comfortable, I want to ask them, how does anyone ever feel comfortable anywhere? Please explain.

"We were in the city and couldn't go out alone. The streets were as narrow as corridors and wound around each other, sometimes ending in steeply inclined stairs, worn slippery and formidable. Some streets covered by crowded terraces were as dark as caves."

"Did you ever become lost?"

Even though my mother was sitting in front of me, it was impossible to think of those streets without the idea of her becoming lost in them. This terrified me.

"I had to remain close to an adult. If I went out I couldn't run around as you do. Sometimes you felt as if you lived on top of a mesa, should you want to run away, you couldn't. It would be the end of you. We looked out at the street from behind window screens. Even children drank coffee so thick you could turn the cup upside down and none would spill."

She overturned a cup so that coffee spilled into the sink as if to demonstrate how pedestrian life had become for her.

"I would go crazy."

"Yes, you would."

"Didn't you ever get out of the city?"

"I rode camels a few times, learning to sway back and forth as I held my breath. It's difficult to stay on." She imitated riding on a camel, swaying back and forth in her chair. She looked like a crane. "We used to go on outings to look at the ruins near the Mediterranean. I thought they looked like limbless parts of a dead giants. Columns were legs, a blasted arch was a kind of crown."

I thought she might be making this part up. Then her tone changed. She came back to earth.

"I was bored, looking out windows so much of the time. I remember very few nomads. All Europeans were called Frank or Franks. Most of the people we knew were Franks." I imagined hundreds of people living within a few city blocks who, regardless of whether they were men or women, were all known as Frank. "There was a man, a Frank of course, in our building who smoked kif, and you could smell it in the hallways."

Kif, kif, kif. What was it? Could you get it in Paris if you grew bored with ordinary cigarettes?

"How did you get to Marseilles?"

"My mother died, and there were violent riots. There was nothing to keep me in Algiers."

"What kind of riots?"

"Against certain businesses. There were violent riots everyday. Zola and Dreyfus were burned in effigy."

"Who were they?"

"Two men who caused a lot of trouble. People were stoned, bludgeoned to death. I thought it would be safer here, and I met a man who was leaving for the same reasons. We traveled together."

I could see her leaning hard against the side of the boat, still bored. The rivets left little round marks on her back. A man, a Frank, said the water was full of sharks, so she stayed away from the edge of the deck. She was sailing away from Algeria, and she would never return.

"There was a woman on the boat who smoked Javanese cigarettes; the smell clung to her clothes, and I picked up her suitcase, mistakenly thinking it was mine. She gave me dirty looks, and I dropped it. Had I taken it by mistake, we might have had an entirely different life. I heard later that it was full of cash. People whose businesses were being torched fled with all their money, and I could have become that stranger, and she could have taken a form of my identity since I no longer felt very attached to it. Toward the end of the voyage the deck became crowded with passengers looking at the horizon: men in red brimless hats, women wrapped in black from head to toe, a monkey on a leash, a parrot who flew off a man's shoulder and was lost at sea."

"Who were you traveling with?"

"I don't even remember his name."

"Sure you do."

"No, I don't. As we approached Marseilles I looked for him, but he didn't seem to be on the boat. It was as if he had disappeared into the air."

"Had he jumped overboard?"

"No. I went to find the captain, who was Spanish and spoke only a little French. He answered brokenly as he looked into the horizon, spyglass by his side. He had seen him; he was on the other side of the deck. I had just been there, but I looked again. He wasn't on that side either. The coastline was growing clearer, and soon I thought I saw minarets in the distance, but they weren't minarets. It was Marseilles, where the houses look like slices of wedding cake. The captain brushed me off, shouting orders for going into port while hurrying away. Just as we were about to dock, my companion reappeared. I asked him where he'd been, and he claimed he was only strolling around the boat. It was possible that each of us turned a corner as the other approached; he was a fast walker; in the street he had often been that much ahead of me, but he was an even faster talker."

Did she put her arm in his? What was she implying he had been doing during his disappearance. Was he my father? I mentally struggled with possible dates.

"We disembarked, and he attended to our bags, but we were separated in the shoving crowd. In the crush of porters, passengers, and spectators with nothing to do I lost him. Later he told me that he thought he saw my head in the distance and yelled my name, but getting no response, continued to make arrangements for our things to be sent to a hotel or rooms or wherever it was we were to stay."

I never met this man. He actually did disappear shortly afterwards. The incident on the boat had been a rehearsal. He was like a tattoo of an old life, my mother said, but the kind that turns out to be erasable; the kind you can peel off and forget about. Armed with maps my mother made her way north, only to discover it was as possible to become lost in the heart of Paris as if one traveled guideless in the middle of the desert.

———·—·———

Cher-ie! Cher-ie! Auguste leaned over the railing and called out to me.

"What do you want?"

"I want you to take me to the church of Saint Francois Xavier."

"I don't know where it is."

"I'll show you."

"It's too far away."

She made a face at me as if to indicate that my recalcitrance was thickheaded beyond comprehension.

"I have to deliver messages." She held out a bag of paper

scraps and waved them at me. I shrugged, ignoring her, but she began to scream, growing increasingly hysterical. My mother came running out and thwacked me until Auguste stopped her noise. I hated Auguste Bastian. I was afraid of her ridiculous and meaningless requests, *take me here, take me there*, and kept out of her way. We put her in that little room where she stayed for days, but she wouldn't talk to anyone, and no one came for her. I left food outside her door and watched the tray disappear inside then reappear at the end of the morning or afternoon. After the first week I tried to see past the door when the tray was taken in. My mother still maintained that she would make us rich, and I thought money or jewelry might be scattered around, lying right out on the rickety table or on the floor, but all I could see were wasps hovering over a half-eaten peach, stone exposed. Auguste's chamber wasn't very clean, but much of the garbage appeared to be recently acquired; how the junk was collected or generated I didn't know. I never saw her leave. One morning she began to clean, scrubbing the stairs. I stood a few stairs below her and poked her with a broom handle. I don't know why I did. She smelled very bad, and rather than tell her, I poked.

"Where the goat is tied it must graze. It's not my fault if frogs don't have tails."

Her brush made a swishing sound as she spoke, and a wave of dirty water cascaded over the stair, lapping at my feet. The knees of her dress were wet gray patches. I only half-minded being ignored, but whether she was only talking to herself or not, her proverbs made no sense until I developed the uneasy feeling that I was somehow their target. I marched upstairs to the landing just below where she scrubbed. I watched her scrub nearer and nearer, then hopped cross legged down each step as she approached.

———

"Why do you sweep all the time?"

"My first job was in a house where one of the daughters refused to let me clean her room. She decided she didn't want to be waited on. Her father used to come up to the maid's room, that was my room, to do some things with me, but I wasn't paid for it like Gilberte and the others who live here with you."

"What did he do with you up in your room?"

"Ask you mother," she taunted. "Anyway this man indulged his silly daughter, let her pretend to be another person, although in a few weeks the mess grew out of control. One day she slammed the door behind her, left her family, and joined the Commune."

"What happened to her?"

"She was killed. Everyone was."

"That's not true. My grandmother was sent to Algiers."

"It's the same thing."

I shoved a book at her, thinking she might read the story out loud, even if only to herself. It was a book of fables by La Fontaine. She held it upside down, and although it was then I realized she couldn't read, I don't think I really understood what illiteracy meant. Meaning was always there, it was right there. How could she not see it? For me, words, language, were closely allied to pictograms — obvious signs, no mystery in them. Not to be able to read seemed a kind of blindness.

"Are the letters too small?" She nodded, lying. I pointed out the book's pictures of lions and monkeys, told her the stories that I could recite, but I wasn't being kind or offering entertainment. Not knowing what writing was, she wasn't very interested, but I showed off anyway. I read the last verse of *The Town Rat and the Country Rat*. The Town Rat invited the Country Rat to dinner, but the latter, I explained, was scared off by a cat. The Country Rat said:

But at home I eat in peace,
And nobody interrupts.
Good-bye, then. And to hell
With pleasure that fear corrupts!

"You see, that's you. You interrupt. You should go back to where you came from if you can't pay for a room." I knew honesty was a virtue. I had also been told directness was an admirable quality, and that goodness wasn't always obvious. I interpreted these injunctions literally. I was trying to be good; it required thought, effort, and action. It's better in the long run, I reasoned, if she knows she should leave.

"A famished stomach has no ears," she repeated another proverb. "I'm not your pet animal, sweetie." She cornered me on the landing outside her room.

"How can you get around without being able to read street or shop signs?" I wouldn't give up.

"You ask people, dummy. You go backward and forward until you get to where you're going."

"That must waste a lot of time." It didn't occur to me that she mightn't have any place to go to.

"I have all the time in the world."

I ducked out of the corner and ran away from her, but in my flight downstairs, I left my book behind. She returned it to my mother the next day. "Nice of you to read to Madame Bastian," I was told. My mother thought I'd finally done a charitable thing. If my mother thought I was being good when that was the last thing I had been thinking of, the rumor of wealth had paid off in some roundabout way. But that misreading of my character aside, a dividend of a sort, it was clear to me that whatever riches Auguste might be connected to could only lie in a fathomless hoax.

Cher-ie! Cher-ie! Take me to the rue de Lille.

"I'll take you there, Auguste, and leave you with the Germans." I'd learned something about her churches and the rue de Lille.

"If you don't go with me, the Syndicate will take over the world."

I had no idea what she was talking about.

One night while my mother was making dinner, which included special soft eggs and soup for Auguste, who had no teeth, she had told me the German embassy was on the rue de Lille near the churches Auguste pleaded to be taken to. They were all in the seventh arrondissement. I was sick of soft food; since my mother had taken Auguste under her wing, we all ate the same things. Auguste didn't eat with us. I thought she was disgusting, and I couldn't understand why my mother didn't find her so, why she let this woman, this attention grabber, come between us. I left trays by her door, knocked, yelled that garbage was served, and ran downstairs. One of the women who worked at night told me to keep my voice down, then went back into her room. I held out empty hands to her as if to say it wasn't my fault, I was the one who had no peace. Madame Gilberte, barely dressed, didn't care what I saw. Her eyebrows were penciled arches, pointed and gothic, but her mouth had smeared to a long sneer. *Donkey walks on four legs and I walk on two; the last one I saw was very much like you,* I sang at Gilberte's door. I still didn't know exactly what Auguste meant by the men who went to her room to do some things, but I was sure it was sickening, nothing you could pay me to do no matter how much I was offered.

It was a long walk across the river to the seventh, but I developed a plan. I was going to get rid of Madame Bastian who made my life miserable with her demands and insults. My scheme was simple, and when it was carried out I could play in the courtyard again without being tortured, without being caught between the two of them. I could be alone with my mother once more. I would take Auguste to her churches, but as we walked, in the middle of a crowd, I would let go of her hand and run away. I didn't think she would become lost because she'd lived her whole life in the city; an anomie, she could never be truly lost and I was certain that all she'd ever done was wander around the city for years. It was just a question of shifting mass from one location to the next. The narrow room my mother shut her into couldn't really be considered home. She could make someone else rich. My mother never explained to me why or how this would happen. When I asked, all she would say was that Auguste had worked in the German embassy; that's all she had time to explain before a tenant rang for his key or came with some complaint or need.

———·—·———

Come on, Auguste, I'll take you.

The next day when my mother was out, I went upstairs and took the smelly old thing's hand; she looked surprised at my surly complicity and grew quiet, trying to figure out what I might be up to. We walked out of the courtyard in what turned out to be a short-lived silence and began our trip to the embassy.

At the corner, deserted and quiet, she whispered to me, "I'm glad you came to fetch me, dearest, I needed you so." I studied the base of a lamppost in acute embarrassment. I didn't know why she'd changed her tune and sounded almost coy, but I suspected she might be plotting as treacherously as I was. Then Auguste handed me a folded piece of paper.

"You can look at it." She paused, waiting for my reaction, but I just looked at her. She stared at the sky as if someone were up there giving her cues, jumping from rooftop to rooftop. I unfolded the piece of onionskin she had handed me. The "writing" looked like knitting. It was illegible, not really script at all. She had probably scribbled this mess of a letter herself. I didn't know what to say. The loopy lines meant nothing at all.

"If you can read, you can make out the message." Auguste nearly tripped on a step as she rolled her eyes.

I pretended to read it and agree with her. "Oh, my God," I said, cynically imitating my mother. Madame Bastian looked up at an apartment building that seemed to lean over the street as if it would collapse onto us.

Auguste explained to me that when she worked at the embassy she was often employed privately by the ambassador's family and his staff to carry personal messages to different parts of the city.

"They thought I was stupid, and so they trusted me. I could go anywhere in their offices and private suites. Behind doors closed to nearly everyone I watched women paint their faces, bottles and pots of color fanned out in front of them." She smacked her lips at her imaginary reflection, evening out nonexistent lip rouge. "I might stand by dumb like a piece of furniture while they spoke about private things: love affairs in which the love was not returned or the desired one was caught with someone else; they talked about debts from gambling, debts from bad investments. I heard it all, but they carried on as though I was dumb or wasn't in the room at all. Then, because they trusted me to be ignorant and obedient, I'm handed sealed letters, and off I go. But I'm not without feelings and curiosity." Auguste switched to the present tense for a moment and mimed someone handing her a letter, which she took with a bow.

"I travel across the city. All kinds of doors are open to me with a wink. When notes are delivered, the envelopes are often torn open while I wait, although some men and women throw them aside carelessly as if I were an ordinary postman who didn't know anything and wouldn't talk. Not so. I couldn't get used to gloves, coats, flowers thrown at me to dispose of. I didn't like being reprimanded, and I knew how to be indiscrete for a price." She made a talking gesture with her hand, opening and shutting fingers as though her hand were a mouth, then she lowered her voice and took on a confidential tone.

We had stopped in front of a hardware store for a moment, its window full of gadgets. I rocked back and forth, shifting weight from one foot to the other. I wanted to appear cavalier when I was actually spellbound.

"In the embassy, especially in the evening, I saw all kinds of things, indescribable acts. I saw men kissing each other behind frosted glass, women swimming naked in the embassy fountain at night." She put her hands over my ears, just for a few seconds, then went on. "I was supposed to burn the papers I collected in the German embassy trash, but I didn't, I harvested them. In the middle of the night I left with my *cônes* under my coat. The code word for my papers was *cônes*."

At rue Notre Dame de Lorette we passed a stand that sold newspapers, that was all, but she became nervous and wanted to go back. We turned around, she didn't speak again, but when we reached our courtyard my mother was standing at her station, arms crossed. Madame Bastian didn't say a word to her, proceeding to shamble up the stairs as if nothing out of the ordinary had happened. She leaned heavily on the banister and put all her tired weight on each foot as if she might go rolling backward in the wind. When the door shut behind her, my mother started to shake me by the shoulders.

"Do you like throwing money out the window? Because what you've done, missy, amounts to the same thing." She grabbed me by the collar. "Someone's going to recognize Madame Bastian and take her from us, then where will you be?"

"What are you talking about? She's been living on the streets for years. She's not your prisoner. Either everyone knows who she is, or no one does, and no one cares."

"Wouldn't you like to move out of this building and live in a nice place?" My mother was employing the stupid question technique.

I was exasperated, felt too old to be hit and badgered, and could sense she was tired. I twisted free, running out the door toward the part of rue Notre Dame de Lorette where women chased drunks away while taking the arms of others.

"Take this scarf, Madeleine. You'll freeze."

"Leave me alone."

I looked back and saw her standing in the street, but I kept running, tripping into someone's legs only to be pushed away with a shove. I knew a few tenants had somehow squeezed the truth from Auguste. She paid no rent and was given free meals. This did not sit well with Madame Gilberte and the others. It may only have been a matter of time before they found out who she was, a former charlady who worked at the German embassy decades ago. I pieced together that she had stolen something valuable from the Germans, but when I asked her, all she would say was *right under your nose*. The last year she worked had been before the World's Fair, the Exposition of 1900.

A week later Auguste wanted to be taken to the church of Sainte Clotilde. She wanted to go so badly and expressed the need with such urgency I thought there might have been a pile of money hidden in one of the apses, something taken from the Germans, a crime much advertised but never resolved. My mother could wait forever, but I would take matters into my own hands.

"I have to deliver my *cônes*." She showed me a bag of sweepings culled from the garbage. Besides papers the bag also contained rotting orange peels, apple cores, lumps of stale bread. In the shadows a silver stream of light, dust motes floating in it, hit the upheld bag.

"Henry will be waiting for me."

"Who is Henry, Auguste?" I thought Henry was an imaginary lover that Auguste had invented for herself years ago. Cradling the greasy bag of garbage she looked maternal and childish at the same time. I hoped no one would see me. Auguste embarrassed me, but I had entered into a kind of bargain with her. Again I took her hand, and we walked into the street. The rain had left the sidewalk cleaner than usual, and I heard an urgent clacking of heels before I actually saw Madame Gilberte.

"Where's your mother? I saw another rat." This was a ruse. The building was full of rats. What did I or anyone else care? Why complain to me? Pulled along the curb by her terrier, she finally planted both feet on the ground in front of us. "This one was as big as my dog." She tossed her veil back over her head so she could smoke, a sign she was going to loiter for a few minutes while he strained on his leash, nose to the ground.

"Where are you girls off to?" Madame Gilberte seemed to take an unusual interest in our welfare at inopportune moments.

If I asked her to leave me alone, she would call my mother. I thought of telling her I was taking Auguste to the bank, but in her meddling way, she would have insisted on accompanying a minor and a nutcase.

"She's taking me to church."

Madame Gilberte's face expressed contradictory and conflicting sentiments: how nice and how disgusting. If she suspected we weren't really going to church, she only said, "Of course, that's what I thought. You're wearing black." Auguste, dressed entirely in black, black rags tied around her head like an elaborate turban and her middle as if holding her together, began to walk away, as if conversational obligations had been fulfilled, and I followed. We left her staring after us.

"There was a nosy functionary in the embassy I didn't like, and I always tried to duck when I saw him coming. A petty intruder, I think he got wind of my courier route or suspected I wasn't burning the trash the way I was supposed to. He was always sniffing around where he wasn't wanted, and he was difficult to get rid of. Once I walked backward in a circular hall in order to avoid detection, only to run into him backward. Slam!"

"Who's Henry?" I asked again. I wasn't really interested in Auguste's ghostly lover, but was surprised she hadn't ever mentioned him before, spilling over with memories of a love that embraced her even in fantasy, a love in which she was more than just a messenger.

"Henry was the man I met in the evening after work in order to hand over the *cônes*." Only once before had she alluded to the identity of her contact by saying that the Army General Staff had more important fish to fry than love letters and she, Auguste, was more than a common go-between.

"First I have to tell you about poor Martin Brucker, an agent for the Second Bureau, I used to leave my *cônes* for him. Some people say the lower you go in the rungs of spying, the more lowlifes you meet, but there are lowlifes everywhere, and Brucker wasn't necessarily one of these. I knew his uncle, a retired pensioner. We lived in the same building. Brucker's three faults were that he liked money, he was indiscreet, and he had a girlfriend, Millescamp, who was up to no good. She was gaptoothed and like to wear a plaid dress that fit her to a T. His uncle told me she slept late, making a living by selling ecclesiastical souvenirs at Notre Dame. She had great pretensions and no alliances to anyone except herself. Millescamp accused Brucker of wanting only money, of not paying serious attention to her, although she wasn't very different. She told everyone he wasn't much of an agent, only a salesman who would sell my papers to whoever offered the right price, and soon Brucker, the middleman of sorts, was finished thanks to his big-mouth girlfriend. I do my job for my country, not for the money. A down-and-out Englishman I met during the trial said of Millescamp that she really was a thousand scamps. She was a piece of work. She stole documents from Brucker when he was asleep and sold them to the Germans. You can imagine this little man waking up in a dark room, alone, looking around and figuring out that the woman he loves is gone with my garbage, my *cônes*, his meal ticket. When he visited his uncle he stormed up and down the stairs talking to himself, growing passionate in his distress. He would have her put in jail, and toward this end he didn't have to do much, and Martin, once roused, was spiteful enough to send a letter here or pay a call there. She was easily caught and sent to prison, but it didn't matter. Martin Brucker still had a reputation for a big mouth, no more spying for him. After his girlfriend's deceit was uncovered, I met only with Henry, a much more important man, and left my *cônes* for him in church. If it hadn't been for Millescamp in her loud plaids, Brucker and I could have gone on for years. He was my kind of man, and I was fond of him, but it wasn't to be. Meeting Henry in church at night I felt kicked upstairs, I think it's called. Commandant Henry was formidable and uncommunicative, a lump of black ice sitting in a church pew. An important man, I know, but I couldn't quite figure him out.

"Commandant Henry of the General Staff, head shaved almost to the skull, thick moustache with waxed ends," she whispered, and beginning with the words *General Staff of the French Army*, the story my mother and the other tenants only had the vaguest grasp of was explained.

I understood about half of what she was saying, but I had no idea how my mother was going to spin all this nattering about tight plaid suits and a treacherous gap-tooth smile into gold. Auguste winked at me when she said the name *Brucker*, and I wondered what had gone on between them. It was clear she didn't like Brucker's girlfriend, but was she also a bit jealous of her?

"My *cônes* were crucial. I was trusted and never caught. Henry wouldn't tolerate any jokes. An important person, he wouldn't have given Brucker the time of day, nor me either, but he needed me. I could give him what he required."

Auguste paused and winked again. I couldn't imagine her as a young woman. She seemed like someone who had always been old. The man, Henry, probably used her in some way she would never recognize.

"I respected Henry, but he made me nervous. I preferred to leave my papers hidden in the church behind a relic or a statue; he could pick them up without ever actually seeing yours truly," she pointed to herself.

"Brucker, in disgrace, was desperate to return to the bureau. He haunted 78, rue de Lille, and once I gave him a letter I stole directly from Schwarzkoppen's pigeonhole. He opened it right in the embassy and ran off, saying it was important, critical. He laughed. He would be a hero. What was in the letter? How should I know? I couldn't read it. His uncle was a friend, I would do what I could for him, to help him get his job back. When the *bordereau* surfaced it was full of secrets turned over by that scoundrel D, it was said. Some say that list of secrets was in the letter I handed Brucker, some say the *bordereau* came via the Ordinary Track. That was what my route was known as."

"What do you think?"

"I have no idea. I couldn't read the letter. Was it the one I gave him or did I deliver it myself? I don't know. It might have been in the garbage. All kinds of things were.

"A traffic in documents. Imagine, if you can, a parade of files, miles of files, marching from Pigalle to the Champs Elysees to Montparnasse, stopping at one office after another, each office or apartment adding more papers to the parade of documents. Many of them are forgeries, pastiches, collages rephotographed and passed off as original copies. Only my *cônes* directly from the embassy garbage are genuine, and I deliver only to Henry."

"But it's only papers that have been thrown away."

"No, you're wrong. Junk is the best. People imagine trash is trash. No one looks a second time at that which has been tossed into paper hell. Those that do, like myself, are rewarded. Great secrets have been found in junk or written on torn pieces of paper. Schwarzkoppen, the military attaché, an attractive and important man, tore his letters into two to twenty fragments. Occasionally you would get a ball, a crumpled wedge of onionskin or blue paper. These smooth out with no trouble. When Henry went home to his wife, I imagine they reconstructed letters and sorted them into piles by candlelight; fragments spread out on a table, on the floor, dinner pushed aside, growing cold."

She stopped in the middle of the street and laughed out loud. I didn't know what to make of her stories.

"Schwarzkoppen, *Tête Noire,* he was called, what a name."

A woman in a red hat stared at her, pulled a black tulle veil over her nose; I nudged Auguste forward, then tried to wipe my hand on my dress. She really smelled.

"I earned 250 francs a week. It was the best job I ever had. My route was the most reliable in French intelligence, and it was called only this: the ordinary track. That's all. Every cigar on the General Staff knew me as the ordinary track. You could ask them even now, except Henry is dead." She stopped speaking. We began to walk again, and she gripped my arm harder.

I've begun to put the American's things into boxes. His books and papers written in English are as meaningless to me as the *cônes* were to Auguste. It all looks like nonsense. *The Shirelles, Litle Anthony and the Imperials, The Chiffons, The Marvelettes.* Looks French but isn't. Every time I clean this room out, I imagine her inventory of bills, receipts, love letters between men and women, between women, between military attachés, cigarette papers, fruit wrappers, and important documents. I've even searched this room for bits of things she may have left behind, but it's been empty, cleaned, and reoccupied thirty or forty times since she lived here. She never saved any of her original *cônes* anyway. They had been taken away from her. That had been the beginning of the Dreyfus affair.

"Schwarzkoppen, the German attaché, was elegant but careless. His trash bins were open catalogs, schedules of entire days, weeks from the most personal to the most secret. It came out at the trial."

Bits of paper tumbled into her bags soundlessly, innocently, in slow motion. She polished an iron grill, she hummed to herself, and sat at a black Dresden piano as calmly as a bank robber in the middle of the night with the alarms disconnected, taking a break for a smoke. I imagined her listening at doors, waiting until everyone had left, before she could depart with her bulky bags, out the service entrance into the night. The elegant and attractive men and women were like movie images. If she put her hand to the screen, she'd feel only canvas; none would shake her hand in return. They lived in the world of written language. Their exchange lay in a milieu of signs that she, though blind to them, had the ability to completely undermine, but the spy in the house of love and intrigue was eventually reduced to living off scraps thrown out the back doors of restaurants. She might have seen one of Schwarzkoppen's lovers dining inside, waving forks, elbowing waiters, knocking over glasses. The contents of the fragments she so conscientiously collected were to Auguste entirely imaginary. What did she think they referred to? Poison gas? A bomb capable of leveling a city? She couldn't even sign her name just for fun across illicitly acquired notes on French artillery secrets.

1. A note on the hydraulic brake of the 120
2. A note covering troops
3. Modification of artillery formations
4. Madagascar
5. The sketch for a firing manual for country artillery

I am off to maneuvers.
Yours,
Auguste

She was like a blind fisherman who caught both rare fish and rubber boots in her net but relied on the boats of other men to get out to sea in the first place. The ultimate word-democrat, she rejected nothing.

We went into a shop that sold secondhand china. Auguste needed a cup and saucer, a bowl, and a plate. She had decided to stay
in our building awhile, and my mother said I might take her to
a cheap place where she could buy a few things. Lazare's was
dark and dusty. There wasn't much in the shop. Auguste picked
through crates of crockery. In the dark only a few rays of light
hit the rim of a plate or glass. An old man with reddish hair and
a long beard slept behind the counter. A younger one came out
and told Auguste to leave. She wouldn't be served in his shop.
She could buy nothing here. He said that he recognized her
and knew her name. I turned red when he looked at me, as if
I was guilty too, without knowing what the crime might have
been. Why did these strangers hate her so much? What had the
Ordinary Track done? Auguste began to sweat and shuffled toward the door. She would have been thrown out into the street if
we'd stayed, I'm sure of it. I followed her to the door feeling as if
I'd been caught stealing, but I had no idea why. What would my
mother say? How could I tell her what had just transpired when
I didn't really know myself?

"During the trial it came out, what I'd done, and so I lost
my job. Everyone knew about the Ordinary Track. I served my
country, but I lost my job, and it was Dreyfus's fault. I didn't care
if he was guilty or innocent. I told everyone. I didn't care who
knew. The papers I brought in proved his guilt. I was glad of it,
and knew they had the right man. Citizens like Lazare might say
evidence of his innocence was discovered in forgeries created
from my papers, but I don't believe it. He was a traitor. I may
be the only one who thinks it was that simple, but I do believe
they should have left him on Devil's Island. People have called
me a liar, a double agent, but I was none of these. How could I
lie? Garbage never lies. I don't even know what a double agent
might be.

"Papers like snow, eddying in drifts. Each paper flake is unique and laced with blue veins, inky writing. That's what gets you into trouble; so I feel innocent when I examine each bit of illegibility. A corner here, a crooked line there. My ignorance preserved my innocence. I sniff things out, rely on instinct, not wayward thoughts, so I'm always right. I have a nose, an instinct," she tapped it and pinched the flange of nostrils as if holding her breath until the end of her nose turned very white.

"In church I think about the hell in the pictures. There must be chars to keep things up, to stoke the fires."

"I thought her family might have found her by now."

"She has no family."

"Madame Gilberte went to the police."

"She did?"

"They weren't interested. Nobody cares about the Ordinary Track."

"I can't have her living here rent free."

"Nobody paid for the room before. The owners will never know."

"I was stupid. She's a lump, nothing more."

"I don't know if she was really just a lump," I said to my mother as she sorted bills. "She had to act stupid. Perhaps that's why she was never caught. We could go to the papers, tell them we've discovered a national heroine who deserves a reward, or better treatment at least."

"They won't care either."

"How do you know?"

"When I first saw her I thought she might be like one of those cases of a celebrity suffering from amnesia; you know, and when they wake up, so to speak, gratitude is showered on whoever rescued them. Now I'm not sure that she wasn't just a minor player who found the spotlight trained on her one day and lost whatever footing she had. I can't remember what it was she retrieved from the embassy."

I told her what I knew. My mother's impulses were doomed to disappoint her. Her get-rich-quick schemes, founded on charity, never worked. Some people bet on horses or bought lottery tickets. My mother bet on strangers, from confidence men to women found living on the street. She sat by the keys, looking into the dustbin. It was full of papers.

"Some citizens will say anything and expect to be believed. You will find as you grow older that they turn out to have a history of it," she said.

"I believe her."

"I remember Henry created forgeries pasting together a piece here and a piece there. Auguste must have believed in the army and in the Syndicate. She went crazy, became an enthusiastic symbol for *La Libre Parole,* and for its editor, Edgar Drumont, for those who wanted all foreigners put in boats and blown up, I think. We'll have to ask her what she did."

"There's no point. She doesn't know herself."

"She's not much of a treasure."

"What do you mean?"

"What do you think I mean? That's the end of the Ordinary Track, then. I can't keep freeloaders here."

She went out into the courtyard to speak to Mademoiselle J., who had come downstairs partly undressed in order to complain about Gilberte's yammering little dog. I was fascinated by her transparent underwear, which showed under her robes. My mother thought there was no point in wearing anything if you could see through it, but the filmy things were curiosities to me. I sorted the mail slowly, and then, since the shops were about to close I went out to buy wine for dinner. When I came back, although she couldn't have left that quickly, it seemed to me that Auguste was already gone.

La Fontaine was full of stories that demonstrated that kindness might not always be its own reward, and strangers were not always benevolent godmothers in disguise. Tricksterism demanded constant vigilance. Behind what appeared to be honest offers lurked one hoax after another, and every possible opportunity to do good had to be examined. There was no way to know which indigent strangers were masked princes and which were devils. The charlady hadn't promised us riches. That had been my mother's construction, but she didn't blame herself. There were, she said, too many hungry mouths in the world to feel badly for too long about any single one of them. I put my arms around her, but she was distant, and so I left her alone. She swept up in the morning, knocking over an oil lamp brought over from Algiers. The metal was already very dented, no genie came out or was evicted by this last battering, but when my mother saw the damage she had done she sat very still with it in her lap and wouldn't speak to me. I went to her post and took keys from the tenants who left them with us in the morning.

During the weeks that followed Auguste's departure I walked to the rue de Lille looking for the German embassy, past Stendhal's house burned by *petroleuses* during the Commune, and past the prints of the Commune (images of churned-up paving stones, smashed windows, firing squads, heaps of dead) sold in stacks on the quai Voltaire, but I couldn't find the building that had been the beginning of the Ordinary Track. I was late for school, and I didn't look very hard. I do believe Auguste really was involved in the trial, otherwise Lazare wouldn't have refused to sell her a chipped cup. I looked in the churches where she left her papers, not so much because I expected to find a fragment someone forgot to sweep up decades ago, but because I wanted to be sure the churches were there. On another empty afternoon after school I would try to follow her steps. In the churches my eyes would take a few minutes to get used to the dim light. Hidden in portals or painted in chapel apses, long, thin, mutilated figures, some standing on the head of another, some beheaded altogether, made me uneasy. I looked at the floor but didn't step on any *cônes* and would soon forget about them altogether.

That fall the older sister of one of my friends was sent away to the countryside. She came back with dark circles under her eyes, and she seemed to spend a lot of time moping around until her father got her a job in a café, I was told, in another part of the city. I didn't see her again. Another friend began to travel by bicycle. She was very tall and had no trouble managing it. Few girls rode them, but I wanted one. Finally my mother got me a bicycle, and the freedom to travel fast and unfettered felt like flight. It had no brakes, and I had to put my foot down in order to stop. As I traveled through the city I might come to a standstill in front of small buildings, houses or structures too little for a city block crowded with taller apartment houses, but which hadn't been torn down and perhaps wouldn't be: *parro-quets*, wedge-shaped angled structures fitted into corners, one-story boxes with or without sloping rooftops, solitary towers or marooned turrets resting illogically on the ground instead of above a castle. Between right-angled nests of modern flats I found isolated places that one or two people might inhabit entirely alone, like Alfred Jarry's decrepit freight-car house on stilts. I wanted to live in one.

———·—·———

I turn the American music off and return to my post. Jean Auric knocks on my door to share a cup of coffee. He's the oldest tenant, superannuated and alone, but knows little of the details of the Dreyfus affair. He only wants to ask that the newly empty room not be rented to Algerians. My grandmother, I tell him, was *a petroleuse*. She hated Napoléon III, burned buildings and was sent out of the country. My mother was born in Algiers, near the desert. He doesn't believe me, and it's true I sound as if I don't really know what I'm talking about, I can barely keep my eyes open, but my mother was born in Algeria. I'm sure she was.

"See the photograph of her near where the keys hang?" Auric has never noticed it.

"Can't you tell," I ask him, "how much we look alike?" He finally nods, and acknowledges, it's true, he's sorry he never met her. He senses this isn't a good time to talk to me, takes his paper and leaves the courtyard walking toward the street.

The building is so quiet I almost miss the Americans and their noise. With their records and English magazines of naked women, they took pleasure where they found it, then blundered on to the next titillation, I would guess.

To hell with the pleasure that fear corrupts, the Town Rat thought, eating amidst threats was no more than life as usual, and food should always be taken with the idea that it and one's life might soon be snatched away. Some might agree that abuse is the normal scheme of things, if not a kind of spice. If it is a kind of odd-ball corruption, combining pleasure and fear, then this building is packed to the gills with Town Rats, and I'm their long-suffering queen wearing a garland of sponges round my head for a crown. They turn out to have a history of it. Auguste was the worst offender with her careful collections and well-nursed hatreds, not realizing that some people have no choice; their fates are sealed by forgers and confidence men and off they go to Devil's Island or El Asnam.

It begins to rain, clearing the last streaks of soap and detergent from the courtyard, but an untapped lode of powdered soap that I hadn't seen before blossoms into an explosion of bubbles. The children from the Mekong Delta tumble downstairs again, carrying small black umbrellas, pushing and chasing the foam in the rain. This spill is better than the last one, more spectacular, more ridiculous, and, although it is raining, the bubbles now reflect colors. From the stairs Auric yells at them and his distress is also directed at me in my rooms. They are making a mess, he shouts. The soap could be toxic. When their parents get home he will complain, he insists, but we ignore him. Between the rain and the confusion caused by a drunk American, the court-yard can be cleaned with no effort. I go out to join the children screaming with delight; the paving stones are slippery, and if one should trip I will catch her before she falls. I don't shout with them, I only watch. It's an uncorrupted pleasure, I think, and there are so few of these to be had.

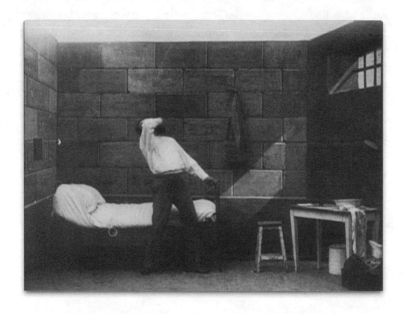

Squirting Cameras and Rubber Noses

January 6, 1935

Principal Commissioner
Place Baudoyer Prefect of Police
Paris

Dear Sir,

After the recent death of my sister, Claire Francoeur, letters addressed to me were recovered that seem to indicate that a certain property was stolen from her a few days prior to her passing. Although she was not well and her judgment not always sound, her sudden death remains unexplained to my satisfaction. If the cause of death was accidental electrocution then the contusions on her neck could not have been self-inflicted. The bruises were disguised for her wake, but I saw them when I was called to identify the body. How did a new and heavy radio find its way upstairs and topple into her bath? I know the radio was kept in the salon like any other piece of formal furniture, and here one could listen to music or news as most people do. No one listens to the radio in a bathroom. Even if my sister had lugged the thing up to the bathroom, as far as I was told, the chair on which it was supposedly balanced was surely placed a safe distance from the water. The detective on the case explained to me how the dog knocked it into the bath, but his interpretation of events seems far fetched. I trust your office to look into such discrepancies, which signal, to me, that a truly wrongful death hides behind your conclusion of "accidental electrocution."

The enclosed letters were never mailed to me. They were found in her desk while arrangements were being made to sell her house. When I made inquiries as to what might have become of my sister's papers, her maid suggested to me that a man who had rented rooms from her was very keen on acquiring the documents. She also indicated that he came and went from the house with some frequency, only spending the night once or twice a week in spite of the high price he paid for the privilege of using them. She believed he had an apartment somewhere in the district of the Hotel de Ville in Paris, therefore I address the matter to you. It will become clear as you read these letters that this is the man you should seek. He is, at first, referred to by the name Fontaine, but if my sister could, even in part, be considered a reliable observer, he is, without question, a man who has an ardent interest in an unpleasant affair of many years ago. I needn't name the incident which, I'm sure we would both agree, should have been laid permanently to rest. It should remain buried, earth packed over it with a spade because if forced out, I promise we will find ourselves struggling with an unspeakable embarrassment. With the acquisition of these papers, this Fontaine will be in a position to reveal evidence that would be very awkward for my family as well as your office and the institution of the army. I realize parts of my sister's letters express doubts as to whether or not the documents in question ought to be left to me, but her will stated otherwise and indicated this bequest without condition. I can assure you just as unconditionally that we were always extremely close. I shall be in the city for a few weeks more before returning to my family in the south and hope to resolve this business to everyone's satisfaction. I will be staying at the convent attached to Sainte-Anne-de-la-Maison-Blanche on the rue de Tolbiac. If there is anything I can do to expedite the recovery of my sister's papers I await only your request to do so.

Yours sincerely,
Lille Charpin

July 1, 1934

Dear Lille,

It's late afternoon, but I'm still in bed after a disrupted night and a bad morning. Shadows moving toward the eaves look like the long arms of frog princes who never really changed into anything else; in this house they are always frogs. Rooms downstairs are very quiet. What else do I imagine? Previously elusive representatives from my daydreams assemble themselves in haphazard sequence and then a pattern emerges, the *tableau vivant* begins to have significance. What is the motivation behind their sudden appearance? I'm looking for the figure in the carpet, outlines that will finally link pesky scenes so I can sit up in bed confident there is some meaning behind images of pens, spilt ink, and the sound of knocking on a thick door.

In my dream, light shines between its cracked panels, and although I know the doorknobs will be ice cold, it takes me a long time to reach one of them. Opening the door on the other side, what do I see? A huge bouquet of flowers with two small feet standing at the threshold; the delivery boy, made invisible by monstrous lilies and roses, moves toward me. I refuse to take the clusters off his hands. I send them back to wherever it is they came from. I don't even want to know from whom or where this bunch was sent. When I return to my rooms, most available spaces are crammed with pens of all shapes and sizes; ink bottles replace washstands, hands and faces dipped in them emerge blue and blinded. I can hear you marking the margins of this letter: this part you'll read out loud to your children, this part will be read through peals of laughter to a confidante if you have one, and to each you'll cluck your tongue and somehow manage to get out the idea that such lines reveal how unhinged your sister has become. Call Charenton if they're still minding hysterics, we'll go hand in hand, but you'll never collect my papers if you do. If I were to rewind the film and review all the scenarios of our past, you would point out, "My sister is a deranged syphilitic in the tertiary stages of the disease, not to be trusted now or ever." I have no deadlines, nothing to rush toward, and the public humiliation and shame I've suffered needs to be put to rights. My half-waking thoughts produce associations that overlap each other like shingles. One touches its partner because a roof would not be functional otherwise, and like squares of slate these pictures have utilitarian logic but no psychological meaning. One just leads to the next.

Yours,
Claire

———·———

July 13, 1934

Dear Lille,

Last night I was awakened by a sound that would cause anyone living alone to turn rigid or sit up in bed: footsteps, soft at first and then more careless, tapping out what I thought might be a figure eight on the rug downstairs. I think it was long past midnight because the trains had stopped, and the sky wasn't entirely black; perhaps it was close to dawn. Standing behind my bedroom door, open and near the steps, I heard a voice. *It's abandoned. We can take anything we like.* The sentence was followed by a vaudevillian clunk. *Watch out for that desk. We can come back for it later.* They moved some furniture around, stacked plates, lifted paintings from the walls, making what I would later discover to be a large pile of my belongings, concentrated like a junkman's pyramid in the middle of the kitchen floor. When I heard them leave and was absolutely certain the gate had slammed behind them, I went downstairs, only to freeze in the doorway, immobilized by the sight of extraordinary disarray. Stacks of misplaced objects teetered in hastily assembled minarets, and I stood there unable to prevent their slow-motion toppling. I sidestepped through a plenum of my possessions. Slowly I began to move small things: a tarnished frame, photographs of the family at Deauville, souvenirs from the 1900 Exposition, the pre-Revolutionary clock that I don't think is really over fifty years old. I moved whatever I could into large closets with secure locks. If they don't return tomorrow, I can use this opportunity to mark off my territory in this empty house, my private Maginot Line. You may worry that the interlopers knew what they were after, but I don't think the thieves knew how to read. The foundation of my guesswork lay in the sound of their accents: the nocturnal intruders were chumps after long-gone family silver, a comforting thought. To an illiterate treasure hunter one box of dated letters is no better or worse than a bundle of kindling, overlooked, neglected old things. *Le faisceau* — bundle of sticks, kindling, carried by the Romans, the root, I'm told, of the word we whisper from time to time: *fascism*.

In the morning when Sylvie arrived she sat in a chair that threatened to disintegrate under her and cried into her fists. My first impression was one of incredulity, why, why bother about this minor tornado? Was she pantomiming her shock in order to appear sympathetic? No, the sobs were real. My loss had in some way become hers. Slowly she began to replace trivial objects, but I urged her to get a boy from down the road to move heavy furniture into the cellar, which can be locked. A little fellow arrived, moved the table, chairs, and the desk with a hundred small drawers and pigeonholes. Many of the drawers spilled their contents when maneuvered down the steep steps. I've left the debris, moatlike, lying on the floor beside a mattress near the stairs: lists, bills, lost buttons, stamps, bottles of ink, ribbon, scraps of paper. The rooms above are still crowded with furniture: bookshelves listing to the north, desilvered mirrors, and a torn-up sofa have remained in their places. By late afternoon, just when we were finishing, I had my bed moved into the attic and looked out a lunette into the street below. I felt wedged into a tight corner perch, but secure. I combed my hair, ringed my eyes with black pencil, painted my mouth red, so I looked like a woman from the kind of print you feel embarrassed by when it tumbles out of a book. *Is it pornography? Look again. Maybe not.* I felt sort of like a parody. Who was I waiting for? The burglars of Bastille Eve were no one I wanted to meet.

From the window I could see Sylvie and the boy standing in my yard, parts of it choked with plants, the edges bare, stomped-earth paths. Sylvie called up to me because the boy was waiting to be paid. I washed my face and went downstairs. There was no one to even imagine seducing. Even in the darkening court the boy dawdled, pulling at the dandelions and weeds.

"I can always find someone, even on the fourteenth, who can put bars over the windows and new locks on the doors," the smart aleck offered. "You want people to know you live here, that this isn't an empty house."

"I won't pay for frills." I thought I sounded emphatic, while Sylvie shook her head and sent him on his way. As it grew dark she looked anxious and offered to spend the night in my house, but I encouraged her to go home after she served dinner, and I think she must have been relieved to be able to turn her back on my disorderly house and botched rearrangements.

Yet an hour after she left the boy returned with a blue-eyed dog borrowed from his uncle. Delphine could be rented for a few francs a day. He handed me leash, a chipped food bowl, and a bag of old bones, then disappeared into the night before I could insist that I wouldn't pay for an animal I never asked for. Delphine ignored me and hid under the kitchen table, tail thumping the floor. I left the whole bag at her feet. The dog, barricaded by marrow bones, may never emerge again.

There are all kinds of chiselers and libel artists who could buy dinner based on information discovered in my penmanship. A scribbling kind of intruder would write books and articles; I worry about him. He might appear in the form of a solicitous young man with hair parted carefully down the middle. Quoting Charles Maurras, the royalist writer who hatched the scheme of "patriotic forgery," to explain the actions of those who framed Dreyfus, he will stand nervously at the door. Sylvie, ignorant of the signification of these references, will show him in. He'll smile, so happy to be here, feeling right at home with a fellow traveler, one with a record. To be sure we have an understanding he'll reveal his membership in *Les Camelots du Roi,* newsboys of the King, known for beating a professor at the Sorbonne whose opinions ran contrary to their own. Then, sitting comfortably on a broken chair, he'll speak of the new pollutants, foreigners from Eastern Europe and Africa, *les métèques,* he'll say. He'll look disappointed when I tell him that the truth is I never cared. My alliance with the spy Esterhazy — what I did for him, I did for a lark. I wrote the letter about spying for the Germans because he asked me to. He told me how to sign it: Alfred, etcetera He took the paper away and that was that. I'd never heard of Dreyfus, I'll say. No one had, and even later, I couldn't care less. At the beginning of the case he was almost released for lack of evidence. The young man will look pinched. He'll think, this can't be so.

France d'abord, he'll *say, France comes first,* as he kicks Delphine under the table for drooling on his ankles. Restoration of king and church, he'll plead. I'll show him the door, but the problem, or one problem, is that I've always been receptive to flattery and his childish face and faltering speech will have its charms. Masses of flowers will arrive. Thinking lightning can't strike twice, I'll accept. He couldn't imagine I would fall for the same trick after the first debacle. Has he no sense of irony?

He knocks again, popping up like a rabbit who won't stay in the hat. *We defend small shops,* he says. *We're against Jewish department stores.*

If I might see the letter his brother, Mathieu Dreyfus, sent you, and a copy of your reply?

I respond very politely that I have not kept a record of my humiliation. He can send all the flowers at his disposal, but I can't produce what was burned in 1920 when Lenin, I remind him, predicted the revolution would spread to Germany. That does it.

He's convinced he's dealing with a dizzy blond who cares nothing about the fate of the republic, and red faced, he leaves again.

If I could trick Mathieu as I was tricked, I would take any opportunity to do so, even now. When I look around this house and see evidence of my own history: photographs of Monsignor Rivette with mother, a row of bronze elephants with small riders, mullahs or muftis, father's medal collection, I become certain of my own innocence. I know a fortune could be made from my letters and their value grows every year, but it's a fortune that will lay dormant, unamassed, dispersed into other coffers, unrecognized.

If you recover childish notebooks, adolescent letters, and scribblings assembled over years, a kind of record could be formed against me and constructed at such a time when I might be entirely disarmed. Death, stroke, senility: I will no longer be capable of defending myself against your memoirs. *She was prone to tantrums and playing tricks.* There have been nights when I've written endlessly, explaining everything from the first time I remember seeing you in your cradle to the image of the dock and the judge, Bertulus. I analyze and document every angle, anticipating every attack that might occur after I'm gone. The construction of my innocence kept a man on Devil's Island, and I'd like the record to stay this way.

July 15, 1934

Dear Lille,

Two days after the break-in another event occurred, unrelated to it, as far as I can tell. I was pulling up weeds that line a path behind the house when Sylvie brought me a letter from a man who wants to see my papers. His letter was different from other requests I've received since establishing residence in Montreuil. Letters like this one come in fits and starts, but when they arrive, they make me feel less forgotten, almost a celebrity. Usually the requests are formal, impersonal, they mark the last step in a research project, when the applicant must leave the archives and actually talk to someone. His letter, however, was full of quirks. First, he quoted La Fontaine, as if this particular verse might be a sign of sympathy for my situation:

> How I've always hated the view of the multitude,
> Which seems to me prejudiced, hasty, and crude
> And alien to God
> Interposing between itself and things a distorting lens
> And measuring other men's
> Stature by its own small rod.

I hate the multitude and small rods, too. Good idea. Second, he referred to the incident of the flowers sent to me from Mathieu Dreyfus under a pseudonym, Antoine Belmonde or Albert Dormonde. I don't remember the name he used.

You remember the story; my maid accepted the card, unwrapped the crinkled, perhaps slightly used tissue paper, put the roses in water immediately. I looked at his card, white, plain, newly printed (I didn't know how new) and wrote to thank this Antoine Belmonde, whom I'd never met. I wrote out one version, then copied it over and had the note mailed that evening. The name Belmonde had been made up, but the address was that of Dreyfus's brother, Mathieu, and in this way I was uncovered and undone. Now he had a copy of my handwriting and could compare it to one of the notes attributed to his brother, a crucial piece of evidence in his conviction for espionage. The handwriting matched. I, or rather, Z, was the real German spy. Had telephone numbers been a common thing, I might have called Albert Dormonde to thank him for the flowers, and a sample of my handwriting would never have fallen into litigious and vengeful hands. Since my innocent forgery came to light I make it a habit never to write back, regardless of whether La Fontaine is quoted, Claudel, or the archbishop of Chartres.

The real spy, Esterhazy, used several pseudonyms, Z was

the one he wrote under; "the benefactor" was another, but Z is the one I prefer. You might say I've been drawn to things that fly under invented banners, labels not really their own. You and mother thought we were introduced through some formal and legitimate arrangement, but the truth is we met on a train from Le Havre to Paris. He sat in my compartment while my companion was in another part of the train.

I was traveling with a journalist, unsteady and truculent, who wrote under the name *Boisandre* for *La Libre Parole,* refuge for racial purists. Mother was suspicious of him, seeing through his moralism to the sponge underneath, but her chilliness only made him more attractive to me, his harebrained causes appeared ennobled, however quick he was to follow the crowd and do so badly. But with the help of his money I was finally able to leave the house, as you know. After a few months Boisandre appeared embarrassed to be seen with me in public. How was I an embarrassment? Did I say silly things, make trite observations? Did I wear the wrong clothes? I endured painful incidents in cafés, at concerts where he ignored me, pretended I wasn't there, sometimes excusing his rudeness by saying that he was looking for someone, a contact, an official, anyone.

So I was still stuck with him when a stranger on a train introduced himself as Esterhazy and offered his card. With his hat pulled down Z resembled a caricature of a silent film scoundrel, or like a child who makes a face, showing off, not realizing that no one is fooled and Mardi Gras is over. His eyes barely showed, and he unbuttoned his jacket as if he owned the train. Despite the fact that he was so small, he slouched in his seat in a cavalier way as if he'd just arrived from the American West. How soon I forgot that first impression of childish authority, annoying and stupid, which presupposed the ease with which others could be taken in. He was right. Very often they were easily taken in. While we whispered in deep conversation Boisandre leaned out a window in the corridor, oblivious to me and to everything else. I was happy to be rid of him.

Esterhazy and I arranged to meet the following week in a café near the Gare d'Orsay. I had difficulty finding a cab and was so late I felt steam coming out of my ears. In the midst of a tie up I jumped from the cab and ran several blocks in anxiety, certain he would have given up waiting for me and left long ago. Had this been true, had we missed each other at that point, I would have been saved from a life of distress, but Z was a patient man. He waited for me. From down the block I could see him looking around, his large head turning toward the station entrance and then back toward the street.

Entering the café I tripped on a nearby chair leg, someone's umbrella clattering to the ground. I was glad to see him, but there was something reserved and uncertain about the way he greeted me.

"Claire, what a surprise to run into you. I'm waiting for . . ." he hesitated, obviously strategizing on his feet.

He whispered, and I felt I ought to whisper in return without knowing why. As he lifted a glass to his mouth, the bottom part of his face turned green from absinthe. Later I tried to remember if he swallowed before he stood up to take my hand and pull out my chair. I decided he had. Swallow first, shake hands second. At times he gave the impression he might be departing any minute, but nothing was further from the truth. He had all the time in the world. A waiter with one eye fixed on the street brought me a drink identical to his. It must have been ordered before I arrived. I placed the trowel-shaped spoon over my glass, poured water through it, and watched the green liquid turn opal.

He took my hand, but no niceties initiated our meeting. He spoke directly with no prologue about his projects, which made little sense to me. His plans involved the army, and although I tried to appear attentive, it was only because he made me feel like a serious person, a woman who could be told about military maneuvers, and this kind of flattery, as you know, was where his charm lay.

Then he asked me for money. He spoke as if the thought

had just occurred to him, but the request came in the form of a declarative sentence, I'm sure of it. "I've been doing favors for General X." (I don't remember who he named.) He owes me, but I haven't been paid yet. I'm often abandoned this way, and left feeling cheated and unappreciated. They know how much they need me, how they rely on the information I bring in."

I wondered why he was confessing to me, not realizing that the deadly combination of confession and sympathy had turned a corner and been brokered into a financial transaction. He took me into his confidence, and basking in his trust, I emptied my pockets. I gave him all of what I had. I wanted Z. He had my compassion and desire. I was nothing if not a willing dupe.

"I'll only use part of this, the rest I'll invest, and you'll be paid back double the amount." He said something about a horse called Pourquoi Pas who would double my money as nothing else could, yet though he spoke with assurance, he also sounded as if it was unusual for him to be destitute and gambling was, for him, a novelty. As I write about this now, the horse sounds like an obvious joke, and Esterhazy seems like a laughably bad con man, but I believed him, and though not a pushover at the time, I believed him easily.

Women walked by in dusty shoes, smelling of lilacs, hair the color of nougat, half-hidden behind umbrellas or broad-brimmed hats. One turned and looked in our direction as if she recognized Esterhazy from somewhere. The world seemed sleepy, on the verge of spring. I did worry about the money a little. I've never been that naive, but told myself this was the only time I would lend him anything. It wasn't, but as we sat in the café I felt the anonymous women who looked at him knew something I was blind to. I wiped my face, thinking it might have become smeared or dirty from an unconscious brush up against something, what? I stared at Esterhazy as he gestured for the waiter. He looked like someone familiar with clandestine arrangements, like procuring abortions in foul-smelling but expensive apartments. If the woman dies a slow, agonizing death, it's nothing to do with him. He's long gone out the back door, hand in his pocket. He'd only been the arranger, but remembers everyone's names because you never know when this information might be important. But on that first day, knowing he was a man who probably hid a distasteful side only added to my curiosity.

He paid the check out of what I gave him, and swimming in his Zeus-like smile, I was certain he wouldn't ask me for money again. Having none left, and convinced his need was enormous (which it was) I didn't dare ask him for a few francs to get home, and so walked all the way from Gare d'Orsay.

The next time I met him in Parc Montsouris. I had difficulty finding the place we had arranged until I recognized the slouching figure waiting on a bench at the end of a lane. I put my hand on his shoulder, and although he told me he was glad to see me, he didn't look in my direction as I sat down. He remained steadily focused on some children sailing boats as if he was in great psychic pain, too great to let anyone near him.

"My superior officers laugh at my innovations as if I'm some kind of crackpot not worth bothering with, then they steal my ideas while I rot in the poorhouse. They have me followed. They play with me. See that woman on the far bench? I see her every day, and it's no accident."

He still wouldn't look in my direction. If a child had fallen in the pond, I don't think he would have really seen it, much less leapt from the bench to offer rescue. I had the feeling it was entirely possible, and even likely, that he would be meeting another man or woman after I left. He would say exactly the same things while never moving from the same park bench. He could perform all afternoon before a steady stream of visitors who were strangers to one another. Powerless and intimidated, I traced a loopy pattern in the dirt with the toe of my shoe. He made me feel that men in bowlers hid behind the trees, eavesdropping and taking notes. The men were quick, they disappeared as soon as one turned around, never dropping or leaving behind the hats that sat high on their heads.

"Listen, Claire, I don't know if you understand the gravity of my situation. The French General X and German Attaché Y dangle carrots in front of my nose, big money, yes," he nodded. "They trip over themselves to get their hands on the services I offer, but the handsome payments promised on Friday seem always to be postponed when Friday comes around. 'We have to wait and see how your artillery lists compare to . . .' To what? In a blast of chumminess they try to cheer me on with cognac and cigars, but have I been paid yet? No. My information is first class, believe me, and they know that it is, but since I'm paid in promises, all my resources have been depleted, dried up completely. For me to be reduced to asking a woman like you for a temporary loan is a sin. They need me, I'm invaluable to their operations, they need to know what one another is up to, but my expenses, as far as General X and Attaché Y are concerned, have as much weight and consequence as spun sugar. What am I to them? A clown? It's the great irony of my life that I have to stoop to their level for a few francs. My humiliation knows no bounds." Then he acted as if he was deeply lost in thought, irretrievably lost in dismal contemplation, and I got the distinct impression I wasn't wanted. I began to walk away, but he called after me.

"I'm at your mercy, Claire. I had to use all the money you gave me just to maintain myself in the middling style to which I'm accustomed, and instead of returning with double or triple your original loan, as I'd intended, I sit before you completely broke."

"I can't give you any more."

"Who's asking you?" He was suddenly infuriated, and it was a frightening spectacle. "Don't flatter yourself. Do you think I'm sitting on this bench waiting just for you? Any minute after you leave," he looked at his watch, "which should be soon, the archivist from the Section of Statistics, Felix Gribelin, will arrive, wearing his predictable dark blue glasses as if I'm some kind of disease you can't look at straight on. He will be accompanied by

Major General du Paty de Clam himself, in black silk gloves and a fake beard. They look like a pair of clowns, and I'm at their mercy."

"Are they going to pay you?" I didn't mean to sound skeptical, but it was difficult to disguise my tone of voice.

"I think it's time for you to leave."

Confused and hurt, I left him sitting on the bench. I believed him, but was unsure whether I should empty my pockets once again. The walk out of the park was long, but as I reached the street I heard footsteps behind me. It was Esterhazy breathing hard, trying to catch up.

Perhaps someone altogether important but anonymous *had* failed to show. I know he did meet his connections in the park, but more likely he was growing tired of his pose on the bench and hadn't expected me to leave. Taking my arm as if he hadn't heard anything I'd said and forgotten his own temper, the simple truth was that he didn't want to miss a free ride. The cab ride was short; he spent half of it chastising himself, then asking me for another loan. Again, I gave him what I had and did so without thinking. He was well dressed and spoke of opportunities that would surely work out soon.

"What I haven't told you, Claire, is that I'm working on the goose that will lay the golden egg."

He had information about the Syndicate. You remember the Syndicate. Mother used to rant about the Syndicate, urbanist financiers who control the banks and the theaters. More well informed than she, Z made me feel that I was one of the few women clever enough to understand such a conspiracy, and therefore could be included in knowledge of a dangerous secret. He had confidence in my intelligence. I was sure he would pay me back. We began to meet more frequently. Somehow he managed to rent a large apartment, far from where he lived with his wife it would turn out, and offered to let me live in it. I never knew how the payments were made but eventually made sure my name was on the lease. During the Dreyfus affair it was to this address that the archivist from the Section of Statistics was sent with a message for Z: *You're in trouble, but you have powerful friends who will protect you.*

Whenever I received a letter from him, there was a moment before I opened it when I could imagine that though the envelope was addressed to me, the letter inside would begin with salutations to someone else. He often signed his messages with only the initial Z, and with Z no transaction was ever straightforward: listening to his speech or reading his letters was always an act of interpretation.

Around the time I moved into the apartment he sent me a photograph of a Japanese woman taken, the caption read, in Yokohama. He explained the woman was a prostitute who, like the others she worked with, was forced to use a dialect which would mask and ultimately obliterate the tones and sentence constructions of her regional speech. If a woman escaped she would be identified by the accent and grammar she had been forced to acquire and would immediately be sent back to her master in Yokohama. I didn't ask him how he knew this story. I understood I was to become complicit, and therefore trapped, but felt I would risk everything for Z. I would learn any dialect he proposed. Was I embracing a concoction of shackles dreamed up by a paranoid? No, replacing one grammar with another was a pleasure, as far as I was concerned.

Underneath Z's explanations for his bankruptcy and misunderstood nature there was some truth, or some need, even if he wasn't telling me exactly what that need might be. Never having enough went hand and hand with another obsession, one that was an absolute reality to him: his talents and abilities went unrecognized in France. In the privacy of my apartment, behind locked and bolted doors, he would grow repetitive, his bitterness and debt burgeoned in tandem. He would walk from room to room, pick up small objects, examine them and return each figure or book to its place. He liked to lie on the floor, stare at the ceiling, and carp.

"My ideas are neglected yet you can't imagine who dogs my footsteps, who repeats my confidences. Powerful people chase and flirt with me in urinals and private opera boxes, then, in cafés, in the street, those same individuals go to great lengths to disown our relationships. Such lousy actors who feel they must pretend they don't know me are themselves laughable." He was lying on the carpet, leaning on his elbows and smoking, bitterly looking for refuge, licking his wounds. His forays into the tiers of power and money and the numerous rejections that followed were meticulously preserved (by him) and much rankled over. The cycle of hope, rebuff, and inevitable disappointment would never end.

"Not me, I'll never betray you." Which was true, I never did, but at that moment I spoke quickly, leaning over the bed, childishly, sincerely eager to make sure he knew I was on his side.

"I've broken off with someone who used to be very close to me."

"What happened?" I grew alarmed. Z was sweating slightly and wiped his forearm across his brow as he rolled over on his back.

"I was hoodwinked." He looked so serious, but at the word *hoodwink*, I had to suppress a laugh. What I could never figure out about him was this: did he con himself or just everyone else? Was there a divide with Z on one side and the rest of the world on the other, or did he believe his advertisements for himself?

"An informer gave me a diagram of a gun, which turned out to be no more effective than a toy, and I passed this information on as if I believed it genuinely dangerous." He rolled onto his back and blew smoke into the air. I didn't yet ask where this traffic in documents was going or what the source might be, but I wondered about the identity of his informer. I was never told exactly, but he gave the impression the former intimate was someone important, a general or a duke. Convinced he was persecuted by everyone, Z could cook up fantastic stories of conspiracy and fraud, but at the same time he was the consummate victim, he always portrayed himself as one innocently mauled and left for dead by the roadside.

"Where can you go then?" I asked. I genuinely believed this layabout was in danger, but had the sense to know there were few places he could flee to where he wouldn't end up hating everybody in sight. (His style: Look, I'm your confidante. I told him everything, even knowing he had a history of bilking even his nearest and dearest of everything they possessed.) The landscape was littered with the friends and relatives he'd swindled, from nephews to dueling partners. He rolled away from my reach.

"Maybe you should get a job."

At this he abruptly changed the subject, picking topics out of the air that had nothing to do with me or anything I knew about. This was his strategy when he felt uncomfortable.

"One night in Cairo I paid a woman the equivalent of fifty francs to go into a private room with myself and three other men. We were led through a series of chambers, one after the next, all of which were practically bare except for a few pillows and rugs." He made a walking gesture with his fingers. "Finally when we arrived at the last room the woman was told to take off her clothes and lie down on the floor. We took off our jackets, rolled up our shirtsleeves, and proceeded to play cards on her back."

I learned to look wide eyed and dumbfounded. He'd never traveled to Egypt, I'm sure of it. The story was lifted from Maxime du Camp. It was an erotic story, but typical of Z, the eroticism was in the suspense, nothing really happened, and he liked the image of a subjugated person who was incapable of putting up much resistance, who for a price would do what he demanded. He lay on my floor, deflated, arms and legs spread out. I lay on the floor next to him, nestling my neck on top of his arm, but he rolled over and stood up. He got up quickly as if he just remembered he had to be somewhere else and began to dress, buttoning his shirt before a small mirror, talking partly to himself, partly to me. He wanted to be somewhere else. He wanted to be someone else. Why did I ignore the danger signs? I was completely taken in. He could say anything, and he did.

"You know, Claire, you shouldn't trust me or ask for what I can't give you now. I carry tales to the adulterer who thinks I sympathize with him absolutely while I size up his catch as well. I take the side of the debtor and the collector. I know how it feels to be in everyone's shoes."

"So why do I feel I'd follow you to the end of the earth? I'm not interested in everyone's shoes, just you."

He paid no attention to me.

Because he had no sense that the various roles he played might contradict one another, he developed a great talent: the ability to be on opposing sides simultaneously. Z spoke seven languages. I watched him change gestures, even height as he switched tongues. He seemed entirely comfortable in the roll of syllables and confident he was enchanting if not convincing his audience, unfurling a carpet of sounds and information, taking them in, then rolling it back up again. A multilingual emperor, unlike the poor illiterate woman who emptied wastebaskets in the German embassy and turned in papers found there to the French secret police. He could easily imagine himself an officer in another army, killing French citizens as fast as he could.

"You can't kill all of them," I poked his elbow.

"No, you can't kill all of them, but you can try."

"I'll tell you one story," he turned from the glass to look at me. "The morning I seconded for a Captain Foa in his duel against Drumont, I rose very early and sent a note to Drumont."

"What did you write?" I was startled. Foa and Drumont hated each other.

He wouldn't tell me, but Drumont, editor of *La Libre Parole*, who was publicly known to want all citizens of Foa's race deported from the country, became one of Z's protectors. If this wasn't enough, Z began a correspondence with Drumont's notorious colleague, the Marquis de Morès, Badlands rancher, founder of a railroad in Vietnam, a firm believer that the Syndicate had ruined him and all its members should be annihilated post haste. Z would sit at his desk writing to Morès yet half an hour later he would compose a letter to Edmond de Rothschild, claiming to have been a former classmate. His aim in the latter case was, of course, money. Both letters went out in the same post. The moment they were dropped in the box he was terrified that he'd put the wrong letter in the two previously addressed envelopes, accidentally interchanging them

"This is what I wrote to Rothschild; I'll recite the letter to you." He quoted, smiling as he stood before the glass, "'Even though we had lost track of each other for thirty years, you were, when I contacted you, good to me, whereas some who could have, who should have helped me out did nothing; I am deeply grateful and although in the more than precarious situation in which I find myself and which can change only with the death of my uncle it seems impossible for me to do anything to convey to you how grateful I am, I might nevertheless be of some use to you.'"

"What uncle? Did he die?"

"Let me finish. 'The extremely cruel necessity which I am forced to confront (without succeeding at it, moreover) has forced me to undertake in secret and outside my profession certain (extremely honorable) tasks which my uniform nevertheless forbids. Those efforts have allowed me to penetrate into circles in which I have learned things of gravity, which I believe you would have an interest in knowing. I repeat that I am neither a madman nor a fool.'"

"Did you interchange the letters? Did you send the letter intended to one to the other?"

"I'll never tell you."

He left a few minutes later, and I rolled over in bed, shutting my eyes hard until I saw blue comet shapes travel across my field of vision. If he was neither a madman nor a fool, where did that leave me? How did he manage to keep all these people from talking to each other? As long as they hated one another, his subplots and counterplots might succeed, and then Drumont had said, *anyone who swindles one of them is a friend of mine,* and Foa and Rothschild were unquestionably two of *them.* Z had a nose for the right track. It's true that we present a different face to each audience, but Z's identity was entirely made up of ever-splitting fractions. I knew, or had met, perhaps five or six of Z's identities, so I had to assume there were five or six unknown ones besides.

Why did I buy it? I don't know, but I did. I let Z become my foreign legion; he could turn me into an amnesiac, a sleep-walker, an automaton whose only possibly authentic feelings lay in a desire for him.

He often wanted to be someplace else, like Cairo or Vienna. He faltered at pronouns, he was rarely part of a *we* but was very clear about *they.* (Ironically, I wonder if Dreyfus came to falter at the plural also? No one would ever tell me.) He was outside everything, and he needed to take revenge. Someone, I won't say who, opened the door and he walked in.

After Z's final swindle, I lost the apartment, but one night I had a statue of Hermes stolen from what had been my courtyard. The theft was a sort of last grandiose gesture as I hovered on the threshold of the poorhouse, and now it's here in Montreuil waiting for you.

So that's the true story of Z.

Still no thieves.

July 26, 1934

Dear Lille,

The man who quoted La Fontaine didn't wait for an answer, which I'd never have written. Perhaps he guessed I was through with thanking people for gifts delivered out of the blue. Acting on intuition and a great deal of nerve, he appeared two days ago. Sylvie, who knew nothing of his letter, let him in. Hearing an unfamiliar voice, I hurried upstairs from the cellar where I was rearranging my papers, but was too late to prevent his entry. The stranger in my hall was a man of medium height with a slight stoop, round eyes like a Spaniard, and a receding hairline. He held his arms crossed over his chest, leaned toward Sylvie like an American who knows little about servants. He stepped back when he saw me approach, held out his hand without smiling. I motioned him into the library. He calls himself M. Fontaine.

I was at a loss over how to begin to speak to him, but he took control of the interview, telling me what he wanted and expecting to get it. For someone who entered the house as a complete stranger he was relaxed, as if he belonged here and nowhere else. The upstart lit a cigarette, holding his hand under the ash while he looked around the room searching for an ashtray. Nothing phased him. I nodded toward the top of a stack of plates piled by the tardy or forgetful thieves, and he took a saucer from the tower. His suit was rumpled but fashionably cut. His face turned toward the carpet as if he were looking for something, then he got right to the point.

"I don't have much money, but will pay something if you require it. I'd like access to your letters."

You would think anyone who wanted to approach me for my letters would try to establish that we had certain interests in common. He might praise Charles Maurras who claimed his prison term was Dreyfus's revenge, but my visitor didn't grow hysterical or mention *Action Française*. His directness betrayed a kind of arrogance, and I lost my footing for a moment. I meant to discourage him, but wasn't sure I wanted him to leave entirely. I liked this overconfident boy. The letters are a representation of myself, I confess, but at the same time they captured only a perverse streak, a grimy, not altogether realistic picture.

"There's nothing left to discuss or to print. All my papers have been read and gone over by everyone from policemen to archivists. The matter has been closed for some time."

"Surely," he asked, "there must be other letters, ones you've never shown anyone." He put his hand under Delphine's chin and called her something like *wise guy* in English. *What's up, wise guy?*

"No. There aren't any letters. None. You're after fool's gold," I lied. Sylvie served him coffee.

"I wouldn't mind having a look at even the old ones. After thirty-five years, many don't remember these details."

"No one will remember me, you mean." Sylvie looked in the mirror, and as I spoke, she patted her hair.

"That wasn't what I meant." Turning red, he must have been born long after the letters' publication.

"If I gave you copies of these letters and copies of the original forgery, hoards of journalists and assassins would knock down my door."

"You could tell them you've given me everything. There's nothing left." He was very sure of himself. Why didn't he just grind his ash into the carpet? He had stiff reddish hair and dull green eyes. They might have been brighter, but in order to save money, the lamps are few and dim. At that moment, for the sake of my own patchy vanity, I was glad of it.

"Why should I give you some kind of monopoly, a cartel of forged evidence? I know nothing about you except you want access to my papers, which I give to no one anyway."

"Why?" He stood very close to me. What was he going to say? Because I like you, Claire? I doubted it.

"Think about it," he said. "I'll be back." Delphine licked his hand, he picked up his hat and left.

When we played in the Luxembourg Gardens, Lille, you would give away your toys, your coat, and you seemed to love everybody, even the tattered men who lurked at the edges of the park. I used to wonder what you were after really, when all was said and done, you were scheming, I'm sure of it. One wasn't supposed to go near those men, even if they enticed you, yet somehow your angelic smile seemed to shame or even cancel the rule every child knows: it's considered dangerous and foolish to talk to strangers. Or did you really know what you were about? I remember once you were seen talking to a man, well dressed, but his clothes were greasy, and from where I stood his trousers looked undone. Honestly, they did, the memory is quite clear. You handed him some bread, and at dinner everyone spoke of your kindness and generosity. They hadn't seen his fly which I, of course, mentioned. *We were just talking*, you said. *He was a nice man. Nicer to me than you ever were.* (Yes, I'm sure that's true.) I was sent to my room. I wish now that I could emulate the way you gave away things while really hoarding the dividends of what passes as good nature. Under the guise of charitable acts and emotional generosity, you got away with murder. When I was left alone, shipwrecked in a dark apartment, you pretended I didn't exist. Smiling at strangers, whenever you had the opportunity, portraying me as someone who slept with riffraff, with pretenders.

It amazes me how some words stick and stick, and not only do they never come off, but they spread like an infection. Within the frame of the word *traitorous* one can be accused of many crimes. Once one is a traitor, one can also very easily be believed to have been a tax cheat, a prostitute, an embezzler, a perpetrator of incalculable frauds. I might define a liar as one who interprets the truth differently from myself, but many give single words the long arms and legs of inference, and so I'm doomed. I think Dreyfus and his family learned this too, ironically, but my family remained pretty much immune from the brush that tarred me, despite the fact that the word *traitor* has legs.

If I could give away something to the young man while actually giving nothing, it would be a pleasure. In reality it wasn't me, but you, who was the first to discover the link between courtesy and danger, and it was a short step from there to a recognition of how pleasure and danger might be intertwined.

Soft rain misted for two days, then turned harder. Just as Sylvie was preparing to lock up, Fontaine rang the bell again. She couldn't leave him standing in the downpour, and I believe he had calculated this. He was drenched, but his eyes were bright, the color of beryl. He claimed to have neglected to bring an umbrella with him when he left the city.

"There wasn't a cloud in the sky this morning," he defended his unexpected arrival as he walked into a front room and found a chair. "After visiting friends just down the road, I wandered through the old Star Films studio, kicking rusty tools and looking at the junk lying around. I saw your light and decided to ring. I didn't think you'd mind my coming out of the rain."

Star Films was abandoned years ago, and most of its panes and spars have been broken one way or another. There isn't a solid wall left, I don't think.

"Do you have any cigarettes?" He held out a sodden pack.

"Check my desk in the cellar," I directed Sylvie while he took off wet clothes, and she soon returned with an old pack of Gauloises, cover faded and shredded.

"They're better than nothing," he said.

Offended, I lit one myself and politely asked if he wanted a drink. (Insult me and I'll still bow deeply, knocking my head against the floor, happy to do so.) He put his stockinged feet up on a stack of books. Muddy water had made a dark outline around his gray socks as if his shoes had been painted on. He saw me looking at his grimy socks and took them off, baring his feet which were long and yellow. He had dirt between his toes.

"I haven't changed my mind about the letters but wish you would be clearer about what you'd like to do with them."

"I only intend to read them."

"If you wanted to print sections of my letters, in what sort of context would they appear? What frame, what caption would accompany the papers?" I didn't believe he or anyone else simply needed something to read on a rainy night. The letters are strong documentary evidence but not consistently accurate. The lines reflect only a narrow moment when I was not myself.

"None. I haven't any interest in publishing them."

171

"How did you find me?"

He paused, looking up from his coffee, as if thinking of the best answer.

"I've kept no memoirs, have few photographs." Remember, you may know a fraud or two here or there, but I was led on by the biggest confidence man in the Third Republic.

"Could I look at some of those?" He perked up at the word *photograph*. He was like the man who wanted to shake hands with the man who shook the hand of Napoléon.

I looked at him closely. Relentless, rude, and what was he really after? I didn't trust him, but my vanity over a few pictures can be stupendous, as you know. I wanted the owner of those feet to see what I used to look like, and at the same time I didn't. It would have been like introducing him to a beautiful younger woman while at the moment I only shared him with a German shepherd. We spent so much time talking that he missed the last train, and I invited him to spend the night. Then I silently bemoaned the bed in the attic. It would be too ridiculous. He would be unable to stand up straight under the sloping eaves. He would knock his head and trip over the detritus that's stored there. I can have the frame and bedding moved back downstairs in the morning. You never know. There may be other rainy days.

I can imagine your anxiety. I'm being foolish, you think, losing my head over an intruder who probably has conspiratorial designs on my papers. *He wants to see you exposed,* you will say, *and not in the way you think.* He can have no interest in a woman so many years older than himself. I counter with this: it is my association with Z that makes me desirable. He wants to shake the hand of the man who shook the hand, so to speak. You're afraid I'll throw away your legacy, and I might, but let me remind you, I want to come out of this innocent. Why should you have a less conspiratorial reputation? I've no doubt you and your children will construct a portrait of me that will be to your advantage financially, as well as to provide a vehicle to clear your name. *She was distant and difficult: a snob. Reckless, never thought about the conse-*

quences of her actions, of what it meant to be the mistress of a spy. After years of provoking my insults you will be able to make me look like Z's dupe, which for a while I was, but remember Flaubert said it's better to be a dupe than a knave. Remember also, Lille, that there came a time I learned to resist your provocation, not to be lured into your trap, not to hit back. I could be a martyr, too. You used to bait me by saying I had the long Francoeur nose, when in fact yours outdistanced mine, but I remained silent. I knew you wanted to be hurt, and so said nothing, would not oblige you in any way. As I said, you were the one to discover the alliance between pleasure and pain.

Before leaving for the night, Sylvie made a bed for him in the large front room. We cleared some minarets still remaining from the intruders' stockpile. At first he insisted on helping move furniture to the edge of the room, but perhaps feeling more in the way than useful among a stranger's possessions he soon gave up. Fascinated by the pre-Revolutionary clock left on the mantle he stood still, clutching it in his hands, then he held it to his ear.

"It doesn't tick," I explained. "I keep it for sentimental reasons, because it's so old."

"It reminds me of a clock I once saw whose back was engraved with a table that translated Gregorian months into Republican months: Brumaire equals October, Nivoise equals September, Thermidor equals July and so on."

I wasn't sure how to interpret this comment: sincere or cynical? The reference to the Revolution, like the quote from La Fontaine, might not indicate the obvious at all. I have known slippery times when insignificant signs hint at circumstances of life and death, but I wasn't sure whether his reminiscence was intended as a republican salute or a wish for the reliable days of monarchy. With his hand on the fireplace, he took on what appeared to be a depressed or thoughtful pose, not unlike Z in the park when he wanted me to believe he should be left alone. I came up behind him and reached around as if in an embrace. He started, but I only wanted to take the clock from him and did so, barely touching his arm, watching our reflections in the mirror above the mantle. Whether he was intrigued by Esterhazy or not, as the mistress of the spy, I know I've been of interest to those who haunt certain kinds of bars in the city: oddball, but occasionally even attractive individuals whose proclivities run in the direction of playing roles. You be Z, I'll be D.

"It has an enameled sun and moon, once in a while they turn." They were jammed, and I shook the clock as if trying to dislodge the planets. I sounded as if I believed the thing were genuine.

"Hey, wise guy." It was Sylvie talking to the dog in imitation of Fontaine's slang. I wondered what she was up to. Sylvie is a small woman with a long neck and limbs that make her appear octopuslike, as if her torso had little meaning to her apart from a juncture of limbs — unlike some women who are all conjunction, all middle. The effect of Sylvie's body is one of adolescent seductiveness, I think, as if those long limbs are signs of entanglement. Sylvie continued to move chairs around, and Fontaine and I behaved as if we were invisible, the way one feels invisible in the back of a cab — you can do anything, say anything, you hope the driver is ignoring you. Finally I could hear her collecting her things, shutting the door to the street, and it was clear she had left for the night. With her absence an awkward silence followed, and he looked at the floor. The clock, after a good shake up, suddenly began to tick loudly. I turned to go, but as I left I didn't close his door all the way, leaving it slightly ajar, just a crack. He was absorbed in his thoughts and didn't seem to notice, unless he was more of an exhibitionist than I ever imagined.

Standing in the corridor motionless as a statue, I listened to the sounds of undressing, writing, and sheets turned aside. I looked in a hall mirror until the light went out, then went up to the attic. I didn't sleep but sat cross legged on my bed reading while moths flew into the light. The house was as still as I'd ever heard it, but I wanted to explode that silence, to change the ordinary course of the night: a man and a woman sleeping in opposite ends of the house. Delphine had been put into the yard, and one couldn't hear any creaks or sighs. I shut my book, crept downstairs, and opened the door to his room.

He lay on his back like Marat in his bath, his clothes spread out and drying on chairs and tables. Hair fell over his eyes, and his mouth was open. I stood very close but didn't touch him. Walking slowly about the room in a crescent-shaped path, the candlelight was dim, and I knocked into a dresser with a soft thud. Fontaine turned over in his sleep, and I heard a voice pronounce a syllable which sounded like *Qui? Qui* and the key were indeed what I was looking for. What if I had sat on the edge of his bed? I used to plonk down on yours, deliberately waking you up, and you would kick the air while I held you down. If I did the same, if I tried to pin him down, I realized he would probably throw me off in horror and run out of the house into the rain. If there is eroticism in terror (or in disgust) the experiment might have been worth an attempt. As I stood at the edge of his bed I thought even anger and humiliation have advantages over narcophilia, but I didn't try to wake him. Overcome by feelings of foolishness, I put my hand on the shape of his hip under the blanket. Even without his waking I felt like a sterile, rejected intruder, a woman left out of a normal life of children and grandchildren because of wasted years siding with cheapskates, the ugly, and the humorless, the dry collector of the parish newspaper. My toe nudged a flat leather bag like a small portfolio. What's this? I picked it up and carefully made my way back into the hall. Flipping on a light I sat on the steps, opened the folder, rummaged around, and without any hesitation began to read. His handwriting was wobbly, some lines scribbled quickly, notes were in no particular order, sprinkled with initials or abbreviations. To tell you the truth the papers were a mess, but a name, his real name was written in black ink on the inside cover on a small square of white canvas stitched into the leather.

Wasserbaum. My guest is actually Monsieur Wasserbaum or

Mr. Waterbranch, a kind of fountain, but not Fontaine. My visitor won't drop names of priests and generals in order to prove his sympathies lay with those who supported Z. To the contrary, his connections were the reverse, and this was what he was trying to hide. He wrote for those who quoted Marx, Trotsky, and Blum. La Fontaine, of animals and moral tales, was a ruse.

As I sat on the stairs, balancing the bits and pieces on my knees, I tried to keep their ordering straight, lest he later discover I'd been through them. He couldn't be a very serious researcher, if this was the kind of archive he produced.

October 31, 1894. Dreyfus's arrest for high treason is announced in Le Soir.

Z, the actual spy, lived on rue de la Bienfaisance. Rue de la Bienfaisance. Practice saying this without laughing and with no sense of irony.

D goes about his bourgeois, probably happy, life as a captain in the army, then slam, in one minute everything changes, and even when vindicated, he will never be able to go back to the life he led before October 14, 1893. His brother described how marooned they felt. I've tried to imagine this. Their house must have seemed transformed into a stranger's territory, even memories of childhood turn alien or seem to belong to someone else. What you thought of as your family life, secure, each respective identity intact, suddenly with a snap of a stranger's fingers, the whole edifice topples over the edge of some constructed horizon, and you're left tottering from accusations that seem to have been delivered in another language and directed at someone else.

Their country house in Carpentras will never look the same. They do return to it, but the place has been lost. Memory + landscape = nostalgia, well, not in this case.

A letter is stolen from the German embassy that refers to "the Scoundrel D," and a man is accused whose name begins with that letter, but the D was really a P. The P, whose tail was short, had been misread as D. Actually the P/D stood for Z. Secondly, if handwriting experts hadn't pointed to D, he could have gone on pretending he was just like everyone else in the army. Many have said that if he hadn't been accused he wouldn't have been on his own side.

I've found myself being stared at by individuals who suffer from some kind of visual disease; they think they're looking straight at you but they're really focusing at a point over your left shoulder. You talk and talk, you look into her eyes, but even while she thinks she holds your gaze in hers, she's looking at the clock or the crackling radio just behind you. This could be called D's disease, except it's the object of the off-the-mark stare that stands in the place of D. "It's not me. I'm innocent. You don't really see me at all."

Mid-March, 1896. Lieutenant Colonel Marie-Claude Picquart, a sharp man, thinks of the army as his family. As head of the Statistical Section, he acquires a document which will determine that Z, not Dreyfus, was the real spy. The story would appear to be over and vindication of D imminent, but the labyrinth of fabricated evidence has just begun. On Dreyfus's side, nothing was forged to prove his innocence, unless you include the gesture of his brother, sending flowers to Claire, Z's accomplice, in order to obtain a sample of her handwriting, but the compilations on the other side were staggering. If I were an out-of-work writer, I'm not sure I wouldn't have applied for a job copying over documents, making changes here and there. The twists and turns of forgeries of forgeries and copies of copies are dizzying. It was crucial to the generals that the accused, Dreyfus, remain guilty, and the convicted Picquart had to be discredited. Nothing arrives in the state in which it was sent. In other words, every breath of air had been inhaled and exhaled by someone else before. All kinds of documents were produced to prove this, and Picquart was sent to prison. As with Dreyfus, everything he believed in must have fallen apart. At the trial at Rennes, Dreyfus was so pleased to be addressed by the generals, even though they were the architects of his suffering while Picquart dared to oppose them. Poor D, so little courage at this point. I weep for him, so sure that X is X with no taint of Y.

The judge might have been the kind of person who, for example, studies a subject about which one hundred facts are known. He only learns twenty of these facts and bases all his conclusions on those twenty

true statements, steadfastly ignoring the other eighty facts and the con-
tradictions expressed by the total number of true statements. He sticks
to the twenty he knows and bases all his blinkered conclusions on them.
The army, therefore, is always right. Am I, in my own marginal way,
just as occluded?

I have faith in nothing and therefore will never be disappointed.
I barter with rats, drink with rats, and I let them debase my language.
I would exploit them if I could, but I with my bad manners, things get
botched up, and I often find myself snubbed. Still I envy them and want
the attention they offer.

I've been to the archives, and even though they are well ordered,
I've returned home again with a nearly empty notebook. Imagine sepa-
rating a mountain of paper into two distinct piles: the genuine and the
faked, and continuing to do so until two opposing walls of documents are
erected. I don't know if I can follow the tangled path, and instead feel as
if I've dragged myself along on my elbows while wind blurs the parallel
walls of paper into one mass once more.

The pre-Revolutionary clock stopped. Delphine began to
bark outside, and fearing she would soon wake everyone close
by, I began to read more quickly.

Colonel Maximilian Von Schwarzkoppen, military attaché in the
German embassy in Paris who employed Z, wrote in his notebooks:
"They [the French minister of war and others] regarded Picquart's
discovery and the great energy with which he seemed to want to pur-
sue it as extremely embarrassing and fraught with difficulties... if he
[Picquart] succeeded in proving Dreyfus's innocence and Z's guilt, it
would be all over for them, for the army's prestige, and for the country's
reputation. They had thus to render the pursuit of Picquart's investiga-
tion impossible and to establish Dreyfus' guilt once again."

November 26, 1897 — File begun on Picquart, intended to present
a composite of information that will incriminate him. A process under-
taken with the same industry as the production of documents constructed

to seal the question of D's guilt. Three months later he will be dismissed from the army. Z sends Picquart forged telegrams in order to throw him off the track. The telegrams were signed "Speranza." Some believe the handwriting of the signature matches that of Claire Francoeur.

Felix Gribelin, archivist of the Section of Statistics, created documents and cataloged them. He became very anxious when a document called le petit bleu *was stolen from Schwarzkoppen's trash. Le petit* bleu *confirmed Z's guilt and Dreyfus's innocence. Later he helped expose the labyrinth of his own forgeries, but he steadfastly believed in the guilt of Dreyfus and Picquart. I suppose he thought his forgeries were a way of replacing the gun in the murderer's hand, nailing him to the spot until the police arrive, a believer in the value of planting evidence. He knew better than anyone that all the evidence was fake, but never doubted the conclusion his fakes led to.*

None of this was news to me. I looked for something more personal and found pages that revealed Wasserbaum is married and has two daughters. Then I found a more recently written entry containing a paragraph that I would guess had been written that night.

No response to Montreuil letter requesting papers, but I'm sure she's Esterhazy's Claire, his accomplice exposed by Mathieu Dreyfus. Check address.

A few pages later:

The address was correct. Found the house in Montreuil and was able to watch from a far corner of the deserted Star Film Studios down the street, in fact it's almost next door. Her house is small, there is a rotted balcony on the second floor, vines hanging from it, cats sleeping in the shade. From the front it looks abandoned, and there is a run-down garden in the back. A woman was sitting in it. She was reading, then shut the book, and began to pull up weeds, easily distracted. Might have been Claire.

Invent pretense for entering house. An inspector of electrical lines in old houses, an indigent relative, an itinerant piano tuner who knew Z.

I skipped ahead a few pages.

Her desk is in the cellar where the servant went for cigarettes. Check it for photographs. She must have pictures of herself and Z, or even some of the false composites published in Le Siecle: *Zola posing with Esterhazy, for example. When published they were entitled "The Lies of Photography."*

I read a few lines over several times: *Invent pretext for entering house. . . . She is Esterhazy's Claire.* The hoax is on me. Shreds of my tottering vanity finally shuddered and crumbled like a powdery model of Pere Ubu. *Help! I'm perforated!* wrote Jarry. Oh, Claire, I whispered out loud, what did you expect?

Newspapers printed rephotographed collages of citizens involved in the affair who were sworn enemies, strange bedfellows, or characters who had never actually met, but if he thinks I would save these relics after more than thirty years, like some kind of repository or museum, as if degradation was something to remember and preserve, he's very much mistaken. His notes were full of these kinds of inquiries, as if in his somewhat sloppy research, he'd come to a blind alley he thought I might provide a blasting tool out of. I pulled out the last piece of crumpled and yellowed paper that had been torn from a book.

She'll pay when her back is turned.

Was she Esterhazy's Claire?

For members of the Syndicate I'm still an object of revenge, so I have to be careful. What measures could I take to defend myself beyond hiding out in an obscure house? Some part of me wanted to be skewered by this man who slept in the other room, to have an odd last night with a man who desired nothing more than my exposure and humiliation. I sat for a few more minutes staring at his door then put the papers back according to their original order, but as I reentered his room I couldn't remember where I'd found the leather case in the first place. Against which bookcase or table had it been propped? I took a few paces backward into the hall, and stared at his face framed by the doorjamb. He turned over in sleep, looking more vulnerable than calculating, much like you did as a child when you slept next to me. I stepped back into the room. He turned over again and I froze, mesmerized, an intruder in my own house. Perhaps he wouldn't remember where he'd left it either. I bent over and leaned the smelly damp thing against a chair leg; when I straightened up he was still lying in bed rolled over on his side, but one visible eye was open and just beginning to focus on me. I jumped but had the presence of mind to invent an excuse for being in his room in the middle of the night.

I crossed my arms as if to control my chest and steady my breathing, yet my voice quavered with sincerity.

"I'm sorry to have wakened you." I hoped he believed me. "I heard a sound downstairs and was going to let Delphine into the house." I jerked my head in the general direction of the yard. "The shortest way to the back door is through your room." This wasn't absolutely true, but he mightn't yet have determined the arrangement of the ground-floor rooms.

He nodded vaguely, then shut his eyes again. I was disappointed that he didn't want to talk to me, make room on the bed, invite me to sit down, or even help defend the place against an intruder. My vanity resurrects itself easily, pieces collecting into a neat pile once again. I went out the door leading to the kitchen and from there was able to let Delphine into the first floor. She was wet and panting with excitement, *the house!* I didn't want to let her in but really had no choice.

The next morning Wasserbaum slept late and stumbled into the kitchen barefoot and unwashed, buttoning his shirt while asking for coffee as if he owned the house and expected to be waited on by us usurpers. Still half-asleep, he knocked into Sylvie while she was trying to grind the beans. In tripping and appearing to lose his balance he grabbed her waist. She turned red, pushed his hands away. The inadvertent shove caused her to upset a dish of butter, and it landed on the floor with a soft splat. Delphine made a mad dive for the mess. In the middle of chaos and growling stomachs, which he did everything to create and nothing to resolve, Wasserbaum put his feet on a chair and actually inquired if he could rent a room from me so that he could come out to write a few days during the week, explaining his flat in Paris was small and cramped. He said nothing about the individuals, wife and daughters, who made it so. I pretended his request was unexpected and agreed to an arrangement, but for a very high sum.

You may shudder that I have consented to this, but your children will eventually benefit from my mercenary intentions. The papers he seeks will be moved, and it will be difficult for him to search the house for them while I'm in it. He'll have no peace. If he appears to be daydreaming I'll make him wash the windows. He'll be sorry.

I followed Wasserbaum around. He talked a lot, but he didn't tell me anything I didn't already know.

"Commandant Esterhazy had many aliases: Monsieur de Becourt, Count de Voillemont, Mr. Fitzgerald. It was feared he would escape France and sell his story, and he did leave, easily, taking a train north as if he were an ordinary citizen. At the end of his life, living in a London slum, he was known to sleep during the day and only go out at night." Wasserbaum mimicked Z stealthily walking across the room, his body at an angle, walking feet first, looking over his shoulder. He knocked back a drink in mime, walked with a cane, and leered at me as if I were part of the game, but I wasn't. I couldn't do it. He waited for me to imitate a character who might cross Z's path, a streetwalker for example, or an informant of some kind. I stood by stonily waiting for him to trip over a leg and fall on his face. I haven't reached a conclusion as to how his performance should be interpreted, was it intended as sympathy or satire? Esterhazy is the bone we fight over, but is his legacy really a bone at all, or is it some kind of slobbered-over rubber ball still capable of shattering windows and rolling out of reach?

August 1, 1934

Dear Lille,

By making jokes Wasserbaum feels safe. *Look, I'm the clown Z, he seemed to be saying, I'm Z, who by his own admission was neither a fool nor a madman.* Both you and I, Lille, have often wanted what we couldn't possibly possess. You became a martyr, but I kick at martyrdom. I have a fit on the carpet.

Even now I'm convinced that whoever refuses me must know the truth, yet rather than saying to hell with them and rallying to my own defense, I find the perpetrators of these acts of rejection and mockery seductive. Acquiring damaging truths about me is the same as acquiring tremendous attractive powers. You might say they go hand in glove, knowledge and interpretation. Can it be that I take part in my own destruction and do so with some pleasure?

Dreyfus is a symbol, like the Eiffel Tower. The only place you can't see it is when you're standing on it. I was in the middle of the Dreyfus affair, but I never saw him. Even the most well-entrenched symbols can be reclaimed and redefined. In a different era, Esterhazy and myself could be reconfigured; we could acquire heroic stature. If you look at the Reich over the border, that new era might have arrived. As cultural and national icons Z and I must be seduced, absorbed, reclaimed. Z desired fame, recognition, money, yet after being treated like an outcast, he would play hard to get. I, too, might pretend not to accept my medals.

I lie in bed listening to branches hitting the side of the house, turn on a light and write for a few hours. Later, looking at each part of my body, arms, legs — what I can see in the glass — it's as if each part belongs to someone else, some older person who made all kinds of mistakes and could make the same ones over and over again with no trouble at all.

"What was behind Esterhazy's conspiracies? Jealousy, that's all," Wasserbaum said, posing and answering his own question. I had seen him idling at his desk, and true to my promise, I interrupted his work, eager to contradict what he thought he knew about his subject. I'd be sure he knew the other "eighty facts."

"It's been said too many times that he was a worm among worms, and maybe he was, but to give him credit, his driving force wasn't desire for position, authority, recognition, or fame. Z desired something much simpler and more vulgar: money."

"That wasn't entirely true, he had wanted recognition very badly; he had wept for it while waiting on park benches, in private apartments, and public urinals."

"No, I disagree. He was in love with Schwarzkoppen. He was jealous of Dreyfus, of everyone."

"Oh, for God's sake," I rolled my eyes to the ceiling. The idea that Z was in love with his victim and jealous of him at the same time was beyond anything I could imagine. In his perverse way Wasserbaum was on the right track about a few things, but I didn't want him to know it. "He might have tried to become the confidante of rivals, incurring risk of discovery and anger; he might patronize mortal enemies, but the goal of all his conspiracies was always financial," I said emphatically.

"Not in the Dreyfus case. That wasn't about money."

I wanted to tell him that if he knew so much he needn't take up my time, but I wanted my time taken up, so I explained. "When Esterhazy approached Schwarzkoppen in the German embassy he was desperate. He was being followed, and he threatened to shoot himself while standing on the colonel's desk. Schwarzkoppen only toyed with his pens and cleared papers off his blotter, giving him space to do so. He knew Esterhazy's information was neither accurate nor of any use, and his indifference only served to make Esterhazy feel more trivial. Provoked into a frenzy, he told the colonel that he would make public his relationship with a certain woman."

"He was jealous of that woman, and he knew Schwarzkoppen liked men, as well." Wasserbaum smiled. With a little knowledge he was jumping off the deep end.

"No, not at all. Z named a name, but I have no idea if the name was an invention or someone who actually existed. The German attaché had him thrown out into the street. His poor hat landed beside him in the gutter. I felt very badly for him."

"How do you know what happened in the embassy? You weren't there. You only know what he told you."

Wasserbaum is a frustrating interrogator. He doesn't understand that many people were convinced by Z. Z was a hysteric who engendered mass hysteria, a kind of fabulous germ capable of grotesque infection, and now, with no living hysteric to animate his remains, I told Wasserbaum that his plans for my papers must be reduced.

"I don't believe you," Wasserbaum walked out of the house and disappeared into the ruins of Star Films. He'll be back. Whether he believes me or not, I'm one of the few participants in the affair still alive.

What I can't tell him: Z was always looking over his shoulder in the interest of self-preservation, but apart from his talent to convince, he wasn't much of a spy. I knew this, yet I was usually taken in and convinced anew. He used to say, *if I go to the guillotine, I won't go alone,* and I always thought he meant others, not me, but the tumbrel did arrive at my door. In return I'll make Wasserbaum pay rent through the nose without ever getting his hands on my papers, my ace in the hole. The exchange, one man for another, doesn't really make sense, but accuse me of thinking like Z, the point is: there is money to be made here.

I could hear Wasserbaum downstairs, and at his entrance Delphine began to bark her head off, jumping at the sills, scratching them, tearing the curtains. I fetched a stick, ready to punish her, but by the time I returned to the front of the house, Sylvie had let her out, and the dog was running around the yard, her destructive hysteria forgotten. I know there are some who push the dog's nose in its business and hit away, forcing memory, but I didn't want Wasserbaum to see me ungenerously beating a dog.

Z used to say everyone can be tempted, or another way of expressing the same sentiment: if one looks hard enough one can find something worth transgressing for.

So here's what I tried: Although Wasserbaum supposedly rented a room from me in order to write, he told me he had business in Paris and would return in the evening. Sylvie, too, stayed late, shortening and pressing a dress I pulled out of storage. It had been one of Z's favorites, but I had hardly ever worn it, and the green silk still seemed new as I removed the rustling folds from a box. It was long out of fashion, and had never been the kind of dress you could wear on the street, but rather it was the kind of dress to receive visitors in, or a certain kind of visitor. The right word escapes me. Still, I wanted to wear it; in fact, I hadn't much choice since my clothes at present are mostly worn, the clothing of a prewar era. Eventually after a combing and painting I was dressed, and I waited for him until past midnight, pacing, unable to concentrate on any book, any newspaper, any radio broadcast. When he finally put key into lock and stepped into the house he was, I think, surprised to see me.

"Why are you up late?" he turned on a second light.

"I've something I've decided to show you."

Holding my hands behind my back I clasped a photograph of Z, then, like the slow arc of a weighted pendulum my hand swung in front of my waist. He grabbed the picture with greedy interest and held it up to a light.

"He's dressed in an extravagant jacket, as if about to meet

Bismarck." He took out a pair of glasses. "I've seen pictures like this one."

I could do nothing to impress him, yet when I spoke he pretended to be all ears.

"You've never seen him scanning a room, performing an elaborate tennis game of eye contact, determining who might be useful and who was dangerous. He said hello to some, but it was hello period, and others didn't even get that much. No conversation would follow unless he could gain something by it."

Z, in his jacket cluttered with what I think were made-up ribbons and medals retrieved from a pawn shop, was the kind of person you wanted to shake by the ankles until all his money fell out. You sensed he had something to hide, he was keeping your banknotes in some hidden pocket, but nothing rolls or clangs into the gutter, the pavement remains bare. Innocence remains intact, as stated. I was afraid I would never be able to get the picture out of Wasserbaum's hands without it being torn in two.

"Oscar Wilde was drawn to him, and he told Wilde that they were both great martyrs," Wasserbaum said.

"I don't know anything about Oscar Wilde."

"Wilde wrote, 'to be a criminal takes imagination and daring. The interesting thing is to be guilty and wear as a halo the seduction of sin,' and Esterhazy confessed to Wilde, he had betrayed secret plans for grotesque weapons and colonial maneuvers while Dreyfus, far away on Devil's Island, was innocent," he said.

"Yes, D." I was sick of hearing about him.

"Can I have a copy made of this?" He handed the picture back to me.

"You would have to take it to Paris."

"Yes, but I would be glad to leave you any kind of security. You'd get it back, I promise."

"I don't know anything about you. It would be easy for you and my photographs to disappear into the city never to return."

"My life is an open book. I've lived alone since I came to Paris. I have very noisy neighbors who argue and fight into the night. We don't speak. I'm as invisible to them as they are audible to me. My apartment faces an air shaft. It is one room, painted yellow with a small sink, the bathroom is in the hall. The concierge has a brain-damaged son who lives with her. She's very old, and I don't know what will happen to him when she dies."

He also claimed he was from Brittany and didn't know many people in the city, as if his provincialism was a sign of the extent to which he could be trusted.

"You don't have the accent of someone who comes from the coast," I said. "One only needs the acquaintance of one scoundrel to come to grief."

"You should know."

"Yes, I do know, wise guy."

Don't fret, Lille, I won't show him Esterhazy's letters. Picture piles of Z's writing stacked as an isolated column in an empty room. Without having to actually see him, the contents of this pile present a far more compelling picture of him and of me. If you don't have to listen to his voice, not only is the audience better off, but a more persuasive case is made for my gullibility as a girl seduced and forced to partake in criminal acts. To a random passerby even now, in 1934, he would look like a cartoon villain, definitely a spy, one would say. A thin man with a drooping moustache whose deep-set eyes appear shifty even in an old photograph — he looked bad and sounded worse. While you made yourself appear pitiful yet good in order to get what you wanted, Z was a man of a thousand transformations. If Z were to walk in the door at this moment I doubt he could rally his old powers of persuasion, but his letters are articulate. Once printed in their entirety readers might understand how I was convinced. Unfortunately, my lodger's opportunism is very discouraging.

I don't trust him. Also, be assured, Lille, that despite my preparation Wasserbaum was no more interested in me than a fly on the wall. He all but said, "Nice dress. See you in the morning." It lies in a heap on the floor still.

August 5, 1934

Dear Lille,

For a few days Wasserbaum appeared to work at a table set up for him in what became his room facing the street. I don't know what he wrote. When he appeared inattentive I interrupted his thoughts, partly out of curiosity, but also because as I've written I was determined not to make his stay an easy one.

"What did you write about alone in your room with fights and beatings going on above your head?" He had been staring out the window.

"Frauds," he answered, smiling. "I write for throwaway papers investigating con artists who, in spite of their success, were shadows compared to Esterhazy." He tipped back in his chair and counted on his fingers. "There was Ferdinand Martin of Tours, who found wealthy widows to invest in harebrained schemes like a costly chauffeur and messenger service between impossibly distant cities. Ferdinand did research on the widows, found out the details of their lives, what their interests were, what they liked to wear, where they went to church. He would be very businesslike at first, then he would ask to use a room in their house in order to organize what would become their mutual business. All bank accounts were in her name, but in the course of their relationship he would ask for loans. As Ferdinand made his way upstairs into the bedrooms the loans became more extravagant. Before the widow knew it, not only was she seduced by Ferdinand Martin, but so domineered by and dependent on him that she was unable to make decisions on her own. When there was no money left, he would leave town to find another victim to bankrupt somewhere else."

I'd heard of Ferdinand Martin, but wondered if Wasserbaum's study of him was as insubstantial as the town in Brittany where Wasserbaum claimed to be from. Did an investigation of matrimonial frauds lead him to the big time of fraud: Z? If so I ought to be insulted; some would say Z was on the level more often than not. I let it go. Easily distracted (he couldn't have been much of a writer) Wasserbaum was always ready to talk, and I sat on his desk pushing ink bottles and papers away as if I were a fourteen-year-old vamp. He never grew impatient or annoyed, never acknowledged how pathetic my coyness must have been. I felt ashamed of myself but couldn't stop.

"I've also written about Claude of a Thousand Aliases who worked Francophone countries on three continents and several islands," he continued, spreading his hands as if smoothing out a map. He grew excited with his explanations. In his small room the fascination of these exploits must have been consuming. "The women he courted were usually less wealthy than those seduced by Ferdinand Martin, but they had some small sum of money set aside. His scheme was simple. He married each and every one in turn, withdrew their money from the bank, then went on to another town to marry someone else." He drew faces on the margin of a piece of paper sticking out from under a book.

"The women all looked considerably similar, as if he thought each was somehow the same woman after all. Like this: round faces and plain features," he continued to draw. "And months or years later they were uniformly interested in murdering Claude should he be found."

Both of these men presented an appearance of honesty and good will, but when they disappeared, their image reversed to negative. What are the contents of the charlatan's bag? How can one be forewarned? Out of the wreckage, one shouts at his dust, his shadow, footprints in the snow, but there's no one to point fingers at.

"Some ruses involve much more than money," I said, trying to sound pragmatic rather than plaintive.

If my boarder was telling the truth, and I doubted that was the case, then he dug up these people for a living. He presented himself as a hack only interested in smal-time frauds. Z was the consummate example of the kind of insect he'd spent his short life studying. Z was a queen bee of con men. I'd never doubted it.

Rather than express annoyance at my interruptions Wasserbaum has begun to avoid me by taking walks around the abandoned film studio, the glass house that in its time provided shelter but afforded no privacy, now reduced to a garden of glass. He brings back relics: a small piece of rusted machinery, a rubber nose, blackened, stiff and split, like genuinely cracked old skin — ironic in something so obviously fake.

Listening, invisible at the head of the stairs, from where I stood I could see four individual feet lying on a mattress left on the floor. I heard whispers and the sound of Wasserbaum pulling her to him, but it was the feet I recognized first.

Did he ask her about my papers, subtly and patiently working his ambitions into his seduction, or was Sylvie really all he was after? She wiggled away with a rustling sound. I stepped back as I heard her foot on the bottom stair and pretended to be busy with Delphine whom I'd actually just kicked out of the way. The audible sound of her sniffing and pawing was too much; I was doing the same, but at least I was quiet about it. That afternoon I moved my papers around.

For the second time I looked in as he slept. The door doesn't squeak, I can open it and walk in all the way. One would never imagine this sweetly sleeping young man had used Sylvie under my nose any more than one could have pictured you, Lille, with Z. I had a kitchen knife in my hand which I was tempted to use. *I heard a sound in the dark. I thought the thieves had broken in again and couldn't see much beyond vague shapes. He'd rented this room. We never knew much about him. Yes, it was in self-defense. His real name is Wasserbaum.* A violent imagination may come naturally to me, but I'm a coward at heart. I wanted to swing at him, the double dealer, but for what, really? As with Z, his pockets were probably bare. I don't know why I bothered, so I went to another room, threw the knife in a drawer, and slammed it shut loud enough to wake the dead. I can't come out of any crime innocent; I'm too much tarred with Z's brush.

"He said he found it in a cupboard in the cellar." Sylvie spoke as if she revealed a secret. "He put the microscope on top of your desk and dusted off the body with the back of his sleeve." She freely tattled on Wasserbaum, but didn't realize that I knew more than she seemed inclined to tell.

"Where does she hide her papers?" I'm sure he asked her.

Sylvie told me only about the microscope. As you read the word *microscope* do you get the chills? Glasses that enlarge, magnify so you can examine every embarrassing detail. *Aplanatic lenses* are those which have been corrected for distortion, lack of sharpness; through them you can see a fly on a rooftop, if not a cell or a microflage.

I wasn't in the apartment at the time, but I picture the scene as if it were a movie cliché. On a late afternoon Z enters the room, jacket unbuttoned, hat pulled low as was his custom. The windows are shuttered against bright sun, and he can't see well. He lies down beside a figure on the bed, thinking it was me, but as he reaches over your shoulders he realizes his mistake. *Lille, I'm sorry, I thought you were Claire. You look so alike.* I'm only imagining this scene, but I'm probably close to the truth. With charming nervousness he suggests you stay and the two of you get acquainted, iron out the unsettling bumps of mistaken identity, a harmless mistake after all, no? Maybe not. You're easily persuaded. To the untrained eye he was reassuring, adult, and in control of his desires as well as his finances. He took you up to the roof, the sun was bright, and you looked out over the city through a pair of large black binoculars, not opera glasses with mother-of-pearl handles, but heavily encased lenses which felt weighty in your hands. He put his arms around your waist, untied, unbuckled, and you dropped the glasses, they fell to the street and shattered. The Eiffel Tower, Sacre Coeur, Montmartre all spun in a blur that tourists would envy for salient compression. You thought I never knew, but he asked me to pay for their replacement without telling me how they broke. Whether spying at a window or from a roof, he enjoyed looking through magnifying lenses, as if innocently scanning the horizon for a dirigible or a rare bird. The glasses had been expensive, and without them he felt denied a great pleasure. Maybe all of this means nothing. I've never been really sure.

----·-----

August 11, 1934

Dear Lille,

Wasserbaum disappeared for three days without a word.

"He needed things from the city. He'll be back soon," Sylvie said. Although she was uncertain, she spoke with authority, and I felt old and foolish in the face of it. What did he really want from me?

The night he was arrested, Z tried to store the most important documents pertaining to the Dreyfus case somewhere in my apartment. We frantically devised hiding places, overturning drawers, dislodging plants, turning paintings around so they hung askew. We spent too much time unscrewing bedposts that turned out to be solid. If we'd only tapped them we would have known they weren't hollow.

We behaved like a pair of clowns, but when the police arrived they searched my rooms on rue de Douai meticulously from six o'clock in the evening until after midnight, as if a key to the city lay in the chase. The evening grew dark and quiet, then it was night. My maid brought them coffee. Anyone looking through the window would think the police investigators were nothing more than late-night janitors whose job was specific: to collect and sort papers. Although careful with the furniture they emptied boxes, tins, turned pitchers upside down, and knocked for hollow places. Some papers were well hidden but despite his care, others were found which revealed the generals had a hand in the fabrication of Dreyfus's guilt and the construction of Z's innocence. The pile finally carted away did contain evidence of that tightly framed facade. Push hard on one part of the construction, and the whole edifice might come down around your ears. He would later claim that letters attributed to him were forgeries fabricated from his handwriting, and that I or someone else had traced the lines from scraps of his original script, completely changing the meaning of his original intention, and doing so out of spite. If anyone knew this wasn't true, it was me.

After the police left with him I expected the worst and told the landlord I was afraid Z would kill himself, and could the lease, which was in his name, be transferred to mine? Even Wasserbaum knows of this incident and has accused me of self-interest before all else. If Z were a hero I'd be considered mean spirited, but since he isn't I get off with being practical, cool headed, suspiciously down to earth. Apartment leases were important and not easy to inherit if you weren't part of someone's family. It turned out that even when confronted by the most damning evidence many would swear by Z's innocence. I couldn't have known it at the time, but the idea of Z as an innocent victim was something you could bank on during those years.

My punishment really consists of the following: the Dreyfus affair won't ever be finished for me.

The morning of the fourth day Wasserbaum drove into the yard in an old Delage, as smoothly as if he coasted on clouds, cats scattered, and I was impressed.

"Would you like to go for a ride?" He held the car door open.

"No, thank you. I don't travel." It had rained again; his trousers and the windshield were spattered.

"Now that you have a car, you can leave whenever you like." I tried to sound more matter of fact than bitter. One reads of characters stuck in houses far from cities; they are miserable and doomed. Once in a while they escape, but in spite of the accessibility of this car I didn't think I was going to be one of these.

"I'm not in a hurry to leave you." He kicked mud from his shoes, scraping them against the stones of the house. He sounded sincere. Practitioners of smoothness have always been my undoing.

As he walked through the door he pretended to ignore Sylvie, and she barely looked at him, but I've watched the way he responds. When she enters a room, snub nosed, reedlike, and passive, his eyes light up. She is perfectly set up for this kind of attention from an urbane man who thinks nothing of using her for reasons she's clueless about. He imagines that because she cleans, she knows every inch of the house, but he'd better move quickly; his money must be running out. I couldn't let him stay without payment, even though I know it's difficult for him to procure the sums I require.

"If I can't pay you, perhaps I can offer you something else." He actually put his hand on mine. He didn't really want me, I do know that, but I didn't remove my interlaced fingers either.

"I'm going into debt, but you're the source of a story that would pull me out of it." He tightened his grip.

Wasserbaum knows he would make more than a little money. A killing, in fact, could be made from the story of my affair with Z. *Esterhazy's Accomplice Speaks!* It seems ironic yet necessary that the killing will ultimately be yours, Lille, not Wasserbaum's, however, as I've indicated, you would be restrained by whatever censorship I chose to exercise over my papers in the meantime.

"The papers the police didn't find were meant for my sister."

"You haven't seen her in years. You don't know much about her. She could do you in as well as a stranger."

"How do you know?"

He gave no answer. Sylvie pretended to dust. I pictured my

betrayal on the wet mattress lying on the cellar floor crowded by junk.

"My sister will know what to do with my papers. Will you? I'm not sure."

Dismissing my arguments for family loyalty with a shrug, Wasserbaum didn't give up easily.

"I know about the generals who had to insure Dreyfus's guilt and toward this end constructed a series of forgeries, but the other side of that coin meant protecting the real spy," he said.

"That had nothing to do with me."

"But they visited Z."

"I never saw them."

"Their disguises were hammy and obvious: Felix Gribelin wore dark blue glasses. Others sported fake beards. Major General du Paty de Clam kept liaisons in the Bois du Boulogne covered by a veil and black silk gloves. There are those who find the spectacle of men in women's clothing seductive; maybe they're drawn to signs of vulnerability. Z also used to meet du Paty in public urinals: caverns with the sound of water dripping in the background." He put his face very close to mine as if to demonstrate the force of his argument, as if to say these were disgusting men. "But I know they came to your apartment. The lease was in your name."

"Z was depressed and anxious. He was going to throw himself off a train. All kinds of people knocked on the door. I remember very few of them." Wasserbaum was going to put me on trial all over again. I didn't know which path to take: a) contrition, or b) insistence on my innocence, my noninvolvement, absence from the premises, etcetera. Which would he find most appealing? Which would get him to stop badgering me?

"Z would never kill himself, he'd twist in the breeze as long as he could. He was going to escape France then sell his story to the highest bidder. Its publication would make things hot for the generals and possibly for you. The General Staff couldn't allow that. The parade to the guillotine would be a long one. Z said so often," Wasserbaum reminded me.

I could sense him weighing the risks. He could remain in my house and pay dearly for it, or he could leave, giving up the fantastic attention that he was certain awaited him if he could acquire my papers. His false hopes were, I think, extraordinary.

"Once the papers are published, you'll be vindicated."

He didn't say: *I'll be able to move into another apartment, employ research assistants, and be able to turn to other subjects. I'll get all kinds of offers,* the word *offers* rolling off his tongue and vaguely sexual. With the publication of *The Private Life of Z* he would be considered a serious writer, an inquirer after the truth, not unlike Picquart perhaps. No more Ferdinand Martin, no more tracing the footsteps of charlatans like Claude of Tours.

"That's all it will take, do you really think so? One sharp lens trained on a botched forgery and you're off, a rich man." I poked him in the ribs yet shuddered to think of what that volume might contain, and who would be enriched by it.

"Don't you believe in holding the torch up to history?" Wasserbaum posed self-righteously, staring into the distance, yet at the same time he looked so hopeful and naive, I couldn't stand it.

"To illuminate or to set fire?"

He looked surprised. Comparing himself to Z, he said, "At least you must be assured I'm honest."

"Thank you," I said, "now I can sleep at night." I wanted to tell him that I had come to believe that repression solves problems that should never find their way to an oxygenated surface. Just don't talk about it, is my motto, and the rest will take care of itself. Wasserbaum, evidently, believes in the opposite, talking, remembering until the sound of your own voice puts you to sleep. He doesn't understand that I want to forget about Z and all the rest of it.

He led me to the stairs. I gently pushed him away, but let

my hands stay on his shoulders for just a minute. It wasn't easy; if I gave in, I'd probably end by handing him everything. My perch is still under the eaves, but no one sleeps through the night in this house.

Before Wasserbaum found me, what were his days like? He sat in an airless room, reading a newspaper or a book, feeling excluded from the world of print. The presses roared without him, he felt neglected, nobody knew his name, and so on. Like Z, he's desperate for attention, filled with envy, yet with less bitterness, I think. Enmity toward all those real and imaginary blockades (the army, women, modernism, Credit Lyonnais) created Z, and he was quite formed by them. Given time, Wasserbaum may become another heel, sort of drunk and miserable in a loud and humiliating way. Z had once commented that Picquart would *become like a garment turned inside out, a reversal of his former self.* He misattributed the quote, almost a malapropism in Z's hands, to Flaubert; the line was not from *Bouvard and Pecuchet,* and he turned out to be wrong about Picquart. The image of frayed seams showing on the outside and the treachery of the dead Z all seem linked somehow. I can, however, see Wasserbaum as a jacket or trousers turned inside out, completely bitter and pessimistic; unrecognizable.

"He needed a way out, the means weren't important."

"He needed you."

"What could I do?" I felt myself sweat. He knew things I'd neither heard of nor thought about for decades, connections I'd thought were forgotten and obliterated now reared their crusty heads. I tried to shove them back into oblivion, all the while hoping I appeared calm, probably failing to do so.

"Handwriting experts claim that the gender of writers of forgeries and fabricated letters can be determined. You wrote with a female hand." The pleasant, accommodating Wasserbaum had disappeared.

"No! Did I?"

"Don't be sarcastic. Madame Henry, wife of Major Henry, wrote some forgeries. You did others."

"Henry killed himself in prison."

"A shut razor was found in his hand. Do you think he had time to close it after he cut his throat?"

"If he was murdered, no one remembers him now." I wanted to change the subject and spun a globe that was standing nearby. Borneo, Tangiers, and Devil's Island whipped round. "You remind me of what Mirabeau said of Robespierre: 'He will go far; he believes everything that he says.'" He was right. Each story was, for Z, indistinguishable from actuality.

"Picquart," he went on, "exiled to Tunis, was on to Z, and so you sent him a short telegram in an attempt to make him appear part of a conspiracy. *Stop the demigod. Everything is discovered. Very serious matter. Speranza.* What was that supposed to mean? He didn't know any Speranza. It was all made up. The generals sent forgeries signed *Esperanze.* You dropped the *e* and added an *a.* You sent the fake telegram to Picquart in an attempt to make him appear guilty and to protect Z."

"One devises a paper trail, invents characters like Speranza and fiddles with the appearances of those who really do exist like Picquart or Picard, as he was known in one fabrication."

I was annoyed. Wasserbaum is an ambitious man. The picture of a solitary man spending bitter months in a cramped garret is both romantic and false. I'm a dupe. I felt foolish, an accomplice in my own discovery, and I wanted him gone. I'm my own Robespierre.

We didn't speak for several days and when we resumed our conversations, he didn't allude to the papers. All kindness and concern, he pet the cats and the dog, spoke to them as if they were human, and pretended to care about how I looked, but he never said *you look ravishing,* only *you look healthy.* Underneath his solicitousness the desire to achieve his own ends peeks through. One night he stood very close to me as I wound the pre-Revolutionary clock. His eyes looked impatient and very green, perhaps due to light reflected off its marine-colored enamel. He put his hand on my arm, but I noticed he had to shut his eyes first.

———•———

August 15, 1934

Dear Lille,

A conversation.

"If I may, I would just study the papers for a moment. I promise I won't take them from the house. You can be assured that I won't name you in whatever it is I write. In a sea of pseudonyms you can pick one out too, or you can remain unidentified."

"In your writings you can refer to me as Marie Antoinette."

He blinked. Marie Antoinette, a name that stands out as simultaneously false and symbolic. How am I like a headless queen, readers will ask?

"What will you write in *The Private Life of Z*? Part scandal sheet, part history, prurient and salacious?"

"There were many women in this story, you don't have to be named," he backed down.

"There was only one woman forger, if you prefer. Madame Henry, wife of Major Henry, was an amateur."

"People are less interested in the affair than you imagine."

"Then why bother to write the book?"

"I think there are new citizens with short memories who would make Z into a hero, and I think you know who they are."

"Who?"

He looked confused, but barged on, putting his face close to mine.

"Don't wait until after you're dead to be pushed around, to be made into something you'd rather not be. Annotate them while you can still defend yourself."

"If I let you print them and comment in the margins, I couldn't defend myself in any case."

"So you have to be dead first?"

Was he threatening me? I returned the favor, pushing him back until he was against a wall. "What if I used the papers as kindling?"

He looked extremely startled; clearly he believed I would burn my papers before he could get his hands on them. Would I have to sleep with a knife in the future? In that moment I indulged in another garish but in its own way realistic and threatening picture: in the middle of the night while moths flew into my reading light, might he put a gun to my head, forcing me to betray their location? Sylvie served dinner, a deaf and dumb machine. She carried plates, rattled knives and glasses, brushed past his chair while he drank noisily. Delphine was let in the back door and ran up to him. I felt besieged in my own house. I held back from telling him his time was up. *(Leave after dinner. Leave now.)* In my discomfort I decided to take a new approach, even if that meant being as cordial to him as possible, in order to see what he would do. I followed your example. Look at Lille, I used to be told, more flies are caught with honey than with vinegar. My smile muscles hurt. He was still paying.

Wasserbaum pulls Sylvie close to him, pushes her hair away from her ear and whispers into it. She turns her head so he has to hold her jaw in order to finish whatever it is he's saying. She's laughing, hiding her face in a cupboard so he won't see her tremors of hysteria. But behind the cupboard door there's a frayed bag of something white, flour or some kind of powder. It's on the shelf that is level with her face, and the bag bursts when she accidentally shoves her nose into it. Whitened and sneezing, she looks like a snot-faced clown. Wasserbaum hands her a handkerchief and, embarrassed, turns to go. In the next room he bumps into me pretending to have a conversation with Delphine.

He pulled his chair closer to mine and began to describe a necklace of diamonds that were reported to have been as big as doorknobs. He made a circle, thumb touching index finger. Since the necklace had been broken up the original 647 stones were now scattered all over Europe.

"Marie Antoinette, accused of every kind of excessive passion, declined to buy the necklace, but through a great con, her name became linked to it. The diamonds grew to symbolize her twin addictions: sexuality and expense. In one cold strand, here was a symbol of avarice and degradation." He rubbed his eyes for a few seconds while pronouncing her name. This gesture, like a tic, made me nervous.

He briefly put his arm around the back of my chair, posing and answering his own question, a condescending and annoying habit.

"Jeanne de la Motte, originally a barefoot girl who claimed descent from the Valois, managed in a few short years to climb up a society ladder, with one foot finally in the court at Versailles but the other toe weighted toward the poorhouse. Jeanne contrived a scheme to acquire the necklace. She found a milliner in the Palais Royale, blond and blue eyed, who resembled the queen. *Un sosie,* to quote Moliere." He looked at Delphine, held her jaw in his hand. "A double, a second self." He dropped the dog's jaw and demonstrated by holding up two identical spoons symbolizing the queen and her double. A dented third with a differently scrolled handle served as Jeanne de la Motte.

"Jeanne dressed her as the queen; she only needed to pose in a garden for a few minutes during which time a man would approach her as if she was in fact the queen, and she would ask him to obtain the necklace for her. This man was de Rohan, the gullible cardinal who desperately wanted favor with the queen. Entirely taken in by Jeanne's hoax, he believed he was doing Marie Antoinette a service by dealing with the jeweler. The queen wanted the necklace. He would get it for her. She would owe him a favor. The jeweler was only too happy to finally get the white elephant of a necklace off his hands." The cardinal was a fork, the jeweler a butter knife.

"What did the double who would later claim complete innocence, think she was up to in the garden?"

I shrugged, although I knew how it would end.

"No one knows. The milliner disappeared."

One of the spoons clattered to the floor.

"Jeanne destroyed the dress *le sosie* had worn in the garden, and in a few days the necklace was delivered to an accomplice. It was shortly broken up and sold all over Paris and London, never to be seen in its entirety again. The jeweler, wanting to be paid, approached the cardinal who still believed the diamonds had been delivered to the real queen. Months went by and no payment was made to the jeweler. Meanwhile Jeanne and her accomplice began spending the money indiscriminately, leaving a trail of consumption from a large estate in the Loire to pairs of silver asparagus tongs." He pressed his fingers together as if they were pincers, opening and shutting, grabbing at the air, then reached over and pinched my fingers as they lay on the table. What am I? I'm asparagus.

"Sooner rather than later the scam was brought to light, and the con artists themselves seemed to sense that this was inevitable. Jeanne de la Motte, branded with a *V*, escaped to London where she wrote vindictive tracts against the queen, claiming she had indeed wanted the necklace all along. Revolutionary sympathies were stirred up." He made a broad stirring gesture with his arm, knocking into my elbow, so that our elbows fit together like a set of quotation marks.

"The queen was accused of having sexual designs on all the participants in the scheme, and when they refused her advances, Marie Antoinette allegedly invented the necklace plot as an act of revenge. What a story. The queen was innocent, but made guilty by reputation. She was portrayed as a harpy, *une orgiaste*." The knife, no longer identified as the jeweler, turned into the guillotine. He made a cutting gesture, not across the Marie Antoinette spoon, symbol of cupidity, but across his own throat.

"Blame landed on the queen and stuck there; her appetites

gave the scandal a reason to be born. Remember, she'd not even been a party to it. Her name and interests encouraged the plausibility of the hoax and overshadowed the bold fact of its undertaking. Everyone knew she was surrounded by corrupt yes-men, but con artists were less on trial than the *ancienne regime,* and as we know, Versailles would soon be reduced to a prison cell memory." He leaned back in his chair, balancing on the back legs. He's not a big man, but I was afraid the wood would break under him, and so I pushed him forward. It was an old chair. He looked annoyed, but only paused for a moment.

"The queen provided an inexhaustible subject for court pornography." Sylvie appeared suddenly, and he removed his arm from the back of my chair. Standing just as abruptly, he walked toward her while continuing to speak to me. "Were these libelous representations, or can we say that given the power to procure any man or woman she desired, she did so with a smile? Was she a devoted mother, wrongfully represented and much maligned? Or was she a woman whose actual life had little to do with the symbolism she acquired? Jeanne de la Motte was branded with a *V,* but perhaps it was Marie Antoinette who was more indelibly smeared. Perhaps not."

I could imagine them laughing at me, an inexhaustible subject of ridicule and parody, and this might inadvertently flatter Sylvie, so patient and unassuming, even more. *Able to procure anyone,* I kept thinking. She knocked a cup off the table, and it smashed to the floor, spilling cold coffee. They bent over the mess, mopping at the spot on the rug.

"It's my fault."

"Let me, sir."

I left the room quite piqued, I can tell you.

Why did he choose to tell me this story? Forks and dull knives aren't the actors here. Which part was really meant to represent me? Cardinal de Rohan, easily tricked, or the queen, easily tarred? Which represented my beryl-eyed alloy of a house-guest? Clever Jeanne and the *sosie* are all the roles that remain to be meted out. I turned to the mineral section of a nature atlas and in distraction looked up the definition of beryl.

Emeralds are formed from beryl, a silicate of beryllium and aluminum, when chromium oxide is introduced. Beryl is found in granite. Crystallized in the hexagonal system, it is sometimes found in huge crystals; one as big as two tons was discovered in America. The alloy produced when beryl is combined with aluminum and copper is uncommonly strong.

From my window out over the steamy garden I could see Wasserbaum wandering through Star Films, picking up a glass star or a rusted saw. He was the rocket in the moon's eye, Méliès's most well-known image, but unlike the moon, I'm incapable of tears.

He asked to see the attic.

"It's hot up there. There's nothing to see."

"When I was standing in the drive I thought I saw a man's face up in the window."

"I've been upstairs. I heard nothing."

"It wouldn't hurt to look."

I shook my head. "That part of the house," I pointed to the ceiling, "is private." He walked around me as if I weren't there.

"I could check. The thieves might have come back."

"Hunting traps are stored in the attic, and hornets' nests grow from the eaves."

He ignored me, and I had no choice but to follow him It grew hotter as we climbed, old lamps and cracked dishes lined the top steps; what would he think when we finally reached the top floor, the space directly under the roof? *She's a pack rat, a squirrel. Or let me describe the rooms another way: objects are so piled up in the corners of her house that you feel you've stumbled into a space which, though engineered by humans, resembles North American beaver dams.* Boxes of things lay scattered around, my clothes folded on top of some of them.

There was no place else to sit but the unmade bed, and we

both moved awkwardly like jointed shadow puppets. I tried to look as if I often had men up to the attic, always expecting them to sit close by, but my efforts at flirtation and seduction are drawn from an arid plane, a lack of experience, from memories so dim and rooted in another time as to be worthless. Feeling something hard under me, I shifted so I was really sitting on the thing. Wasserbaum moved closer, so I inched back as best I could in the few feet of space, knocking into a bedpost. The ceiling slanted close overhead. There was so little space to move around in. If he had kissed me I'd want to advertise that kiss so all scopophiliacs with eyes glued to binoculars or noses stuck to windows would be jealous, but the only view from the attic lunette is the ruin of Star Films. And no one can see in. As I squirmed around a leather case slipped out from under the mattress. I heard the thud and hoped he hadn't recognized the noise. I said, *It's only Delphine.* Somehow the thing did produce a doglike sound in its fall. He looked down, and I felt as if an accordion-shaped photoroman had unfolded in a fall from a chair. Each frame of this imaginary object represented a moment of personal embarrassment, yet I know a photoroman is a constructed thing, a montage made of drawings and colored-in photographs; a few images may be factual in some way, confirming an agreed-upon truth (gravity pulls downward, arms and legs grow in place) but other images confound me at every turning. I swiftly reached down to pick up the package of papers, but he kicked the thing with his foot so it flew out of my reach and into his corner of the universe. I grabbed at the papers, clutching an edge or two, but his grasp was firm, and he easily knocked me aside as if I were nothing more than a mosquito. He tried to pull up his pants with one hand; I hadn't even noticed he'd undone them.

"It wasn't my fault. Everyone agreed on that. Many still believe in Z's innocence, it's true, but I hadn't spied for the German embassy or committed any crimes." I tried to sound as if I were reciting facts, keeping my grip on the papers. "Everyone knows. It's public record."

"You stayed with Z and protected him long after he was found guilty." This was a fact, too, and it seemed to matter to him although he didn't sound particularly accusatory. His voice was distant, which made me feel even worse. It was as if my corporeal self were no more tangible than a voice at the end of a phone line ringing from Rouen or Marseilles.

I pulled at the case, but he held onto it, pants around his ankles. With one hand he pulled up his pants and yanked the case away from me completely. I reached out, and he pushed my dry hands away.

"I only served as a shadow who had no choice as to who I followed, *I was of no real importance.*"

"I don't believe you. Everyone," he said, "insisted it was someone else and not himself who was involved."

"The generals were the most guilty of all," I shrieked. "You're making *me* into the Marie Antoinette wives of despots and criminals, rich men and presidents always are. I spent those nights in Saint Lazare prison. Can you imagine what that was like?"

"Others paid more dearly."

"You should know, Wasserbaum."

"How did you find out my name?"

"You shouldn't leave your papers lying around."

"You snooped."

"You did a bit of looking around yourself. We'll see what the next ten years have in store for you, Wasserbaum. At the time of the affair, some wanted you people burned in glass furnaces. Glass, so they could watch and be sure the job was done properly."

In a few long steps he was out the door. There was a dressmaker's dummy in the corner, moth eaten and fly specked. I'd left a hat on its head, and as I slept up here I'd come to think of it as a companion. Now it looked derelict and lewd.

Don't write to me of betrayal and exposure. The construction of my life based on those letters will be hideous, *she stayed with the miserable Z until the end,* but you would have done me in much the same way. You often asked me why I kept the papers, but I couldn't destroy them. They point the finger at me and away from me at the same time. What I mean is this: as long as no one read the papers, few remembered me very much. As long as I held onto them I disappeared, and time stood still.

The furniture, bed, desk, small bronze elephants, and looking glasses have been moved back to their proper places, and I've insisted Delphine be returned to her master. Let thieves steal what's left. Tripping over damp bones is no way to end one's life. Wasserbaum left his final payment on a table by the door, one of the spoons and the guillotine knife weighting the bundles of francs. I don't know if he left the money under those things intentionally, hastily searching drawers for those particular pieces, or if Sylvie had left the silverware there by accident — the bell rings, she's polishing, she drops the spoons on the nearest table without realizing the contents of the envelope they fall on top of. It makes all the difference in the world, but I haven't been able to ask her. I'm sending half of this amount to you, and you will find the sum enclosed.

Claire

———·—·———

January 23, 1935

Inspector F. X. Barque
1, rue Jules-Cousin
Lyons

Dear Saturnin,

We were all distressed to hear of your mother's accident and hope she recovers very soon. Zazie especially sends her regards and wants to let you know that she will post a duplicate of last week's reports since you haven't yet received the original. The city moves slowly. It has rained six days out of seven. You're lucky to be away this time of year.

I have been working on the Francoeur/Charpin case, and find the track of stolen papers not so much a dead end as a street that may go absolutely nowhere anyone would want to tread. You smelled a rat from the moment you unwrapped the post, but I don't think we're so much knocking at rat holes as chasing paper ghosts and invisible ink.

First, after examining Claire Francoeur's bundle of letters I decided to retrace some of the prominent footsteps. The way was clear: locate Claire's house and those who knew her, call on neighbors — inquire whether they observed anything suspicious — then attempt to gain entry to her former dwelling. I took a morning train out to Montreuil, using this opportunity to review some of the evidence. A few questions pull insistently at my coattails. One, knowing that Wasserbaum was in pursuit of her papers (which meant her reputation) and could have little interest in herself, why did she let him into her house? Is vanity the only explanation? She didn't appear a gullible or tolerant woman.

Second, why did she hide the papers in such an easily discovered spot? Was she tempting fate, thinking he couldn't possibly find her desirable, however much she wished it, and so her bed was the last place he would look? If the description in the letter dated August 15 is accurate, the folio was lying just beneath a sheet, not even under the mattress. Perhaps she had been reading them in bed the previous night and the incident occurred as she described it. Or was she lying to her sister in order to save face? Perhaps the letters were a lure that would turn out to backfire. For all but this last moment of his tenancy Wasserbaum was always only a few floors below. She took an inordinate number of chances with documents that meant so much to her. The papers were her black silk stockings, her backless dress.

Third, her sister must have a thin skin or want the papers so much that exposure takes a backseat. Claire's picture of her is hardly flattering. Aspersions cast in her direction are quite damning.

With these questions needling me I was, at the same time, looking forward to taking a peek at what was left of Star Films Studios. As a child I had always wanted to watch a film in production, and if such a tour had been possible I imagined exactly what I would see: Méliès's tricks occurring literally before my eyes. I dreamed of being selected for a part. He would pick me out of a crowd full of perfectly well-behaved, starched children. *I want you, little boy, the slob, the one dripping a cherry ice down his front.* I would step forward to be launched into a cardboard galaxy or a chemistry lab whose beakers and rubber tubing would give me the capability to pierce anyone who made my life difficult. I particularly recollect being mesmerized and frightened by *The Diabolical Tenant*. A man entered an empty room with a small valise from which furniture, possessions, family, and finally dinner flew out, settling gently into place only to be sucked back into the satchel a few minutes later when the landlord threatened. The films were frightening because of what was left out: logic, gravity, naturalism; yet they weren't dreams. The physical tricks had actually occurred somewhere in the studio. Méliès made this film when he was about to be evicted himself. Have you ever wanted to disappear into a wall? It's often occurred to me that if I could slip between particles of plaster and come out intact on the other side, many problems would be solved.

A woman in black sat across from me on the train breaking off bits of bread and staring out the window without eating. The crumbs fell into her bag and onto her skirt. She was far too young to anticipate the flying chairs, playing cards, devils, and houris I expected to find when the train stopped at Montreuil.

I had no trouble locating rue Francois Debergue. The house said to have been the domicile of Claire Francoeur is empty and appears to have been abandoned for many months if not longer, although the letters imply the place wasn't kept up. The front and back yards bristled with frozen over weeds. Windows and doors were locked. I walked around the entire building looking through dirty windows. Rooms inside were empty as far as I was able to tell. Will make further inquiries as to the identity of the property's owner.

As the city becomes choked with refugees and emigrés, as you know, some spill out beyond its boundaries, even living out in the suburbs. Claire's neighbors on the east side, for example, did not speak French well and were reluctant to open up until I shouted *police inspector* at the door. The woman who finally opened it, holding a cup of tea as if she had all the time in the world, told me they'd only recently moved into the neighborhood, and hadn't ever seen anyone coming or going from the house directly next to theirs. There were packing cases behind her and thin, worried faces. Someone was translating as I spoke. A man's voice, in a language I supposed to be Russian or Polish, expressed disagreement. Whether the tone of disagreement was in response to a domestic situation or to my questions asked from outside the threshold, I had no idea. A hand in a black fingerless glove appeared clutching at the doorjamb only to be pushed away by the one holding the teacup. I wasn't able to see the body or even the arm attached. The way she pried fingers loose was deliberate yet the hand clung so tenaciously, I expected she might pour her tea on those stubborn digits just to get rid of it. They were packing up, she said, moving to the west. Nobody, a voice in the back said, trusts that the Maginot Line will hold. I heard the sound of the speaker being thwacked, and imagined someone saying in Russian, *Stupid old man. You talk too much.*

Their limited French vocabulary was soon exhausted, and we were left communicating by a kind of sign language, so I thanked her and departed without feeling very hopeful. The next house, a narrow, listing dwelling, was further down the road. Sitting in the middle of its front yard was a large model of a camera, the sort of camera used perhaps thirty years ago. This oddity was enough to make me question the reliability of anyone I would find within, and I was inclined to skip the house altogether, but then changed my mind. Although I have seen pictures of actual overblown cameras used in the desert, this monster couldn't ever have been a working machine. An elderly man scraped frost from its body. When I approached he introduced himself as Doublier, greeting me before I could speak.

"It was a sight gag. Used to shoot water. If the thing might be made to work again I would aim the lens at all these new strangers. Squirt, squirt." He made an obscene gesture. I didn't ask him what it was used for now, only nodded in blind agreement, then inquired if he knew anyone who might have lived in the house down the road.

"A woman lived at that address, but I didn't know her. She kept to herself, never any conversation. I'd like to have gotten her with this." He patted the camera.

Stuffing a rag in his pocket, he asked me in, and I agreed, following him through a green front door into a hall so cluttered there was hardly any place to put one foot in front of the other. The old man limped ahead of me, sometimes hopping, sometimes holding onto a coatrack or a shelf for balance. If I weren't a thin man, I would never have been able to penetrate his house, yet here in these rooms filled with rubber feet and false beards were shreds of my childhood dream tour of Star Films, but the shreds had been transformed in some grotesque way, ridiculing me as I stepped with difficulty. His laundry hung drying near the stove. I picked up a rubber nose feeling as if I were being taunted or secretly punished although I didn't know what for. The rooms were airless and smelled of something sweetish and rotting.

"Have you heard of any break ins or thefts nearby, especially around last Bastille day?"

"Yes, at that house you asked me about. She hated everyone, but no one from this neighborhood would have robbed her. They must have come from elsewhere. The barbarian is at the gate. I tell everyone."

"Did you know anyone named Sylvie, a maid in the house?"

"Yes. I told her to get a dog after the house was broken into."

"Do you know where I might find her now?"

"She disappeared sometime after Claire Francoeur's death. Did she steal something?"

"I don't know, but I'd like to talk to her."

He seemed confused about days, so I wrote names and dates on a large chalkboard that served as a tabletop. Bits of chalk and pencils were crammed into a tin cup near my elbow.

"This chalkboard was used in a film too. *French Cops Learning English*. I played a student policeman." He made motions with his hands miming the gestures of writing and looking stupid.

"Did you ever hear screaming or arguing from next door? Ever see anyone burning papers?"

"No. I'm a retired *cascadeur*, a comic stuntman, everyone knows me, but I don't know everyone."

This line of inquiry seemed to have reached its conclusion. I thanked him for his time and decided to continue my investigation elsewhere. I may return to question him if photographs of the sisters become available. On the other side of his house there were a few buildings and houses with small frozen gardens, separated by fields and low stone walls, perhaps filled with more retired actors and stuntmen who walk their dogs through the flapping hinges and empty mullions of Star Films.

I inquired after Lille Charpin with the sisters at Sainte-Anne's. They'd had a Lille Charpin staying with them, but she had to leave suddenly. They described a younger woman. Too young to be a sister of Claire? It's difficult to say with certainty.

Did Lille really lose valuable documents? I've spent an afternoon talking to a man who's still somersaulting through burning windows and swimming in a blown up fish tank.

Remember the case of the Marie Antoinette forgeries? Her friend and supporter, Baron Feuillet de Conches, had several of her letters, so he invented a few more. Even now many aren't sure which came from Versailles, Bastille, or from the cabinet of Baron Feuillet. She'd written so little, everyone wanted to believe in them. *Tell us more, please!* Then every hairdresser, every fourth maid, every prison guard had a book to write. What if all that survives from one's life are the enthusiastic forgeries that reinvent from birth to death in virtual similitude, and who's to know the difference?

Apart from inquiries regarding any possible sale of Esterhazy letters, the question remains, is there a Wasserbaum? Will have Devereaux check his anarchist files for a writer who fits his description as she gave it to us. A woman might invent such a man out of guilt or desire. He might not exist, but suspects can be found and questioned. Will also inquire at the morgue.

Best,
H. LeMaitre
Inspector
Commisariat du Arsenal
1, rue Jules Cousin
Paris

----·•·----

April 1942

Paris, Germany

Dear Chantal,

Here in a storage vault in the cellar of the Musée de l'Homme, I pass time going through relics of dead or dying societies. The curators would prefer that we not unpack their crates, but you like to know what you're sitting on and who your neighbors are. We're careful not to leave spears and things in disarray or mix up Dogon bowls with those attributed to the Kwakuitl. One minute you're running down a street in what you thought was the twentieth century, the next you're hiding in the Bronze Age and lucky to be there. I knew where I was running to. It had been arranged, but I couldn't tell anyone, not even you.

Lying in one box: Asmat sculpture from Dutch Indonesia. A naked man and woman, tab and keyhole, they grin from ear to ear, elbows resting on knees. I sleep on top of a crate of masks belonging to the Iroquois False Face Society. I leaned over the side of the crate in order to read a card meant to be displayed alongside them: *The False Face Society is made up of men and women cured by a man who crawls through the doorway of their house wearing a False Face in imitation of the deformed, crippled spirits in the forest. They rattle shells and skins of snapping turtles. They were believed to cure not through themselves but from the power of those they imitated.* "Crippled spirits" might be a wounded bird, mashed bugs, a broken twig. If I could take on the form of dented North American phantoms I might be able to walk unnoticed from Clichy to Passy. I put a snapping-turtle shell on my head and wave a rattle. Nothing happens. I'm still hiding in the museum basement. The very presence of these masks make me wonder who the native informants might have been. Who told the curators or anthropologists what object cured by virtue of imitation? How do we know what we know? Perhaps the rattles and beetle shells were used for no purpose whatsoever, relics from a garbage dump. Spells misfired. The tribe died from malaria or smallpox. I'm still here in hiding, untransported. No walking through walls.

Paintings have been carefully ferried in fireproof wrappings from the Louvre to mansions and municipal museums in the south: Veronese, Dürer, Caravaggio, the Mona Lisa. Objects of less importance have been kept on display. I am neither on display nor able to escape to the south. I stayed too late. Above me circulating around the city are obscene cartoons intended to portray the "real" parasite, the "real" foreigners; pictures of *lynchage* festivals appear in *Paris-Soir* and *Le Matin*. The stereotypes didn't scare me. I saw my face parodied in all of them, but still I stayed.

You yourself won't need false papers, but you should destroy mine, which you'll find taped under the sink. Monsieur Fontaine, as you know, looked just like me. False papers, even crudely done ones, weren't difficult to obtain, and mine were nearly flawless, but my face isn't. Face and name didn't match, and because the French army isn't invincible, I have to hide. In one month France is overrun, conquered. As escape routes were cut off (Holland, the Channel, the Pyrenees) I relied on the name La Fontaine to save me from my face, but eventually, in a public bathroom, I was identified, so I ran.

You knew about the Fontaine identity papers, but not the papers I stole from Claire Francoeur, and these you should also destroy. I left Montreuil quickly, eager to be out of that house and done with her. I didn't tell you at the time, but as soon as I was within sight of the city I stopped the car by the side of a road and began to read what I expected to be a gold mine, the correspondence between Claire Francoeur and Esterhazy. What I found were inventions. The pages I held against the steering wheel were indeed letters, but letters someone had tried to pass off as Dreyfus's Devil's Island correspondence. The handwriting looked accurate as far as I could remember from examples I'd seen, but these were clearly written by another kind of prisoner. I threw them across the seat in disgust. I was so sure I'd taken her correspondence with Esterhazy, Mr. Z, and she seemed to think so too. Where she actually hid those papers, I was never to discover. She was such a confused old woman, perhaps she no longer remembered where she hid what. How did she get hold of these Devil's Island letters, and why were they written? I've no answers, only guesses. Get rid of them. In certain hands the forgeries might pass as genuine and only provide more material for *lynchage*. What if the actual, the "real" forgeries were all that were to remain one hundred years after the trial? On the other hand, what if Claire's false forgeries were to become the only papers to survive? I have one with me because the forger seems to have mirrored the condition of imprisonment so well, and when I hear certain boot steps overhead, I think Devil's Island has been transposed to the middle of the city. So far, of course, soldiers haven't unlocked the cellar door to have a search. We continue to review the objects we pick up and put down in blind ceremonies. They are a source of mystery for a man from Le Havre, a source of indifference for a Czech who describes unthinkable train rides, dreaming delirious while he lies in a Guinean canoe. Rimbaud believed poems should be begun from the end, and here we are with nothing but the end, thinking about the beginning or the middle is like trying to put a stalled car in gear when it's mired, hopeless, even sinking, and to think about the road ahead or behind is to think like a boy scout. Useless. The Czech sits up in his bark boat and out of the blue quotes Bakunin who "urged one not to take power but to destroy it." I hold an electric torch up to his face.

"Fat chance," I say. "Where's your war paint?"

I'm hoping one of the curators will bring you this letter, otherwise I might fold it up and stuff the wedge between the legs of the Asmat sculpture, hoping someone will one day find it. I receive no letters; there is a poverty of written communication here just as there is above ground; any information is obtained because someone told someone who told someone else. This is not intended as a reproach, I realize the danger of writing to the late La Fontaine. In whispers we've asked for a radio with headphones, but we've been assured we'll hear nothing accurate on it. Children, the curator informs us, sing along with the radio to the tune of *La Cucaracha Radio-Paris ment, Radio-Paris ment, Radio-Paris est allemand!* He imitates them to keep our spirits up.

If you and the children need a place to hide, go to Madeleine's. She's taken over her mother's place in the building, and I'm sure there are empty rooms to let. I know there's a small one her mother cleared out a few years ago that can't be seen from the street and has its own entrance and stair at the back. She might let you have it for almost nothing.

Signed,
Wasserbaum

The Section of Statistics

Maryse saw a girl in the park filling page after page with small cramped script. When she had written to the end of one page, she turned it over, filled the reverse side, then began another sheet. Maryse sat opposite her, staring, but the girl never looked up. She looked familiar, although Maryse was sure she didn't know her. The girl seemed like a kind of distant imitation of herself, writing paragraph after paragraph, noting everything that she saw or overheard, everything that entered her head. Maryse had thought the observed life was a way to step outside things, to put herself beyond the restrictions imposed by her mother. Her mother's constant vigilance was a series of snares: button up, confess, look clean. When Maryse ran away she discovered the water was full of sharks, and not knowing how to survive she swam with them for a while. The dangers left behind in her own house seemed frustrated and toothless by comparison.

The swimming began when Maryse followed her older sister, Aurelie, defiant and annoyed, in the process of driving their mother crazy.

"What did you do to your hair?"

"Nothing." Aurelie twisting a chunk of artificially lightened hair around a finger.

"You always look as if you just got out of bed." Her mother grasped at replacements, ways to imply what she couldn't say. She couldn't use vulgar words to convey vulgar meanings.

Aurelie knew this about her mother and goaded her to the edge of incoherence.

"What are you trying to say?"

"Where were you last night?"

"I was right here. I never left the house."

At night when she thought everyone was asleep, Maryse listened to the sound of Aurelie's door opening, followed by the sound of footsteps down the hall. At first she wanted to creep out after Aurelie but the security of her room pulled too strongly, a kind of irresistible gravity that at first overcame any impulse she had to run away, too. Then one sleepless night she got out of bed and stood in the hall with her shoes in her hands, not sure whether to come or go. From a stairwell Maryse watched Aurelie lock the door and run off into the night. Maryse had no idea where she went or what Maryse herself would do in the street except to feel foolish and risk being assaulted by whoever waited for her there.

One evening while Aurelie and their mother were arguing downstairs, Maryse went up to Aurelie's room to have a look around. She searched her sister's desk for letters or names and addresses written on scraps of paper, but found nothing. The little drawers were empty or contained balled-up cigarette packages, broken pens, a dry inkwell left uncapped. The closet overflowed with clothing and boxes. She looked for letters or other papers which might be found there. After feeling around in pockets she pushed aside jackets and coats, including a man's tight-fitting cutaway suit. She wondered how her mother had never found it. The more Maryse looked the more she realized that she knew little about the woman who wore these clothes. In her frenzy to find something, anything, she wasn't paying attention when the sound of arguing stopped. Maryse was reaching for a box hidden in the back of the closet when Aurelie grabbed her violently by the shoulders, turning her around in a rage.

"What are you looking for?"

The box fell. Men's clothing, black trousers, a black jacket with shiny lapels, and other objects Maryse couldn't identify tumbled out of the box. Her face red, her sleeves wrinkled from the effort of pulling things apart, Maryse waved a man's shirt above her head. "What are these?" She knew the men's suit was nothing more than armor to wear when she traveled alone at night. As soon as she got where she was going, Maryse guessed, the flowery Aurelie would change her clothes and stash the armor somewhere until she had to hit the streets in order to return home.

"Leave them alone. Nothing." Even when confronted with evidence, Aurelie ran over Maryse every time they argued, and she felt completely helpless. "What were you doing here?"

The first crime had been Maryse's: trespassing. The more ambiguous transgression of keeping men's clothing in her closet dwarfed that in comparison, and Aurelie knew it. All Maryse could do was try to mollify her sister by letting her think she was on her side. Was it possible to make a deal?

"I won't tell anyone." Maryse's face was red with the effort of tearing through boxes, looking through pockets, and from being caught.

"There's nothing to tell."

"How do you get out? Where do you go at night?"

Aurelie, with the air of someone who didn't like to waste time, sat on her bed smoking stolen cigarettes and fanning the air to disperse the smell. Maryse could hear their mother sighing on the stairs, but they both knew that she'd been beaten and wouldn't resume the fight with Aurelie for a day or two.

"I have a key to the apartment. I can let myself out, lock the door, and come back again. What's so sneaky about that?"

"So what's all this?" Maryse jerked her head in the direction of the pile of clothing.

"The idea is not to look like yourself, but some idea of yourself."

These things had to be hidden from her mother who, even if she found only the trousers and nothing more, would have had Aurelie locked up. Once she was on the street, Aurelie's guide was a former classmate whose independence had been the envy of the school they had long since left. If she could manage to slip away from her guardian at night, so could Aurelie. It would still be relatively early in the evening when she met her friend on boulevard Saint Germain, still filled with people. Wet iron grills, slick sidewalks, steamy windows, horses blinkered and slavering, snatches of conversation flew by as they made their way north past what were known as kebab joints, though she'd never actually seen the few Algerians said to run them, and boarded-up shop fronts toward the Café des Truands and Café des Assassins. Her friend was only a guide who over time became lost in the crowd and forgotten, but in trying to look like her, Aurelie acquired a closet full of long capes, high boots, and clothes their mother would have identified as the dress of a prostitute.

Her mother wasn't the only person who had to be avoided; Aurelie didn't realize domestic watchdogs took many forms. One night Maryse overcame fear and inertia and did follow her. Block after block, keeping her distance in case her sister looked back, being careful to stop short when Aurelie turned to check her reflection or have a conversation with an acquaintance she might run into, especially if the chance encounter was with someone who knew Maryse as well. Under the terms of this awkward surveillance Maryse learned her way down streets she'd never seen before, but once she followed Aurelie into the cafés, she no longer knew exactly what to do. She become conscious of wearing the childish clothes of someone who rarely left her mother's house, and she wore them without irony. A few people stared at her. She pretended not to notice.

From a rat's-eye view, each room at the Café des Assassins was a forest of chair legs and smoke. She eavesdropped on conversations that made reference to subjects she didn't understand, and in her initial impression of the crowd, its character was only one of belligerence, its members critical of presidents and bishops, colonial wars in Haiti, Tangiers, Algeria, and most of all they derided the academy, moldy and somnambulant, fortress of the sentimental and the nostalgic. As nights wore on and she thought about her mother sleeping alone in an empty house she believed to be safely occupied by her daughters, the small rooms of the cafés gradually revealed not only compelling and explosive qualities, but an escape from her mother's restrictions, her insistence on the appearance of buttoned-up virtue. In contrast, nothing was sacred in rooms that smelled of tobacco and spilled drinks and where every rectitude was subject to parody. Logic was suspended, women dressed as *sans culottes,* Marie Antoinette clowned with Quasimodo on the way to the guillotine, impostors claimed responsibility for bombings committed by the anarchist, Ravachol, and were laughed off the stage. Soon she went out all the time. Maryse listened to the constant hum of voices: nasal voices, metallic voices asking her to participate in stagings of all kinds in rooms kept so dark only faces lit from below as if by solitary torches were visible. She kept watch for Aurelie who, if she discovered the invasion of her territory, would have her thrown out on the street, and although Aurelie would be furious, Maryse had no doubt her sister would also enjoy her humiliation, and so she tried to keep her secret not only from her mother, but from her sister as well.

One night in the back, near the bar, she saw a small figure dressed in white from head to foot like a kind of drunk Pierrot, feet hooked around chair legs. The figure resembled Aurelie, but in the smoke and with her vision partially blocked by the crowd Maryse couldn't be sure it was her sister. She had no one to talk to, or perhaps didn't know how to talk to the knots of people on either side of her. A man grabbed her arm, *you in the boots, write on my shirt.* She put her hand on his back as she prepared to write. His shirt was made of white paper, but he sighed deeply at her touch, clearly enjoying her surprise and the rustling noise the paper garment made as he shrugged his shoulders or twisted his waist. The pen he handed her was sharp and pricked his skin when the surface was pierced. She could think of nothing to write and so pretended to form script, tracing loops, dotting nonexistent i's and crossing absent t's, drawing oversized swooshing accents. She could feel the movement of small muscles. If the weirdly gummy shirt was going to stick to him in jabs of ink and blood she didn't want to be the one to peel it off. He seemed to enjoy it when she stabbed him. From across the room she saw Aurelie leaning back in a chair, then her sister got up abruptly, left the room, and went out into the street. Maryse was stuck. She wanted to leave but couldn't risk running into her sister. The man in the paper shirt had moved on, and she inched to the door, thinking in the smoke it might not have been Aurelie at all. When she got to the street there was no sign of her sister.

In the morning she looked for traces of white powder on Aurelie's clothes, finding streaks of unknown origin which smelled salty when she pressed a dirty stiffened seam to her nose. Aurelie slept late. Her sister appeared to have shape and substance, but for Maryse she had begun to evaporate. A few days later Aurelie moved out of the house to live with a man who acted in films.

Her mother didn't understand what the man did for a living. A doctor, a lawyer, a shopkeeper, these were professions she understood, but her image of a man who performed in cheap entertainments was one of irresponsibility: a man who went to bars, who wore bright colors, who didn't wash.

"What are films?" Their mother screamed. "Bits of nothing with no future. Never mention your sister to me even in passing. Never say her name."

Left alone with her mother Maryse kept going to the cafés which offered her a promise of inclusion; she would do whatever anyone asked her to, but nobody read the pages she wrote furiously week after week in her journal. The hum of *Truants'* voices kept up, and her interpretation of their intent was a construction of fraternity: *us against them, us against them.* Maryse thought she was part of us, but as the nights passed she felt increasingly excluded from us, although she knew she wasn't *them,* and so she floated in a pronoun limbo not of her devising. The sympathy *us* felt for one another left her pushed to the margins, writing on paper-covered bodies, sticking pens into them, if that's what they wanted of her. She participated in spectacles but never initiated one herself. She saw Apollinaire, Satie, Marie Laurencin, and their many shadows. She recognized not only Alfred Jarry in the costume of a bicycle racer, tight trousers tucked into bright yellow shoes, but a few of his imitators as well, and none paid any attention to her.

At night Maryse lay in bed thinking about a riotous woman she might have invented for the sake of writing a story on a paper shirt, a woman who led a double life like herself. She would search the streets and piers for her, and once found, ask her how she managed to do it, to peel in half, as if this woman would even speak to her, a sleepwalker who really needed the comforts of home and hearth, a stray noctambule in funny clothing, who had invented her, after all. She wasn't a double. The double life was a failure, but it changed her and she learned something from it.

———

Maryse recognized the man as he came out of a shop carrying rolls of paper wrapped and bundled together with twine. Jules had a bottle nose like a fighter's although he wasn't a fighter at all. Without the usual beard, only a moustache, his features looked bare and clean. Because he caught her staring, she felt she had to say hello. He didn't remember her, appeared nervous at being identified, and asked what she wanted of him with more irritation than curiosity. She used to see him sitting against a back wall at Café des Assassins. She was on her way home and didn't really care whether he wanted to talk to her or not, but in the moments following her anonymous greeting, if it was possible to stumble in place, he did. A short, awkward man, not much taller than she, he didn't keep walking, and so she stopped also.

She wondered what made him so awkward, so unsure of what he wanted. Would that make one so hesitant? How could insecurity be expressed so physically, like a stutterer? He didn't go away, but followed her along the street, finally asking Maryse if she wanted to have coffee with him. She said no thanks, and continued on her way alone, leaving him to catch a carriage by himself.

A few weeks later they ran into one another again on a train platform, but this time Jules saw her first. Maryse was preoccupied by a journey and was trying to devise some kind of script. Each family member visited the elderly aunt in Montreuil separately with different expectations of how they should behave and what they would find when they arrived. Her mother refused to go at all. The aunt had been her husband's sister, and the two women hadn't spoken since their husbands' deaths. Aurelie had been the favorite and stood to inherit the house if she played her cards right. Maryse almost felt there was no point in going to Montreuil. Even with failing eyesight the aunt appeared to examine her body like a sculptor looking for flaws. It made Maryse very uncomfortable. Convinced there was nothing to be gained by the journey, but as a dutiful, if financially overlooked niece, she bought her ticket early in the morning to get the sorry trip over with.

Jules watched her at the ticket window, came up behind her, and introduced himself again. Maryse jumped. She wanted to pretend she didn't remember him, but knew she couldn't carry it off. Unable to think of any way out of it, she agreed to share a car with him. He changed his ticket to first class in order to travel with her and made a point of telling her he was doing so. His eagerness and gracelessness both pained and annoyed her, but she didn't offer to change her ticket. There were few travelers leaving the city at that hour. No one else entered their car, and he made no attempt to hide his glee at finding himself alone with her.

"Do you go to the Assassins often?" she asked, leaning her head against the window.

He told her he'd given up the cafés full of artists moon-lighting as anarchists on holiday. He detested the *blaguers* who never had a real job.

Maryse didn't know what to say to him, and not knowing what to say made her increasingly nervous.

"It's not so bad. I entered Café d'Enfer through the gaping open-mouth entrance and left by a back door." She explained her weariness, her sense that she was excluded from the party no matter how hard she tried to drink until dawn and say things that made no sense.

He nodded as if he understood her need to at least appear as if she were having a good time.

They began to meet often. Jules took to her to silent films, and she never told him that she actually preferred the realism of Pathé and the Lumière brothers to the fantastic *preconstructions,* as they were called, the filmic tricks of Georges Méliès. One evening he asked her to meet him in Montreuil. Intrigued, she told her mother she was going to spend the night with the old aunt, and she took a crowded late train out to the suburb. He met her at the station, and they walked the short distance to the glass structure that housed Star Films. It was dark by the time Maryse arrived; everyone had left for the day. The silent glass building looked ethereal. Jules picked the lock easily and they broke into the studios. They walked through underwater landscapes, castles of pirates, laboratories of madmen. Jules lifted her onto a wooden rocket destined for the left eye of a moon that Méliès himself had painted. Maryse leaned over and, feel-ing like a figure from a sentimental postcard print, kissed him on the mouth. Jules stepped back, gave the rocket a slight push so it swung gently back and forth for a few minutes, then he lifted her out of it. The two of them spent the night lying in the midst of a lunar landscape, newly painted for a shoot due to begin the next day. In the middle of the night Maryse awoke to the smell of paint, with starkly outlined black and white stars and planets overhead and the sound of heavy, determined footsteps getting closer. They fled through the studio and made their way back to the city.

———·•·———

"At school I used to carve obscene words into my desk, and, stupidly, gouged my name and the date underneath so everyone knew what I'd done. I was caught and punished, which meant staying late and being caned."

Maryse felt a wave of sympathy for the battered boy, exactly the response Jules was banking on.

"In revenge I made up a play in which I dressed as my teacher and parodied his speech. Stuffing a pillow under my shirt, I made a long nose out of stiff paper, and spoke in circles about astronomy and Napoléon's surrender at Sedan. The laughter among my classmates was stupendous. I drew cryptic diagrams on a chalkboard set up behind my house, as if I were demonstrating for the class. Everybody howled at them, and in this way other boys were drawn to me. I invented more roles. Everyone, even the most shy, wanted to be part of the parody. So, for me, I've learned pleasure can grow out of pain. So I'm willing to wait for you."

This story was almost identical to Alfred Jarry's well-known schoolboy parodies, but Maryse pretended she didn't know this.

"Do you still write plays?" She drained her glass, hoping to turn the conversation elsewhere.

"No. When my parents died I was sent to Paris to live with my uncle and his family. I no longer had an audience, nor did I have a subject to parody. It's difficult to make things up out of the blue."

Jules talked in a stream that give her no possible entry. Noticing she wasn't paying close attention, he asked her a question that caused her to snap back to earth.

"You need cash and you're unhappy. Would you like to make a lot of money, Maryse?"

She moved her chair slightly away from him.

"I want you to work for me. My uncle used to say that the boulevards of Paris are paved with blocks of cash but we're all standing on our heads in the middle of a street and can't get to any of it, but if you're clever, you can pry one of those bricks loose with only one hand. I can do it, believe me, but I need someone to help me, someone with brains, dexterity, flexible hands."

He took one of her hands in his and studied her palm, stroked her fingers. Too much time passed, and she withdrew it in order to finish her second drink.

"You have beautiful hands."

He used words like *verité* with a kind of hardness, but Maryse hadn't, she was certain, ever hear the word *fraude*. She would have remembered. Again he offered her a lot of money, and she agreed to his terms, although she had missed the word *collusion*.

Jules hadn't told her that at school he had been called *Gasconade,* meaning blather, and that the name had stuck for many years. Every action he took came with an explanation, but the explanations had ways of veering into terrain that had only tangential connections to the original subject, but Maryse remained interested. As she walked from room to barely furnished room in his apartment, she said nothing about the house she'd left behind, while he discussed the history of his business, how he inherited it, what he did when he arrived in Paris from the provincial town where he had been orphaned. He spoke as a kind of distraction, as if he didn't want Maryse to look too closely.

"To most people my uncle seemed the picture of concern: a solid citizen, a salesman of ship engines who also worked as a notary public, penning signatures for illiterate workers, a man who went to mass and whose opinions were as square and conventional as paving stones, yet this image couldn't have been more false. His children drove him mad. One was a chronic petty thief, but because of his father's position he was generally treated with some lenience. As he grew up he turned into a layabout. His wife was a fountain of aphorisms and banalities," Jules said as if trying out the phrase.

"One trivial remark followed the next until anyone would feel he or she would go mad. I used to fall asleep at the table as soon as she opened her mouth. The discussion of inanities, the price of X or Y, were, I suppose, a bulwark against the disorderly life of his son, the deadbeat brother, yet my uncle couldn't stand the flood tide of talk coming from his wife and police reports about the other, so he began to lead a double life. At first I couldn't figure out what I was supposed to be doing with this family so I would sit around drawing caricatures of anonymous citizens: a man from the Bourse, a woman observed window shopping across the street. I was bored, too. Seeing I was quick with a pen my uncle began to take me with him to the shipyards. As I proved curious and a good listener he confided in me rather than in his lazy son. At this time he was working out a scheme to back the pirating of ships on little-known straits, and to have the ownership papers changed while still at sea, so the ship, then transformed, became his. During the day he appeared the same as he ever was, stolid and patient, but his family drove him to seek another identity. Like his ships, he adopted another name, began to work out of a second office, kept nocturnal hours and, in secret, married another woman. At night he dressed in expensive but worn clothes, and used a combination of populist, slangy, and arcane figures of speech. He leered and rolled his eyes as no one ever saw him do in daylight."

"Perhaps his wife led a double life also."

"No, she didn't live long. The shipping venture made him a lot of money but became too risky, and he had to retire from it. In his later years he developed a quieter occupation. The rare book business provided traffic on little-known straits as well. Books, like ships, could be disguised, and again I was enlisted to help him out in the trade."

In this way Maryse was made to understand that Jules had learned his vocation from an uncle who had more schemes than sleeves to keep them up, a man who promised easy money. The city was chocked to the gills with paper to be had for almost nothing: old books which could be taken apart and re-assembled, cheap modern editions easily aged, and so a book which appeared over one hundred years old might actually be of relatively recent publication. The city was full of foreigners who couldn't speak the language well, if at all, and *faubouriens* who lived outside the metropolis but ventured into it once in a while, just as Jules himself once had. When his customers were Americans or provincials Jules offered Rimbaud, poet of the Revolution, killed during the Terror, or Verlaine, favorite of Lafayette, for sale at high prices. Jules was a persuasive sales-man. He gained customer's confidence easily, sensed anxieties and reservations quickly, knew how to give assurance of quality, and was quick on the street when he needed to be. He himself was rarely fleeced and never caught. The fin-de-siècle desire for the antique was overwhelming, and in a reflective moment Jules told Maryse he considered his clients' obsession with looking backward the result of being on the brink of a new century. She disagreed. In the age of electricity, when tiny things, molecules, were found and named, what appeared rare and unique would only become more dear, representative of a collection of un-known and unknowable oddities.

Nostalgia is your friend, his uncle had said. As a salesman he had learned how to imitate the signs of class. English-style bowlers, waistcoats, moustache wax, all of it, and he occasionally found himself believing in those signs, wanting to be the thing he wasn't. Don't be afraid of the word *arriviste,* his uncle said, the parvenu is always someone else, probably your customers who will buy rare books by the yard and never read them. If the circulation of money could be compared to a river, his uncle proposed a dam while Jules could think no further ahead than the next swim. A dam required work and planning.

Jules's uncle, a man who was said to have no enemies, was found dead in an alley. His partner disappeared that same night. What was unusual, Jules told Maryse, was this: no pens were found on the body. He always carried several, and not the valuable kind anyone would steal. Maryse imagined the old man had signed too many signatures not his own, but she said nothing to Jules. The shipping money must have been lost somehow. His uncle's "dam" paid for the burial, but little else. Those who came to his funeral had nothing but praise for him, *a man beyond reproach*. That was how he had wanted to be known and remembered. Jules was on his own.

———·—·———

"A man who buys and sells rare books?" Maryse's mother screamed. "He'll leave you without a penny."

She disappeared after Maryse's wedding, rarely emerging from her house. She gave up on her children and barely spoke to either daughter again.

———·—·———

Hearing the coffee boil over, Maryse ran from the window and took the pot off the stove. Liquid bubbled into pools, and a sticky brown film covered the burner. Her daughter, Caroline, sitting close to the stove, absorbed in tearing pages from an old book, seemed deaf, unaware she was in danger from a scalding burn. Maryse shook her by the shoulders, but she twisted away, knocking over a stack of books and nearly overturning a tub filled with hot water. Pouring coffee into the tub, face buried in steam, Maryse watched water dilute the color. Their hands, faces, and clothing smelled of coffee. There was no end to it. After sulking in the hall, Caroline returned, and according to their system, handed her mother four or five pages with exaggerated yet sarcastic care as if the leaves might crumble into dust

232

at any minute. Maryse dropped them into the tub and stirred the papers with a long wooden spoon.

Promises of piles of currency disappeared in ripples of liquid. Expenses exceeded their income and debts were spiraling out of control. She checked a few other leaves drying flat on a table far away from any window. In the tedium she separated thoughts from her body and imagined herself a figure in a melodrama, her miserable portrait formed in steam over a cup entitled *Slave of Java*. When dry, the slightly warped papers would be dashed with a few drops of black coffee from a stronger brew. Lying on a nearby chair were pieces of limp, battered parchment Jules had picked up from the floor of a bookbinder's shop. While Maryse waited for the papers to dry she scrubbed the stove in a frenzy, back and forth as if, Caroline thought, she were rowing a boat during an electrical storm

The meticulous process of assembling what passed for rare books and the routine Jules had developed became a form of rule, a series of timings and physical laws that ran their lives. As far as she was concerned, it was simpler to bake the pages in the oven. The results appeared just as antique as the coffee procedure, but Jules insisted this method produced objects which were too brittle and could be easily detected as fakes. He peddled their rebound books to dealers, some of whom knew they were faked, and to others who didn't, tourists or whoever might believe he offered singular volumes. Jules kept a list of his sources and their addresses folded into an eyeglass case. He came and went from the apartment, keeping up with his business, selling in private residences and on the street.

Maryse had seen a lithograph of a morphine addict sticking a needle into her leg called *Eater of Dreams*. She had heard of caffeine addiction that ended in death by poisoning, and felt she had become this kind of addict, not by choice, but because someone had twisted her arm behind her, someone had handed her a needle. Remembering the spontaneity with which she had taken the needle seemed ironic to her now, but she didn't feel like a prisoner, believing she could walk out anytime.

Bertillon, a small man with closely cropped hair and a big moustache, wheeled a blackboard into the assembly hall and began to draw. Isolated lamps shone on his chalk lines and the white backs of his hands.

"My system will prove that Dreyfus forged his own handwriting. The *bordereau*, the list of artillery secrets, the letter he offered to sell to the Germans, was written in an amalgam of his wife's and brother's handwriting. If you follow the pattern of this trench," he drew a series of lines, *the trench,* which led to the center of diagram that looked like a maze with redan-shaped branches and crenellated wings, impossible to read without expert intervention, "at the center is the arsenal of the habitual spy." He pointed out features of the accused's handwriting then drew another series of parallel lines, *the corridors.* Arrows led all over the surface of the blackboard. Measurements from tails of letters to upper loops were taken, calculations made in the margins of the diagram.

"I see the evidence of self-forgery as indisputable proof that the Syndicate was involved," someone in the room said.

"The operation was planned a year in advance; the Dreyfus family spent hours practicing a script that combined features of each member's handwriting, hoping that the amalgam would elude identification." Fingers traced Bertillon's corridors and channels, convinced. There was a murmur of agreement like the hum of machinery.

"Let's call him D, not because there is any doubt about his identity but for the sake of brevity and because the incriminating D is how he signed the letter offering to sell French military secrets that was found in the trash of the German embassy. Look at this," Bertillon pointed to his labyrinthine diagram, *"D is trying to retreat to a citadel of graphic rebuses."* The generals and others applauded. Bertillon wiped his chalky fingers on his jacket, bowed, and left the room. As soon as the door shut behind him, someone in the back near the door coughed.

"There is no unity on the subject of who wrote what." The speaker was barely visible apart from the glowing end of a cigarette and the curve of a lapel. "Another expert compared D's handwriting to the letter stolen from the German embassy. He found no similarity between the two." The lit end of the cigarette bounced to emphasize no similarity. "In his opinion D couldn't possibly have written that document."

"Yes, I know your expert, an expert who works for the Bank of France, an expert with ties to the Syndicate." Felix Gribelin, the archivist for the Section of Statistics, stood up and hammered at the dissenting opinion. "We aren't naive here, randomly trying to tie pontoons together. We know how things work, how patterns are established and connections made. D has ties to the Syndicate, as does the Bank of France, therefore a handwriting expert who works for the Bank of France will not give a reliable judgment in this case."

The Section of Statistics, the headquarters of the French intelligence agency, had an immediate concern with the trial, but as the room filled with smoke, the archivist wanted only to go out on the terrace. He wanted the meeting to end; there was no more point to it. He was convinced of D's guilt, but didn't want to appear to jump to conclusions. The divisiveness of the speaker, whom he couldn't quite make out, was irritating. He wanted to know the man's name. At the same time what he wanted most of all was to be in his office downstairs.

"Felix makes a point," one of the generals nodded at him. "Bertillon is head of the Prefecture's Service of Judiciary Identity. We depend on him. His system for identifying criminals based on bone measurements and numerical theory reflects the infallible logic of algebra."

The room burst into applause, not quite unanimous, but close to it.

"He has a reputation as the founder the Anthropometric Department of the Police."

Felix stood up for a second time. "Whether we trust him or

not doesn't matter, but when the judges hear his blackboards and diagrams roll down the hall, they'll remember that Bertillon has been called 'the stubborn defender of the unintelligible.' That's a fact. There's nothing you or I can do about it."

Felix peered into the dark recesses of the conference room. The lit cigarette continued to emphasize his points. "Remember your numbers man was publicly embarrassed by the failure of his system in the La Boussinere case of a second will. A blind man could have detected that forgery. How can we be sure that he hasn't become trigger happy, claiming that every document that passes through his office is either a bad copy or a self-forgery?"

"A man who covers his tracks, who has an overly elaborate explanation for everything, isn't a good witness," another voice trailed off.

Felix remembered the case of multiple wills. He doubted others would, but they might notice the chalky stripes down the front of Bertillon's jacket as he left the room, and in noticing that the man with the passion for algebra was a slob, conclusions might be reached about the undeniably ridiculous aspect of his theories.

"We need more evidence."

"What are the informers bringing in?"

"There was a report that D frequented the Café des Assassins, gambled, kept prostitutes."

"That's very good, very useful."

"No, not at all. The report was about a Max Dreyfus, no relation to the accused. Max D. had a police record. Our D has none. He is wealthy, sees only a few close friends. He has no motive."

Everyone had information to sell about Dreyfus. Passing through many hands of various nationalities the so-called secrets Felix was asked to pay for often turned into nothing more than old shoes stuffed with domestic shopping lists. His desk was spread with documents when he called his colleague, Major Mercier du Paty de Clam, whose close-set eyes and severely pointed nose were all centered in a face left with too much space, too many broad margins. A man who liked chaos, when du Paty couldn't find confusion he would create it. He had arrested D with enthusiasm, never telling him why he was being taken away. If his pleasure was staked on something as flimsy as handwriting, measures had to be taken to ensure that pleasure wouldn't be squandered. Brought into Felix's confidence, he calmed the archivist's nerves. Du Paty was convinced of D's guilt and therefore believed the script of the letter found in the German embassy matched D's handwriting, and the problem of a motive could be determined another time. Taking the situation in hand, du Paty had strolled down to D's cell armed with a variety of writing instruments and different kinds of paper. *Try writing lying on your back. Now turn over and pull your legs under you.* Du Paty made D write in as many positions as he could invent so as to elicit or force as many samples of D's hand. Precision instruments, originally designed for lunar photography, were brought in to analyze the handwriting. Du Paty, swishing around Felix's desk, laughed at the results, and Felix joined in. *We'll tell everyone D forged his own hand. That's what happened.* Du Paty informed Bertillon of D's guilt long before the handwriting expert could look at the samples, and du Paty, who knew everybody, was believed.

Felix sorted through documents as he waited for du Paty, only to be told that the general had left for the evening. At eight o'clock Felix walked some blocks west from his office on the rue de Lille to the Ile Saint Louis where he took his dinner regularly in a small restaurant, a recessed corner behind law offices, near the end of the island. After being served he made it a practice to write down what he had eaten and what he paid for each item. *Escalope de foie gras aux truffes, 2 ft. 50. Poulet a la Grèque 8 fr. Vin Graves, 6 fr.* When he was finished he asked for a cognac, insisting it be poured from the bottom of a nearly empty pyramid-shaped bottle so he would be ensured a larger drink for the same price. He was convinced larger portions came from the broader base of the bottle. Dinner completed, he took a cab back to his office in the Section of Statistics to find the building nearly empty. He had an office in the War Ministry, a large office, one he enjoyed. During the twenty years he'd worked at his post Felix had learned to be both memory bank and camera, reliable and silent. With an eye for minutia, he would spend hours recopying and filing documents into the night. Two notebooks kept by the Section of Statistics were part of his province. Notebook A cataloged the names and addresses of adult aliens living in France. Notebook B was a directory of residents who were suspected of espionage, regardless of whether they were aliens or French citizens. Tonight Felix turned the pages of Notebook B, reading over his notes until late into the night.

How is a camera like a gun? He had seen a camera squirt water at a man, right in his eye, and he had laughed at the joke in spite of himself. The camera/weapon had appeared in a film, not a presentation by an arms manufacturer who entered a conference room with a portfolio full of diagrams and codes. Felix turned to M in Notebook B.

Before he made films Méliès drew cartoons under the name Geo. Smile. In his file Felix found a caricature drawn by Smile, a cartoon of General Boulanger. The figure was inflated and blown apart by gusts of air from a white bellows labeled *pression electorate, a* nonsense tautology. Judges priests, ordinary men of all kinds, the drawing implied, blew through the lethal piping which lead to the bellows. The engraving had been featured on the cover of a magazine, *La Griffe.* Following the cartoon Felix found a handwritten note.

If we categorize his films based on actual events (the American interventions in Cuba and the Philippines, the Dreyfus trial, and so on) as subversive, then his imaginary films, too, must bear greater scrutiny. When is a trip to the moon more than a trip to the moon? We say with confidence there is more here than meets the eye. Examine his film The Man with the Rubber Head. *The exploding head, disembodied and recalcitrant, had, through an optical trick, been Méliès, own, as if under the cloak of a joke, Méliès could take revenge on his double. Note: subject calls his Kinetograph "my machine gun." (Incidentally, the camera is a counterfeit.) His motto is* The Whole World Within Reach. *He is known to run Star Films like a crown dictator, and one can conclude that he in some way identifies with the authorities parodied in his cartoons.*

Was his double, doomed and flammable, supposed to be a reference to a darker and perhaps exploitable side of Méliès? Could he control his double or did the double that he persistently created in film after film, control him? Felix wondered if the double could be recruited. He doubted it. He needed someone meticulous and obsessed with small details, someone who led such a narrow life that he or she would never be suspected, the sort of citizen whose loyalty to the army would never be questioned by themselves or by others. He suspected this ideal profile of a forger belonged only to either an idiot savant or an impressionable provincial too ham-handed to commit thoughtful, artistic forgery. Another profile of a potential candidate presented a second option: a criminal, refined and educated, yet still a criminal who could be blackmailed into writing whatever was needed to add to the Dreyfus file. Felix returned to his notes.

Méliès has a cameraman who sells obscene photographs on the side.

Felix needed someone whose eyes were in his or her fingers. A pornographic arranger, though inducible, probably wouldn't have the delicate touch.

Méliès employs an assistant, Fabien Leclerc. The file contained a photograph clipped from *La Libre Parole. He lives alone, separated from his wife and daughter. Leclerc has been observed staring into the river for long periods of time, but he never jumps. His impulses are anarchic. He might have once asked why there are rules which are only selectively held to, and he answered that question by working for a man who clearly believes in none, including gravity, and the most elemental physical laws. He is well suited to the anarchistic humor and chaotic at-*

mosphere of Star Films. Is known to collect Revolutionary costumes, but is easily duped into believing he bought Robespierre's shirt, for example, when it could have been anyone's. He does meticulous work. It is usually destroyed within a short period of time, and another project is begun. If there is a banana peel in the vicinity, this citizen will slip on it.

Felix needed someone who drew well or who was clever with penmanship, a man whose dexterous fingers were in so many pies that he would have to be careful not to engage in contradictory interests. He wanted to create someone like an informer who would be in his pocket, one who would have to tread with caution. The trial was no secret, everyone followed it and took one side or the other, and so an automaton, a man who wouldn't ask questions, would be hard to find. He capped his inkwell as if letters might escape from it; in its depths he imagined a soup of half-formed sentences more dangerous than a ton of dynamite. Scratching his thinning hair with one hand, he poured himself a brandy with the other. Footsteps pattered down the hall. A door shut, then the section was quiet again. Apart from night cleaners in another wing of the building Felix was alone. He needed someone who had something he could hang over his or her head, saying, *if you don't do this for me, there will be consequences.*

In Felix's employ there were men who saw spies everywhere, but none of them knew anything really incriminating about Dreyfus. There was bucktoothed Brucker whose job it was to keep German diplomats under surveillance, and he in turn employed an army of maids, messengers, butlers, and errand boys; professional flies on the wall who felt it their responsibility to overhear conversations, poke around in drawers, pockets, hatbands, and steam open letters, but so far they hadn't turned up anything of value for the case. Documents would have to be created. He needed a writer with a facile hand.

What he did have disturbed him: something called *le petit bleu* had fallen into his hands, stolen from the German embassy garbage. It was addressed to a German attaché, Schwarzkoppen, and it was from, not D, but the real spy, Z.

The entries in Notebook B kept Felix up for several nights. His light could be seen from the street, an illuminated window set back on the third floor. A short woman in a felt hat slipped out the back door of the German embassy carrying battered shopping bags. Rats waltzed in the gutter under her feet. She noticed Felix's silhouette at the window, wrapped her coat more tightly around her chest, lit a cigarette, and walked on.

———•———

Stacks of postcards lay on Felix's desk. First he looked through satirical postcards of men with big heads and tiny bodies shoveling shit, looking for what the caption said was "the pearl of truth." It was a reference to the trial, and the three caricatured shovelers were recognizable as men he knew and respected to one degree or another, and so the caricatures made him bristle. He thumbed through a series of cards entitled *History of a Crime* and tried to read a handwritten message scrawled on the back of one of them. He was annoyed by a drawing of the minister of war, a scythe in his back, *Au Beaucoup de Faux* written under the blade. *Faux* could mean forgery or scythe. He wanted to humiliate, to force the hand of one of these postcard artists, make him work for the Ministry; he was looking for the thing he could hang over a head, but all he came up with were cheap prints, photomechanical ephemera, and lousy puns.

The Dreyfus trial confirmed Felix's belief in the Syndicate, a vast network of businessmen, lawyers, shopkeepers, theater owners, actors, all kinds of people from bankers to newsboys. No one was exempt from suspicion of membership, but if a citizen crossed the street when a church came into view, that pretty much guaranteed association with the Syndicate as far as he was concerned. Felix believed in the magnitude of the Syndicate, and if anyone questioned its far-reaching influence he gave as an example the incident of a contractor who cheated the army, bilking it of great sums of money by supplying faulty hardware, yet the man was never prosecuted for his extortion. This was one of many examples that Felix felt proved the Syndicate protected its own. Anxious as he was to expose the conspiracy, the network of stool pigeons who worked for the second floor was, in his opinion, less than satisfactory. Informants were usually paid by the piece, creating an enterprise any eavesdropper or riffler could dip in and out of and many did. Crooks who needed cash or revenge put on a patriotic face and endeavored to acquire information which might be useful and lucrative. Felix was convinced that ideas about allegiance, loyalty, and commitment grew flexible, or at least highly subject to who found what in whose garbage, whose mail, and what they did with it.

According to the Section of Statistics, apocrypha didn't exist. Felix squared the postcards so they formed neat stacks, bound them with twine, and took out a set of pens.

He searched Notebook B for information on a prisoner he had interrogated years ago, but he couldn't recall her name. She remained frustratingly anonymous, but he remembered fragments of her speech. She had detected conspiracies between the two of them that he would not have imagined.

When is a bed not a bed?

He had looked in her cell, seen dried blood on her dress, signs of torture, but her pain had been entirely invisible to him, even while he participated in her interrogation. Her wounds, he had told her, were self-inflicted. He shut Notebook B and called his secretary who did remember her name and brought in her file. Some pages she'd written had been found and confiscated.

Everything in this cell apes the idea of home, house, a shelter. There is an iron bed with a mat on it, home to bugs of all nations, one chair, and even a basin. I've had my head beaten against these so they are no longer signs of comfort: bed, chair, metal rim. The signs of homeness ridicule a desire to go home. In spite of accommodations which imitate a residence

I'm certainly not in one now. A bricked-over window is only the footprint of a real window. Hatch marks on a wall parody a calendar and the idea of deadlines or pressing time. Limericks, names, verse scrawled overhead mimic the idea of narrative, something to read at night whenever night is. Something to read before bed. The objects in this cell bear so little connection to their definition that some other prisoner, an English/French lexicographer, wrote a list in a desperate attempt to remember definitions and make them stick.

le logis – home
la loi – law
la logique
loin – far, distant
louche – dubious, suspicious
louer – to rent, to praise

Or perhaps he or she was bored or could only make L sounds with their tongue and broken teeth. I think the message is as follows: a doubtful or distorting version of law which is not law has provided me/us with this home which is not a home. When a person is in physical pain, logic is a far, distant thing. How can renting be confused with praise? My relationship with my cell is not one of rent paid out, but it isn't a space I own either. In English someone wrote: home, hostage, hostile. A slice of alphabetical coding I don't understand. Where is I, J, and K?

Since my body is an agent of pain I hate it, I sting myself, bite my tail, and what's worse is that none of this is private. You and your doctors and soldiers watch all of my most private functions and agonies.

Your questions are allied to the administration of pain so sharp and all encompassing I'm left inarticulate, reduced to cells and sensors at your service. I imagine our sessions as a kind of dramatic dialogue that begins with the sound of a door opening. The parts are well rehearsed. The questions matter so much to you. My confession is your possession. You've taken my body as a testing site without my consent.

I'm altogether sensored.

Had she called him a nightmare with a human face? Or had he been Torturer with a Human Face? War with a Human Face? He couldn't remember. Cliché after cliché emerged from all that nonsense, delirium, that absence of language. He had shut her door soundlessly. That really scares them, he had been told. She was a them, and that was all.

He remembered the rest of that night just as clearly. Afterward he went to the opera and nearly wept for Mimi when she died of cold in the snow. He hummed an aria in the cab and watched men and women on the street as he passed them. Although it was late, there were a number of people still to be seen out the window of his carriage. One woman walked quickly and appeared to be talking to herself. She was well dressed and alone; he might have offered her a lift but didn't. A man crossed in front of the cab abruptly, in danger of being run over, yet smiling to himself, oblivious. Felix's driver had yelled at him. Felix envied the man's absentminded oblivion. He remembered that he was pleased to arrive at his home. He ran up the stone steps, undressed, and sat on his bed, unsure of what to do. He played with a brass reading lamp, turning if off and on until he finally decided to lie down. The base of the electric lamp was in the shape of Winged Victory, the bulb, concealed by a green shade, had been placed where her head would have been. He hadn't fallen asleep immediately but reassembled the scenes he had just watched, inserting himself in small roles, dressed as a tailor or soldier. Apart from the pleasure and gratification of imaginary curtain calls, which was immense, the idea of performing on a stage frightened him. Drapery would brush behind him, he would look up at points of light on the balconies, then he would bow deeply with gratitude and humility. Somewhere in the audience he was even applauded by the anonymous prisoner, *this is a form of pleasure for you.* She wasn't referring to the opera.

Now, sitting in his office, cognac-colored light filtered through his glass and fell on Notebook B. Still taking imaginary bows, he remembered that she had once worked in the Section of Statistics until something about her had been discovered. She had been a Communard whose background had escaped research by the Section, or she had belonged to a Marxist cell in Belleville. He wasn't sure; his usually exceptional memory was failing. He did remember one of the jailers saying, one man's informant is another man's hero, what can you do? He was looking for an artistic sort of writer, not an informer, and went back to his reading.

The body lay sprawled on steps just below the level of the sidewalk. On his way back from the bindery Jules saw her as he looked down. He hadn't heard any footsteps running away as he approached the street from place Maubert, he was certain. The woman's big legs had folded under her in an awkward angle, and he thought of calling for help, but the street was empty. At first he did nothing but stare. He leaned over the iron gate to see if she might still be alive. Her torn skirt fluttered in the hot breeze. It covered her face and then blew away in another direction so the bruised features became fully visible. The inert body had a heavily made up, mannish face. A camera had fallen down the steps near the basement door. Jules stepped over bent knees, picked up the camera and examined it. Part was nicked, but it didn't seem to be badly damaged. Sticking the camera under his arm, he climbed the steps, skirting the body, and walked quickly away from it just as the door at the foot of the steps opened a crack.

There was a secret file filled with forgeries that contained copies of so-called originals written by employees of the Section of Statistics. Each copy had been authenticated. The General Staff guaranteed each copy had been made faithfully and reproduced a genuine original. When the minister of war was to leave the General Staff, he wanted to be sure the dossier on Dreyfus would, should it be examined in the future, contain no cause to doubt Dreyfus's guilt. A dossier of 365 documents were added to the file and these documents had to be copied in turn. The need for writers was urgent and kept Felix awake at night. The material in the files was extremely sensitive. He did some of the writing himself. Undated papers were dated and each document was numbered and initialed by a different general. Some dates were changed. The file was designed to show that Dreyfus passed on valuable documents wherever he went. Leaks were made to seem to follow the trajectory of his assignments with calculated regularity. Felix felt confident his files were as solid as polished rocks.

"What's on your shoe?"

"Dirt."

"It doesn't look like dirt, and your shoes smell as if you walked through a slaughterhouse."

"Why would I do that?"

"I don't know."

"Polish the shoes and then make some coffee."

"Balzac died of coffee poisoning," Maryse said.

"The man is feverish, said the doctor to Monsieur Gault; "but there's always a bit of fever in an accused person at this stage, and," he whispered to the sham Spaniard, "to me it's always a proof that there is a criminal guilt of some kind."

Jules tapped Balzac's words so they sank in brackish water, a murky substance which had the capacity to pull the wool over his customers' eyes.

There were some documents that Felix thought best to destroy. He did so reluctantly, imagining trees arriving from the Loire valley by train to be milled and turned into pulp. For higher-grade paper, rags were used. Yet experiments had been made with recycling paper, mashing it, repulping, returning the inky document to a clean piece of paper once again. So the mill becomes like a giant moth which will eat everything: plants, old clothes, lice, secondhand books, cigar wrappers, medicine bottle labels, stacks of old newspapers whose headlines proclaimed the Franco-Prussian War, the strike of Paris World's Fair workers, the first celebration of May Day, old love letters. *(No! I might want those back!* Oops. Too late.) Everything is swallowed, no sentence or word can resist mastication. In the middle of a pristine white or cream-colored page, one will not find the ridge of a cryptic watermark or fragments of words: *possibil, etoricat, your assig.*

An inkwell bubbling over with a morass of troubling or convincing words was no match for this kind of erasure. Felix saw himself as a kind of Goliath standing between the chomping jaws of one and the ink-stained press beds of the other. Take consolation in responsibility, Felix said to himself. Stories convincingly formed, backed up by hard evidence, will always ring true. Then the anonymous prisoner stood opposite him, jamming both the presses and shredder.

Or she stood on the side of the stage, faced the audience, and explained to all those rows of upturned faces exactly what was going on behind painted flats as he pretended to sing his heart out.

Louer, logis, louche
hospital, hostage, hotel

Looking out the window he thought he saw a man looking up at his window, just in the shadows outside the gate. He rang for his maid who was slow, and when she did come in with a tray she seemed somnambulant, her thoughts elsewhere as if she had been hypnotized. Her cap was askew, and it took her several

247

minutes to answer simple questions. Perhaps the man had been waiting for her. If a man haunted his garden it could mean surveillance just as easily as encounter. When she left the room he hummed a few bars from *La Boheme* over his glass, then, drink in hand, he closed his curtains. The man was gone.

"This man claims you tried to sell him an eighteenth-century edition of Mallarmé's *Divagations* including 'A Throw of the Dice Will Never Eliminate Chance,' a poem not even found in the book." Feix examined the accused's hands and eyes. The man appeared slightly athletic, but like a cat burglar, not like a pugilist. He had a reason for taking interest in what may only have been a nuisance arrest or a minor charge of theft.

"No, he said the book was a copy of *Pere Ubu,* story of a Cistercian."

Jules recognized the speaker, a little man in a black suit who appeared to fawn over Felix Gribelin and who spoke much better and more formal French now in a dark, high-ceilinged office than he had on the street. He didn't know why he had been taken to the Section of Statistics rather than a precinct house. Gribelin had the curtains drawn. Desk lamps made small pools of light. Jules tried to scrutinize blocks of figures in a painting of a Napoléonic battle back in the dim recesses of the office. He didn't know exactly who his interrogator was beyond a name, but the large room was a sign that Felix Gribelin was a man of some stature, and this was puzzling to him. His crime was minor and easily dealt with in a police station. What did a man who worked in rooms like these really care about small-time cheats?

"We misunderstood each other. I was trying to sell him a camera." He had tried to throw the camera into the book deal just to unload the instrument, damaged and useless without a tripod. Jules hadn't expected the man in the black suit to go to the police. He had always bet on the embarrassment of his dupes.

To his surprise when he was brought to the police, special interest had been taken in the camera. He couldn't imagine why.

"Where did you find the camera?" Before Jules could answer Felix turned and dismissed the man who'd made the charges leading to his arrest, making it clear he was no longer needed. The case would be taken care of without his testimony. Jules watched his disappointment and hesitation at the door. Unable to witness a miscreant's full humiliation, he hovered like an afterimage until Felix finally waved him away. Turning back to Jules, Felix repeated his question.

"I do business with a book dealer who often asks me to sell things for him."

"Did you look at the lens?"

"Why?"

"Did you look at it?"

"Yes."

"Why didn't you clean the glass?"

"I didn't think there was anything wrong with it."

"What do you call this?" He pointed to a smudge on the lens, but in doing so, left one of his own fingerprints on it.

"How should I know?"

"Glue. Glue for parchment. It's sort of brownish color when it dries." Felix took a book off a shelf and ripped it so the binding split. Fragments of white thread from its stitching and flakes of white glue fell onto his desk.

"The lens cap was on when it was given to me."

"You were seen at *La Libre Parole* last week."

"What could I have been trying to sell them?"

"You were seen at their printing works, near place Maubert."

"No, I was in Lyon."

"How did you get there with a railroad strike on?"

"I walked."

"From Paris? You're a fast walker, and you could walk fast to jail. You could disappear in jail."

"Who'd I taken it from then?"

"A woman who was found dead in the alley adjacent to the printers."

"No, I don't think she was."

"Dead? Indeed she was dead, as you were the first to know."

"Didn't look like a girl to me."

———•———

Jules poured coffee-water out the window and turned the tub over to dry. He gathered up stained pages and old books, tied them together with lengths of twine, and stacked them in the hall near their upstairs neighbor's door. When the table was swept clear he laid out pens, bottles of ink, pieces of gummed transparent paper, onionskin, several kinds of writing paper, and graph paper with blue-gray squares. There was a box of letters and other papers said to have been gleaned or stolen from the wastebaskets of the German embassy. Jules was to cut, paste, scratch out, recopy, and construct a series of documents that would create crushing proof, Felix had said, against a known guilty party. As far as initials were concerned, P's had to be changed to D's, and Z's left out altogether. Jules pulled a handful of creased letters out of the box with attached explanations and instructions. The instructions read:

> These love letters were from an Italian military attaché, Panizzardi; to his German counterpart, Schwarzkoppen. Panizzardi signs his letters Alexandrine. Construct a letter from these fragments that will make reference to D and payments made to him.

Jules poured a cup of coffee, looked out the window for a few minutes, then returned to the papers and began to read more fragments, footprints of some kind of love affair between the two men. He had no idea who any of these people were or who the initials referred to.

My beautiful bugger. I was in bliss, and am returning to you the three pieces. Farewell my beautiful bugger. Your friend.

Jules put the fragment aside then selected another letter. There was a part missing between the two halves of this one.

My dear Bugger,
I am forwarding to you you-know-what. As soon as you left, I studied the questions of those called and saw that certain questions of address, etcetera are all subordinated to a major one whose direction is this...
. . . for it must never be known that one attaché has dealings with another. Farewell, my little dog. Everything.

The last of the three was a whole letter, but it seemed an unimportant note.

My Very Dear Friend,
Last night I ended up calling the doctor, who has forbidden me to go out. Since I am unable to visit you tomorrow, I am asking you to come to my home in the morning, since P . . . has brought me many things of great interest and since we have only ten days to us, we shall try to divide the work.
Try then to tell the ambassador that you can't give up.
All yours,
Alexandrine

Jules practiced his calligraphy, drawing upper- and lower-case letters, numbers, filling sheets of paper with lines of words. He knew handwriting experts mainly paid attention to the outer shapes of letters. When Felix asked for results he told him he was practicing, and in this way the uncertainty of what he had been asked to do could be put aside while he sat alone in his apartment drawing letters over and over just to pass time without ever looking at the examples he'd been given, talking to himself about how he felt backed into a corner. It all began with lifting that camera from the corpse. His uncle, had he been arrested for the same theft, would have been quick enough to invent a story about how the camera had come into his possession. Though a talented mimic, Jules wasn't quick at inventing stories on the spot. He could hear his uncle berating him: you exposed yourself by telling the truth, you're the architect of your own predicament, your misery is of your manufacture. "But I had no choice!" he shouted back. The apartment was empty. He balled up page after page so neither Maryse nor Caroline would have a clue as to what he was engaged in.

———•———

Jules circled the stairway near place Maubert, afraid to get too close to the iron railing. He felt shaky, yet as he walked he tried to remember what he had heard or seen that day. He had heard nothing. The block had been as silent as if he had walked onto a stage set while an invisible audience, impatient to get it over with and go home, waited for him to begin the last act. After only a few minutes standing at his corner post he saw a short, blond man emerge from the stairway where he had found the body. Red-faced, talking to himself, the man walked in his direction, looking at Jules in anger as he passed. Jules wanted to follow him, tap him on the shoulder and begin a conversation just to see what the result would be.

"Say, do you know me?"

"Never saw you before in my life."

"Me neither," Jules laughed.

Perhaps the man was always angry, and the anger had nothing to do with Jules, but he disappeared behind a doorway on the next block.

Copies of *La Libre Parole* weren't hard to find. Jules didn't want to be seen reading it, but on a crowded street he glanced at one lying on top of a stack and was able to make out a column headline that told him that the only lead the police had in the murder was a camera. It was as he suspected: the camera he had stolen linked him to the body he'd found in the stair-well. He didn't know whether to believe what was printed in *La Libre Parole,* nor was he sure that Felix was telling him the truth. Gribelin had never really told him why he was writing what he wrote, but all these questions had an immaterial aspect. The Section of Statistics knew his address, his identity. *You are,* Felix had said, *engaged in fraud. I know it. You know it. What can you do but work for me?*

He could ask Maryse to break his hand by slamming it in a door. Disabled, he would climb the stairs to the second floor of the Section of Statistics. *I can't write anymore, Felix, you'll have to find someone else.* He might wave bandaged digits with mirthless sincerity, but Felix's glassy stare, he knew, would remain fixed. The archivist wouldn't care about Jules' medical problems, and pain wasn't something he handled stoically.

----·----

Jules determined easily that Felix had torn the *bordereau* into six even parts and pasted the squares together again so the list would appear to have arrived in the Section's hands as if it had been found in the rubbish of the German embassy. The *bor-dereau* read:

> *Without news indicating that you wish to see me, nevertheless, Sir I send you some interesting information:*
>   1. *A note on the hydraulic buffer of the 120 and the way in which this gun behaves;*
>   2. *A note on the covering troops (some modifications will be made under the new plan);*
>   3. *A note on a modification of the artillery formations;*
>   4. *A note about Madagascar;*
>   5. *The preliminary Firing Manual of the Field Artillery.*

He examined the sloping, rapid handwriting on one page. It looked natural and unforced, though slightly irregular. He had been instructed to add prices to each item, reproducing what Gribelin had said was Dreyfus's handwriting, indicating what Dreyfus's fee would be for procuring such information. The prices were to be followed by comments, annotations in the margin executed in the kaiser's hand. He had no conception of what believable prices might be. *I'm Dreyfus. No, I'm their idea of Dreyfus.* He put his fingers in his ears, tried to imagine hunting with the kaiser, unleashing the greyhounds, speaking German. Jules wrote in the kaiser's hand, *"The rogue is asking too much — nevertheless the delivery of documents must be hastened. W."* It occurred to him it was possible that Kaiser Wilhelm might not write in French, nonetheless, Jules followed the instructions he was given. Examples of Dreyfus's handwriting didn't bear a close resemblance to that of the *bordereau* Gribelin insisted he had written, but Jules formed the numerals designating prices as best he could, becoming proficient at writing convincingly over the strips of glue although the writing should, technically speaking, have appeared under the glue. If Gribelin was careless it wasn't his problem. His pen floated over a grid of gummed transparent paper.

A sound in the hall made him jump, causing jagged lines to come from his pen. The paper was wrecked. He would have to start all over again, but Jules couldn't muster the concentration to start from the beginning. He walked around the room performing parodies of the people who had made his life miserable, from schoolteachers to those who passed him in the corridors of the Section of Statistics, but there was no audience.

On another evening as the iron grill from his balcony cast a curling shadow over his papers, he told himself the writing he invented signified no more than a police drama dreamed up by someone who was bored at his job and rankled by the late nights he felt compelled to work, someone who had access to papers kept in vaults on the rue de Lille. There was no Dreyfus. There was no trial. It was all a conspiracy to help someone win an election. He switched to another pen. He didn't know where Maryse was, and Caroline was either in the hall or had disappeared too. In the middle of the silence he had heard her talking to someone, and then the sound of conversation stopped.

"You shouldn't be here while I'm writing."

"You aren't writing, you're copying," Maryse corrected him.

"No, I'm writing. If people didn't want forgeries to exist, forgeries wouldn't be created. If there wasn't a need or an audience, no one would bother," he said, wondering if he were as big a phoney as those he parodied. "Where will you go?"

"We're out of coffee."

"I don't think we'll need as much as we used to."

"There are rumors of riots due to break out when Méliès tries to show his film about the trial."

"Méliès is incapable of subversion. He has his head in the clouds. Dreyfus goes to Saturn."

Caroline was bored. Her boredom marked off the hours of the morning, and then the afternoon, as if she lived in a city where she didn't understand the language, only the patterns of speech and so was excluded from most activity. She understood the formations of sound that indicated meals would soon be served or that she should go outside. The verbiage her mother and Jules spoke had the pitch and rhythm of language but the meaning, as far as she could tell, yielded only nonsense. With no more books to tear up, no more coffee to stir, she was excluded and superfluous to their industry, whatever it was. Jules rarely left the apartment anymore. He spent hours filling pages with careful script, and while he was writing he didn't want her in the room or even on the balcony. She looked over his shoulder.

Alfred Aid Alfred
DDDDDD

"Who's Alfred?"

"Nobody. Watch it, you'll knock my elbow. Go play in the hall, sweetheart."

He sat at the table with solidity, unbudgeable in every way. Once he had taken her to the wax museum. When her father wasn't looking she had pitched a pencil at the Napoléon display, aiming for his open mouth as he lay dying. She ran past the freaks in glass jars, and he comforted her. Now he barely noticed whether she came or left.

In time I, too, will turn into a two-headed monster. It's inevitable. There nothing I can do about it.

Jules shut the door behind her and went back to his pen nibs. She heard a cat and followed the sound up a flight of stairs to the top floor where it disappeared. Curious about the animal she knocked on the apartment door, its paint blistered and coming off in temptingly long peels, and while waiting for an answer she pulled one off. A cat could be heard inside along with the sound of someone moving around, but no one answered.

"Fire!" she yelled.

"Get lost!" A voice within seemed to issue from close to the door.

She wondered why this door and hallway were so shabby while the others in the building were relatively well kept. Stripping another long paint tail from the molding she turned at the sound of coughing several floors below her. It grew closer, and from the landing she could see a man's head between flights of stairs. He was near their landing, then he passed their door. If he wasn't coming to see Jules, he could only be a visitor for the man they never saw. A young man with a tightly knotted scarf, elfin face, and curly hair came into view. As he grew out of breath from the stairs, his compact body became more racked by vibrations of coughing. He said hello to Caroline, walked past her, straightened his clothing, and knocked.

"No one will come to the door," she told him.

"Do you mind?" The coughing man looked down at her, telling her, in effect, to scram. Caroline sat on a stack of books and stared at him.

"This is my hall, sir." He ignored her.

"Louis," the man got out between coughs. "It's me, Antoine."

Caroline decided not to pester him further; his tone when he spoke to the door was personal and desperate. She walked down to the next landing. Sitting cross legged in a niche meant for a small statue, she could listen to his conversation with the door while allowing him the illusion that he had some kind of privacy.

"Louis, listen, let me talk to you. I have to leave the city tonight."

Caroline could just make out the voice of the man behind the door, and his garbled syllables sounded like, "You'll be back in a few days."

"Why am I under suspicion, Louis? When have I let you down?"

Caroline strained her ears but only heard more quasi-unidentifiable sounds.

"I had nothing to do with that." Antoine raised his hands to the door as if it were animate. "This isn't a trick to get you to open the door. I really mean it, Louis. I've brought you food. I won't be able to come again. I'm leaving the city tonight."

"Leave me alone."

A coughing fit followed that was so severe Caroline jumped out of the alcove and ran into her apartment to get the man a glass of water. A hot breeze blew through the open windows, ruffling Jules's papers. He snapped at her as if the racket in the corridor had been her fault. When she returned to the hall with the glass, the man was descending the stairs, wiping his face with his scarf. A bottle of wine had been left before the locked door overhead. She ran downstairs to try to see where the man might have gone. When she returned a few minutes later, the bottle had disappeared.

Facsimiles of Jules's writings were reproduced as posters and pasted to walls, kiosks, and lampposts. The documents, which bore Dreyfus's signature, were meant to convince skeptical citizens of his guilt. A very thin man, so thin he looked like he was made of pencils, stopped to read the posters. Renard wore a velvet coat, soft felt hat; his clothing was frayed at the edges, but he had assembled himself as if he gave his dress a great deal of thought. As a writer he was captivated by what he read and imagined the texts were inventions if not composite forgeries, but then he wasn't sure. Studying them he felt the desire to write some Dreyfus stories of his own, complete with anecdotes about family, school, army career, and if he had any resources at all he too would plaster his fictions all over the city, signing his name, or one of his names. He was drawn to the idea of being falsely accused. It was something he felt familiar with. At the school where he used to work he had been accused of showing children too much attention when he had only been trying to help them. One child had told a story using dolls to show what she claimed he had done to her. Acts of love were confused with acts of violence. It is possible to love something so much you end by destroying it, he wrote melodramatically.

Felix waited for Jules. Men passed him with hats pulled low, lapels turned up. Women didn't look at him; veiled, squinting, smelling of burnt sugar, they held each other's elbows as if they might topple in the wind. Felix clutched his documents, loosely bound and intended for Jules. He was anxious. If the pages of instruction were blown out of his hands and dispersed down the street, not only would the case against Dreyfus be lost, but Felix would become the fall guy. He didn't want to end his life in a prison cell as a convict whose inevitable murder would be made to look like suicide.

Write letters declaring that D has new contacts. Even on Devil's Island there is no cessation of his betrayal and subversions. He writes of them to his wife. He can't get off a treadmill of betrayal because it's in his character. Be sure your handwriting matches D's to a T.

He would have that fool Jules done away with before they got to him. It grew late, shops were locked up; he clenched his papers even more tightly. Hat spinning in the gutter, Felix imagined trying to run after the incriminating documents should they slip from his grasp. He would try to catch the papers, but they become pierced on the ends of canes, umbrellas, made into paper hats, gliders, boats. Stuck to the bottom of a shoe, a word might catch the eye before being thrown away, *my beautiful bugger — use Alexandrine's phrase.* The accidental reader or readers would expose his scheme. The cat would be out of the bag. Dreyfus would be released, a hero. Felix grew impatient and cursed all those whose facility with a pen made him their victim, and he also damned those who had no sense of what it meant to be on time.

By the time Jules arrived Felix had left, but he ran north toward the rue de Lille, soon catching up. Following the archivist down the block, he continued to walk in his shadow, imitating Gribelin's loping steps, unable to say *Felix,* incapable of pronouncing even similar sounds: *felicitas, felicité* stuck in his throat. A stray dog nipped at his heels, finally giving him away to the man whom he both mistrusted and relied on. Turning around to face him, Felix looked disappointed, but it was the lofty disappointment of one in authority, one who condescended to be disappointed, one who expected atrocious slip-ups from those who worked without direct supervision and control. He handed Jules the package.

"The administration of the prison at Devil's Island is confiscating and burning Dreyfus's letters. Neither he nor his family ever see the originals any one of them sends."

"This is a shorter street if you're going back to your office," Jules pointed.

"Letters sent to and from the prison must be copies."

Jules put the package under his arm as if it were nothing more than a pair of shirts. "I'm going to get a cup of coffee. I've only just gotten out of bed and would like something to eat."

"I'm walking in the other direction." Felix examined Jules's rumpled hair and wrinkled trousers.

"I wasn't asking you to join me."

"You know your work would be considered a serious crime in Italy, *plagio,* taking over an individual's will," Gribelin needled Jules.

"Who's the real counterfeit? Your D or me?"

Felix shrugged and stepped off the curb and into traffic. "The messenger will pick up your letters next Wednesday."

"Good-bye, Felix." Jules coughed out the name and waved at his black hat as it disappeared across the street. He looked at the package under his arm, then walked toward a café, away from the archivist. If they were to run into each other in public they would behave as strangers. He would be nervous, and Maryse would point her finger at Felix writing prices in a notebook. She would say, "Is he the one?" They would all be found dead in an alley, just like his uncle who thought he left no *t* uncrossed. He imagined Gribelin in his office referring to him as M. Loophole, one that would soon have to be closed. Uncrossed *t*'s had become his specialty.

He didn't know who Maryse might talk to given an opportunity. *Night and day Jules manufactures messages from kaisers and diplomatic errand boys.* She was a liability. Since the rare book business was finished he didn't need her to help him anymore. He planned to tell her to move out. He was tired of her whining, and her cynicism no longer seemed as witty it had when they first met. It would be a relief to live alone again in a state of badly needed calm, an experience he had forgotten to the point where he had begun to doubt such a thing as a tranquil room could actually exist anywhere in the city at that particular moment.

But I've never met Dreyfus.

As you write, you're engaged in a kind of extortion of identity.

Plagio, *but not plagiarism. The letters are my inventions, my words, perhaps modeled after Dreyfus, but the sentences are my own.*

A pigeon nearly flew into him, and he realized what he was doing, speaking out loud. No one seemed to be staring at him, apart from Caroline a few paces behind, and he didn't notice her at all.

———•———

Rabbit with cucumbers, 7 frs. Braised guinea fowl with tarragon, 8 frs. Felix wrote in his notebook, put it back in his case, and pushed his empty plates away. He turned to Jules's letters, which should not have been taken from the rue de Lille office. They were useless; their content was rubbish. He would add them to the D file, although he couldn't claim the letters had been sent to or from Devil's Island. The handwriting was exceptional, the slant of the letters looked unforced and natural, a photographic copy of any sample of Dreyfus's writing, but the content of the letters was the jabberings of a lunatic who screamed alone in solitary confinement. He wanted a cold-blooded Dreyfus, levelheaded and calculating, in touch with the Syndicate even from his island. He knew that Dreyfus did scream alone in his cell and throw himself against its iron furniture, but the letters Felix wanted were supposed to be penned by a rebellious prisoner, a man like Méliès's double, unrepentant and plotting still.

———•———

The first Caroline saw of him was the soft crown of his hat, his long hair and shoulders underneath as he made his way upstairs slowly, as if it was a chore. Leaning against her door she watched closely until the rest of his body came into view, climbing the stairs. He was carrying a box, and she guessed he intended to try to see the man who lived above them, but he stopped when he arrived at her landing. Sitting on a stack of old books Jules still hadn't cleared away he lit a cigarette as if he had all the time in the world. They both knew the man upstairs wasn't going anywhere. He smiled, unbuttoned his jacket, and asked her name.

"What do you like to do, Caroline, when you're not in the hall?"

"I do drawings."

No one had ever asked her questions about herself or how she spent her time. On sheets of paper Jules had no use for, she drew only what she could see out the window or in the park, and what she could see was ordinary, so when he asked her what she drew she proceeded to describe pictures that she didn't draw, pictures of things she couldn't see or hadn't seen.

"I draw women and men."

She meant to say people and immediately regretted her answer. She felt as if she had stood on her hands for one second, then fell flat on her face. The refuge of a show-off, her father used to say, was the province of a girl who wanted to make startling gestures of talent and intelligence when everyone around her kept telling her she was just as difficult and ordinary as any other thirteen-year-old girl. "What makes you think you're special?" her mother might add from time to time. Renard still smiled at her.

She had seen men and women behind open doorways, through windows, in posters. She knew what they did together. Caroline watched him smoke and thought in his carelessness and indifference he looked like a man who could take care of himself, not like Jules. Jules, grown red eyed and disheveled, made her want to puke. Her mother pandered to his complaints, but expressed contempt for whatever it was he wrote and tore up and wrote again. Renard was clever and friendly. Jules ran on a cycle of nervous energy and despair, a series of impulses trapped in his hunched-up body. Go ahead, she wanted to say to her father and mother, make yourselves miserable, see if I care.

"I have to find the tenant who lives one flight up."

He didn't seem to mind that Caroline followed him upstairs like a puppy dog and watched as he knocked on Louis's door.

"Is Louis in? I have some things for him. My name is Renard. I'm a friend of Antoine's."

Louis's response, though barely audible, was angry. "I'm not opening the door. Leave whatever it is you've brought and go away."

Renard shrugged, pushing a box against the door with the toe of his boot. "Suit yourself."

He took Caroline's hand and led her down a flight of stairs, making as much noise as possible as they descended so Louis would think he'd gone. The sculpture alcove was conveniently empty, and pulling Caroline onto his lap, they sat in it. He smelled of cloves and tobacco. She nestled into his thin shirt and as he put his arms around her she felt self-conscious discomfort on his bony knees and awkward pleasure at the same time. They watched the food disappear and the door shut after it.

"We might have rushed in," he said, "but what would we find inside? Old socks, dirty playing cards, and opium pipes." She made no effort to get up from his lap. He remained with her in the alcove, and for a few more minutes they watched the peeling door as if a wind might blow it open. He finally stood up, removing her from his lap with his hands around her waist.

"You feel like a strong girl. I'd like to see you the next time I make a delivery."

"Don't knock on my door. If I'm not in the hall, I won't be in." This wasn't strictly true, but she didn't want him to ask Jules or Maryse for her. "You wouldn't want to meet my mother."

Caroline had watched her mother flirt with all kinds of people, from shop boys to Jules's clients. It was easy to imagine the door slammed in her face, her mother and the tall man laughing behind it. Her mother and her new friend needed to be kept well apart.

She watched him make his way downstairs. Caroline was smart enough to guess that he probably wouldn't actually knock on her parents' door to begin with, and the possibility of Maryse coming to the door half-undressed was not the reason why.

She daydreamed about running away with Renard. When her mother spoke to her she answered as if Maryse's voice interrupted the most spellbinding melodrama. The man who held her on his lap for a few minutes was transformed into a lethal weapon, a man who would settle scores for her; the image of Renard doing no more than leaning against a door sent shivers down her spine. She couldn't come back to earth.

Seeing him was a matter of chance. She considered skipping school, taking her plate into the landing and eating just outside her door in case he made deliveries while her family was having dinner, although they rarely ate together anymore. She considered moving into the hall, taking over the stairwell and a few of the steps, as if this were her own private dwelling put together from the architectural details (alcove, corner, ledge). It was a space few paid attention too since only her family lived near the top, and the man above them was never seen to go out. Apart from the others, she would balance her plate on her knees, arrange her clothes in boxes, and undress when the building was quiet. It was a futile plan. Maryse wouldn't even let her leave the table. She went back inside and noticed her mother poking through Jules's papers. She stopped long enough to say that Caroline caused them nothing but trouble and anguish.

"Even Marie Antoinette had to behave herself once in a while."

"Why Marie Antoinette?"

"What do you mean? Marie Antoinette, that's all."

"Why did you pick her? You'd just like to see me with my head cut off."

If her mother couldn't get what she wanted, she took her pleasure where she found it, even if the taking was at Caroline's

expense. Caroline looked forward to sleep. Lying in bed she re-
viewed her minutes on the landing with Renard, reinventing the
ending so that he carried her away in his arms. Feverish images
of Renard rescuing her from the brink of enslavement to a grotesque taskmaster (in the form of the shut-in upstairs), gave way
to the reality of her parents' constant arguing. Jules talked while
he ate big gulps of food. Her mother slammed doors. Caroline
stretched her hands over her head until each one grasped a bedpost, then put her hands over her ears.

Maryse wanted to kill Jules. He slouched over his desk or the
table or wherever he came to a physical stop as if he were melted
over the surface, his elbows like support struts holding up his
curved back, so neither of them could see what he wrote. When
she asked him what the pages were for, he wouldn't answer, and
she grew convinced his industry was directed toward a useless
end. He sat in a wrinkled suit, sleeves covered with bits of ash,
face like a nut. Deaf and mute, he refused to answer her, and this
was only more infuriating.

"You give no thought to anyone but yourself." She grabbed
a page from his hand so that a long line of ink smeared the writing. Jules smacked her as hard as he had ever hit anyone. Ink
bottles fell to the floor. Black ink splashed on Maryse's dress.
Caroline ran into the hall, upstairs to the invalid Louis's door
and knocked without knowing why. There was no answer, and
she kicked the door as if the stranger's obstinacy was keeping her
in her apartment, and at the same time keeping Renard away. It
was a meaningless thing to do. She ran downstairs, certain he
wouldn't open the door and at the same time embarrassed by
her impulsive kicking. His voice trailed after her.

"Get lost, girlie. I can't do anything for you. It's not my fault
that your parents are assholes. Why don't you go kick a moving
train?"

Alone in the hall she stuck her knobby knees out straight, stockings had collapsed around her ankles, one shoe buckle was about to fall off. Hours passed. She wasn't missed. She sat on the old books waiting in the hall. The books slid out from under her as she shifted around, and she collapsed into a heap on the floor, knees up to her ears. Caroline could hear Louis and his cat moving around in their apartment. Perhaps, in spite of himself, he was expecting a delivery soon. She waited.

Jules sat in a hard chair opposite Gribelin while the archivist read the letters Jules had brought with him. It was growing dark; Felix had clicked on a brass desk lamp, and dust motes floated in its cone of light in a small pool on his desk. Someone entered and shut the curtains. Occasionally Felix smiled as he read, but Jules felt on pins and needles; *look, you carved your name on the desk, we know it was you.* He hadn't planted jokes and sight gags in the Devil's Island correspondence. Why had he been called in? What was wrong? He'd done what they'd told him to do. Usually a messenger was sent to pick up his work, but this time he had been asked to come directly to the Section himself. After a sharp knock, a man in the uniform of a general, maybe, Jules couldn't be sure, and also not sure whether to stand when the man entered, so he just twisted back the other way and faced the windows. The man told Felix he wanted a word before he left for the night. Looking down at his shoes so he wouldn't witness Gribelin's subservience, Jules heard Felix push back his chair and leave the room. The heavy door clicked shut and the sound of footsteps could be heard outside in the hall.

He walked around Felix's desk, a broad U-shaped piece of furniture, sat in his chair, and took a sip of a drink he hadn't been offered. The glass lay outside the pool of light, and he replaced it in its original position. He opened a drawer. Under a blotter lay a dead watch, a blank notebook, pencils, erasers, and a few boxes of gummed labels. A second drawer contained several documents. He picked up a sheet of onionskin on which individual words had been traced from a crumpled dinner invitation from the Italian embassy. Jules put it aside. He picked up a letter written on a piece of graph paper. The letter had been torn and pasted back together, just as many documents were, to insure they would appear to have been resurrected from the dustbin when in fact they'd never even seen the trash. All were newly made. The forgery Jules held up to the light was particularly crude. Half the letter was written on one kind of graph paper marked by blue-gray lines, the other half bore claret-gray lines and the graph's squares were slightly larger. The shapes of the letters were hesitant; they had obviously been traced, not written freely. A name, Henry, was scrawled on a piece of paper clipped to the back.

Jules heard footsteps down the hall, causing him to jolt upright, nearly knocking over Felix's glass. The sound of a man's step, a man who loped but did so with conviction, grew closer. By the time he managed to half stand, the footsteps had turned elsewhere. He sat down again in the padded chair. The drawer closed with a click. Noticing it had a lock, Jules wondered why Felix had failed to secure the papers before he left, perhaps he intended to show him an example of a forgery badly done.

Opening the drawer again he found more papers. The second forgery wasn't his work either. Brittle paper had been reassembled as if from bits of a sloppily produced puzzle of thirty or forty very small pieces, glued together with strips of transparent paper. A photograph of the document also lay in the drawer. A letter-telegram, it had been photographed to delete any trace of having been torn up. It was labeled *le petit bleu*.

"If he doesn't like it, he knows what will happen."

Jules froze, statuelike, holding *le petit bleu* up to the light.

"Does he know?"

"I've always made that clear to him."

The deep, authoritative voices belonged to the profiles of

two women who appeared in silhouette against the glass half of Felix's door, then they moved down the hall accompanied by the sound of brooms.

It was only night cleaners talking about cooking and what would happen if their husbands didn't eat what was put before them. He looked at the Henry forgery again. He had been writing letters as if from Devil's Island for weeks, but the letters and documents the Section actually used appeared to be written by another forger, without regard to the fact that they were crudely done, much inferior to his own. Felix apparently didn't realize the difference. He closed the drawer for the last time, took one more sip from Felix's glass, then returned to his chair and waited.

"Fifty francs will get us through this month, but no further."

"That's all he would pay me. I couldn't get any more."

"You write all the time. He could pay you twice as much, it's worth it to him. If anyone were to find out what he's hired you to write, the whole case against Dreyfus would fall apart. If any anarchist wanted to blow up the Section of Statistics they couldn't find a more powerful bomb." Maryse startled him with her political acuity. But he had decided he wanted her to move out, and he was impatient for the two of them to go.

"While I'm negotiating a higher fee you and Caroline should move to a smaller apartment."

"In the sewer? What will we live on?"

"Your mother could help you."

"You make me sick." Caroline accidentally kicked Maryse's chair while she was aiming for the table. Her mother thwacked her in return.

"Shut up," Jules said.

"Don't tell me to shut up. I've seen what you do on the street."

Caroline didn't want to rub her cheek, didn't want to let them know the slap stung.

"I walk on the street. What's wrong with that?"

Since the book business disappeared her mother and father had become preoccupied with money. They calculated and came up short, counted notes, then began again, making lists of what they needed to buy each month, trying to shrink the margin by which they fell short. With sweaty meticulousness Jules pored over documents, holding them up to the light, tracing, cutting, then writing again He never seemed to get it right and was paid very little for whatever it was he worked so diligently on. She had read of poor farmers who murdered members of their large families because they couldn't afford to feed so many children, smothering them in hay or throwing them down a well. It wasn't supposed to happen anymore, and not in the city, but she could imagine her parents selling her to Star Films, for example, as a worker bee, or dropping her off at a pawnshop somewhere on the rue des Rosiers.

Before the Revolution, she had also read, children had been known to murder aged parents who could no longer work to earn their keep. She went into the hall. Bakery boxes, a bottle of wine, and a bundle of sausages had been left for Louis. Caroline opened one of the boxes. She could make out the name *Bluette,* but the rest of the writing was smeared and illegible. She pinched a rose from the side of the cake, probably stolen from a bakery, and replaced the box. Renard had come and gone again. She was furious.

"It's all your fault," she yelled through the open door. A pot had hit the jamb as she slammed it. Caroline ran downstairs and out into the street. "I'm leaving. I'm going to live in the park."

She wandered past old women sitting in front of their buildings who looked at her as if she ought not to be out alone. Their stares had never seemed censorious before, but now they were full of approbation, as if they'd heard and seen everything. *A bad girl, willful and full of ideas.*

"Piss off, you."

They didn't hear her. Turning a corner she looked in the window of a shoe store; her heels were worn, that had been one of Maryse's constant complaints, and she was sick of both her shoes and the nagging. A man's reflection appeared beside her. He tapped her on the shoulder.

"How do I get to the Bastille from here?"

He stood very close, brushed her arm with his sleeve. Everyone knew where it was, not far from where they stood. He smelled like petrol. She pointed and ran away from him, past the old women, past the high windows of place des Vosges, and away from the Bastille.

———•———

It was glued to a wall, part of a series of posters Caroline had seen splattered around the city although she'd never stopped to read the tightly spaced lines with almost nonexistent margins. Renard stood still in the middle of the empty sidewalk reading one. He had his hands in his pockets, his head tilted back while he read. The task of reading owned him; he was inaccessible. She wasn't able to shout in a voice loud enough to travel across the street, and he didn't seem to notice her, or he was deliberately ignoring her. Even the way he put his hands in his pockets excluded her. She began to walk in the opposite direction, but two men huddling in front of a doorway snickered at her, and she quickly turned back the way she'd come.

"Hey, girlie." It sounded like a net hidden between them, ready to catch her as she passed, but when she turned around and looked over her shoulder they were only handing a bottle back and forth from one to the other.

Renard was gone from his post, but seeing him down the street, she ran to catch up. Her footsteps clattered behind him, still he didn't look back. She touched his sleeve. He turned around with a start and looked at her with hostility. Caroline crossed her arms over her chest. She couldn't retreat. He had to be made to be sympathetic to her predicament. Perhaps he was only surprised to see her, unused to meeting anyone by chance in this way. A man who spent his days going from place to place looking after crazy invalids like the man upstairs probably led a quiet, introspective life.

"Where are your parents?" His expression softened a little as if he were figuring something out, adapting himself to the situation.

"My mother is out," she lied instinctively in order to protect herself. Maybe he wasn't the man she thought he was. Maybe he would try to get her to go back home. Caroline tried not to sound out of breath; she tried to sound as if she hadn't been looking for anyone in particular and finding him on a street not far from her apartment was an unexpected coincidence.

"Where did she go?" He made aimless conversation.

"I don't know." She wanted to sound as detached from her parents as she felt, as if she hadn't seen them in years.

Then she couldn't stop talking. Words poured out of her mouth about subjects as trivial and as serious as her hunger, the men who followed her in the street, the cost of new shoes. She had spent so much time imagining Renard that she was certain he would be sympathetic if she confessed how miserable she was. Renard didn't seem to be listening to her, but he clasped her hand anyway, smiling, nodding vacantly at a passing woman. He hailed a cab and took Caroline to his apartment, a single room in Montmartre.

⁣————

"You could be sent to Charenton." Felix leaned over his desk.

"I don't know how to write any other way."

"This is a warning. You could spend the rest of your life writing on stone walls."

"What other kind are there?" Jules scratched his head.

"Can I stay here?"

His room was very small, closetlike, and windowless; there was only a narrow bed in it that seemed to fill the room, and this was discouraging to her. She had imagined he lived in a place with a large kitchen capable of making enough food for Louis and other charity cases, its bedroom on an upper floor would be enclosed by curving glass doors, and on one side there would be a balcony with a view of the city. In this setting she would seduce him. His imagined innocence made her the aggressor, the one who offered unknown and unknowable gratification. She had no acquaintances who lived in a ground-floor flat in the back of a building that smelled of mold and industrial cleaner. The sound of a train ran close by from time to time, so she knew she was near a station. Caroline wasn't sure she wanted to stay, but she had convinced herself she had no place else to go. She wanted to have no place else to go, to ensure that whatever happened to her was out of her control. If she had no choices, whatever happened wasn't her fault. Outside the province of Jules and Maryse there could be other rules, and she could find a new language, one that might sweep her up and make her a child bride. She would never have to see any of them again.

Renard put his clothes on a chair. Unclothed his tight little body looked vulnerable, but raw and terrierlike. Caroline thought of a small, nippy dog you couldn't escape or control, but she didn't scream. His hands were stained yellow from smoking, and in the harsh light it looked as if he had gloves on. He stroked her hair and unbuttoned her dress, and the touch of his fingers gave her chills. Her dress was blue, ink spots near the hem. She smelled like school paste. He decided he would write about Caroline as if she were a smart aleck, a wiseass with a dirty mouth, a girl who got what she had wanted and deserved: a girl who would have to leave when it was over. He would put her in a cab. She could go wherever she pleased. He might stop bringing packages for Louis. It was getting tiresome, and if he stopped Louis would be forced to take care of himself. No one else would. That would be the best thing for him. Renard, after all, had things to do. The inky dress on the floor reminded him of how his pleasure produced leftover things; they seemed to go hand in hand. Like eating lobster, there's more left over when you're done eating than when it first arrives on your plate. He would use that metaphor somewhere. The building shook slightly, and he could hear someone going upstairs just on the other side of the wall. He hoped she wouldn't be sick. He had no reassuring gestures, only what she could misinterpret as comfort.

Back on the street, Caroline felt she had emerged into a world placed on a spit and turned upside down, as if what had happened in Renard's room happened suddenly to absolutely everyone else at the same instant.

———•—•———

The police didn't search the apartment. They arrived on cat's paws, careful not to displace papers, overturn coffee cups or ink-wells. They stood in the doorway as if separated from a museum exhibit by a velvet rope, as if they'd been explicitly told: Don't search. When they read out the arrest they cited the victim's name.

"I've never heard of her," Jules said.

"That's nothing to us," they answered. "Finish getting dressed and come along."

Jules had put on his jacket before he realized what they were talking about: the corpse clutching a camera.

"She was a man, a man dressed as a woman, but still a man." He took a few steps backward. In their confusion about the identity or sex of the murder victim there might be a way out for him. "You must be looking for someone else."

Maryse felt she had woken up at the wrong address.

"What woman? What did he do?"

"It wasn't a woman's body. The corpse was a man dressed as a woman."

"That's not what we've been told."

"You said she was stabbed near place Maubert?"

"Yes."

"I found the body, it's true, but he was already dead."

"Did you report what you'd seen?"

"No."

"Why not?"

He didn't have an answer.

"Then don't be stupid and come along."

"A man dressed as a woman, what is he talking about?" Maryse grabbed one of policemen's arms. "Why are you wasting your time arresting the wrong person when you ought to be out looking for kidnapped children?"

An officer wrote something on a piece of paper that read *Inquiries for missing children can be made at the rue de Rivoli office,* and they led Jules downstairs. She leaned out over the railing as they took him away. At the sound of heavy boots stepping almost in unison people peered out of their doorways. Jules looked up at her, imitating the bug-eye stares on faces as he descended. He didn't get it. He didn't understand how serious this was. The arrest had something to do with the writing he'd been doing that he never let her see, of that she was certain. Even if the accusation of murder was a trumped-up charge, the wall of uniforms, as they spiraled down the stairs, paralyzed her.

"No one answers my questions at the rue de Rivoli, or anywhere else," she shouted at the retreating police and at Jules. Caroline had disappeared into thin air, as if a Méliès cinema trick.

Murder or forgery, whatever Jules was involved in, she never knew the full story, he'd stopped telling her everything. She was cut off from him, and from every person she had ever known. Her mother and sister, all were estranged from one another, and she wasn't even sure where her sister lived anymore.

But what was worse, far worse, were Caroline's clothes, school books, and drawings that screamed at her every waking minute, which were most of all possible minutes, since she rarely slept anymore. She would refuse to move out until Caroline reappeared or was found. Above Maryse's head even the recluse had opened his door a crack.

Alone, Maryse lay down fully dressed and tried to sleep. She knew a few things. She knew what Jules wrote and who he wrote for. Once he was locked away the police might come back for her. Instinctively she wanted to leave the city so that no one could find her, but Caroline would be part of that "no one." Slowly and silently Maryse became angry at Caroline, invisible and deliberately remote. When she was next fully awake it was late afternoon. She sat in a chair without moving for hours, facing Jules's desk, mentally cataloging what objects could be sold. Toward evening she went out looking for her daughter again, asking the old women who sat in front of their buildings if they'd seen her.

"She walked north toward Montmartre."

"No," another one said, "she was running away from a man."

"Can you describe him?"

"An Algerian."

"Jewish."

"None of those. He was a tall white man with a turned-up nose, thin moustache, and a goatee, fashionably dressed, but his clothes weren't new."

This seemed to be the description the three finally agreed on, and Maryse described him to all she met. It was turning colder and darker, and in a park children milled around, able to see their breath, pretending to be smoking before mothers or older children came to take them home. There is no "not there" like a child's "not there." All the children were younger than Caroline, but she asked them if they'd seen a blond girl, thirteen years old, wearing a blue dress. They shook their heads. Maryse walked to Montmartre and back showing Caroline's photograph to shopkeepers, gendarmes, to other old women who watched the streets.

At night she walked past the closed cafés.

———•———

After the riots in front of Houdin's theater, no one on nearby streets wanted to talk to her about a missing child.

The nearly empty street was littered with broken glass and drifts of torn paper eddying in the breeze. Newspapers, posters, wrapping paper, advertisements, shoes, hats, clothing, even a marble counter broken into pieces, all kinds of objects looted from the shops blew around her while soot-gray men with brooms tried to contain the piles they'd worked so hard to assemble before wind blew the papers into anarchy again. Maryse picked up what looked like a personal letter, handwritten and crumpled into a ball. She smoothed it out, but rain had smeared the letters into a bluish watercolor, a series of horizon lines, nothing intelligible at all. The piece of paper, she realized, was cut into the shape of a human foot. She tossed it back into the gutter. One of the men shook his broom at her and told her to watch her step.

There were many other missing children, too many. She couldn't bear to read or hear anything about the fighting or the trial, and found herself avoiding newspapers of all kinds. She kept Jules's papers locked away without telling anyone, but the police didn't return.

———•———

Caroline found her way to the station. In the confusion of the panicked crowds she was able to slip unnoticed onto the train to Montreuil, and from there made her way to Star Films.

A devil sat in a wooden pumpkin coach crying. His tail swung back and forth, half a ham sandwich lay on the seat next to him. A blond woman in a long transparent dress sat at the other end of the set. The dress was hiked up above her knees, and she twisted her hair up and then let it down again. They didn't see or hear Caroline, and she didn't know how to begin to talk to them. The glass house was plain, not castlelike as she had imagined it would be. A sort of partitioned-off studio or office lay to one side of the set, half wooden walls, half open windows, and she stepped inside it to get out of the way of whatever was going on. Fake beards hung from pegs to her left. No one noticed when she took one down and twirled the beard around by its elastic, twisting the cord on her index finger. She pulled a chair close to the open part of the partition and watched the devil and the barefoot woman in the strange dress sob without comforting one another. Sooner or later, she thought, they would get back to work and see her watching them. When asked, she would tell them without hesitating that she intended to stay forever.

———————

Outside, the courtyard was being swept; the concierge leaned against a statue of Hermes and looked up at Claire's window on the lower floor, the better class of tenants lived here. The man who usually visited Claire Francoeur would, she knew, return at night. These two had a kind of partnership which was different from some of the others who'd rented apartments from her in the past. The swipes of her broom echoed across the courtyard. Her niece had left her some newspapers before she bicycled off, and she went into her office to read about plans for the 1900 World Exhibition. She thought of the new century as an artificial yet dangerous precipice. A cataclysmic change might not be marked by anything as recognizable as four numbers marked on a calendar but might occur on a Thursday afternoon or Monday morning when nobody was looking. She would ignore the fireworks and stay indoors. Walking outside she looked up one more time, but Claire's windows were shuttered. She was supposed to move out soon.

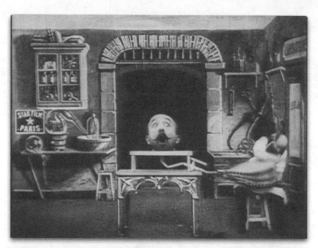

Actualities and Preconstructions

On the morning commute to his job at Star Films, Fabien looked up from his lists just once, quickly, and in that random glance out the window saw two boys clenching boards with long nails hammered through one end. They stood on the edge of a runnel that ran parallel to the train tracks. A few days earlier the stream had been deep from rain, but it was now stagnant and green. The boys were killing frogs. They pounded each frog so that the nail pierced it, then they pried it off. He used to kill frogs the same way as a boy, putting them into a bag or stringing them around his neck so that the frogs, until untied, fried, and eaten, looked like a twitching garland, an Elizabethan collar made of green legs. But there was something else in the water that the boys pointed to suddenly, screaming and shouting at the train as it rushed past. It was a long shape like a body, which, if that's what the shape had been, must have surfaced as the stream dried up. He was alone in his compartment and didn't know if anyone else on the train had seen what he had seen. The image of the boys went by in a flash, but Fabien was sure he had seen slimy hands, muddy clothes, and a body lying facedown in the water.

Méliès was an adored man. His silent movies drew larger crowds than the Lumière brothers' films. He offered escape hatches, transformations, jokes. No one wants to see what they can see every day, he said, they want to see what they can't see. Then he began to think about filming what everyone looked at but didn't really see. The Dreyfus trial had split families, including his own. *Is Dreyfus a spy? Yes, no, maybe.* Méliès didn't think so, and if he could film what he believed he saw, others might agree.

A man dressed as an apothecary examined glass bottles, beakers, jars with arrogant, obscene-looking snouts, and coils of tubing going nowhere. He placed a head, identical to his own, on a small table and after selecting a stop-cock and curved pipe, connected a length of tubing from a whitened bellows to the base of the head. Rolling up his shirtsleeves, he proceeded to pump the bellows. As it grew, the severed twin head expressed mute alarm. Its eyes rolled upwards, a febrile sweat broke out on the brow, and its mouth opened in a silent scream, then just as it seemed to near the bursting point, the apothecary smiled with grace and deflated the head. The apothecary, Georges Méliès himself, wiped his hands on his full-length apron. He was bald and against a black background his head appeared free floating, able to look at his smaller self with terror.

"You play the apothecary's assistant dressed as a clown," he said.

Fabien waited offstage, his face covered with cracking white paint. When the head was reduced to its normal size, Méliès walked on, picked up the bellows, and began to pump again. The terrified head grew larger and larger, finally bursting in a cloud of smoke. Fabien, with Méliès's help, was thrown out the window. On his way past painted fenestrations, Fabien accidentally kicked a box which had held the allegedly rubber head. Although the box was a real cardboard box, the head hadn't been rubber; it was Méliès's own. The illusion of its isolation in space and subsequent enlargement was an optical trick. *Poor frangible hat filler.*

Georges Méliès loved the severed head trick as much as he enjoyed domineering his real and imaginary assistants.

Out the window, Fabien, out the window and to the moon.

"At least," an actor in a bottle suit reasoned, "the fractious decapitated head is usually his own, and that it's a fat head is only natural."

But I'm the fool, Fabien crossed his arms over his chest, as if proud of his role, as if by declaring his position he was pulling the rug out from under everyone before he could be knocked over himself. During his first months at Star Films Fabien had tried to manage his pratfalls by attempting to detach himself from his body, to try to feel as if someone else was being thrown around, but he couldn't really convince himself of the separation. His head had remained firmly attached to his shoulders so far. Georges told him his humiliation was part of the constructed illusion of a film, and therefore his embarrassment couldn't be real. It was only a byproduct of Méliès's bonhomie. He wanted everyone to laugh at all times. The actor adjusted his bottle costume, twisting in it so his eyes appeared in a slot directly under the stopper.

"I think you have it out for me," Fabien yelled through the flimsy window.

"No, no, Fabien, I love you, you're my right-hand man. I want everybody to be happy," Georges said, dusting himself off.

"This is too much. I'm always the fall guy." As hard as he tried to turn the tables on Georges, fatherly and slaphappy, Fabien continued to trip on his own shoelaces. In his frustration, he remained the boob, the knucklehead, the one who falls in love with the most hopelessness, with no sense of how maladroit he appears. Even though he made intricate and delicate props in a studio to the left of the stage he was perceived as the one with two left hands. Méliès treated him like a thickheaded boy picked from the audience for a prank while he, Georges Méliès, was the elegant master of ceremonies.

"In tricks I like to take all leading roles, for I can never make my players understand the thousand and one skills needed for a complicated sleight of hand to work well. You're not really flying out the window. It just looks that way."

Furniture had been overturned in the fake explosion. Fabien picked up a gauge that had been attached to the bellows and looked through a black aperture used in constructing the optical illusion of the growing head. Most objects were gray, black, or white in order to register more sharply on film, and sets painted in a persistent trompe l'oeil played tricks on the inattentive. A less clever man might walk into windows, knock his head against spaces between painted trees, train cars, or corinthian columns. Ladders, hedgerows, rooms whose painted checkered floors had carefully plotted diminishing transversals, all these were painted or constructed so they narrowed to a point on the horizon. Fabien was careful, but the vistas of distorted linear perspective were so common among studio flats, the landscape of Fabien's days, that he often felt off balance, as if he were caught in a Uccello painting he couldn't step out of until he was on the train back to Paris, and even then, as the landscape rushed by, he wasn't sure. *Uccello, fellow lover of practical jokes. Is the horse rooted to the plinth or does he float above it?* There was something inaccessible about the pleasures offered by the films he worked on. He built false ceilings and imagined sinkholes. He wanted to ask Georges, "Who laughs, who's taken in, who splits his sides over your gallows humor?" Georges talked about *the profane gaze of the audience,* all his optical illusions and sight gags were attempts at second guessing the desires embedded in that profane gaze. Fabien sometimes sensed this future ogling as he prepared to be thrown out a fake window. This is what the spectators want, *do it,* he said to himself, jump *out the window.*

———•———

When Fabien offered his future wife a retreat into a small apartment filled with drawings of a complicated series of ramps, dollies, and camera plans, she accepted. His two-room apartment was a kind of trial stage for his work for Méliès. Drawings and cardboard models of lunar landscapes and castles covered floors, tables, chairs. At first she was utterly enchanted, but soon grew annoyed at having to pick her way across a floor littered with wood shavings and pencils. Fabien made an effort to clear some room for her, but his work commanded too much space, and he couldn't afford a larger apartment. Soon her belongings and clothes were seduced into becoming props in entertainments acted out at home.

They had a son who slept in a cradle made from two crescent moons, discarded props, and he played with paper rockets that crumpled in his greedy, willful hands. Fabien restrained his anger at the boy's destructiveness. He moved self-consciously, knocked into tables, chairs, spilled glasses and folded newspaper pages into all kinds of objects, wiped inky hands on his wife's dresses, which she refused to wash as she grew increasingly restless and impatient with the constant invention. One day she took the boy and departed.

With its warped floor and only one window, now his apartment choked him. He didn't like to spend time in it. Each morning he would look in the mirror with a disconnected stare as if shaving a mannequin, then wash up and be on his way. Hair sticking up, often crackling with static electricity as he pulled sweaters off and on, he drew attention in the glass-walled studio, if not on the street, but women avoided him. His wife and son had left him, disappearing into the south, or so he had been led to believe. Then he discovered they had been in Paris all along. Their things, a few pieces of clothing hanging in a closet and toys his son had outgrown, remained scattered around the apartment. It was easier to get rid of himself than to throw these things away. He had met the man she left him for, and held nothing against him, really. The man was apologetic and tended to confess to Fabien as if out of guilt, as if to declare, yes, she left you, but I have all these problems I'd like to tell you about. They met a few times by chance in a bar on the rue du Bac. Fabien didn't care to spend much time with him and began to avoid that street altogether.

A woman across the street received other women in her rooms, sometimes the visitors were agitated, sometimes impatient, frightened, or weepy. At night he watched them come and go, one at a time. Each one would place money on a table, then she would shut the curtains, never looking up in the direction of his window, although she might have known he was watching. When she reopened the curtains the visitor would have disappeared, only to be replaced by another within the hour. The episodic visitations and disappearances were not unlike a Méliès film. He had removed his own curtains, not only in order to see out at any time, but so he could be seen as well. Anybody who had the desire to watch could do so, but there was nothing much to see in the rooms he quickly abandoned each morning. Pictures of his family, too small to be seen from across the street, had been put away.

For him the most trivial coincidences transformed even the café next door into a fearful, tottering street barricade he would go out of his way to avoid. The topography of familiar zinc counter and marble-topped tables had always seemed like an airtight escape hatch he descended into after returning from Star Films, until one day in July a deeply tanned European, sensing an opportunity in Fabien's self-consciousness, sat down at his table and tried to strike up a conversation. He wanted to talk to someone, anyone. The man said he had lived in Algiers, but had returned to Paris during the winter, having lost everything through bad investments. Fabien shrugged, hoping to discourage his monologue, but the man didn't give up. He said he no longer understood France. He knew, as soon as he opened his mouth, people believed he'd gone native to the core and avoided him. He couldn't figure out what gave him away, what nuance of speech or gesture did it. He gave up trying.

"Let me show you something. Here's a stripe in the marble that imitates the route of the Nile, a series of parallel lines like the veins on the inside of an arm." He traced a pattern on a table top. Fabien couldn't see what he was trying to illustrate. While spilt coffee spread into Lake Victoria the man reminisced about Berbers, Tuaregs, sandstorms. He'd kept a boa constrictor that became lost one winter night and was eventually found frozen solid in a field in Montmartre. The man made an S curve with his hand. As he demonstrated he brushed Fabien's lapels and jacket buttons.

The man seemed to turn up every time Fabien went into the café. He tried to avoid the stranger, not looking up when the man entered the room, ignoring gestures to join his table. Invariably he would join Fabien anyway, buying him drinks however much Fabien tried to discourage him by barely responding to his questions or descriptions of the Sahel. If he shrugged instead of answering, the man shrugged in return, but went on remembering. He had begun to wear a haik on his head because, he said, of the heat.

For a while Fabien stayed away from the café, even remaining in his apartment in the morning, having coffee alone, and he crossed the street at night in a hopscotching strategy of avoidance. He blamed the former Algerian with a cloth on his head and took more care watching the woman he believed was an abortionist.

———·———

When Bluette Bemon first appeared at Star Films she used to stroll past Fabien's office what seemed like a hundred times a day dressed as a playing card or as a succubus clothed in black so that only her face registered on film. She wouldn't speak to him, and though at first she barely addressed anyone in the studio, Fabien felt singled out because she crossed his path so often and looked at him with what he interpreted as a cloying expression. He tried to avoid her and decided that her body, pinched into an hourglass shape, struck him as forced and a little repellent. *Love is a crime one cannot commit without an accomplice,* he quoted Baudelaire to her dressing-room door. He assumed the room was empty and no one could hear him, but Bluette suddenly opened the door and looked at him as if he were some kind of nut. It never occurred to him that he might have it wrong. If, when he arrived at the station, she was waiting for the train back to Paris, he would walk to the far end of the platform, pretending he hadn't seen her. So he didn't realize it when in fact she had begun to take steps to evade him.

A plaster volcano, replica of Martinique's Mount Pelée, lay in the center of Star Films. Edison had filmed a version of the volcano in which the eruption was represented by a barrel of beer left in the sun until it exploded. Méliès wanted to eclipse him, to make Edison look like a cinematic primitive, but when Fabien looked around Star Films, he felt as if he were in a nest of unrelated frenetic activity, nothing more. The weight of boredom was crippling, and as he completed one small task only to be presented with another, his uselessness overwhelmed him. Georges had once cast himself as the Leader of the Institute of Incoherent Geography, and it seemed to Fabien this role never ended for any of them. The wolf could be at the door yet a model universe born just outside Paris spun on its course as if it could always continue on its way untouched.

Off to one side of the set Bluette waited for him. Fabien needed to measure her for the construction of a skeleton-key costume. He walked slowly in her direction but she kept her back turned to him as if he were an insignificant irritation. He tried to talk to her, but she would barely answer him. It occurred to him that to see himself as the object of her occasional glance when she'd done nothing more than walk down a much-used corridor of Star Films was to tip the spotlight on himself when, in fact, no one had been looking. His imitation of Baudelaire rang in his ears. He was the one people laughed at behind his back, not her.

He held the measuring stick up to Bluette's hip, putting a finger against her flesh at the point where the stick ended. The second placement of the stick brought his finger to the side of her neck. She shivered, as if brushed by something unpleasant, then walked away. He wanted to explain that he wasn't like the *pied noir* from the café, who had no idea there ought to be a barrier between thought and speech, but she ignored him, and Fabien was left to petition empty film sets. He followed her, walking close to the stage without watching where he was going. The model volcano convulsed, showering him with flour, cinders, and chalk dust. Flashing lights, another effect, were dim, sputtering on long past their cue.

"Idiot," Georges coughed.

A washroom attendant who had played Edward VII rushed to help clean him off. Fabien sputtered, blinded and whitened. Bluette passed by, staring through him as if he didn't exist. Fabien renewed his efforts to follow her, not knowing what to say. It was worse than if she had laughed directly at him. Without really knowing why, he felt as if he had collided with the series of levers and winches that caused backdrops and sets to tumble from the ceiling. He had imagined he was being pursued and desired when she barely knew he existed. In a white maillot she was barely dressed, and even with his flour-occluded vision he could see that she was carefully stepping around his dust, as if the particles might have been deadly germs. A set painter ran outside in a coughing fit, violently gagging.

Georges felt he needed to interject a laudatory distraction. Pounding Fabien on the back he shouted as if they had all been made deaf.

"Apollinaire was interested in how I would reproduce the effect of the volcano. I told him I would do so by photographing cinders and chalk, and he replied: 'Monsieur and I have the same occupation, we enchant ordinary materials.'" Georges smiled, pleased with the comparison.

Edward VII wiped and swept until all the flour, chalk dust, and cinders were gone while Bluette disappeared into the back corridors of Star Films.

LABOR OMNIA VINCIT

Fabien painted the motto, invented by Méliès, on a plinth supporting a plaster statue of Barbenfouillis, commander of a trip to the moon. The statue would be completed by the time Méliès was ready to shoot the last celebratory scene. *A Trip to the Moon* was a fantastic preconstruction, a film meant to project the future, borrowing from the mathematical and empirical domain of Flammarion as much as from Wells and Verne. Fabien loved this film and was happy to dive back into the world of lewd entertainments. His hurricane of tasks continued to spin into the nothingness of sets made and then dismantled, but after the volcano film he realized the actualities frightened him in some undefined way, and he was happy when Méliès took refuge in preconstructions. So what if the wolf was at the door? A brush fell, spattering his trouser leg. Méliès kicked it aside as he stood with his arm around the plaster statue, which was essentially a portrait of himself. He smiled as if they were old mates, which, of course, they were.

Creatures with lobster claws, spiked heads, and sharp knees did cartwheels and stood on their heads with the agility of monkeys. They were acrobats hired to play Selenites, creatures who lived on the moon, a moon who cried a custard tear when pierced by the rocket sent by Barbenfouillis's Astronomy Club. One acrobat, needly points growing from her skull, was poked by an astronaut's umbrella and disappeared in a cloud of smoke. This would be the film Méliès would be most remembered for. The image of the moon with a rocket in its eye would be reproduced in other films long past Méliès's death.

Bluette Bernon played Phoebe, rocking on her crescent moon. She caused a snowstorm that woke the travelers on their way into the stratosphere; now she rubbed her back where the wooden seat had irritated her. Bluette, swinging in superlunary space, appeared fearless. Even the vertiginous momentum of the crescent moon she jumped from didn't seem to scare her. Fabien watched her argue with Georges. The backs of her knees were tense and straight and her bare toes curled against the floor. She didn't want to sit on the moon swinging her legs like an ornament in the wind.

"If this is a preconstruction, then there aren't any rules. I can play any part in the script and I want to be an astronaut."

"Girls can't be astronauts, dear."

"Do me a favor, Georges?" Bluette looked bored. "Wake up."

"You, Bluette, can go to the moon." Georges meant this as an insult.

"Exactly."

On film Bluette had been transformed into a houri, an opium dream, a large key, but she stared at him now as herself, in open hostility, and turning on a silver heel, put her arms around a passing stagehand. Georges was blind to her signs that seemed to say *I am loved, allegiance isn't where you think; it's turned elsewhere.* Perhaps because he knew there would be no coup. Star Films wouldn't be overturned by a recalcitrant Phoebe, but Bluette's gesture bothered Fabien, because it seemed to him that she flirted openly with anyone, but not him.

Georges surrounded himself with women in chaotic chorus lines that looped around the sets and went absolutely nowhere. None of the grotesque but agile Selenites, like clay in Méliès's hands, held any interest for Fabien. One complained that her costume prevented her from sitting down; she was tired. She had unfastened her monstrous head, technically fashioned after deep-sea diver helmets, and held it in her hands, blond hair falling over her shoulders. Were they half crab, half monkey, or humans with complicated histories? What were their individual and collective identities? Fabien had no idea. The project of finding out would involve too much peeling back layers of costume and too much effort. He painted over the *it* of *vincit* and watched as the crescent moon was removed from the stage and carried off into storage.

"Subjects dependent on the imagination are infinitely varied and inexhaustible," Georges said, smiling and looking around the set as Fabien searched for his hat. Fabien didn't quite believe Georges would rest in those subjects, pleased with himself and languidly pleased with the women who looped brainlessly in and out of his films. There would be other actualities, more terrifying than the sugary dreams trick photography was capable of creating.

"Tomorrow you can dismantle the moon!" Méliès shouted after him.

While waiting for the evening train back to Paris Fabien watched for her. She approached as he looked in the opposite direction, and when he turned around he saw her. One of the actors carried her bag. It was a tall man Fabien recognized as a character who often stood in front of the other actors and had a tendency to look directly into the camera lens. When the film was screened it would appear that he, and only he, addressed the audience, upstaging the others whose gaze was directed at painted sky. Fabien stood a few yards behind them and watched as they boarded. He remained on the platform and waited for the next train.

The man beckoned to Fabien with such urgency that he couldn't pretend he hadn't seen him. He was talking loudly to someone else in the café, but still signaled frantically. As he sat down Fabien heard the word *Kabyles*. Fabien didn't know what he was talking about and wanted to leave the table at once, but inertia kept him sitting, listening to the *pied noir* who, bareheaded and anxious, now denied ever having owned a haik.

"An Algerian tribe of the south Sahara," the man turned exclusively to Fabien, "a kind of Berber, but more dangerous. They're coming into the country now through Marseilles." Unscrewing the cap of his pen with a flourish and a jerk of his elbow, he drew a picture of one with a big nose and a knife in his mouth. Fabien told him the drawing looked like a cartoon.

"I'm not an artist like you." The man was hurt and annoyed.

"Why do they want to come here?" Fabien asked.

"Drug trade. They make a fortune."

Fabien found it hard to believe these particular Algerians could assimilate with the seamlessness and speed needed to make large amounts of money in a land which the man himself found foreign and unpredictable.

"They're like an infection, gangrenous, that you fight in someone else, then it turns out you've caught it."

"So what do you do?"

"Throw them out."

"But you cut gangrene."

"Self-amputation if the infection has spread to oneself."

Fabien drank another absinthe trying, in a blurred way, to figure out who and what the man was talking about. Others listened to him with interest, writing down names and talking of traveling to Marseilles to loot or riot, but Fabien was utterly convinced they were as harmless as schoolboys plotting their turf wars. He wasn't going to lose sleep over Kabyles. Wrapped in the sense of security that came from extricating himself from the café he returned home, only to fall asleep in a chair. He dreamed about Bluette as a succubus, cunning and sinuous, defying gravity like smoke. Consciousness and daylight didn't seem to diminish the memory of the dream once he awoke, and throughout the next day he felt embarrassed whenever he saw her in the distance, sitting on the discarded hull of the *Maine* or sticking her hand into the volcano, now cold and pushed to the side.

———·———

Star Film Studio was large; it filled an entire block, but Fabien's office was small, cramped, his desk covered with papers and props: army uniforms, helmets, fake guns, and rubber chickens.

False beards hung from pegs along one wall, a winking face had been daubed behind one, and he snapped the beard so that it boinged up and down. Large rubber shoes leaned against a windowsill; a filmy pair of gray wings, torn, wires sticking out, were propped in a corner; a cardboard sword had been placed across his cluttered desk like a threat or a kind of dare. It might have been left by an actor between rehearsals, or one of the set painters might have entered his work area in order to throw the gauntlet on his desk. Dares and the transgressions they hinged upon made Fabien nervous. Without glad-handing or behaving obsequiously, without compromising his reticence, he believed that maintaining cordiality in the studio was very important; it kept people at a safe distance.

Letting himself be kicked around was part of his strategy of passive resistance, but sooner or later he would get Méliès. Georges might one day slip on the tail of a costume and land with such force he would crash through the set floor, and the cuts and bruises of battered or broken limbs would put him out of the way. The lesson: real injury can lie behind apparent puff-balls. No one would suspect Fabien of loosening wheels, cutting wires, greasing the rails.

As he drew models of scenes, as he discussed props and costumes or when he was tapped on the shoulder to perform, Fabien didn't argue with the other assistants or actors. He appeared not to care about having his own way, and by seeming to be indifferent, he often got what he wanted in the end. If two painters couldn't agree on who should drive death's coach he would suggest a skeleton, as if he'd just that moment connected the idea and its symbol, death's driver and bones, when he had in fact had the image in mind all along. They would agree with him and pour out white paint, as if the connection between the notion of death and the image of skeleton had only just occurred to them, too. Without thinking he ran his hand over a camel recently cut from a sheet of wood and several splinters became embedded in his palm. He opened and shut his fist, pushing out the yellow bits of wood. The cardboard sword didn't carry any dare or threat. It was just part of the mess. He felt narrow rays of sunlight as he dropped the rubber shoes to the floor and opened shuttered windows. The others left him to himself in his cluttered end of the studio. He was careful not to offend anyone.

"Move to the left, more slowly, look shocked. Try to express panic, see like this." Eyes bulged, eyebrows shot up to widow's peak, jaw dropped.

Fabien could hear directions being given outside his door. He had a view of the stage, only half walls separated his quarters from the main part of the studio. He knocked over an empty flea circus that toppled down from a pile of crates, crashing to the floor. Fabien picked up the home of the fleas and put it on his desk. A beetle crawled out of one of the turrets. He squashed it with a giant rubber nose that lay on his ink blotter. He had bought the circus, a castle-shaped house, as a theoretical shortcut should a castle set need to be built, shaking out the bugs on the sidewalk and stamping them flat. If Méliès could enlarge figures, Fabien expected he would one day reverse the process and shrink them as well. The camera would be moved very close to the door, and optically reduced actors would lower the cardboard drawbridge, but by the time *Gulliver's Travels* was shot the castle had fallen apart, its crenellations frayed and its turrets dented and miserable.

While rinsing the rubber nose under a faucet, he watched Méliès position a pair of actors dressed as soldiers. Fantasies, preconstructions had been suspended at Star Films, and Georges had decided to concentrate on a dose of reality, perhaps dangerously so. Méliès had experienced the abrupt slamming of body against stone floor.

Years ago Star Films had produced several reconstructed newsreels. They were more like filmed documents; Georges called them *actualities*. When America intervened in Cuba and the Philipines, Méliès brought in headlines clipped from American papers, patriotic and sensationalistic, spreading them out on the studio floor. He knew about William Randolph Hearst, who had sent an artist, Remington, to Cuba to draw evidence of Spanish aggression toward American interests on the island. When Remington found none and wanted to return, Hearst wired back, *You furnish the pictures. I'll furnish the war.* Méliès liked the idea of hatching images and propaganda, but he would work against Hearst's designs. He would furnish pictures of American trespasses, and so began work on an *actualité, Divers at Work on the Wreck of the "Maine."* When Méliès spoke of the film, Fabien pictured American cowboys in Cuba killing campesinos, until he was cast as a diver and instructed to move in painful slow motion, as if he was plodding along under miles of ocean and had been doing so for years.

The *actualité* now being arranged as Fabien washed his rubber nose required no optical illusions apart from trompe l'oeil backdrops. For this film, Georges would not use any trapdoors or fantastically painted flies. No creatures would bounce off springboards, glide through the air, or dance behind special effects. The stage set was ordinary, a prison cell.

"Find an actor who looks like the accused."

"Don't you think this one is a very good likeness? Tell the truth, in a uniform he's not bad." Fabien brushed off the man's jacket.

"No, he's too tall."

Captain Dreyfus, played by an ironmonger, had overheard, and he crossed his arms over his chest. Fabien had looked for professional actors in Chatelet around the corner in Montreuil, but the resemblance of this ironmonger to Dreyfus, he believed, was remarkable.

"Take him down any city street dressed this way, and you'll risk a lynch mob." Fabien strained his voice, as if he actually wasn't sure and didn't really want to get involved. The point of the film was to take on the mob. That was Méliès's intention. Fabien bent down to tie his shoe, but in his affected nonchalance, he wondered if Méliès realized the depth of violence crowds were capable of when issue of the trial was raised. City streets, as he walked them, contained the potential to take on many possible characteristics, benign or animated. Paving stones uprooted and guns fired — these things didn't reverse themselves — nor could the metamorphosis of an urban landscape be controlled just because the camera was dismantled.

The ironmonger he had found down the street appeared, to Fabien, to be a perfect likeness, perhaps too perfect, but he pretended as if he didn't care. When a set was complete Georges often found it wanting; when a set was in a fragmentary state, he was charmed, imagining what was not yet visible. He saw planets in a sky intended to be empty. He saw crowns on launderers and those who worked in abbatoirs. If Fabien suggested that a particular prop or costume wasn't very believable, or in some way not the best choice, he was reprimanded with the obvious: *this*, Méliès would point to the scaffolding behind the moon, *was not meant to be authentic, we are no longer in the material world.* In other words, Georges had license to imagine the dance of the skeletons, the grimace of a lunar crater, but not to tinker with Devil's Island. Many pictures of the captain had been printed, more than of any other subject he could remember, and Fabien knew the ironmonger's resemblance to Dreyfus was uncanny. *Dreyfus c'est moi,* Fabien imagined Georges saying, putting a fraternal but dismissive arm around the ironmonger, as he had around Barbenfoullis before he left for the moon, and Fabien would scream, *You're not Dreyfus, who do you think you are?*

"Do you have pictures?" Méliès asked.

"Of course."

Newspaper photographs and postcards Fabien kept in a drawer in his office provided unquestionable proof that the actor and the accused spy were as good as twins. Georges relented, and Fabien was, in this case, made to feel he had not yet made his inevitable mistakes, so he went further. Something was wrong with the cell.

"When the prisoner is in his cell he should have chipped cups and cracked plates. The cross should be removed from the wall." He walked up to the stage and pried it off.

"But perhaps every cell has one, regardless of who is interned," Méliès argued, then, after a moment of thought, gave in. "Take the cross down."

The Dreyfus look-alike lit a cigarette and slouched against a wall that was unstable and in danger of collapsing under his weight.

On the train back to Paris he looked out the window. He'd neither heard nor read anything about a body discovered near the tracks, but he was sure the boys had been shouting at the train because of what they had discovered. The stream had prematurely aged into pools of algae and in spots was completely dry. The boys were nowhere in sight. Fabien added prison uniforms and cracked plates to his shopping list.

He knew on which streets he would find secondhand clothes, prop furniture, facsimiles of medieval armor and plaster imitations of Renaissance Italian saints. He knew the shop in the Galerie de Valois where on the morning of July thirteenth Charlotte Corday bought the knife she used to murder Marat. It was a few doors away from the former Café Mécanique where before the Revolution patrons were served by invisible hands from dumbwaiters that opened out into the middle of each table. Disembodied hands might have predicted the explosion of headless bodies soon to come. The Mécanique went out of business, outlived by Dr. Guillotine's machine, which operated nearby. Directly next door was the Chinese Shadow Theater, once an entertainment for children and convent girls, then, by a transformation that would have puzzled even Méliès, it became a place where men could procure boys in crumbling rooms stripped of oriental decoration, all identities unknown. Now the building was empty, its windows boarded up, and a bitter breeze came from a smashed-in door that had once been painted red and gold. He watched a rat pull a long vegetable peel of some kind along the gutter. Then the rat turned on the peel so it cloaked its neck like a noose and ran on.

Working for Méliès, he learned where to find everything in the city. For secondhand china he went to Bernard Lazare & Frères on rue des Rosiers. The window of Lazare's contained stacks of plain white plates, irregularly shaped glasses, a polished but dented teakettle, otherwise it was bare of any display trimmings. A red-haired man in a black overcoat buttoned up to his neck who must have been Bernard's brother stood behind the counter slowly moving cups and saucers to the shelves. Fabien leaned on the counter and picked· one up. It had red stripes running around the edge and leaves winding around the stripes as if trellised.

"Thirty francs for the set. We have one left. Not a complete set." He offered to throw in an ashtray from the Hôtel Coq d'Or.

Fabien weighed one of the heavy cups in his hand. He explained that he needed something very plain.

"Something one would be given in Cherche Midi or Santé."

"You're not going to prison."

"Not me. An actor."

"Try someplace else, down the street you might find what you're looking for. I'm closing up soon."

"It's Friday."

"Yes, it's Friday."

"Where's Bernard?"

The man continued to position plates as if they were valuable china without answering. He didn't know what he had done to offend the shopkeeper. The cardboard sword seemed to hang over his head, its hilt of paste rubies glinting behind stacks of heavy-lipped bowls and rows of wine glasses with crooked stems.

"I know Bernard. I do business with him all the time,"

Fabien started to say. His voice sounded feeble, as if unconsciously acknowledging unknown and unknowable's transgressions. He, Fabien, wasn't one of them. If he had been a member of their own tribe things might have gone differently. It wasn't always easy to identify them. One made embarrassing mistakes.

"Are you certain Bernard's not here?"

"Yes, I ought to know, shouldn't I? I'm always in the shop," the man said, as if Fabien was an idiot if he'd never seen him. His tone discouraged Fabien from asking if something had happened to Bernard. Deciding to buy something, anything, for more than it was worth he pointed to a water pitcher on a shelf behind the counter. Greasy dust came off on Lazare's fingers as he wrapped the object in newspaper; remaining expressionless, he wiped them off on the front of his coat. The bundle was tied with twine and handed to Fabien.

"You should leave from the back door." He looked over Fabien's head as he spoke. The man's accent blurred the conditional tense; words sounded almost guttural, as if he'd lived in Holland or Germany. Matching the man's aggravated manner and not really understanding what had been said to him, Fabien took the awkward package in his arms and walked out the front door in a pique. Neither one of them said good-bye.

The door hit him from behind as it closed, and a camera flashed; the sound of an explosion followed a sharp burst of light. He slapped one hand over his eyes and groped in front with the other, a cartoon blind man whose packages crashed to the pavement. Blinking and confused, he felt like Méliès's moon who found a rocket stuck in its eye. In the moment he was disoriented, the photographer quickly folded up her tripod and began to run. When he took his hand from his face he could see her dimly, a spiked shadow, yards away, and he began to chase her, trying to keep her outline in sight, but each foot felt as if weighted by an enormous gummy rubber shoe. The woman was big and powerful, but she had so much to carry that before she reached the corner he was able to grab the legs of the tripod sticking out from under her arm. He yanked it and jerked her around. He faced a mask painted with long black lips and clumped, pointed eyelashes; it was starkly black and white the way masks were often painted at Star Films. As she shook free of him, they screamed at each other.

"What do you think you're doing?"

"Scumbag!"

"You're out of your mind. Get lost!"

Fabien tried to tear the mask from her face, but she managed to parry all attempts to get near her head.

"Why did you take my picture?"

She didn't answer.

"All I did was walk out of a shop!" he screamed at her.

She mumbled something about foreigners or foreignness. Her voice was deep yet nervous.

"Foreign to what?" he yelled, shaking her. He felt ridiculous yelling at a mask, especially a very plain manufactured one that was chosen not just to obfuscate, but to deliberately strip even the *idea* of a mask from having any sort of identity of its own. He was out of breath and humiliated. She dove for a cab which appeared out of nowhere, and was gone. He returned to the sidewalk before Lazare's window where the pitcher lay in lumpy paper-wrapped fragments. Lazare's door was locked, and no one responded to his knocking. He sat on the curb, unwrapped the package, then balled up the broken shards in their paper and threw them away. The ashtray from the Hôtel Coq d'Or remained whole, and he stuffed it into his pocket. All the shops surrounding Lazare's were closed as well, as if in the flash of his screaming, everyone had locked and shuttered their tiny, marginal businesses. He took cigarettes and the ashtray out of his pocket and smoked on the street in front of Lazare's, holding the ashtray in his left hand. He couldn't call the police. She hadn't broken any laws. Anyone can take your picture. Rain began to fall, so he got up from the curb and stood under an awning for a few minutes. The street was deserted, and when he was sure no one was looking he dumped the ashes from the Coq d'Or bowl, let it fill with water and watched his reflection, swirled the water, then tossed it out.

"You're a lunatic." A boy in a checkered vest whom he hadn't seen huddling in a doorway yelled in his direction. Fabien looked at him while the ashtray filled with drops again. The boy wrapped his jacket around his narrow body, darted out into the rain, and vanished.

———·———

Fabien stirred his coffee, making the spoon hit the sides of the cup with a repetitive sound. While he drank he drew pictures on scraps of paper littering the table: a prisoner looking at a calendar whose pages flew off into the distance, a train of camels, a disembodied hand drawing an S in the air, an escaped boa constrictor, an empty checkered vest. He heard no one on the stairs outside his door, so at first he didn't notice the delivery. As he stood to pour more coffee he looked down; the paper lay where a minute earlier there had been only bare floor. The gap between the bottom of his door and the floorboards was high enough to accomodate a large rat, so the folded journal had been easily slid into his rooms. It was a very slight paper, *La Libre Parole*, a paper he'd seen before but never read. Leaving his coffee half-finished, he picked it up and unfolded the damp pages. The first page carried his picture, blurred but recognizable, coming out of Lazare's, carrying an awkwardly shaped package. The caption read that these businesses weren't French, and the people caught coming out of these places therefore stood accused of partronizing businesses that weren't French. The paper contained caricatures of beards who resembled Méliès a little, Méliès when he dressed as a devil, one of his favorite roles. By the time he emerged from his doorway thousands of people would be able to identify him. The power of the photograph was such that he felt accused and exposed, though all he'd done was buy some rubbish from a secondhand shop. The photograph would make him famous to a number of fanatics who felt he was part of a large piece of machinery engineered to ensure their betrayal. Putting dark glasses in his pocket before he walked into the street, he didn't know if, when he traveled to Star Films, he was risking his life or not.

On the train to Montreuil, he saw a woman with his picture folded under her arm. He stood up to go into another car, but the train was crowded, and he couldn't find another seat.

The act of taking his picture without his consent had betrayed hostility, but he'd thought the nature and intent of the hostility could have been random craziness until he saw what had been done with his photograph and where it had been printed. They weren't after him in particular, they were after the Lazares. Until the paper was slid under his door the photograph was a vague, unexplained prank, as inexplicable as the boy in the rain who had called him a lunatic; and anyone who would wear a loud-checkered vest like that might well have a few screws loose himself. Those who read *La Libre Parole* had little interest in the North African wars, the Panama scandal, or General Boulanger, nor were they obsessed with an accounting of who in the city bought what where, but they had ideas about race and infection, and somehow in their desire to rout out those they perceived as foreigners, Fabien knew he'd been caught up in a campaign of eradication that he felt certain had nothing to do with him.

As the train continued east he drew sketches on the margins of his newspaper of the prison yard that needed to be built at Star Films. No object in the studio had a fixed identity. The ties that held object to name, use, and meaning were loose and flapped in the breeze. His picture was being circulated all over Paris. By the time the train reached Montreuil his drawing of the prison set ran into columns of type. He looked at the woman who had folded up her copy of *La Libre Parole* as he walked past her seat in order to exit the train.

He's a member of the Syndicate. It was in the paper.

Fabien was sure he heard her whisper, but when he turned his head she was looking out the window.

Syndicate. S - S - S Syllabant with the steam escaping from the train.

From the station platform he watched until the train was out of sight, then he walked toward the glass building at 74, boulevard de l'Hôtel de Ville, at the intersection of rue François Debergue. The two-tiered network of spars and panes dazzled in the sun. Under its steeply pitched roof he felt safe.

When he unlocked the door to his rooms the studio was already noisy with hammering and crowded with actors silently and independently acting out their parts in a pavane of unrelated gestures. He wondered if any of them had seen his picture, even by accident, and what it meant to them. While waiting for Méliès he stared at the flea circus absently, finally taking the thing down and unscrewing one of the turrets in distraction, just to see how it was put together. Dry husks, specks of dead fleas tilted toward his hand and a cuff link fell out. It was in the shape of the letter *M* and studded with fake diamonds. Fabien left it on the floor. The identity of the person who slid the paper under his door was another question. He didn't understand how he could have been identified by that person. Someone at *La Libre Parole* knew his name. His concierge, quick to exchange favors for payment, was the first suspect, but her name had been Madmoiselle Lazard before she married. The abortionist, though he watched her, didn't seem to watch him in return. Even the frog killers who had seen him on the train, even they, were suspect. The former Zouave who missed the desert knew his name and address. The truculent boy who watched him in the rain and told him he was a lunatic seemed the only one free of suspicion. By yelling at Fabien, by accusing him of madness as he watched his reflection in a secondhand ashtray, he had called attention to himself as well. The paper might have been delivered by a friend who knew he would never see it otherwise, anonymously offering a gesture of explanation if not caution. Someone who didn't want to get involved himself, and so didn't knock, didn't wait around to answer any questions. There had been a headline in *Le Siecle* once, not long ago: *Les Mensonges de la Photographie.* In altered photographs deadly enemies appeared to be enjoying one another's company. He remembered thinking these images must have caused everyone who saw them to doubt the veracity of photographic evidence, how could it be otherwise? To see Zola and General du Paty de Clam, the man who first accused Dreyfus of being a spy, to see them as comrades made the films that emerged weekly from Montreuil look like reinforcements of common sense rather than contradictions of gravity, simple logic, and most appearances.

A woman leaned in his doorway. It was Bluette dressed as a figure from a painting that came to life in the last scene of a film Fabien had forgotten about. She played Manet's Olympia, but in this scene only her head was needed. Since the Dreyfus project was still only in a rudimentary stage, other films were being wound up.

"Your entertainments are shown in amusement parks. Hard cases and poor sops on their days off laugh themselves sick, I think. What a place for Manet," she said. A picture frame was fastened around her head. Why did she say *your* entertainments? Angry at Méliès for not casting her in *The Dreyfus Affair,* she didn't include herself.

"Maybe you're right." The film about a painting come to life might be a flop of no interest to anyone. "That hasn't stopped you from working on them, has it?" He didn't know why she was suddenly talking to him, and because he was distracted, he answered her sharply.

"Do you wear a lot of secondhand clothing?" she asked. Fabien had thought his clothes looked new apart from a few ink or paint stains around the cuffs.

"My work takes me to such places . . ."

"I know, I know," she didn't let him finish. "Say, you might need one of these yourself." She unfastened the frame and put on one of the false beards hanging from pegs near Fabien's desk.

"What do you mean?"

"A disguise, dummy. I saw someone reading that paper on the train. I saw your picture. Are you going to ask them to print an apology?" She laughed. "Their address is right on the front page. It isn't a secret." She snapped a false beard hanging from a peg. "Listen, my friend, you may not know it, but they mean business. If you cause trouble for them, they'll cause trouble for you."

"You're either sure Dreyfus was a spy or certain he was framed." An actor dressed as a sleepwalker joined them and added, "If you challenge them, take an arsenal." The cardboard sword and prop guns would do him no good.

Fabien ran his fingers through his hair. In *The Eclipse* sexless planets became male or female and fell in love, skipping cheeses became agents of revenge, a painting could come to life and walk away from a wall, the sun could swallow a train, and cardboard guns could do injury.

Poor sun, Georges had said, *I must make him swallow a nausea pill. Where is my nausea pill today?*

If his morning train had been eaten by the sun, he'd be traveling in some giant solar stomach instead of designing a prison cell, and it seemed to him that an imaginary trip might present a reasonable alternative to the glare of light through glass and Méliès's testy continuation of the debate as to whether or not there should have been a crucifix on the cell wall. Fabien watched the sleepwalker put his arm around Bluette, who still wore his fake beard, and she swung the picture frame, her arm like a pendulum, and the frame a weight. As they walked down the hall she nearly hit a man in a cheese costume when he passed her.

"Careful with that thing," the cheese complained.

The sleepwalker only held his nose.

Fabien put one of the wooden guns in his pocket and walked out of Star Films as silently as he had arrived that morning. On the road to the train he skirted the cheese walking in the same direction, and he realized that the panes and spars of Méliès's studio no longer made him feel removed from the city and safe from its inhabitants.

———•———

Fabien became obsessed with the idea of finding the photographer who had taken his picture. If he could speak to her, if he could ask her what demons set in motion the act of stalking, the endless hours of waiting in front of certain shops in order to photograph strangers; if he could dissolve the opaque mass of these questions into something transparent and clear, he could regain enough sure footing to throw stones at the offices of *La Libre Parole* itself, to take a crack at their door with a sledgehammer. He already knew part of the answer: by intimidating potential customers the paper forced a boycott that would in turn cause those businesses to fold and their owners to flee. He knew that, but he wanted to ask her what drove her into the street with a camera, that was all. Finding her presented certain problems. The offices of *La Libre Parole* were out of bounds. Even messenger boys would recognize him, but he learned the paper had its printing operations in a basement near place Maubert, and the printers, perhaps just doing a job without particular allegiances to one side or another, might have some information about those who took the pictures. Photographic plates were delivered directly to them. On an afternoon shortly after the incident he looked for their address, walking in circles as if he didn't actually intend ever to come face to face with his destination but finally arriving at the east end of place Maubert, a street he knew well. He asked directions of a boy whose back was to him as he glued bicycle advertisements to a brick wall.

"Look," the boy pointed sarcastically at the row of posters

with the end of his glue brush. Men raced around a velodrome. "If you were to follow the direction in which the bicycles point, you would come to it."

The ruelle off place Maubert was more like a narrow lane than a street, and as he turned down it, he heard what sounded like shrieking in a foreign language. A woman knocked on a smeared glass window, gesturing for him to come in, pointing to the door, but he ignored both her and the shrieks. The number he sought was a few doors down. Barely visible it was painted in white on the glass transom of a small apartment building that contained a butcher shop on the ground floor. It was obvious no printers had their works in this building. Looking for an explanation he entered the butcher's. There were no customers, and the place smelled of rancid meat hanging on hooks. Its walls were smeared with dirt and blood, peeling paint fell near a few cuts lying on a table. A young man, probably the butcher's assistant, laconically arranged a roll of sausages into a starlike shape.

"I'm looking for some printers who have a shop at this address." He shaded his eyes from a nonexistent light. They surely knew what went on in the building. An older man, the owner of the shop, came out from behind a striped curtain.

The boy pointed to stairs outside the shop, dropping a leg of red meat as he did so. He quickly picked the leg up, wiping the sawdust that clung to it off on his apron before replacing the joint on the counter. Fabien thanked him and left. As he unlatched the gate before the steps leading down to the basement he noticed the butcher had come out from behind his sausage counter and was staring at him as he descended. Fabien stared back. The man's apron was covered with fresh red marks and old stains. He held a cleaver in one hand and clutched a leg of some kind of meat under his arm, and he stood frozen like a statue.

An unmarked door abutted the last step. Fabien flattened his hair with spit then dusted it with white powder and put on a pair of dark glasses. Among the tricks he'd learned working at

Star Films was how one could disguise oneself with very little effort. He pushed the door open and found himself in a large cellar, much broader than the building above; it was at least several cellars combined.

"Hertobise, down boy, goddamn you to hell," someone called out to a dog that barked in the distance.

Damp, badly lit rooms were partially separated into smaller cubicles by a series of partitions. The presses were quiet; he saw no printers, only neglected typecases and composing sticks. A dead rat lay on its back in a puddle of dirty ink near one of the press legs. They would never get rid of the rats with the meat just upstairs. Two men sat in the back hunched over a table, and they seemed to be the only ones present in the rooms smelling of ink and petrol. The cellar was dark, only their faces were lit. His hair began to rise, and he ran his hand over his head, hoping to flatten it, brushing the powder from his shoulders, hoping his attempts at changing his appearance would be successful. He was skillful at his profession but feared this was not a film set, and what read as on-the-job full makeup in one place might appear cartoonish in another. Their voices were barely audible, and at first they didn't see him; they appeared to be penciling out lines of type on the pages strewn over their desk. One sported only a beard, no moustache, and as he approached him, Fabien was tempted to pull on that clump of hair, so wiry looking against the deadly white pallor, that he half suspected it would snap back, a fake. A long, scratched counter separated Fabien from the two men. Initials had been carved into it, indicating the plank might have been purchased secondhand and had once served as a bar or part of a table. The bearded man rolled up ink stained sleeves. He took off his glasses, rubbed the lenses on his sleeve and pushed them back on his head. In the distance his colleague scribbled on a pad and poured himself a drink. Between the bad lighting, removed glasses, and preoccupation, he didn't appear to recognize Fabien, although a copy of the paper with his picture in it lay open on the counter.

"My name is Jean Belmonde," Fabien said. The man squinted. "I'm interested in your front page."

"What can you do for us?"

"I'm a photographer. I offer my services and my experience."

"What kind of pictures do you take?"

"Portraits."

"You need to go to the main offices."

"They sent me to you. I'm meant to accompany one of your photographers just for a day or two, to learn the ropes, so to speak. I was told you would give me the address of the woman photographer because she most needs help."

The printers were silent. Fabien kept talking.

"When you publish someone's picture a signal is sent, notice is given. I've been swindled by cheapskates and foreigners." Fabien thought about Bernard Lazare and how he sometimes paid him more but also sometimes less than an object's worth. He hoped the man would put the two halves of the sentence together without Fabien having to spell out what it was he was trying to say. He had learned his lines from the man who had transformed a table into a map of North Africa. Unlike Méliès, Fabien didn't care about the Dreyfus trial and felt no strong convictions about his guilt or innocence, but the photograph had attacked him when he didn't want to get involved. His image became the agency of their campaign. What did he want from these people? He wanted them to contribute to their own exposure, but it was exposure launched from spongy ground. There were moments when he wasn't sure the raving prose spewed out every week by the men who scuttled in the dark cellar before him actually hurt anyone. He felt himself sucked into a morass. He barged on.

"We're overrun by clappers and syphilitics who prey on Christian charity and goodwill. They live in charnel houses with unwashed children, training them to be just as rapacious as their fathers," he picked up steam, "pimping, preying, contaminating, especially in Alsace." Alsace, he believed, was a code for the Dreyfus situation. The man nodded. Fabien felt encouraged. "Landlords, factory owners, harassers of all kinds, polluters."

The printer put his elbow on the counter and leaned in closer to Fabien. He sensed he was gaining credibility.

"Barracks should be built to isolate them, and then they must be sent back to Asia where they came from. Or they could be put on boats to be set adrift in the Atlantic or blown up, even better. Only when they're separated from the rest of us can we really breathe freely."

The printer nodded. Not enthusiastically, but it was clear he was listening closely. Fabien returned to his original reason for visiting the printers.

"To shame people by publishing their photographs and put others out of business is a strategy that requires patience, but I'm also fast and hide easily." Fabien ducked under the counter as if to demonstrate, realizing as he did so that it might have been a mistake to infer that their operation was in any way clandestine or sly because these men were, in some ways, quite open about what they saw as their work.

"You can take pictures fast?" the man bent down to ask him.

Fabien nodded. Standing quickly and still feeling frustrated at his ineptitude, he concentrated on the printer's beard and equally fake-looking eyebrows, dark and wiry against white skin, the kind of deliberately aggressive hair that might provoke an agitated child to tweak it. The man slowly looked down at the paper lying open on the counter, then looked up at Fabien.

The man turned his back on Fabien as his colleague approached, and they whispered to one another. Fabien heard the words *risk* and *intimidation* so he affected a nodding response that could be interpreted as agreement, despite the fact he had no idea what they were actually talking about.

The other man, compact as a jockey with a pencil moustache, folded papers with a sharp crease and handed his colleague a printed page, which he held at a distance without reading. This second man was almost doll-like. If he had been taller he might have seemed less tightly wound and his attractiveness might have been unnerving; instead he was the kind of person who could be compared to a whippet. Weak light filtered through the sheet he held up, and Fabien was able to see the lines but couldn't interpret the reversed words. The beard returned it to his associate, a man who even when he spoke in whispers, clearly believed in his own importance.

Elbowing in front, the Napoléon interjected himself between them, upstaging the other who leaned over in order to hear his whispers. He looked at Fabien closely as if he finally recognized him. Looking at the paper then back at Fabien, he began to frown and turn beet colored. Words Fabien couldn't quite hear were spoken with a kind of sibilance, then straining, he heard a few explosive syllables and saw the bearded man wiping his face. The Napoléon seemed like a child suspended in the seconds between injury and scream, but the beard suddenly took the paper from his hands. *Too quick sometimes,* was all Fabien heard. Too quick to make accusations, perhaps. Too quick to jump to conclusions. Too quick to suspect. He wanted them to believe he shared in their cause, but was at a loss as to what slogans, other than those he'd already voiced, might serve to dispel their doubts. Against sounds of paper folding and crackling, Fabien interrupted them.

"Ridicule, I find, is a very effective weapon." He hoped his loud voice reaching back into the basement sounded convincing. He gave the *r* sound in ridicule as extra high trill. The pencil moustache looked at him with suspicion then retreated into the inky distance, walking straight and turning corners as if every one measured ninety degrees.

"You can work with this photographer." The beard wrote a name and address on a piece of paper, smirking just a bit. "The paper will pay for whatever prints we use." He spoke about their well-placed contributors but their identities (a bishop, an abbé, a general) were only alluded to, the artists and writers themselves were not named.

In the distance a dog began to bark again, and Fabien wondered what they paid, although he had no intention of getting behind a camera. He felt uneasy, pocketed the address he'd been given, and left the two men to their schemes. Upstairs, the butcher shop was shuttered and locked as if it had never been there at all. Fabien turned the piece of paper over: Roger Artois. It was not the name Fabien wanted. When he got to the street he threw the address away, then went back to retrieve it, putting the paper in his pocket, folding it into quarters, then folding it again.

———·———

In place Maubert Huguenots and heretic printers had once been burned along with their books, and though it was now the site of blooming trees, wide boulevards, and busy shops, a man had recently been found dead of opium poisoning in a public bathroom at the square. To find the cellar under the butcher shop one had to walk away from place Maubert and infiltrate a web of streets, full of sliver-shaped cafés whose business transactions resembled those of the men who had lurked in the deserted Chinese Theater. The names of these streets, he knew, were followed in speech by the word *malfamée*. New buildings elbowed out the medieval ones, and some spoke of razing the tortuous streets altogether. He felt as if the desires of inquisitors or burnt printers had screwed themselves into this dark corner, taking root in the cellar beneath racks of meat not intended for sale.

In order to obtain the address of the woman photographer he had to return to the cellar offices, but thought it a good idea to make his inquiries when the two men he'd met were out, when someone else would be at the presses. He returned and positioned himself under a short flight of stairs across the ruelle and watched the empty street. No one bought any meat at the shop. No one opened a window or left their building. It was as if all had been evacuated, but at midday he finally saw the pair come up from under the butcher shop, and as they disappeared into place Maubert, he descended into the cellar. The cavern-ous space was quiet; only one figure sat minding the presses. In silence Fabien watched her, a woman in yellow, until she noticed him. Startled and annoyed, she jumped then stood in front of the table as if hiding something on it.

"The men will be back in an hour." She slowly unwrapped a grenade-shaped cheese studded with peppercorns and wiped her hands on her dress.

Fabien looked at his watch. He had neither the time nor the desire to wait around in the basement; the smell of ink and machinery made his eyes smart. The woman's clothes were very bright against the dim cellar walls, and she examined the pages left on the table slowly as if to convey a seriousness and grav-ity that excluded him. In the dark, without the witnesses of his past performance, he felt it easier to slip into his role as accom-plice. The subterfuge of allegiance suddenly seemed effortless. He made his usual comments about traitorous shoppers and the need to cleanse the city of foreigners, then his voice trailed off. She agreed with him, and he remembered to apologize for star-tling her.

"I've lost an address, one I was given the day before, the ad-dress of a woman who takes photographs."

She pulled a pen from behind her ear and wrote a few lines on a corner of paper. "She may not be on the street this after-noon," she said, tearing it off, "one of our photographers was attacked last night."

He didn't answer her, wondering if it were possible to snap blackmail pictures with no conviction whatsoever, as if taking them was just a job. They might not realize what they were do-ing, these photographers who snapped pictures as an assignment and nothing more, but some, Fabien was sure, might be moon-lighting doctors, lawyers, or lamplighters; people who would chose to sweat in the sun or freeze in front of shop windows waiting for someone to emerge, so sure of themselves and their assignment that it meant nothing to stand for hours in the rain outside Lazare's and to do so with zeal. No one even brought them coffee or brandy or held an umbrella over their heads as they waited in the rain. He didn't think anyone could take the pictures without realizing what they were about.

"Self-defense is important, even when you know you're doing the right thing." He stressed the first syllable of *important* in an effort to sound sincere, even tutelary, but she went back to the table cluttered with bread, sausages, wine glasses, sheets of scribbled paper, and jars of ink. The paper she'd handed him smelled of brine.

When he reached the street he unfolded it. She had written an address but no name, as if she had assumed he knew the woman's identity. He hadn't even seen her face, only the mask, and there were many just like it. The studio owned a trunk of them. All he really knew was her approximate size and that she carried a brass-legged tripod. Waiting at the entrance to her building, watching for the appearance of a big woman carrying a tripod, bleary eyed, perhaps covered with mud, out of breath as if she'd been running, he would emerge from the shadows himself unshaven, hands dangling. Then what? He would do nothing. It was getting late; he needed to return to Montreuil. The Devil's Island sequence was due to be shot soon. A desolate shore and stunted plants had to be painted, a prison yard constructed, and hands with decorative ambitions had to be kept from tampering with the sparseness of his cell. Dreyfus had only one bucket of brackish water for drinking and washing. Mosquitos swam in it. He had no privacy. The prisoners who worked in the laundry ripped the hems of his clothing open, looking for hidden messages.

He turned away from place Maubert, but instead of walking directly toward the train station, his steps traced the trajectory of a wider arc, across boulevard Saint Germain, past cafés and shops. Her address would only take him a little out of his way, but as the arc widened further he passed large buildings set back behind gardens; white facades were covered with balconies and long glass doors, shades drawn halfway like lidded eyes. He had expected vulgar, explicit, angry buildings, larded with ironwork and signs about dogs. He stopped and looked up. Water dripped down the damp wall he was leaning against, soaking the back of his jacket. Most of it was vine covered but, despite the apparent wealth of the neighborhood, initials and parts of words had been carved into some of its surface. Fabien leaned against wet leaves again. He saw two figures embracing as he looked up. He had expected she might live in a large apartment building with so many tenants he would have to stand and watch for days, and he would never be able to truly identify her, but there were no crowded buildings on these blocks. He went on counting numbers, white on black.

The address was less grand than the others, an apartment house set close to the street, and unlike the neighboring buildings, no trees grew in front of it. As he stood across the street mentally dividing each floor into separate flats, a man with a portfolio walked out of the building. A woman in a fur coat entered, and he took advantage of her preoccupation with a cigarette, easily following her into the courtyard. A dry fountain was stuck in its center, bracketed by statues of Athena, Pan, and one of Hermes that looked as if he had been added recently because he was carved in a different style. Although it wasn't a *hotel particulier* the building was still more elegant than he would have imagined. He looked for the concierge who had seen him first and was knocking on a window with a key; the glass that separated her quarters from the courtyard was partially frosted, and she was a black and white blur behind it, bearlike and annoyed. As she opened a window, leaning out to question the interloper, her voice rang high and shrill.

"Who do you want here?" Before he could answer she beckoned him inside. Fabien avoided her inquisitorial look, glancing upward from shuttered windows to the lunettes that faced the courtyard, still figuring possible divisions of each floor as he stepped into her rooms.

She had been reading, but shut the book and put it away before Fabien could see the title. A cup of black coffee that must have been drunk slowly all morning lay on a table; rings marked the levels at which it had been sipped and then abandoned. The wall behind her was covered with photographs. Children in carriages, aunts or uncles in stiff suits standing before painted backdrops of Greek columns or flatly rendered but highly detailed rooms. Fabien didn't recognize the woman herself in any of them. Her post in the building wouldn't allow her time to be the photographer, but the person behind the camera might have been her daughter or some other relative.

"You have so many pictures." He reached to touch the frame of one. The woman pushed his hand away. He asked her if she had any floors to let.

"Three floors, three apartments, all occupied." She looked at his clothes, which reflected the dust and paint of the Dreyfus film: bits of the fence of Devil's Island, frayed threads from the underside of a judge's wig clung to his trousers. The woman turned from Fabien and squared one of the frames. He explained that the apartment was for his aunt who was returning to Paris in a month. "I was asked to find something for her," he said to the woman's back. He could have given her money, but he didn't have enough to make the gesture worthwhile.

"Three floors, three apartments, no vacancies."

Thanking her in what he considered an obsequious voice, he took another look at a photograph of a woman in a clown suit posing on a Venetian terrace, a photograph done in the style of Nadar. The venture had been a useless waste of time. He stopped long enough in the courtyard to strike a match against one of Pan's elbows. She watched him through the frosted glass as he lit a cigarette then gazed up at the windows and balconies overhead as if he were looking for someone. When Fabien disappeared out the entrance she checked the statue's elbow for scratches, running a rag over Pan's stone arms and hollow flute. Satisfied they were unmarked she ran upstairs and knocked on a door.

On the train to Montreuil he looked out the window, unable to study his lists. In a flash he saw one of the frog killers near the tracks being beaten by a man in a torn shirt. Fabien twisted around to try to see more of the beating, but the train sped on, and they quickly disappeared from sight.

For several hot nights cafés spilled into the streets and marble tables gleamed with glasses of beer, green wine bottles, red brandy, and chips of potatoes fried in oil. As he moved from crowded pavement to empty silent ruelles, he came to the river, and standing on a bridge, he looked at the dark shapes of barges anchored below. Light hit the face of a man sleeping on a top deck. Fabien couldn't remember if this was a place where the current was strong, and the water was too dark to see. He rubbed his eyes, hands still smelling of the gasoline he'd used to remove paint. Someone caught his arm, pulling violently at it, and he allowed himself to be turned around, passively expecting to be robbed.

"I thought you were about to jump."

The woman was angry, her voice was knifelike as if he'd caused her unnecessary, wasted alarm. She ran her hands through short hair, picked her fedoralike hat up from the ground. He explained he was just looking into the river. She apologized for interrupting, but he wasn't sure she really was sorry. Embarrassed to be rescued when no risk had really been taken, he tried to detain her by thanking her too many times for preventing a suicide attempt never considered. His attempt at conversation went nowhere. She shrugged in response to his questions, rejoining friends when it was clear he was all right and had never had any intention of tipping himself off the edge of the bridge. Her friends pointed at him. They had seen his picture. They knew who he was.

"What's wrong with you?" He shouted after them. People

stared. They had seen his picture, too. Someone under the bridge yelled in mimicry.

"What's wrong with you?" The phrase echoed, bouncing against the stones and back.

"A woman is moving out at the end of the month." She twisted the top buttons of her dress. "She isn't home. I can show you the floor."

He slipped franc notes into the book left by her cup of cold coffee, and she moved the book to the side of the table, then dropped it into a drawer, which she locked. She took him up a curving marble stair to a series of large rooms on the first floor. Letters that had arrived by the morning post lay on a table in the hall; he tried to lean over to read the addresses, but she swooped them up and turned them over. As if it were routine she unlocked the apartment's entrance with a quick twist of the right set of keys then threw open door after door as they wandered through each room. In the bathroom, small marble tiles felt icy under his touch despite the heat outdoors. In other rooms clothes lay scattered on floors and chairs, and when he thought she wasn't looking he picked up a red dress, but she unexpectedly turned around at the door catching him holding its shoulders. It was too small for the photographer he was chasing. He made a gesture with his raised hand across his neck as if to cut his throat. The pantomimed knife made no sense, but he felt he had to do something. He dropped the dress to the floor, tripping on the folds of material as he left the bedroom. She took his hand as if to say she recognized him as an interloper touring a museum of opulence. The concierge must have sensed he had no aunt. Her hand was dry as if she'd been counting money.

"My aunt is too old for this," he said, looking at a painting of naked women sitting on a grassy knoll with clothed men.

"The painting will not stay."

"Also, she's very short. She wouldn't be able to reach the light switches or shelves in the closets." The image of a tiny relative who, though rich, was more at home in the country, came out of nowhere.

"The police have already been here."

"Why?"

"I think you know."

She pressed her lips together; she wouldn't say much more to him. The meanness of his tip and the weakness of his story might have indicated to her that he was some kind of policeman, some kind of investigator, the kind who didn't appear to pay attention, the kind who made a poor pretence of reading the paper or examining traffic signs, so you never really knew who he was or what he wanted. The tour ended, and the woman led him downstairs. He thought he saw a bundle of tripod legs and the edge of a black coat disappear into her quarters, but she steered him away from her own rooms, and they stood in the courtyard. The fountain had been turned on, and Fabien struck a match against Hermes's wings.

"Are you trying to scratch that?"

"My aunt might want to see the rooms herself."

"The police have already been to see the departing tenant, the woman who lived in the rooms you just saw. They asked her to save them trouble, but I don't know what kind of trouble. They were looking for something, papers, documents, letters. I don't know anything more than that."

"I don't understand."

"They had rude manners and asked questions about flowers delivered with notes from a man who turned out to be Dreyfus's brother. They were very thorough. While she looked on they turned drawers upside down, tapped for concealed sections of furniture and walls."

Fabien looked over her head toward the door and considered that he could wait in a café across the street. The photographer would have to appear again.

"Who was she?" he asked.

"A friend of Esterhazy, maybe he's the real spy, maybe not. He used to come here often, and he was a charming man."

"I meant who was the woman who disappeared behind the glass."

"There wasn't anyone in the courtyard besides yourself and the three statues. They often give the illusion of moving into my sentry as you descend the stairs because of the reflections in the pool and glass."

The nice man who visited the former tenant had probably given the conceirge money, but not enough. Money for watching and for knowing who came when, but not enough to stop her from dropping hints once in a while. Fabien couldn't keep up with the bribes either. His nonexistent aunt would have to find another empty apartment. He didn't really have time to sit in the café across the street and watch the doors of the photographer's building, hoping one of the people who walked in and out all day might be her, but his picture on the front page of *La Libre Parole* haunted him, and he relived its taking, helpless before the power of the printed pages circulated to thousands.

On his way to the train station he walked past Lazare's shop. Another photographer, a man, was stationed in front, although the storefront was shuttered. He was silent, immobile, like a statue or a figure in a wax museum, and he looked as if he would wait forever. She might have been haunting other shops, but he wouldn't travel across the city to find wherever it might be that she stood waiting. The bits of newsprint with the addresses of the two photographers written on them were in his pocket, and the one that bore her address still smelled salty. He rolled them up into balls and threw them from the train window.

On Fabien's charts the Dreyfus film was divided into eleven scenes. It would be Méliès's longest film, 780 feet, thirteen minutes in duration. Some of the sets were based on illustrations from the weekly papers, and information about the case came from many sources. Postcards had been printed portraying the trial, and these flying fragments of news, small bits of paper intended to disseminate facts, were, Fabien imagined, channeled through the mail, a chorus of evidence. A Dreyfus display in the wax museum, Musée Grevin, where scenes of recent and historical events were presented as if frames from newsreels, this was one of Fabien's destinations.

"Let's say you live in Paris, and let's say you can't read," Méliès explained. "You visit Grevin's to learn what's going on. This way you get as close as you possibly can to events, reenacted, the museum claims, with stunning accuracy."

"I'm not convinced of this project." Fabien argued with Méliès one last time. "The story isn't one of strong images. Why bother? People want the preconstructions."

"It's an *actualité*."

Méliès felt there was no longer any point in trafficking in nostalgia and amusements.

"I look at Lumière, and I fall asleep. Lumière, impressionist of reconstruction, favors haystacks and boats on a lake, cheerful and romantic images as useless and as ephemeral as greeting cards. The urgency of the story under your nose — a monkey trial, featuring garbage collectors and transvestite generals hiring forgers to fabricate evidence — is mesmerizing, impossible to ignore."

Fabien didn't respond. The voyages to the moon kept him from thinking about a locked closet of a woman's clothes and a child's toys. The fantastic preconstructions kept him from thinking about the footprints they had left in his apartment. The *actualités* offered no escape.

"The trial presents a ready-made story. The characters are well known," Méliès persisted.

"Too well known."

"There's no such thing."

"I'm at a loss as to how to depict the details so important to the story." Fabien showed Georges the palms of his hands as if to say, look, nothing is possible here. "Scenes of forged handwriting, copied, traced, torn up, reconstructed, photographed, and rephotographed are didactic, graphic minutia; it's not the kind of story that can keep an audience rooted to their seats through silent images. Everyone knows which side he or she is on, and everyone knows how the story will end. It's a bad idea."

"If they're on the wrong side, the film will change their minds."

"You're playing with fire," Fabien resorted to clichés. He knew trying to convince Méliès of his folly was useless when the foundation of Star Films was and had always been folly. Folly reigned supreme. He said nothing more to the director, who would not listen to him anyway. Georges left Fabien sitting in his office drawing another prison. Bluette loitered near his doorway kissing the sleepwalker.

———·——

The conductor looked at him twice as he punched his ticket. Fabien fixed his gaze in another direction, staring out the train window at the landscape so familiar he could see it in his sleep. Two dogs tied up in the same yard barked at the train, running the length of their tethers before being snapped back. They were tied to opposite trees so they couldn't get at each other, and they barked at one another in frustration. Each time the rope jerked them back, they seemed newly wounded and shocked that this jolt had happened to them. Their choking was self-imposed, but they couldn't stop, and it seemed to Fabien he was no better off. Mind blank, he sat in the train like a strangled mass with no cognitive ability to determine what a rope or a collar might be. Through an unshuttered window he saw a woman angrily trying to clothe a naked boy who struggled to get away from her. In frustration she hit him, and the boy wriggled and resisted her even more. Everywhere he looked he saw ordinary irritation and suspicion, which only served to make him wary and to remind him of things out of reach: rooms he couldn't rent, rooms that would startle Bluette in their opulence, although she would never see them. He chafed at the threads that determined his identity, tied him to the house of cards that was the Syndicate, tied him to newsprint, tied him to a woman and a child who had disappeared.

The train drew into Paris, and while he no longer expected to find the woman, collar up and face down, carrying a brass-legged tripod, he still looked at women who seemed to walk quickly with the air of a mission undertaken. Leaving the station he saw the men from the printing operation walking toward him, and he turned his face to a shop window in order to avoid them. Although they appeared deeply engaged in conversation, he suspected the Napoléon had caught sight of him. He didn't know what they could or would do to him for pictures never taken, but their appearance made him nervous, then as rue Serpente turned into rue Danton he did see a figure in a long billowing coat, tripod legs sticking out like a brass tail behind. Forgetting the two men Fabien caught up to and passed the phantomlike figure, who turned out to be a man. His long hair had been deceptive from the back. *La Libre Parole* laughed at him still.

He bought a few postcards of *The Degradation;* they were useful, but contained the obvious elements, reminding him that they would need many more swords and army uniforms, boots, and hats. Fabricating sunken boats, assembling a madman's lab, or reconstructing Manet's *Olympia* complete with backless shoes, all these presented concrete problems. For such tableaux he might not have to leave the studio or engage in the pretence of small talk with shopkeepers. Moreover the prison scenes were dull to look at. Acquiring facsimiles of military accoutrements (or the actual objects) often necessitated a kind of acting, presenting himself to a distributor of such things in the guise of a citizen who cheered on military campaigns. He winced at the jocularity and false bonhomie, the hale-fellow-well-met attitude he was habitually greeted with if they mistakenly thought him one of their own, but when Georges reminded him of his picture in *La Libre Parole* he realized that if recognized now he would be greeted with coldness and suspicion, doors would be shut in his face.

Fabien turned to pay for the postcards. Beside the stand, glued to a stucco-faced wall, a poster from the Museum of Horrors series glistened, slick and new. Zola's head had been drawn on a pig's body, and the pig painted a map of France with a brush dipped in a bowl labeled *Caca International*. He sat on copies of his own books. Dreyfus and others had appeared in the Museum of Horrors posters with their heads attached to various animals: cows, snakes, donkeys, and elephants. At intervals the Horrors could be seen all over Paris, pasted on houses, shops, kiosks, empty walls. Fabien expected to see Méliès's head attached to a drawing of an animal, but he wasn't yet represented in the gallery of monsters. Perhaps the manufacturers of the Museum of Horrors didn't know how Méliès felt about the espionage trial. When the film was shown they would find out. One day while on an errand looking for a hookah or fez Fabien would turn a corner, and plastered to a wall he would come face to face with Georges's head attached to the body of a rat or a dog. Or the artist might draw Méliès as the moon, a rocket labeled *J'accuse* hitting him in his eye, round and terrorized. If Fabien tore the drawing down, new ones would appear in its place. The Horrors were that kind of poster, springing up in triplicate wherever they might have been expunged. After *The Dreyfus Affair* was shown, he and Georges would be linked in a kind of fraternity of publicity, their portraits reproduced and scattered around the city.

Now the grotesque caricature of Zola caused Fabien to question the postcards' accuracy, and he examined them once more. Perhaps the image of cardboard facts carried through the mail was a distorted one, and what passed as small mirrors of actualities were, in fact, more of the hysteric expressions and shrill voices of those whose sympathies were more aligned with the Museum of Horrors. *You can't trust anyone,* the concierge had said, leaning against the statue of Pan.

The Musée Grevin was quiet and nearly empty. *One can almost see them breathing and hear their hearts beat! See history come to life!* Fabien smiled at the man who took his entrance fee. If Star Films were to go bankrupt he could get work here. He could make molds or construct sets in studios located on the floors above the tableaux vivants. The rooms were dark and drafty, and he hurried through most of them. He saw a portrait of the last hours of Victor Hugo, blue-white from the attack of pneumonia that would kill him, several scenes from the battle of Waterloo. Napoléon's last cancerous hour on Saint Helena was also represented, and, most intriguing so far, a mechanized Raft of the Medusa. The raft was pitched over canvas waves, wax figures clung to creaking boards. Although he knew better, Fabien imagined a homunculus sitting under metal ribs cranking the canvas waves. Jack the Ripper followed, himself (or themselves) undepicted in the tableau. Only Mary Kelly stood alone on a corner in Spitalfields, waiting for what the audience knew would be her murderer. This is where the fear enters, Fabien thought, and it seemed to him that now he understood Méliès: one can be afraid even when one already knows the ending. Even knowing the ending, one can wish things will turn out otherwise, one can still be terrified and angry at the inevitable outcome. He passed Mary Kelly and walked on to the scenes of the trial.

At the depiction of the assassination attempt against Dreyfus's lawyer, a wax figure of Labori lay under a lamppost, a woman bent over him, fanning his face. Fabien took notes: *lampposts, see storage.* There were stacks of lampposts left over from other films. A crowd of wax figures gathered around

Labori, forever slumped and bloody, or at least until a hot August when no one was in the city to notice him melting away. He went on to the next small room, a display of two soldiers carrying a basket of files. The prosecution had assembled over four hundred secret documents and transported them in wicker baskets; Fabien made a note of the basket. The scenes were not in any particular chronological order that he could figure out. A man held a stuffed carrier pigeon as if he were about to release it. Another pigeon appeared to be flying out the window. Its back half had been to the taxidermist's. Its front half was painted as it intruded into two-dimensional space. Painted birds dotted the sky. They were being dispatched to carry news of the trial from Rennes to Paris. A cage containing three pigeons sat on the floor, near the edge of the stage, far to Fabien's left. A velvet rope separated spectators from the diorama, a kind of room within a room. He took notes about clothing and furniture while standing in front of it.

Madame Thullier, the colorist for Star Films, had said in advance that she refused to work on any film about Dreyfus. If it were to be colored, the work would have to be done elsewhere. The ironmonger dressed as Dreyfus would not pass under her brush. He remembered that when he met her she had given him her hand, fingers still bearing the indentations of sprocket holes and smelling of aniline paint diluted by alcohol. In her rooms rows of women sat over strips of celluloid. One painted only blue then passed the film on to the woman next to her who painted only red, and so on until all colors and all frames were accounted for. As he stood in the wax museum it seemed to Fabien that this film shouldn't be colored. It wasn't a *preconstruction*. There was no color match for torn prison laundry or an ordinary courtroom chair. The frames should remain black and white.

The dark walls and smell of wax figures closed in on him. He put his notebook in his pocket and walked away, but as he turned to look back at the tableau he noticed one of the pigeons had been taken from the cage at the left end of the diorama. Now only two remained. A woman with a lumpy shape under her coat disappeared across the threshold into the darkness of the next display. He watched the back of her long coat, only the white of her neck and ankles was visible. She seemed careless, unhurried, as if certain no one was watching her. He'd seen no one else, then he gradually heard voices coming in his direction. A gang of men who seemed to be working in concert moved from display to display. Leaving Napoléon and Hugo untouched they slashed each tableau representing the affair and trial, beheading each Dreyfus, throwing paint and smearing obscene phrases over backdrops and furniture. No one stopped the vandals. The rooms grew raucous. Spectators jumped ropes and stole clothing, a wax assasin's gun, swords, a gavel, a wax moustache. Fabien ran. The gang followed, smashing the Siamese twins, the octopus man, and other freaks cast in wax. They were all aberrant, all Dreyfus.

As he stepped out of the museum a man brushed past him, almost knocking him into the marquee. He pointed at the woman now lingering on a corner, possibly waiting for the gang to finish in the museum. Wisps of hair stuck out from her black hat, and she had Bluette's walk, occasionally mannish, but her authority was tentative. She began to run before he could get a close look at her face, running fast, without turning to identify the man who shouted after her. The man chased her, calling out. Fabien quickened his pace, only to collide with the other pursuer when he suddenly stopped in his tracks.

"She melted into the air," the man wheezed.

Fabien apologized for the collision. Once again the phantom was like the succubus in black who barely registered on film.

"A lot of people," he continued, "are looking for that woman. She takes all kinds of pictures." He coughed again into a handkerchief. "She took my picture as I turned away from a newsstand. She was fast as if she had been waiting for me, but I hadn't stolen anything. As the camera flashed, I grabbed at her, but she got away."

"Did you see her face?"

"No."

Introducing himself as Antoine Notelle between fits of coughing, he described how the incident had happened so quickly and unexpectedly that he could remember nothing concrete but her coat. "As fast as a thief," he said. He had searched crowds for her on streets and in arcades but met with no success until that afternoon when he recognized the flaring black skirt in front of the wax museum. He knew no reason anyone would want to take his picture and then run off. Notelle's eyes rolled back and forth as if on a pendulum. He pulled at his frayed cuffs, but scanned the crowd like a professional on the lookout for tourists, provincials, vulnerable naïfs who left wallets where they could be easily lifted. Fabien wasn't sure that he, at Antoine's hands, couldn't become just such a mark. He was easily pushed around. Even though he knew what sent the photographer to that particular kiosk and what drove her to wait for Notelle to turn around, even that knowledge had little currency for a man who worked the streets. Antoine thought she worked for the police. If Fabien told him the real reason, what would it mean to this stranger who clung to him? *So they want to scare some people, so what? Leave me out of it.* The Dreyfus affair, dragging on for years, had nothing to do with him.

"I'm sure we're walking in the same direction." He took Fabien's arm as if to steer him, and although Fabien wasn't sure what direction that might be, Notelle couldn't be shaken off. A volatile and animated person, once he had decided to take Fabien into his confidence, Notelle seemed to take up more space on the sidewalk, appearing to double in size when he spoke. He wound a black scarf tightly around his neck, a kind of noose or tourniquet that ought to have arrested the flow of speech but didn't. Sometimes he coughed into its ends, which flapped over his chest. They stopped at a street corner and stood before a poster advertising cigarette papers. A boy posed smoking a cigarette, and the letters he puffed spelled *Moi, je fume le papier . . .*

C.A.P.I.T.A.I.N.E. Fabien felt his pockets while Antoine stared at some women evidently window shopping across the street.

"Have you any?" Fabien asked. He pointed at the poster.

"Boys?"

"No, cigarettes."

Antoine stared blankly. It was, Fabien felt, like suddenly discovering someone you'd been chattering to in a queue or on a train was, although nodding along, stone deaf. Notelle couldn't read. Lines of print or script looked like graphic clutter, sinkholes of possibility, boring and frightening at the same time because he had no way to unlock their signification. What had he been doing at a newsstand if he was illiterate? He would skip over written language, whether cartoons or the caricatures of the Museum of Horrors, lines of print didn't register in his field of vision. Antoine squinted at the poster as if he could read but had only forgotten his glasses.

"You know, don't you, where these photographs end up?" Even if Antoine had traced his photograph as far as the butcher shop near place Maubert, the activities of the basement would have been a mystery to which he had no access. Yet he brought out Fabien's desire to twist arms until he heard a scream.

"I told you I don't know."

"I don't understand why she bothered to take my picture. I didn't steal anything." Just as Fabien had guessed, Antoine couldn't care less about the trial. He hardly knew anything about it.

"Who's Dreyfus? Let me tell you an actual story," Antoine said. "I have a friend, Louis, who's afraid to take a single step beyond his door. He lives in a top floor garret with dirty lunettes for windows, which he covered over with papers. Why? He believes policemen dog his steps. He looks out at the street from between tears in the papers, and should he see anyone looking up at him, there's no question that they are agents of the police. In fact," Antoine explained, "it would be difficult to see a specific face in one of those lunettes. They are so small and recessed, even without the paper coverings, you'd have a hard time making out anything if you're standing on the street. People often do look up. A woman in a building next door has a habit of leaving her windows wide open, and she attracts attention. This has been pointed out to Louis, but to him all the voyeurs, all the dirty old men are really the police, and they're after him. The police probably don't know of Louis's existence. His crimes are all imaginary. Believe me." He stared into the distance as if overcome.

A sandwich man passed them, took off his boards, and went into a café laughing uncontrollably. Antoine ignored him, but Fabien turned and watched the man slip out from his signs advertising a seer at place desVosges. Despite his empathy for Louis, Antoine wasn't easily suckered into anything. Even hysterical laughter could be an act, a ruse. Not just anyone had the ability to recite a story designed to entangle strangers. Some could do it convincingly, some couldn't. Fabien didn't know whether to believe this Antoine, a lung case, a noctambule who didn't need light to read, a man who claimed he had a vulnerable spot: a sealed room in Montparnasse. Why? What did he care about a man who never went out?

"According to Louis the police take many forms. Anyone can be an enemy. His apartment is full of old newspapers. He never throws anything away. He's been trying to dovetail parts of newspaper stories together as if they're all sections of a grand conspiracy. Everything is connected, everything is contaminated. The dirty air outside his door has been exhaled by someone else somewhere, sometime. He has all these crackpot theories. He's talked about Dreyfus, the spy. He was part of a plot I couldn't follow."

This Notelle was a man of no words other than those that evaporated into air. His friend Louis had nothing but words, threads of logic that served to prove the existence of the terror outside his door.

"In an effort to get him out of the house I was finally able to convince him that lightning wouldn't strike the same place twice. I mean they'd gotten me already, and if the photographer worked for the police what were the odds she'd get him too within a matter of days? To my surprise this made some kind of sense to him, and he put on his shoes."

Fabien shoved his hands into his pockets and looked into a shop window for a clock. He had to get back to Montreuil.

"There's a reason I'm telling you this. With myself along, Louis took a few steps outside his door. For the first time in years he walked through the courtyard, opened an outer door, and crossed the threshold. No one was there to notice the event, who would care, right? Looking behind him, one hand on a wall as if for balance, the other shading his eyes, he made his way down the deserted street. We were going to buy something at that newsstand. I don't remember what anymore." Antoine took a few long steps hand on the wall, constantly looking behind himself, imitating the fearful Louis.

"I considered this a great victory until suddenly a camera flashed in his face. Louis hadn't even gone into the shop; he had only looked in the window. He began to scream, and again I chased the photographer who disappeared behind a door on the other side of the street. The door locked behind her."

"So she lives in the building."

"I don't know. She may not live there at all. She ran out a back way for all I know. An old woman who sits by the window day after day claims not to have seen anything. I took Louis back to his rooms, but he'll never go out again. Others have to bring him his meals. He would starve otherwise, but he won't eat the food I bring because he no longer trusts me. I stand outside his door with soup in my hands but he won't see me." Hands cupped, he appeared sincerely distressed. Although they weren't near Louis's address Fabien looked up at a building whose garlanded lunettes looked as if they'd been squeezed from a pastry tube and imagined Antoine standing in front of a door, food falling from his hands.

———

Fabien shuttered the windows against a storm and tried on a pair of rubber feet with large hammer toes, putting his feet up on his desk, singing to himself and flapping the feet back and forth. Drawings of the degradation scene were scattered on the floor. He could no longer look at them. He still didn't understand why Georges wanted to shoot this *actualité*. The verdict couldn't be changed. There was no point to the project. Fabien felt so mired in the hopeless story with scene after scene of humiliation and degradation, and so sick of the gray objects around him that he gave up, and in giving up, he flipped the drawings facedown, turning instead to the ridiculous. The oversized feet had their own logic and gravity. Georges spoke of film as a form of agitation, political agitation, in some ways not unlike the pictures taken in front of Lazares'. Fabien had nodded, and his agreement was more than acquiescence, but as he slapped the rubber feet together he considered why he had given up on newspapers, no longer even inquisitive about headlines and smeared pictures. Like the unknown Louis, he was sure every external feature of the world, from his own corridor to the islands of Micronesia, combined to form a gluttonous polyglot beast that sooner or later would devour him whole. If a man or woman could be found to bring food to Fabien's door, the only actualities he would recognize as he sat with a view of an angled wall would be of his own invention or memory. His days searching the city for plates and uniforms were the antithesis of those that occupied the man locked in his room, but Fabien had no choice. No one would bring him food, pleasure, or entertainment. He was always outside, even in the rain, looking at his reflection in an ashtray. He couldn't escape.

The ironmonger who played Dreyfus walked past, leaned against a winch, and lit a cigarette. Bluette rarely came to the studio during the shooting of this *actualité*. He addressed one of the trial postcards to her and was about to throw it away when two men suddenly appeared in the doorway.

"Hello? My good friend who knows the stars of the movie business?"

It was the stupidest line he had ever heard. Fabien never imagined he would see Notelle again, and hadn't wanted to renew the acquaintance in any case, but the man knocked and stepped inside without waiting to be asked, only saying he and a friend had come all the way from Paris to speak to him. The second man was even thinner than Antoine, but well dressed and confident. He wore a velvet coat, soft felt hat; he'd spent a lot of time deciding what to wear to this meeting at Star Films. Antoine, stepping around the open jars of paint that lay on the floor, introduced him as Renard, a writer or dramatist of some kind. This introduction could only have consisted of what Renard told him to recite. Words written in verse looked like rows of marching ticks to Antoine. Renard must have trusted Antoine, or perhaps hardly knew him.

"Listen to this," Antoine said, still standing. "This is an important man." He pointed to Renard who pulled up a chair without offering to find one for his master of ceremonies.

"I don't object to being photographed for any reason if the result means my appearance on the front page of anything that resembles print. What is humiliation or so-called humiliation? The attention will make the temporary indignity of appearing in an asswipe paper worth enduring."

Antoine nodded. It was suddenly as if the studio was deserted. Fabien realized that no one would rescue him from these two. There was no point in telling them to go away. They could see he had work to do. It made no difference.

Renard looked Fabien in the eye and described how he spent his days parading or loitering indiscriminately from the Theatre Ambigu-Comique to the Louvre, following celebrities, trying to crash their parties. While Antoine, a man who Fabien imagined felt uncomfortable in his own skin, traveled from place to place reflecting the personality of whatever quarter he found himself in at any particular moment in order to lift wallets and merchandise, his friend Renard behaved in exactly the opposite fashion. He spoke breathlessly without a break. He wanted his picture taken everywhere with everyone.

"Why are you telling me this? If you want to be in a film speak to Georges."

"I don't want to be in a film."

"Listen to him," Antoine leaned against a wall.

"After Antoine and his friend had their pictures taken, I hung around shops."

"Which ones?"

"I haunted shops that trafficked in stolen firearms, new shops with big windows, shops that sold pornography under the table, but I was always wrong. My picture wasn't taken. Now that you've pointed out to Antoine which businesses were targeted, I realize I was stabbing in the dark." He stopped speaking for a moment and picked at one of the rubber hammer toes still fitted over Fabien's feet, which he still had propped on his desk. Fabien jerked away and put his feet back on the floor.

"If you want to find the photographer for *La Libre Parole* I offer my services."

"Why?" Fabien asked. He imagined that in spite of whatever assurances Antoine might have given Renard, Notelle would jump the photographer and smash her camera without a second thought. Renard's picture wouldn't appear on the cover of anything. Antoine smiled and fiddled with a rubber chicken, as if he was a frequent visitor to the studio and could make himself at home. Then he left the room. How much of Star Films could he steal in twenty minutes? Not much if all he had were his pockets.

Fabien grew bored listening to Renard's desires to advertise himself and while half listening sketched Dreyfus' degradation, the scene in which he was stripped of his medals before the troops in the yard of Les Invalides. He had grown more obsessed with this scene than any of the others.

"Humiliation," Renard said, "is temporary, means nothing."

"I can interpret that absence of shame in two ways," Fabien

said without looking up from his drawing. "Either you ignore feelings of shame as soon as they rub up against you, or more likely, shame is a daily and acute circumstance so one way or another you manage to live with it and carry on."

He himself had felt it when he leaned over a bridge or looked out a train window. In this buffered cosmos mortification and disgrace were reduced to the snap of a cardboard sword. Could the actor, unaccustomed to the use of arms, break a real sword across his knee? If not, one could be made out of something else, like a thin strip of wood, a material that might render the effect of snapping in the silent universe of black and white film.

Fabien nodded toward Renard, inking a drawing of a close-up shot of military medals that lay scattered on the ground. He left Dreyfus's face blank, focusing downward. Telling an actor how to look wasn't his job. He glanced at his notes: leg irons. Dreyfus, the ironmonger, might be willing to make his own. After his brother leaked a false story to a Welsh paper that Dreyfus had escaped Devil's Island, he had been put in irons and strapped to his bed. His brother had intended only to draw attention to the case because he felt it was slowly being forgotten. The scheme had backfired badly. Immobility, enforced paralysis, leg irons rubbing into skin, wasn't the kind of humiliation one could absorb like a daily cup of lousy coffee.

"What do you think it would be like to be strapped into a bed so that you couldn't move?"

"I'd be afraid of a fire."

Renard returned to the subject of his writing, quoting Henri Murger. *I am on the path to the path.*

"It's important to be recognized, and deleterious to work at anything not connected toward this end: recognition." Like Antoine, he was a noctambule who slept until late in the afternoon and wandered around the city until morning. He had no money but managed to scrape together a job from time to time.

"I worked as part of a mill of *feuilleton* producers, penning episodic fiction which suited my working style of fits and starts. I sent characters to the guillotine one week only to have them rescued at the last minute by another writer a week later. Then I would pick up the story again and engineer the details of the escape. *Their two faces were very similar, so it was possible to walk out past the guards.*" He moved his head back and forth like an Indo-Chinese dancer. "*No one looked twice.*"

"That's been written about before, one man going to the guillotine in place of another," Fabien told him.

"Borrowing is the point," Renard looked at Fabien as if he were an idiot. "On the other hand I don't like to corrupt my own identity too often because this kind of subversion creates potholes in the road leading to notoriety."

"So you wouldn't become a ghostwriter?"

"Yes, in desperation I've composed banquet speeches for the tongue-tied, proposing colonial expansion in Algiers or New Caledonia one night and revolution in the colonies the next, all obviously written under another name. As much as I would do anything, I decided finally to draw the line at writing for hire. Next, I collected information for an emigré, a count, a man with an accent and scarred face, who treated me like his servant. *Use the back door, please.* I was hired to watch who came out of which doorways, note who spent time in royalist restaurants and who was seen leaving the former Chinese Shadow Theater in the middle of the night. I gave up one set of notes when I quit but kept another copy for myself."

The flood of Renard's memoir was getting on Fabien's nerves. The interloper engulfed in a cloud of self-importance as he walked around the city thinking of himself in the past tense, reliving and rewriting.

"There was no mistake, when I walked into the café all eyes were on me, and it was obvious as soon as I entered, even if some pretended to be indifferent." While Fabien was removing his rubber feet, Renard picked up the postcard addressed to Bluette and put it in his pocket.

"You might ask who are my characters, who do I write about?" Pushing aside the prison plates and rubber chicken on Fabien's desk as if clearing a surface for his own production, Renard explained.

"Recently I've gotten work inventing alternative identities for people in trouble. False papers are easy to acquire, but fictional histories to match them in case one is questioned — complex, detailed, rare, and more desirable — these can't be found on any street corner. Antoine, for example, was the former Monsieur Meuble from Amiens." He leaned close to Fabien's ear and whispered the alliterative *m*'s, although Antoine was no longer in the room. He was awash in language while Antoine groped in the dark with a smile on his face and a knife in his pocket.

"Monsieur *Meuble*," Renard repeated.

Fabien didn't believe him. That name, too, had a made-up ring to it. Renard claimed to have performed the same service for so many other citizens that perhaps no one in the city was really who he or she claimed to be. They were all his inventions. He tapped his chest and misquoted Apollinaire, *The city is full of Columbuses like me, who, in order to survive, must discover a new continent every morning.* Fabien kept his doubts to himself. The photographer from *La Libre Parole* would put him on the path to the path.

"How did you first meet Antoine?"

"He needed someone to sign his name for him, since he cannot do so himself."

"Did it become a habit? A kind of arrangement in which you are always the one who signs his name?"

"Yes, I think so. He trusts me. He told me he stabbed a man, disposed of the body, and was never caught or even suspected. Soon it was if the man had never existed. I think the fight had been over something unimportant, but there are occasions when, out of pedagogical necessity or otherwise, homicide seems an appropriate option."

He used grand words in place of simple phrases. *Teach him a lesson* might do just as well as *pedagogical necessity.*

"Why are you telling me this story?" Fabien asked Renard. "A murder, covered up and perhaps forgotten, isn't the kind of story you should repeat to someone you hardly know."

"I'm suggesting Antoine might go to town here, and we should be careful. His picture has been published because of her. Someone might remember him, someone might have seen him from a window the night of the knifing. Someone he hadn't counted on might have seen him hiding." Fabien translated: go to town equals murder.

Fabien imagined Antoine as a spinning top, impossible to arrest. "If that's the case there isn't much that can be done to stop him." Confiding in Renard, spiller of beans, was clearly a mistake, but Fabien was curious enough to set all the pieces in motion. Antoine returned to the room, and Renard stopped talking for a moment.

"I know your cameraman," Antoine said. "Interesting side business with nudies. We've been talking."

Fabien slammed the gigantic feet back on his desk. He didn't want any connection between the two intruders and his work at Star Films. He didn't ever want to arrive at the studio and find them waiting for him. Antoine winked then pretended to take a bite out of the rubber chicken.

It was decided that the three of them would meet at Lazare's and wait inside the store. The whole street, Fabien knew, was staked out frequently. Sooner or later the photographer would appear on the sidewalk, and Renard, posed as a shopper, would emerge on cue.

———·———

"At least let her take my picture before you jump her," Renard looked in a mirror. "Don't damage the camera, whatever happens, eh Antoine? I'm talking to you."

Bernard Lazare had returned but wouldn't tell Fabien where he'd been. While he made them coffee and spoke in his

Russian-accented French, they sat in the back between stacks of chipped plates and rows of dusty glasses. They waited.

"Others," Bernard said, "were photographed in front of the shop earlier in the month, and then the picture-taking stopped, but they'll be back. She didn't always wear a mask, you know. This is a woman with a big face. Sometimes she wore a lot of paint. I watched her from the shop window. I waved to annoy her. Her makeup was so theatrical and caked on, she looked like a caricature of a woman. She could scare customers away just by looking. Once I yelled out the door to her, 'So why don't you firebomb me and get it over with?' My nephew pulled me back in."

"I'm falling asleep." Renard wasn't used to being awake during the day. He kept dozing off and had to be caught from leaning against fragile objects. Antoine was bored and agitated.

"I'll get you some coffee. I'll go for a walk. No, I won't do that. What if she arrives as soon as I'm gone." Antoine had drunk double cups of coffee, which Renard claimed he didn't need. He talked mostly to himself. "No, I'm not budging. I'm not going anywhere."

Customers were few; they came and went undisturbed, none of them noticed the group, three lumps in black clothes, huddled in the back of the store. To pass time Fabien drew the scenes he had yet to build. Dreyfus returning from Devil's Island for the trial at Rennes late at night, in the middle of a gale. Flashes of lightning would be drawn on the film by hand. The next scene was to be the assassination of Dreyfus's lawyer, Labori, who would be played by Méliès. The assassin waited at night at the foot of a bridge. Fabien wanted to play the assassin, but Georges gave the part to someone else. He shut his eyes picturing the scene. As it darkened, Antoine could barely contain his disgust, and his impatience only served to make Renard agitated.

"You'd only wear a mask if it were lined with a mirror."

"Shut up Antoine."

They heard the clacking sound of Bernard closing up his

shop, and he finally called out to them that the doors had to be locked.

Fabien left Renard and Antoine in front of a café, walking south as it grew dark. They made no arrangements to meet again. He walked until he came to the building that he thought was hers. Fabien stumbled at the entrance as if drunk. The statue of Hermes was barely visible in the shadows. He thought he saw the boy in the checkered vest and the woman from the cellar printers huddled together under a street light, smoking and whispering, but he couldn't be sure. He walked on.

He saw a stuffed pigeon in a poulterer's window. It was part of a display of feathered birds hovering and nesting beside those which lay plucked and raw on beds of ice. This particular bird sat beside a nest but was posed similarly to the one stolen from the wax museum. Was the merchant connected to the vandals? Even whisper the name, Captain D . . . and many clamored for the guillotine. Many citizens would have wanted to deface the Dreyfus tableau, yet the museum didn't have a guard patrolling the display's proscenium, and so, it was a ready-made effigy, easily destroyed. Fabien looked at the arrangement of expensive food with a revolutionary's fascination regarding bourgeois wealth before the rock was thrown, but then entering the shop self-consciously, he bought the display bird. Ice clung to its feet and, although it was wrapped in paper, the melting ice left wet patches on his trousers as he sat in a cab on his way to the train station.

———•———

Star Films was deserted at night. He walked past racks of prison garb and army uniforms, a train wreck, half-painted, half-constructed. Light was dimly reflected in its broken windows. Bluette sat perched on the jumble of wreckage, her fluffy hair framed by two enormous rubber ears. If she hadn't been wearing them he would have assumed she was waiting for the sleepwalker or the astronaut or the cheese, but she looked so absurd, her head sandwiched between two elephant-sized human ears. She might have been waiting for someone and deliberately wanted to be deaf to the man's approach, to be surprised. He whispered into one of the artificial ears: Why do you torture me? Why do you get under my skin? She couldn't hear him. He left the stuffed pigeon in her dressing room. If he was a ventriloquist he would hide behind her clothes and through his voice across the room. The pigeon speaks. Seen me before, huh?

As he traveled through Paris Fabien saw special effects as links that created logical connections between otherwise entirely disparate events or objects. What does a flea circus have to do with Gulliver's Travels? What does a hotel ashtray have to do with Dreyfus? While he searched for props, he created or participated in another event, a parallel set of circumstances and phenomena: the photographer, Antoine, Renard. Everything, every object he encountered in the city, and the routes he had to take to find those things, turned into its own whirlwind, its own journey, and its own tale. He felt like the natives of New Caledonia who marked out territorial boundaries by singing a story, or he felt like Zeno, he would never get to point B. He went to look for plates and his picture was taken. He made a trip to a wax museum, and he met a murderer. He looked for words in the steam billowing over a cup of coffee. He would accept clues or notes of affection in it. He found neither.

"What are you staring at?"
"It's you!"
"It's that man whose picture was printed in *La Libre Parole*."
He yelled at those who pointed and shunned him but worried that some frightened, panicky part of himself that agreed he deserved to be elbowed out of the way, remained firmly en-

trenched. He deserved to be shunned, not because he did business at Lazare's — that, like the trial, no longer mattered to him, if it ever had —but because he was afraid somehow that the idiots who yelled and talked about blowing up boats with people on them had, in their gross stupidity, somehow discovered some truth about himself: he was a coward. He wouldn't even do a decent job of defending himself, let alone defend the risky gestures of Méliès or those like him. That the toadies of *La Libre Parole* should be the unveilers of this was unbearable.

———•———

There were many short films about weary travelers, travelers who had terrible nights persecuted by boots that walked by themselves, shirts and trousers that had a life of their own, even unzipping for a monstrous pee. He had developed "pyrotechnic furniture," tables that grew human legs and walked away with dinner, and automobiles, when they did appear, went on "rampages," as if human and angry with vendettas to settle. But Fabien was sick of images of departure and arrival. Boats, trains, anything that moved, seemed to mock his daily routine. He was happy when trains and rockets crashed, or bridges collapsed, their anthropomorphic features splattered across the set. It should be an *Impossible Voyage,* he screamed at Bluette's rubber ears. His travels through the city made him the reverse of Louis, the agoraphobic, but he would have preferred to stand as still as possible. He wanted to go into the studio as flats were painted and hammered and say, *Look craphead, I'm a statue. I'm not going anywhere.*

Méliès liked to run film backwards, and this always seemed to be funny to him. The audience, Méliès believed, never tired of the joke, but Fabien wasn't sure the joke didn't wear thin. Méliès was intrigued by reversal, as if he could turn back clocks, defy gravity and logic. His *preconstructions* were an answer to Lumière's straightman realism. A meal could be regurgitated. If the clown always threw up, he would go hungry. This, Fabien decided in

341

disgust while Georges roared with laughter, was a model for all his failures.

"Help me into this, will you?" Bluette was struggling with a musical–note costume.

The staff needed to be taped to her right side. Fabien taped the black wooden bar to her body. The round part of the note began at her waist and ended at her knees. She spoke to him condescendingly, as if he were a servant.

"What are you going to do in this costume? It hasn't been used in years."

"I'm going to run across the stage while he's shooting the scene of the trial."

"Why do you want to interrupt the shoot?"

"Because, dummy, this film is going to get us all into trouble."

From the other side of the room Bluette blew him a mock kiss with her eyes crossed. *What are you saying? I'm a dunderhead? Get lost yourself.* He felt he was getting somewhere, and at the same time he was getting nowhere. *If dissolves are like conjunctions, the conjunctions of film, my efforts are one dissolve following another with no substance in between.*

A-N-D B-U-T Y-E-T

Dreyfus saw her coming, pointed across the stage, and Bluette was stopped. Fabien watched, leaning out of his office door while Georges snapped her costume in two. She threw the halves of the musical note on the floor, put on her clothes, and marched out of Star Films as if never to return.

"You just want to play Lucie Dreyfus," Georges yelled after her. "Well, you can't, and you know why."

Fabien returned to his office. He spent the afternoon unable to work, drawing figures swimming from Devil's Island while holding onto goats raised by the leper colony housed there. The fiction had arisen that the sharks that infested the surrounding sea would eat the goats so the swimmer would live and escape. Although it was a fantasy — no one could escape this way — the goats had been removed after Dreyfus arrived at the island. Fabien drew the swimmers like mythological creatures who knew nothing of deprivation. With each frame Devil's Island receded into the background.

Bluette returned the following day, though there was no work for her. Fabien knocked on her dressing room door balancing a box of Revolutionary costumes on his arm: guillotine earrings, tricolor socks, the jacket Danton wore to his execution. He pulled objects he thought of as bait from the box as they walked back toward his room. He fingered Danton's collar, made a chopping motion with his hand.

"It's authentic. I bought it from a woman whose great-grandfather had been a guard in the Bastille."

"How did he get it?"

"I don't know."

"Where are the bloodstains?"

"It was cleaned."

She let him put the gold blades in her ears. At first he was happy she was paying attention to him, then she kissed him as if his cheek were a disembodied rubber feature, walking out the door without thanking Fabien or even saying good-bye.

———·—·———

Fabien believed that if he stepped behind one of the house facades in the Musée Grevin, and there were several in the Jack the Ripper display, he could hide, easily escaping notice only to come out later after the museum was locked up for the night. It was an idea. An imitation of life could be lived here. If there wasn't enough space behind the painted flats, he could crawl under Napoléon's or Victor Hugo's respective deathbeds. Alone, he would approach the display of Monsieur Automata, a mechanical man who could do both factory work and household drudgery, and hinted at a certain freedom from industrialization. In the silence Fabien asked if he might eventually be able to take over his job. He knocked M. Automata's tin arm. A hollow, tinny sound emerged.

A man announced that the museum was closing, and Fabien walked quickly through the remaining rooms. The area of the Dreyfus tableaux was closed. It was growing dark outside, and he had nothing to look for here anyway. The filming of Méliès's last *actualité* was finished. The ironmonger rarely came to the studio anymore. He continued to receive death threats, as if by playing Dreyfus he became the accused.

She stepped in front of him as she emerged from the most remote displays, the freaks: the shriveled heads in preservative baths, the wax copies of Siamese twins. He saw no tripod or camera, only the black hat and a flaring coat that covered a dress, but he recognized the mask. Behind the eyeholes lids flickered as if tired and troubled by deciding where to go next. He reached out his hand. She didn't move. He yanked the mask from her face. A man stood before him. Longish hair fell out from under the cap. The mask crashed to the floor, and its nose broke off. The man grabbed up his white face and put it back on so that his own nose and a stubbly upper lip poked out through the hole. He carried no camera, but clutched a leg from a tripod, unscrewed from the rest, as if a kind of cane. It was dripping wet, and fragments of wax and paint clung to it. He had smashed the glass jars that held the museum's freakish specimens. *Contaminants. Impurities*, he whispered. The vandal of the wax museum struggled to fasten the strings of his mask as he ran down the street, black skirts billowing, feet running soundlessly toward place Maubert.

———•———

The woman, the one he had waited for, was a phantom. He looked for Artois's address, tossing props and costumes right and left, then remembered he had chucked it from the train weeks ago. He tried to find Antoine or Renard, but found no trace of either one. The talent for disappearing into the city was one Fabien envied.

He was folding the damaged and faded flea circus, preparing to throw it into a heap of trash to be burned. The cardboard walls collapsed easily, but he was so preoccupied with its disintegration that he jumped when he heard Renard's yellowed fingers tapping on the door. His nails, the first part of him to appear on the edge of the jamb, appeared long and dirty, and the rest of him as he slouched into Fabien's office gave the impression that he hadn't been working lately. His usually neat clothes were creased and grimy. Before he actually spoke, Renard picked through the trash, draping a coat he found over his shoulders.

"No one will miss this." He didn't sit down. "I can't stay long." He pulled the coat closer around him, preparing for a dramatic presentation, deciding which tense to use. Fabien read his tone to mean that this was going to end in a request for money.

"Do you remember Antoine?" Fabien nodded. Now he was sure the story was going to be about cash.

"You were the one who told Antoine about the printers where the photographers delivered their plates. Though he couldn't read, Antoine remembered the address, and he knows the city well. He waited around the butcher shop, hiding under the stairs or watching from an alley across the street. The wait was rewarded. He saw all kinds of people come out of the cellar: generals covered with braid and medals, others arrived in a state carriage."

"A general wouldn't have gone into that cellar in uniform."

"How do you know? If Antoine had a camera we could identify them now, couldn't we? Antoine wanted one. You might have gotten him a camera. You have a lot of things here.

"He waited at place Maubert. Sooner or later the photographer stepped up to the gate, as he knew she would. She didn't notice him across the street, although he could see that her disguise had been knocked around, and she held her hand up to her face as if hiding a smirk. He didn't jump her yet, but let her go in, thinking that if she were expected in the cellar offices, they would grow impatient at her absence and might begin to look for her, so he would continue to wait until she came out again.

"Sometimes he was very canny, sometimes stupid," Renard said, "either way. When she emerged, he caught her under the stairs and slit the woman's throat without even looking at her face." Fabien imagined the body slumped on the stairs, head wedged between a tread and a riser.

"She was wearing a mask, and as he climbed over her to escape, he knocked it to one side with the toe of his shoe." Renard paused, then took a drink from a cup of coffee Fabien had on his desk. "He shouldn't have been so quick. He should have followed her and done it someplace else, not right on their own doorstep. When the body was found, articles appeared immediately calling for revenge. It's bigger than an eye-for-an-eye business. They believe one of their eyes is worth thousands of other eyes. Didn't you ever look at that paper again?"

Fabien shook his head. He hadn't.

Renard didn't believe him. "They asked for demonstrations that would end in riots with the looting of certain businesses. These businesses, the articles said, were part of a Syndicate, a conspiracy to destroy the whole country."

"I don't read those papers. The film about the trial is finished. I've been working on *Dreams of an Opium Fiend,* on *Cinderella.*" He wanted Renard to leave.

Renard rolled his eyes to the ceiling as if to indicate Fabien lived in a world of phantasmagoria, useless and remote, but for Fabien his indignation had a false ring to it, as if Renard were looking for a part. He took the noseless mask from a crumpled bag and laid it on the floor; sorry-looking, etiolated strings curled wormlike at Fabien's feet. It seemed to Fabien more like a thing one shouldn't touch, a poisonous jellyfish or snapping turtle one might poke with a broom handle, rather than the memento mori it appeared to be for Renard.

"All that," Renard made a sweeping gesture with his arm

which was meant to signify the activities of the cellar near place Maubert, "meant nothing to Antoine. All that raving effort and plotting ended on the edge of a razor belonging to a petty thief with a short fuse, illiterate and able to disappear into the city, to melt into the air, as if he'd never been corporeal in the first place. That's the conspiracy. Nothing."

Renard asked him if he would like to hear one more thing. Fabien noticed Renard pocketing a box cutter but said nothing.

"The paper stated the photographer was a woman."

Georges enjoyed playing the part of the devil, whom he envisioned in many different forms from a sixteenth-century courtier with horns to a man wearing almost nothing but tights. The morning following Renard's visit Fabien found Méliès in a remote part of the studio wearing one of these suits and eating a ham sandwich. The devil wiped his hands on his legs.

"Look at this."

It was a neatly written threat to burn Star Films down in retaliation for the Dreyfus film. Delivered with the mail, the paper was dirty and scrappy from several foldings. *This is how it will look. The panes of glass will burst in the heat. The rocket that traveled to a paper moon, Selenite suits, prison uniforms, Mount Pelée, and cardboard swords will all burst into flames. They will do it at night. They will never be caught.*

"I'll sleep in the studio for a while."

Fabien imagined Georges naively playing an unarmed guard, still in his devil's suit, horns falling over the side of his cot. These would be among the first things to catch fire.

It was difficult to imagine the threat was a joke. Most things from sets to costumes had been painted in grisaille. Caught on orthochromatic film emulsions, a painted blue sky turned into a gray mass and a red dress was transformed into mourning so everything was painted in black and white. Some films were painted over later, others not. Georges like to quote André Maugé when he called his films *salvoes of comic go-getting,* but even a brief glance through one of the greenhouse windows of Star Films would indicate a funereal appearance. Although gray and cool-looking, the sets were highly flammable, and fire, once started, would spread quickly.

Georges believed in the camera; it would serve as the press, the judiciary, and even replace religion. There was nothing more beautiful than a box of perfect, flawless convex lenses. He held one up to the light and every object around him appeared more solid and authentic. His possessions, the wobbly props and the actors who surrounded him every day, had definition assigned to them by virtue of being seen through curved glass. Fabien took the lenses from him, put them on a shelf.

"Finish your sandwich," he said. "There's nothing we can do."

———•———

Fabien had traced Bluette's foot on a piece of paper, lead pencil nudging each grimy toe. The foot smeared, and they had to start over again. He held her foot down, skirts brushing the back of his head and began to trace again. Finally the paper foot was accurate, and he cut it out, folded it, and put the paper foot in his pocket.

———•———

Out on the street looking for a glass shoe for Cinderella, he had just turned the sharp corner where the allée des Brouillards ran into the elbow curve of avenue Junot when he saw the former Algerian, the man he usually tried to avoid. No longer wearing a haik, he had the preoccupied air of someone like Renard who woke in the late afternoon. At the same time, as he looked right and left and from side to side, he displayed the nervous vigilance of Antoine. Fabien followed him a few blocks, soon losing sight of the man as the streets became increasingly crowded. Men bumped into him, there was less and less room to walk. He wasn't far from the street of shops on which Lazare's was located, but the intersection was blocked off. The crowd seemed enormous; suddenly, as if planned, hundreds of people clogged the streets, and Fabien was caught in the crowd as if it were a vice. There was no room to move. The woman in yellow who worked at *La Libre Parole* shoved into a spot a few yards ahead of him. She grabbed a boy and turned him around to face her. It was the boy in the loud checkered vest. Unlike Fabien who had only stumbled into the crowd, they gave the impression of knowing they had come to the right place. The concierge from the expensive apartment building was also part of the mob. She stared at Fabien, but without recognition. As the pressure from the crowd grew she was lifted off her feet. Fabien watched her grab the cape of another woman's coat until she was shaken off with a violent twist, but he couldn't reach her to help. Faces bobbed up and down in waves of a stampede, some open mouths screaming unintelligible slogans. *Put them all in glass furnaces.* Men threw rocks at windows, smashed in doors. A woman shoved him and called him an idiot. A man with a club and another with a broken bottle told him to get out of their way, and he squeezed behind a kiosk.

For a few minutes he stood several feet from the mob, then the crowd swelled outward, and with a pulsing movement he was swept from behind his post, carried along like a dead fish. At a corner the pulsing stopped, and the crowd seemed to freeze. Fabien pushed against a man's stomach or a woman's solid legs. They didn't react. No one gave way, and unable to see the edges of the street or the mob he panicked, but the panic had nowhere to take him. He was sandwiched in, paralyzed. There were no longer landmarks, lampposts, statues, trees, or visible storefronts, just bodies. The crowd began to move again. He strained, looking upwards at the tops of buildings, but nothing appeared familiar until he thought he saw the facade of the Musée Grevin and a theater that showed films as well as other entertainments, but he still didn't know what he was tangled in until a man yelled a taunt that became a chant: *Méliès guillotined and Star Films burned to the ground*. A few people took up the chant, then their voices petered out in the chaos of jammed bodies. It was like a circus with no markers between audience and performers, and the animals ran unfettered. A woman near him tripped then disappeared, either trampled or carried away. He realized too late that he had seen her before on the train; she was the one who read *La Libre Parole*. She might have recognized him, but as it was, he felt oddly anonymous.

The Dreyfus film was being shown somewhere nearby. The next to the last scene was the "Battle of the Journalists." It began with a room at the courthouse full of reporters who took opposing sides; then an argument between *Le Gaulois* and *Fronde* turned into a fight. Actors playing journalists rushed the door. He remembered the close-ups of their faces, Méliès as a reporter, papers flying. Fabien had thought it looked real, but now he saw how staged every fight or mob scene had been.

Finding a gap, Fabien tried to squeeze out of the ball of people. He imagined he would be discovered unconscious and robbed, with nothing in his pockets but a paper outline of a woman's foot. He crumpled the foot into a wad. Bluette would presently be leaning out the window of her coach, telling her footman to whip the horses. The door wasn't very well hinged. She might fall out of it. As he imagined the tearing of thin wood, a man punched him. *I know who you are. I know who you were.* The trial scene had been staged so as to appear very ordinary, dry, here's Dreyfus, here's the judge, here are the generals. The audience knew the verdict and knew the end of the story: Dreyfus descending the steps on his way back to prison.

Fabien recognized sounds of shooting and the shattering of windowpanes. Glass flew through the air, crunching underfoot, and people pressed against him so closely that he could barely move or even turn around in the panic of so many bodies. His feet were lifted from the ground for a moment, and he heard sounds that reminded him of the frog hunters. Thwack, squish, thwack, squish. He put his hands over his eyes. He tried to melt into the crowd, grasping arms and legs and body parts, perhaps rubberized like the exploding head, or waxen and warm from the molds, but as he felt himself falling, losing consciousness, he realized too late that this was impossible. The people who trampled him were real.

Every Man His Own Illumination

The end of the film contained no secrets, no murderer revealed, no scenes of riot and pandemonium. Dreyfus walks down the steps of a building, soldiers stand with their backs to him. I shut the door to an empty Alphabet and made my way home.

When I reached my building, I looked at the mail left on the hall table. Folded menus from an Indian takeout restaurant lay in a neat pile beside flyers from a district councilman and drugstore advertisements. Letters addressed to the building's tenants who sublet, tenants whose mail didn't always end up in their boxes, these also lay stacked too neatly. Footsteps pattered on the stairs above, and instinctively I looked up. Half a body: yellow untucked *guayabera*, black trousers, the white heel of a running shoe seen in a triangular mirror placed in a corner where ceiling met wall. I couldn't be sure. The mirror was dented and covered with dust. Every person reflected in it looked like one of Munch's screamers; every leg or object, as a corner was turned, looked like a marshmallow, stretched and melted. I stood frozen, listening, unable to finish turning the key in the mailbox, climb the stairs, or open my apartment door. I imagined drawers turned upside down; boxes of sugar, salt, coffee, and soap emptied into a heap. Pictures would be knocked off the walls, plates broken, the floor slippery from cracked eggs and an overturned bottle of olive oil. Mice, roaches, and bugs of all kinds would celebrate in the anarchic landscape. If with each step forward I expected to be met with a half nelson, then a step backward when the halls lay entirely empty meant I was a limp dishrag, easily spooked, afraid of my own shadow. Walking up my steps again I thought I saw a flicker of a yellow shirt near the banister, just past a glass door. I worked up my courage and went upstairs. No one was there.

The entrance to Jack Kews's building was bricked up with cinder blocks, and the blocks were covered with notices from the city declaring the property to be condemned and extremely dangerous. The gas leak had not only killed a tenant, but caused an explosion, and two of the floors had been partly destroyed. All tenants had vacated, even the naked, paralyzed Lewisohn. A line of laundry still remained across a fire escape, a coffee can with paint brushes sticking out of it, and a quart of milk still sat on a ledge. I was standing, tipping my head backwards to stare at those windows when the super once again emerged from Mail Boxes Etc.

"Frances, you still looking for your boyfriend?"

"He wasn't my boyfriend. Your building was in the news, huh?"

"It isn't my building. Not anymore, but, yeah, this was the one." He pointed upward. "Gas leak. Boom. I was on the news."

"Were you here when the building exploded?"

"No. I was at my girlfriend's, Gladys Knight, really, that's her name. She lives on Atlantic Avenue, couple of blocks away. The cold was too intense. I couldn't take it. Who could blame me?" Breath misting in the air, he rubbed his arms. "I called the landlord. I called the boiler company who never showed up. I did what I'm supposed to do in an emergency. My nose is clean. I knew they wouldn't show up, by the way."

"So you left without warning anyone?"

"Frances, Frances, I tell you what I told the police. How was I supposed to know some moron would turn on his oven for heat, and a few crummy apartments would hit the sky?"

"Did you see Jack?"

"The dead guy?"

"Presumably."

"By the time I got here the body was taken away."

"Who identified him?"

"How should I know?" He shrugged and picked up some supermarket newspapers that had piled up near the door.

"I seen your Spanish friend here a few days before the explosion."

"Antonya?"

"I don't know her name, sweetie."

"You must mean Clarice. Clarice was his girlfriend." I tried to remember when Clarice was supposed to return to London.

"I told you I don't know her name, but I know I've seen her before."

———·———

Alphabet was locked and shuttered, only packing boxes visible through the glass doors. It was the middle of the day, I wasn't sure where to find Antonya but tried her cousin at Burrito Fresca. The restaurant was jammed full of lunchtime customers. Luis was yelling at a cook who had screwed up orders. I stood around reading the illuminated menu above the counter, waiting for a lull in the argument, getting pushed and shoved by customers pressed for time.

"Where's Antonya?" I shouted when Luis finally left the cook alone.

"Next door getting her nails done, but that was an hour ago. She might be on her way home by now. You know I asked you not to come in when it's busy like this."

"I'm not here for a free lunch, Luis."

I walked out of the restaurant and slowly approached Hollywood Nails two doors down, not knowing exactly how I would confront her. The idea of a collusion between the phantom, Jack, and Antonya made no sense. If she were in complicity with him, they really had made a fool of me, but I didn't understand why they would bother. Neither appeared to be spiteful people who would construct an elaborate tease of letters and clues, goading me to try to find Kews only to fail at it. Hollywood Nails was busy, but she sat in the back chatting with another customer seated nearby while a woman with peppermint-striped pigtails bent over her hand.

"Frances, I'm over here." Antonya gestured with a drying hand.

I threaded my way past small tables cluttered with bottles of polish, files, and scissors, inhaling the sweet chemical smell. As I got to within a couple of feet from Antonya's table I could see the nails on one of her hands had been painted half sky blue, half sand. The manicurist was painstakingly affixing palm-tree decals to the horizon line where the two colors met.

"How can you have your nails done and still do martial arts?" I really wanted to know.

"I get them done a lot, that's all."

"So, tell me about Jack." I didn't know how else to begin and sat down on a stool beside the manicurist who pretended to be deaf.

"Jack is a nobody."

"I know he's a nobody. He's dead. Why did you find him and not tell me?"

"I never met Jack. Forget about him already."

"Antonya, I'm like someone who's so late for dinner that by the time I arrive the meal is almost over, but I will sit down and try to catch up anyway. In other words, I may be slow, but I'm trying to understand. The super said he saw you in the building with him."

"Late for dinner? What is this? Late for meeting a man is what you're talking about, isn't it? Listen, ding dong, it's like this. For your information I didn't go looking for Jack, he wanted me." Antonya studied her palm trees while the manicurist began work on the other hand. "He called me to let him into the studio at night so he could view *The Dreyfus Affair* himself. You know that — no surprise. You weren't very cooperative on this point. You did your job, you preserved that hockey puck of a movie, if you could even call it a movie. He didn't believe there was nothing at the end of the film like you told him, *and* he paid me, which is more than Julius's dreaming ass is going to do."

"Why didn't he want me to see him? Why did he go to you?"

"Am I such a dummy? Why shouldn't he ask me? I worked there too."

"But why didn't you tell me?"

"I didn't think it mattered. What do I care about these rotting films? I needed the money, and you're going to need money, and like I said, your Jack paid me cash. When you have two children you got to feed then you can talk to me about some guy who's stuck on a murder that may or may not have happened so many years ago nobody in their right mind gives a shit.

"Look, I'm sorry, Frances, but listen, I never saw the guy. Honestly. An envelope with my name on it and cash inside was slid under the door. It was waiting for me, but Jack Kews never showed up. Get yourself a real human, not a ghost. I couldn't find the can anyway. That film is gone from the studio, no question about it. It's not in your editing room. It's not packed up with the other films waiting to be shipped. He paid me anyway. I'll take you out to lunch."

"No, I'll take you."

One copy of the film was in my apartment, but the other was in someone else's pocket now. Several people had access to the office, not only the staff of Alphabet, but even the renters, those who, for unknown reasons, watched Godard films and *Felix the Cat*. But only Julius, Antonya, and I had the key to my editing room.

———————

At night the statue of Hermes, lit from below, looks menacing, as if warning intruders. Although the Mayflower Building mostly shuts down at night there is a doorman/guard because a few offices employ a graveyard shift. Murray greeted me with raised eyebrows. The building was under new management, and he was to be replaced by a younger, handsome, more pumped guard who would be paid far less. Mirrored panels in the elevator had already replaced the dented metal siding, scratched with telephone numbers and names, and the framed inspection certificate had been removed because, I guess, it clashed with the decor.

Alphabet didn't look different or unusual, at least not from down the hall with the sound of a vacuum cleaner in the distance. I had expected it to be dark and locked, but I hadn't expected that my key wouldn't work in the door. The lock had been changed. Through glass panels I could see scattered packing boxes; the office was in complete disarray. On the floor close to the entrance lay the picture of Julius and Montgomery Clift, cracked as if someone had thrown it against a wall. I sat on the pink carpeting outside with my back against the doors, my hand inert on a salmon-colored leaf pattern.

What I was afraid I'd lost was something I didn't even know if I'd had to begin with. Through the glass I could see that the Méliès films had been crated up and labeled but had not yet been returned to London or Los Angeles or wherever they were supposed to go. If someone wanted to hide and preserve footage that depicted scenes of a murder they might splice it onto a badly eroded film, one not likely to be examined too closely. Some of the films had degenerated so badly, they were not destined to be viewed often, if at all. As far as I knew, only one other person had the skill to splice ancient film.

I returned to the lobby, called information, and got the number of the super from Jack's building. Fortunately, I remembered his girlfriend's name, since he was at her apartment, having no place else to go. Also, I had guessed correctly; among his handyman skills he would, for fifty dollars, happily pick the lock I required. I didn't think a licensed locksmith would agree to break into Alphabet for me. A recessed light flickered out, and the guard briefly looked up in my direction. The pay phone was only a few feet from his station. I whispered into the receiver, *break in,* but Murray paid no attention to me, focusing on a tiny television and talking to himself.

It was after midnight by the time Gladys Knight's boyfriend was through picking what he said was a piece-of-cake lock. He carried all kinds of wirelike tools and keys with him in a red toolbox.

"The case of a Hell's Kitchen Houdini," he said, referring to his place of origin.

At the moment the door gave I remembered one of the first things Julius had told me about the Méliès job. In 1907 fifty negatives were stolen from the New York office of Star Films. Looking around me I felt like a thief who wasn't sure what was of value in a sea of papers and detritus, but who had gone to a lot of trouble to achieve the break in. The former super picked up the Montgomery Clift photograph and put it in his toolbox when he thought I wasn't looking. He poked his nose through some doors, but could see nothing of interest in the wreckage.

"Fifty dollars is a low rate for this kind of work. I made the trip in the middle of a freezing-cold night. I might have to charge you more."

I emptied my pockets, anxious to get to work.

"Thank you for thinking of me. Please call again should the need arise."

Then he disappeared into the elevator. I waited until the doors closed behind him, just to be sure he was on his way out. Two minutes later I was making my way past emptied drawers, overturned wastebaskets, chairs placed on top of desks. My office was still fairly untouched. I moved the boxes of Méliès films from the entrance, unpacked them, threaded up the first film and began to consider what lay in scenes I might have overlooked. The footage of each film seemed to match the length of time stated on the box. *Fugitive Apparitions* came and went. *Extraordinary Illusions, The Infernal Cauldron, The Melomaniac,* all consisted of exactly what their labels declared.

Finally *A Miracle Under the Inquisition.* I remembered this film. It looked much longer than two minutes, ten seconds. I threaded it up. In a gothic prison, very different from Dreyfus's bare cell, a woman is tortured and finally burned at the stake. An angel appears, and phoenixlike, the woman rises from the ashes. Not only is she brought back to life, but the sleeping jailer replaces her on the pyre. Accompanied by the angel she disappears through the wall as two monks enter. In the last scene the monks run out of the frame in horror, but there was, just as I thought, more film to watch. The monks ran into a courtroom, the courtroom at Rennes. It was the Dreyfus trial. What had Julius done? Perhaps by copying, drawing, and splicing many bits together, somehow he'd created the ending he desired.

Innocent, the judge proclaimed in subtitles. *Cleared of all trumped-up charges.*

Rejoicing in the streets followed. Lucie Dreyfus cried and hugged her husband. Shamefaced, du Paty de Clam shook his fist at the camera as he was led away, presumably to a prison no angel would help him escape from. The real spy, Esterhazy, recognizable by his dark hollow eyes and pointed, ferretlike nose, slouched at the edge of the frame. He tried to slip away, but he too was dragged off to jail, arms and legs struggling in protest. The forgers, a man and a woman, were apprehended on the street. *I followed orders from Z, that's all,* the subtitles declared. The woman, well dressed, large hat blowing off her head, was angry. *I'm an ordinary citizen just trying to live my life. I had no idea who D was, I really didn't. No opinion about him whatsoever. Why should I be carted off?*

The man, whose ink-stained hands hung at his sides, offered no resistance.

The film was very eroded here, nothing but grain appeared on the screen giving way to a mass of bodies, a riot scene; it was a postscript, the scene following the credits that few stay for. A face was visible in the crowd, then it shifted to the bottom of the frame. The man looked like the actor, the ironmonger who had played Dreyfus in the film. He and another man holding a glass slipper appeared to yell at one another in recognition across a sea of faces. The ironmonger was swept out of the frame, but the other man was swept closer to the camera, an expression of panic on his face. It looked as if he was being trampled, but the crowd turned into fog, and the film all but disintegrated under the light.

I pushed back my chair and bumped into bare shelves. Even the happy ending hadn't saved Alphabet. Julius's business was finished. I unthreaded the film and put it under the guillotine splicer. Slice. The trial scene with its false but true verdict was cut, chopped into bits and dropped into the trash. Just as the citizens of Krasilov had relegated the papers reporting Dreyfus's guilty sentence to the rubbish heap, never to believe those papers again, I tossed empty coffee cups and other garbage on top of the footage so no casual observer of the wastebasket, no Auguste Bastian, could fish it out and say, *See, this is what really happened.*

I replaced *A Miracle Under the Inquisition,* but before sealing the large box it was meant to be shipped in I added *The Affair* to the lot, taking it from my pocket and packing Styrofoam peanuts around it. Had I done the right thing? Julius had disappeared, and I knew what he'd say if he were around. I slipped the guillotine splicer into my bag. You never know when it might be useful, now that I'm out of a job. Though harmless to live humans its blade is oddly sharp and lethal to filmed ones. It made a muffled clanging sound as I walked. There would be other jobs because there are always other stories that need to be preserved, Julius himself said so the last time I saw him. His picture with Charlie Chaplin winked at me as I secured what remained of the lock and left for the night.

ACKNOWLDFGMENTS

Thanks to the many people who helped me along the way with the writing and research of this book. Richard Kaye, Esther Allen, Linda Collins, John Foster, Leslie Camhi, Tom Bissell, and Shirley Miller Daitch read early drafts for which I am very grateful. Conversations with Sander Gilman and Stephen Brown at the Jewish Museum about Dreyfus and Thomas Gunn about Méliès were immeasurably helpful. David Kehr's Méliès collection was an invaluable resource and John Pollack of the Lorraine Beitler Collection of the Dreyfus Affair, Rare Book and Manuscript Library, University of Pennsylvania, provided generous assistance. Thanks also to Marion Falk, Bill Kanemoto, Mary Kanemoto, Debarati Sanyal, Radhika Subramanian, Mark Cohen, Ivone Margulies, Anna di Lellio, Sam Crawford, Jennifer Gordon, Karen Weltman, Jon Sterngass, Sunita Viswanath, Stephen Shaw, Brooke Stevens, Margo Cooper, George Seminara, and Magui Nougue-Sans. To the incomparable Elaine Katzenberger for her confidence and enthusiasm, through actualities and preconstructions, I'm grateful and in awe.

Susan Daitch is the author of two novels, *L. C.* (Lannan Foundation Selection and NEA Heritage Award) and *The Colorist*, and a collection of short stories, *Storytown*. Her work has appeared in numerous publications and literary venues, and has been the subject of various critical studies. She has taught at Barnard College, Columbia University, and the Iowa Writers' Workshop. She currently lives in Brooklyn and teaches at Hunter College.